STRANGE WEATHER

BOOK ONE

CURSE & QUANTA: THE ENCHANTER'S THEOREM

A.N. HYATT

First edition published by Hunt Press, Los Angeles, California, June 2006
Second edition published June 2010
Reprinted by Ursa Major Books January 2025

Ursa Major Books
California

ISBN 978-1-62530-030-0

10 9 8 7 6 5 4 3 2 1

DEDICATION

For my Father

Hugh Marvin Hyatt

I miss you every day, Poppa Bear.

TABLE OF CONTENTS

Chapter I – Onset of Turbulence

Heathrow International Airport, United Kingdom

Fucking State Department. How long had they had waited to flag her passport? Five minutes? An hour?

Sabine Parsons displayed her most winning smile and crushed the sigh she wanted to breathe out. The handsome young man behind the Customs counter in his starched white Oxford shirt and blue tie still saw something in her passport that made him pause. One minute stretched to five as he consulted his computer, her passport, and her face in mild bafflement.

Sabine's smile grew fixed. Her imagination supplied the security advisory. *Blue eyes, blond hair, average weight, average height, horrible passport photo, yet... A person of dubious quality, of the Gray sort, ex-Intelligence, Watch with Caution.* The $50,000 question remained. Had they issued more than an advisement—or a full block? Wasn't it enough that she had quit? Wasn't it clear to them that she never wanted to have anything to do with any of them ever again?

The young man couldn't seem to decide whether or not to bring in a superior, so Sabine turned up the wattage on her smile and with a shrug, the young man stamped her passport.

"Enjoy your stay, Miss Parsons."

Ari Doran, Sabine's best friend, who had waited at the Customs exit, had the good grace to wait a full minute before pealing out in laughter. Dark circles lay under her friend's violet eyes and a disarray of dark brown curls haloed her long angular face, her grin a little askew as she waited for Sabine to join her, all six feet of her leggy form leaning against a wall. Ari had sailed through Customs, even looking jet-lagged to death and bearing an Israeli passport. Sabine restrained the urge to glower holes into her.

"Don't even say it," Sabine growled.

They escaped Heathrow and Sabine set her weary self down on an almost empty train, her black travel clothes already wrinkled, her black travel bag propping up her feet. Ari stared out the window as the train came up out of the ground into the outer London suburbs. Gray sky lay like a lid across the landscape outside.

Great start to a vacation. Oh yes, she thought with no humor.

Jet-lagged or not, her situational awareness wasn't gone. Sabine caught odd looks from the woman across the aisle. Sabine glanced down. Except for the uniform black of their clothes—black made for only one load of travel laundry—she couldn't figure out what possible interest the small gray-haired woman could have in them.

Sabine locked gazes with the woman, which seemed to make the woman focus in on her with even more intensity.

"Can I help you?"

The woman smiled, leaned forward…

And vanished.

Sabine froze. Her heart shivered in her chest.

"We're staying where again?" she asked.

"A Ramada in Earl's Court. Close to everything," Ari replied.

"I hope we get there soon."

Yeah. Vacation, what a fucking great idea, Sabine thought again and shut her eyes tight. *Nothing strange or horrible could happen on vacation. Yeah.*

Coils and coils of blackness, she dreamed. Reflective as water, warm as blood, from slender tendrils to limbs the thickness of tree trunks. The coils caressed her, invasive strands even under her pale white skin. The entire mass of coils moved down towards a black stone-paved floor, a controlled fall from a great height.

The dream shifted and now there were clouds above her, she stood in a different place, the clouds black and destructive. They swallowed a broken and fragmented shred of brilliant rainbow, the darkening clouds a devouring gigantic beast.

The beloved coils returned and then were gone in the next instant.

Sabine stood in a huge hall, more a cavern than a gathering place. She turned in place, peering up into the deep shadows of the great room. Cold, white-veined black marble numbed her bare feet and, stark, roughhewn pillars of dark gray stone disappeared into the shadows that hid the ceiling.

Bare feet. Sabine stared down. She wore only torn black pants and a sweaty, dirt-stained black sweatshirt.

"Where are my shoes?" she asked the emptiness.

Another place then and...

He was there.

So close she could taste his breath. From far off came a drumming. It pulled at her blood. His eyes were on hers. Pale blue, lighter than her own and fiercer, filled with the same agony that she knew from every one of the previous dreams.

Sabine wanted to scream.

Rough hands on her, pulled her away, bound her arms with coarse rope that cut flesh. Appalling smells of unwashed bodies. She saw only Him.

And like every other time, she watched the blue leach from his eyes. A leprous non-color, black, but not, rose to take its place.

Sabine screamed as Edward Quintaine lost his soul. Again.

Which was impossible, since Edward Quintaine had been dead for thirteen years.

Gentle shaking woke her later.

Sabine cracked gummy eyelids and managed a smile at Ari.

"It's almost ten. Wanna get up?"

Sabine tried to answer, but a yawn grabbed her and felt like it was going to crack her jaw off her skull. Despite that, she propped herself up on one elbow and waved a yes.

Two hours later, fortified by a shower, tea, and toast, Sabine stood outside, blinking her eyes in the sunlight of an alien city.

"Where to first?" Ari asked.

"Ain't got a clue. Need a map," Sabine muttered in return for her friend's contagious enthusiasm.

"British Museum! British Museum!"

"Okay, museum it is," she drawled.

She yelped when Ari grabbed her arm and dragged her to the edge of the road to flag one of the ever-present London black cabs screaming along Knightsbridge Road.

As they passed the security checkpoint and coat check of the main foyer of the British Museum, Sabine rubbernecked with all the other tourists, even as she worked on getting her breath back. The cab ride over had imperiled her tea and toast and she wanted to keep it inside her body. Ari hadn't given her much time to ogle the façade of the museum either before dragging her inside.

Maybe Ari had been right, Sabine had needed a vacation far from nightmares, or omens, or whatever.

They chose the west wing of the museum, following the signs to the artifacts. The first room didn't bother Sabine and neither did the second. The third hammered into Sabine's brain like knives of Memory.

Sabine walked into the Elgin Marbles display, the Parthenon in all its lost glory. Her time and place slipped away from her, even as she tried to hold on to it, her fists clenching in bright terror for the intangible.

The moment passed in an instant, leaving behind new knowledge, for she remembered this place. Not the British Museum, but in the place that wasn't memory, but Memory, Sabine remembered.

Sabine never debated the existence of past lives; she remembered lives the way some people remembered where they put their shoes the night before. Not something ever-present, but if something shook Memory loose... Then, she could get lost in a remembrance of things so far past that the people in those Memories, whom she saw so clearly as alive and breathing, were long since dust.

A tug still remained on her soul from the swift in-and-out tide of Memory. Something she had made was in the building, but she shook the feeling loose, refusing to pursue it.

Every room after that was the same, swift currents of Memory that came and went. Sabine quailed only once when Ari led the way into the Egyptian displays. She took one look at the replica of the ancient walls of Egyptian mourning, felt more than saw the countless mummies on display, and turned tail.

"What's the matter? Are you all right?" Ari came out to ask.

"I know your passion is Egyptology and stuff, but I'm not going to be able to go in there."

"Ah," she sighed. "I get it. Too many?"

"I'll just wait out here, if that's okay."

"No prob. I'll be quick." Ari nodded and left Sabine on her step in the stairwell.

They wandered in a fairly circular manner, museum crawling in earnest after that, the Memory tide coming less often, until they rounded a corner into the back of more Greek displays. Photos displayed the ruined glory of the Parthenon. The familiar chill that she felt whenever anyone described the Greek temple of Athena, never mind showed Sabine pictures, came over her.

She'd always had an affinity for Pallas Athena. Any god of wisdom couldn't be all bad in Sabine's book, but of all of Athena's incarnations, Nike Athena called to Sabine the most, the figure of Victory in flight.

Time fell away, as she turned around and came to face the statue of Athena as Nike, and knew it for the thing she had made.

Her heart broke. The head was gone; the arms, broken, only a torso and wings remained. The statue was a shadow of its former glory. Sabine gasped, eyes stinging.

"What have they done to my Nike?"

Ari snaked an arm around Sabine's waist.

"Christians and Mongols and whoever was sacking the city that time. They smashed all of them, remember?"

It was obvious that Ari knew this statue too, though not the way that Sabine did. Their similar gifts were one of the things that had made them friends to begin with.

"But I worked so hard on it!"

"I know, sweetie, I know, but that was a long time ago."

"Did they have to break her? She was just a statue. She wasn't hurting anyone."

"I know."

"Do you mind if we stay here for a minute?" Sabine asked, her voice tiny.

"As long as you would like."

Sabine wanted to touch, but knew alarms would sound if they did. So she stared, saying nothing, and Ari didn't fill the silence. Which meant she had plenty of time to observe the two men who entered the room from opposite entrances.

Sabine scanned from long habit, taking her attention away from her broken Athena just long enough to do so. She was startled by the fact that the body language, (furtive and scanning), on the two visitors screamed "Clandestine Drop." After all, why would anyone use the museum for a drop?

Too exposed, she thought.

The one who had come in from behind them was a nervous professorial type, complete with graying hair, tweed coat, and glasses. He glanced around too often to be anything but a Watcher, down to his comfortable shoes. Sabine noted him and kept her attention to the Nike.

The other man might as well have worn a sign labeled: Shooter: he walked straight-up the swagger of a professional killer or a field operations man. Dark hair, dark eyes, and a black cloth jacket. Sabine did not roll her eyes.

Ari maneuvered around to Sabine's back, appearing to be taking in the other sculptures in the room.

The bulge of the Shooter's weapon was quite obvious, and Sabine wondered how the front security had been stupid enough to miss it.

Too soon, the shooter went out of her sight, but Sabine trusted Ari to watch her back.

"Gun!" Ari gritted out of her teeth.

"Not the Nike!" Sabine yelled and flung herself at the statue.

Three shots rang out, thunder-loud.

Ari dove behind a bench, a Beretta Jaguar .22 materializing in her hand like magic. But the Shooter was already gone, leaving behind a body in a spreading pool of blood.

Sabine let go of the Nike, checking for damage. None, but she took one final look just to be sure. She locked eyes with Ari and they made for the exit.

"I've had enough of Greek sculpture for the day, how about you?" Sabine asked.

"Oh yes, very boring after a while."

They headed for the coat check without running, but by way of the Egyptian section, mummies and all, though Sabine had her eyes closed and clung to Ari to get through. They slipped by the museum guards by mere seconds and stepped down the front steps and into the spring sunshine at the same moment that London's Finest rushed in.

"Well, this museum crawling has been an exceptional idea, Ari. However did you think of it?"

"Just flag a cab," Ari said in a withering tone.

Luckily for them, a cab arrived in seconds. Ari turned and to all appearances, took a last appreciative gaze at the sculpture on the front lawn, a gigantic stone face, as they climbed in. Sabine knew she scanned for anyone following them.

They turned away from the coat check at the Dorchester Hotel thirty minutes later, the choice made *en route*. Sabine had regained some of her equanimity, but only just.

Ari, as usual, looked at her ease, window-shopping through the little display cases along the hall as they made their way back to the lobby. The usual jeweler's wares were presented with other items of interest to the well-heeled traveler, but of course Ari was drawn to only one thing.

"Oh look, Sabine, a spy tech shop, wanna go?" Ari asked in an evil little voice.

"Are you out of your mind, and have my face plastered on every bulletin board at MI6? No thank you."

"Ah, come on, it's not like they don't know who I am already," Ari shrugged.

"Yeah, but I'm with you. Hello? Retired?"

Ari chuckled.

"It's not funny," Sabine said, even as she giggled in turn. If they didn't get tea soon, Sabine was certain she would collapse right there in the hall.

"In case you had forgotten I have sworn off all of that and do not want to get back involved again," she continued.

Ari's airy wave of acknowledgement did nothing to make Sabine feel better.

The big warm golden hall of the Dorchester's tea room welcomed them. Tall columns and tiled floors set off a group of tables scattered about with a variety of plush chairs and small divans in tan and scarlet brocade, and Sabine felt knots let go in her shoulders.

A server in black tie and tails appeared out of nowhere.

"Two for tea, ladies?"

"Oh yes," she breathed.

Sabine gave a deep contented sigh as they settled into matching tan armchairs the waiter pulled out for them. The pristine white tablecloth and elegant Wedgewood china laid on their small tea table forced the rest of the knots out of her back.

"Tea at the Dorchester, now this is more like it," Sabine said.

"Will it only be tea then, ladies, or the full high tea for you both?" their server broke in.

"Bring out the whole thing," Sabine said, with a dramatic wave of her right hand.

"So," Ari said when the butler left.

"We're not speaking of it, Ari."

"We're witnesses."

"They'll kick me out of the country."

"We should say something."

"We don't know a damn thing."

Ari said nothing further and they ate in heavy silence.

Ari emptied her teapot for the third time. She set up her cup with cream and sugar in the bottom of it anyway and flipped the pot's lid upside down, the universal signal for, "Please fill me up again."

Sabine had mentally wandered off into her own little world of overfull contented daydream when the server appeared with more hot water.

"As you can see, I was prepared for you," Ari said with a flirtatious smile.

The waiter grinned and leaned in closer to pour, closer than he had on previous stops.

"Ah, are you in the Game as well?"

Sabine froze, a plastic grin glued to her face, daydream shattered. Her monkey brain gibbered. She locked gazes with Ari and saw an identical plastic grin on her friend's face. "The Game" was a term used by members of the intelligence community. His use of it not only outed him as a spook, but it also indicated that their slips were showing rather badly. Receiving no response, the waiter nodded, still smiling, and withdrew.

"Did he just say what I think he just said?" Sabine asked, finding her voice with difficulty.

"Yes," Ari replied in a small voice.

"That's what I thought." Sabine said, hysteria bleeding into giggles around the edges. "Oh shit. Oh shit. What have you gotten us into, Ari?"

"Me? I haven't gotten us into anything! I swear it!"

Sabine looked her in the eye, but not with any accusation, just the look to see how much truth Ari gave her.

"I swear, Sabine! Nothing! I'm on vacation!"

"They didn't ask you to run any little errands while you were away?"

"No! Well, you know, the usual keep your eyes and ears open stuff, but nothing else! I swear it, Sabine. As the *Shekinah* is my witness."

"I believe you. But are we wearing signs or something?"

"Um..." Ari looked embarrassed and pointed. Sabine stared down and she could have kicked them both.

The tan trench coat slung over the back of the chair, the ancient black sweatshirt and equally ancient black jeans, her black walking boots, looking only two steps away from combat boots, her dark blond hair pulled back into a tight pony tail. Sabine saw herself in the uniform of most paid assassins taking a break between hits. Ari wasn't dressed much better.

"Well, I feel sheepish," Sabine said with a grumble. Old habits were hard to break.

An American couple went by and Sabine made herself not do a double take. The man wore a tan jacket and a loud Hawaiian shirt, his wife in an almost matching ensemble.

"I see that the "Christians in Action" are still using male/female pairs." A quick scan of the room and Sabine realized that she had been so lost in contented thoughts that she had missed the obvious. The Tearoom was occupied almost exclusively by intelligence operatives from various fraternities. Somehow they had wandered into a Spook watering hole.

"No wonder he thinks we're Players," Sabine said with a sigh.

"Can you believe it?" Ari asked.

"Do you think they would get really pissed off if we started putting little cards on the tables to identify who is who?"

"It could be like a game. Spot the Agency! We could ask them to tell us if we're right or wrong."

Sabine snickered. The image of the two of them running around the hall with little place cards, labeled with the names of various intelligence agencies on them, amused her no end. Even if this was no way to handle the situation. Dead Watchers. Random Shooters. Spies in the Dorchester.

They spent the next half an hour playing a mental version of Spot the Agency by themselves instead. They decided that the only thing that really seemed to peg the difference between MI5 and MI6 were the umbrellas carried by MI5. The MI6ers were clearly too cool for school and eschewed such additional accessories. It still made them shockingly easy to pick out in a crowd.

"Do you think we should let them know?" Sabine asked.

"Nah. They probably don't even notice amongst themselves."

"I know. That's what frightens me. How could they not notice?"

"Well, this is clearly neutral territory," Ari pointed out.

"Honor among thieves and all that?"

"Certainly."

"Guess they don't care as much here then, but, it's not like they probably don't know who everyone else is," Sabine thought out loud.

"That's why they're watching us like hawks," Ari said, dropping her head and directing her voice to her teacup, an old anti-lip reading trick.

"I had a feeling," Sabine said, then grinned; their unspoken agreement apparently needed speaking. "You know, it won't make a lick of difference to try and be subtle if they've got the teapot bugged."

Ari straightened like a queen. "But one doesn't have to make it easy for them either."

A tall man in an impeccable gray suit walked into the tea room and glanced at all the diners, coming to rest on Sabine and Ari. His face lit up and he headed straight for them.

"Good afternoon, are you perhaps with International Filmworks?" The tall man asked.

"Huh?" Sabine asked, and then recovered. "I'm sorry, uh, no, we're not."

"Oh, bother. I was sent here to meet some of their representatives and you looked likely. Well, please forgive me, I didn't mean to disturb your tea." He made a small bow and withdrew.

Sabine turned to ask Ari another question, but Ari stared at the tabletop. Sabine followed the line of sight and there, on the immaculate white linen, lay a tiny jar. It had a gold lid, a silver gardenia flower design on the sides, and tiny gold print lettering.

They both leaned in.

"Tell me that he didn't drop that while he had me distracted."

"Okay. I won't," Ari said.

Sabine groaned. "What is going on?"

"Don't know."

"Did you peg him as anyone?"

"He's not wearing any of the uniforms, if that was what you meant."

Sabine felt a faint chill. Everyone had something that stuck out. The fraternities couldn't help it. But to have no marks, no jewelry, no nothing...

"Oh my." Sabine sat back abruptly, while Ari reclined at a slower rate.

"So, it's a bomb," Sabine stated, knowing it wasn't. She'd made enough bombs in her day to know one when she saw it. For one, you didn't drop one on a table, no matter how sturdy. They were delicate things and harsh treatment had a tendency to excite an exothermic reaction before one wanted one. In other words, you could blow your fool head off being that kind of stupid.

"Ha," Ari deadpanned.

They drank more tea. Ari kept her eyes glued to the jar, but Sabine made sure she didn't look at it at all.

"Well," Sabine said after a while.

"Well, what?"

"Are we leaving it or taking it?"

"It's meant to be taken."

"And both of us being contrary, the tendency then is to immediately leave it if they want us to take it."

"But it doesn't answer why," Ari said.

"No. It doesn't. Open it here or at the room?"

"Here," Ari blurted.

Sabine figured it out. If it turned out a bug or locator, no reason to take it back to their rooms.

"Who's opening it?"

"You are," Ari answered with a crooked smile.

Sabine snatched up the jar before she could change her mind.

Gold lid went on the tabletop after close inspection with her little white Swiss Army knife that TSA had completely missed; there were no creases, no seams, just a lid. If there were anything embedded in it, it was cast at the making and that didn't look likely. The jar was a wealth of non-information. Despite the words "Gardenia: Refreshing Eye Cream" emblazoned on both sides, the jar was filled with ten tiny silver pellets, not a cream.

"Oh shit." Sabine handed the jar over to Ari, who took one look and frowned.

"Pills?"

"I have to ask. What are the chances our tall man dropped them on accident?"

"None. He distracted you deliberately and I pretended to be oblivious as well, and he did a nice bit of sleight."

"Could this be a bad drop? Did he mistake us for someone else?"

"Not enough data for me to theorize with," Ari chastised.

"Shit." Sabine took the jar back from her friend and capped it, setting it back down on the table.

"We take it with us."

"I won't ask you if you're kidding."

"I know what's on the market and that's not anything that will land us in trouble. It's weird, but not that kind of weird. If anything, you can say they're cold cream pills that break apart when squished."

"Well, maybe they are." Sabine started to reach for the jar again.

Ari shook her head in the negative, a slight gesture.

"They're not."

"That sure?"

"I'm sure. I don't know why I know it isn't, but they're not."

Sabine scooped the jar off the table and dropped it into her pack.

"Well, no reason to leave it out in full view of God and everybody. For all I know he just put up a sign over our heads, that neither of us can read, that will get us into trouble."

"I think we're already in trouble."

Sabine had no comeback to that. After a firefight, being made by their waiter, and now this, it was obvious they had problems. They finished their tea in more silence and niggling unease. When the bill came, Ari piled pound notes on the bill, not even blinking at the cost.

They stepped outside and Ari stepped away to flag a cab. Sabine glanced up at the sky, and did a double take.

She felt something quiver in her belly. The exact clouds that she had seen in her dreams, hung in the sky over her head.

That night, her dreaming self watched a teacup that sat on the table in front of her. She sat mesmerized by the rolling liquid in the delicate porcelain.

"Turbulence," she thought, watching the distinctive rolls begin, the steam rising and obscuring her sight.

From out of the mist, a set of Gates appeared wide and gaping before her, a terrible light poured out through them, screaming into her eyes.

The Gates of Hell open. She held a sword in her left hand. A feeling of horrible loss tore her belly like shards of glass. Rage squeezed the rest of her so hard that she wanted to scream. Only one realization pounded through her brain, through her entire being.
She had to go in. Get someone out, or get something back, she couldn't tell which, but the terror overwhelmed everything, except for one impulse.

Jump.

Sabine woke in a cold sweat.

Chapter II – Daffodils and Fractal Smoke

The next morning dawned brilliant and sunny. Sabine sighed in silent relief when she saw the sunshine, stepping out onto the sidewalk in front of their Ramada. The traffic on Knightsbridge Road barreled by fast and thick, throwing her off kilter with the sense that they were on the wrong side of the damn road.

"So what's the plan for today?"

"V&A?" Ari asked.

"You want to do more museum crawling? Wasn't yesterday enough for you?"

"It could have been a fluke."

"Sure," she drew out the syllable with a roll of her eyes.

They weren't far from the Victoria & Albert Museum, a prime example of the type of architecture that Queen Victoria demanded after the death of her beloved consort. Large, beautiful, and gaudy, it was meant to dwarf the beholder.

"Is everything named Victoria & Albert around here?"

"She was in mourning," Ari said with some asperity.

Their bags were searched again on the way in. Sabine didn't think she'd get used to it. Like the wrongness of the traffic pattern to her, part of her found it irritating. However, the vial of pills they'd been gifted with caused no remark.

The V&A didn't impose the way the British Museum had. Less overwhelming. But it made up for it in real estate. By the time they decided to take a rest in the center courtyard, Sabine was more than ready to not move again for a while.

"I think my favorite was the life-size windup tiger mauling the British soldier," Sabine commented, sinking onto the stone fountain's ledge at the center of the courtyard.

"It would be, what is with you and bloodshed?"

"What did you like best?"

"The dresses, the dresses, and the dresses." Ari was a passionate collector of vintage clothing. "Want them all!"

"Of course," Sabine laughed and something caught her eye. She said nothing, knowing her friend would have noticed long before now, but unless she imagined it, two men stared at them.

They wore round, black, circular glasses, and identical gray suits with mandarin collars, which was a style she equated more with the '60s, and her friend, Chaz, who had an obsession with the Beatles. But there was nothing friendly about these two men. The tall, skinny one had a shaved head, but she doubted he was a skinhead or a punk, while the shorter one was dark-haired and broad through the shoulders.

She got up and took a picture of Ari in front of the fountain, adding to the five rolls she'd already shot. She thought about getting a picture of the Twins, but decided against it.

"Seen enough?" Sabine asked a minute later.

"Yeah."

"What next?"

"Wander?"

"Good for me."

Sabine stopped a couple blocks later, on the pretext of admiring some more London architecture, but in reality to check their back-trail in a convenient window. The Twins loitered half a block back.

"Ari, are we being followed?"

Ari answered by way of staring across the street, playing oblivious tourist. "I thought I was imagining it."

"Any ideas?"

"Well, if they're muggers they're about to get the nastiest surprise of their life."

Sabine grinned, a trace of good-natured malice in her expression. It was true. Between the two of them, they had a combined knowledge of martial arts guaranteed to break most people in two.

"Shall we start pausing to make sure we keep them in sight?" Sabine asked.

"Nah. Let's go to Harrods!"

"Ooo! Good idea."

"Hail a cab, sweetie."

"You got it." Sabine leaned out into traffic. She flagged a black cab on the first try and they clambered in, double quick, even as their followers scrambled to flag one of their own.

"Ha!"

"Amateurs," Ari said with a disapproving frown.

A couple of hours later, well-fed and somewhat overwhelmed, though in a good way, Sabine took in Harrods's Bridal Department.

Lunch had been found in the food court and had driven all thoughts of their incompetent tail out of her head. More than likely they were young agents for the MI6ers and no need for concern.

Ari promptly found the Toy Department after lunch had been accomplished. Sabine knew there would be no getting Ari out until all was seen and ooh-ed and aah-ed over.

"Our bozos are back," Sabine said, catching a reflection in a mirrored panel.

"Where?" Ari asked, her ecstatic expression never changing, as she looked at all the Play Mobil characters in their bright blue boxes.

"In the stuffed toy section. What do you want to do about them?"

"I'd say let's not worry about them, until they make a move."

"I just wish I knew why they were following us."

"Well," Ari straightened from her covet fest. "That, we won't be able to figure out until they do something. Where do you want to go next?"

"No tea?"

"Tea would be fine! But, whatever you'd like."

"I'm beat. Can we go back to the hotel?"

"I thought you'd never ask. I'm not actually feeling very well."

Sabine's head ratcheted around at her friend. Sure enough, Ari looked a trifle pale.

"What's the matter?"

"My throat's scratchy."

"It's all this air-conditioned air. We'll get you back to the hotel," Sabine said, all briskness. "Let's get you to the taxi stand. And to think, they'll probably think that we're trying to evade them."

The ride back went with no further adventures. Sabine got Ari into one of the hotel beds and tucked her in, then waited till Ari fell deeply asleep, before letting herself out of their hotel room in search of a strong cup of tea and a pack of cigarettes. The concierge in the lobby pointed her in the direction of a pub. Sabine headed out into a darkening afternoon of threatening rain clouds. She scanned now not from habit, but because she knew someone in all probability had her back-trail and she didn't want to be stupid.

A chill crept over her, independent of the dark clouds.

I left tradecraft behind, Sabine thought. The ease with which things came back to her, frightened. Which led her straight into another old technique, a mental one she had long used to suppress fear.

"Game on," she whispered to the clouds and felt the old mindset settle back over her.

The pub turned out more than decent, Sabine mused later, very pleased. Down the road from the Earl's Court Underground station and around the corner from their hotel, the Stanhope Arms was everything an English pub was supposed to be. Dark wood paneling welcomed, even if the cigarette smoke overwhelmed. Loud music pumped out from the CD jukebox and the 'tender, a large, balding man in a clean white apron wrapped around his ample middle, waved and smiled as she came in.

A cigarette vending machine stood at the right hand corner at the back and Sabine gave thanks to the Gods of Travel. The logo for "Silk Cut" caught her eye and she fished change out of her pocket.

One of the tables next to the big picture window at the front opened up and Sabine made a beeline for it. She was probably asking for a drive by to come gun her down like a dog, but she would at least have a chance to see it coming. She'd be damned if she'd sit with her back to the door. Some habits could bugger off and die. A very pretty barmaid, with ringlets of red hair pulled back in an untidy bun, came to take her order. Sabine ordered tea and peeled the plastic wrap off her pack of cigs.

Her gaze drifted back like the needle on a compass to polar north, back to the window, as she lit up. The rain clouds had not bordered to black yet, only to a dark and steel gray.

The street's only denizens were people coming back from late hours at whatever work they held and the beginnings of an evening crowd, even on this weekday. She spotted no pursuers and no refugees from bad '60s spy films.

Sabine frowned, as she listed off her problems in her head. Prophetic Dreams, broken rainbows, handoffs gone bad, and the Twins, who worked for someone in the fraternity of spies or she'd eat her hat. She didn't know what to think. She'd been careful to keep no ties to her old life, including any that might have fed her any sort of information. She went on one vacation to Europe in her entire life and all the old ghosts came back to haunt her.

She closed her eyes and went very still. She searched for her most neglected of old gifts, the one that was more than just remembering past lives and the ancient Memory of the world.

She Reached for the first time in thirteen years.

It was the only way that she could describe it. Somehow, whenever she had needed things, she had been able to Reach into some strange void or into the World itself and well... Make things happen.

The Waking Dream was not available to her yet, the ability to catch a glimpse of a possible Future or Futures. It slumbered too deeply within her. But it would wake, that much she could feel. Where Memory told her what had passed, the Waking Dream told her not of a definite future, but gave hints of Possibilities.

Sabine's eyes snapped open. She felt the imminence of her abilities at the edges of what she had been able to touch. But no answers.

"Quintaine," she thought and didn't know that she mouthed the name as well. Edward Quintaine, long dead, but not forgotten, even in her Dreams.

A long hour later with no bolt from the blue to illuminate, Sabine stepped out of the pub, the last light fading from the sky. But even in the darkening gloom, the fresh air braced, a tonic to her senses. She stood half a world away from more mundane troubles. The fact struck her heart like a blow.

Spring in England, in London. Sabine found her breath taken away for a moment. The brilliant yellow of daffodils, like small suns come to rest in the green grass by the sidewalks, caught her eye. Trouble might be afoot, but daffodils still found time to bloom.

She crossed to the flower vendor across the street without a thought for the traffic, heading for the buckets of daffodils for a pound a bunch. A moment later, armed with a bouquet and feeling sunnier for the expense, she turned back for the hotel.

She walked, her tan trench coat wrapped around her blacks, a bunch of yellow clutched in one hand, while smoke wreathed her head from the cigarette on her lips like an ashen halo.

The next day brought a fitful, clouded London. Sabine took Ari straight back to the pub for breakfast.

The pub lay empty, the morning crush already off to work. Pink Floyd played on the jukebox and Sabine had to laugh, identifying the live album, Delicate Sound of Thunder. More weather omens. She sighed.

"I'm going to put some more money in the juke. Any suggestions?" Ari asked.

"More Floyd," Sabine said and lit her first cigarette.

Ari went for longer than just a little visit to the jukebox. Sabine assumed she'd run to the Ladies as well.

Why was she in London? Going to Europe? Granted, she felt she had to accept when Ari announced that she'd bought tickets, EurRail Passes, and none of it refundable, insisting that Sabine needed a vacation. *Fait accompli* and Sabine fumed, but Ari got what she wanted. Sabine said yes and worried about getting a passport for the first time in thirteen years.

The broken rainbow swallowed by the angry clouds. She couldn't push the image out of her brain.

"What are you worried about?" Ari asked coming back as Sabine lit her third Silk Cut cigarette. "You don't smoke like that unless you're pissed off or stressing. Which is it?"

"The clouds..."

"Yes, I saw them, too."

"I'm imagining it, I'm sure."

"Honey, you had another of your patented scream fest nightmares last night, someone was shot dead at the feet of Nike Athena, and we were pegged as members of a fraternity at tea. What else do you want to happen before you feel okay about worrying?" She wrinkled her forehead at Sabine in dismay.

Sabine widened her eyes at the tall brunette; she had thought her friend hadn't noticed her nightmares, and that she had managed to be quiet.

"Of course, it could be nothing. There could just be some big op going on right now and we had the bad taste to step in it." Ari threw off with a shrug.

"Uh huh. Sure."

Stepping out of the pub later, breakfast safely put in their bellies, a strange thought occurred to Sabine. Out of all the places they had been, the pub had been the only place where nothing had occurred. They hadn't been tailed, or in any fashion disturbed. And then she spotted it.

"Holy ground," she said and Ari turned around from stepping out onto the traffic of the sidewalk.

"What?"

Sabine just pointed. There in the lintel, tiny white tiles described the tools of the mason's trade.

"Oh my!"

"Indeed. Do you think our concierge knows something we don't?"

"If he does, we owe him a bigger tip next time."

They stepped out of one of the ubiquitous London black cabs the next morning into another gray blustery day. The previous day had been uneventful, much to the calming of Sabine's nerves. She also had a grin plastered to her face as soon as she took in Tower Hill. The gates and the gray stone walls were as familiar as her own reflection and yet unfamiliar all at the same time. They walked to the tollbooth to pay their entry fees and have their bags searched by the polite Bobbies, but Ari stopped halfway.

"Okay, picture time!" she announced, and had Sabine pose, the stone of the Tower of London rising behind her. "Oh, man, I wish you could see your face!"

"That good, eh?"

"Better."

Walking through Sir Walter's apartments later, all Sabine could think of to say was, "Man, everyone was short."

"Let's go look at the baubles!" Ari caroled.

Sabine laughed. The baubles of course, were the Crown Jewels. But one also had to wait in a line.

"Well, who knew?" Ari asked with a shrug.

"It's no surprise, really. The historical stuff isn't probably what they get people here for. It's the jewelry."

"True, true."

The line into the Crown Jewels exhibit moved at a fair clip, but did not take them in a direct path. They wandered through first one entry room and then another and at the third, Sabine felt as if she had been struck a blow right between the eyes with a steel crowbar.

Against every wall were thrones placed one next to the other and above it, the names and dates of every King or Queen who ever sat the Throne of England. But to both Sabine and Ari's sight, the ghosts of the Kings and Queens sat there and as they entered, they rose, staring straight at them.

"Oh shit," Sabine said in a small voice.

"You can say that again," Ari said.

None of the shades spoke. Sabine scanned the dates and found the one she sought. Henry V. A young man stared back at her, tawny hair cut in a soldier's cut. She paused in front of him.

"Hello, Hal," she whispered.

"Merry met, little sister." He smiled at her.

"Why?"

The other tourists passed them like water around a stone. No one looked. Whatever allowed Sabine and Ari to see the Dead, kept the tourists from seeing anything out of the ordinary. Their eyes slid right off the two women.

"A part of us always remains."

"But why are you here now?" Sabine kept her voice low. "What's going on?"

"The first move in a great game has begun."

"I'd begun to gather that."

"Yes, but the players think thee merely a pawn, my sib."

"How can I be a pawn when I'm not even in the Game?" Sabine kept none of the outrage out of her voice.

Hal laughed and laid a spectral hand on her shoulder. A coolness sank into the flesh under her black shirt.

"Ah, but you forget, when all's lost and crows count the quarters, pawns have often become Queens."

Sabine froze. She knew she heard a capital Q in that word.

"No," she said.

"Oh, aye, little sister! And there be the rub, for the players think thee not capable of crossing their board and taking your right."

"I don't understand."

Henry the Fifth, once King of England and France, general of one of the smallest armies to ever win a victory on a foreign soil, lost his smile, the one that made him look like a boy.

"I know it well. But before all is done, the choice will be yours again."

"What choice?"

"I cannot speak of it. As it stands here, I have spoken naught." He cocked an eyebrow at her.

"I hear you," Sabine whispered.

He smiled and faded to nothing, the shades of the others vanishing before him.

Sabine closed her eyes, eyes stinging with tears for a young man dead more than 700 years.

Outside, the clouds too cool and too oppressive. Sabine hugged her trench closer, but nothing seemed to get her warm. The cold cream jar in her pack felt like a ticking time bomb.

Without Ari saying anything about needing food, Sabine aimed her steps towards the tourist cafeteria. It was more of an outdoor café with seating under a large metal arbor. The coldness of the day didn't lend itself well to outdoor dining, but Ari went in to find food anyway.

While Sabine patted down her trench for her lighter, she twigged to their new tail. Another pair, men again, wearing tan trench coats not that different from her own, non-descript, average brown hair, average features, both of average height. They were the kind of men that most people's eyes didn't stick to. They weren't obvious, like the bozos from the previous day, but their eyes lingered too long and the hairs on the back of Sabine's neck stood straight up.

Ari came back with food and tea. Sabine busied herself lighting her cigarette. She sipped the offered tea through the first lungful of smoke.

"Heads up," she said with a grin at Ari, who was trying to remove the slices of cheese from her sandwich.

"Yeah, them. What about 'em?" Ari said around a mouthful.

"What? You spotted them earlier and only now choose to say anything?"

"Nope, I saw them when you did, but I think they've probably been with us for a while."

As if on cue, one of the men, the taller, sandy-haired one, looked straight at their table.

"Oh boy," Sabine breathed and buried her mouth into the lip of her teacup. "What's that mean?"

Ari stopped eating and locked gazes back with the man. A moment more, and the two men just left.

"What the fuck?"

"Okay. That was brazen as shit," Ari muttered.

"Let me translate to make sure I got that right," Sabine said in confusion. "Did they just fucking make it clear that they are watching us and we're to keep our noses clean?"

"Yep." Ari had forgotten her sandwich.

"Okay. What the fuck is going on? Ghosts prophecy doom, clear as day, and now two members of another fraternity give us the bloody hairy eyeball!"

"I'm really sorry, Sabine," Ari said.

Sabine nearly snapped her neck, bringing her full attention back to her friend.

"What?" she bit the word out so hard that she felt her teeth snap at the end of it.

"I don't know. I just feel like I've dragged you into something really bad."

Sabine relaxed and sipped her tea.

"You know what?" she said, forcing brightness.

"What?" Ari asked.

"Fuck 'em."

"Huh?"

"Fuck them," Sabine enunciated. "We are on vacation. Until someone picks us up off the street, guess what? We don't know jack."

CHAPTER III – RATES OF DECAY

London, United Kingdom

Two days later, nothing had happened.

Sabine wanted to grind her teeth. Their encounter, if it could be called that, with the two men in tan had somehow banished all the weirdness from their trip. Granted, they had taken it easy the last two days. She should have been happy. Instead, she went through two days of strong tea and cigarettes and glasses of Coke coming with slices of lemon, and her fill of English suburban gardens. She was getting used to the lemons. But not the feeling. The oppressive waiting.

The sky had gone overcast again, threatening rain. Sabine saw neither hide nor hair of a rainbow.

"Where today?" Ari asked.

Sabine drew out the Underground map and one of the tourist maps of London, while Ari tried to hide a grin. Sabine ignored her. Because of her maps, they'd found a Laundromat the day before without wandering across half of London.

"Well, we haven't wandered over and had tea at the Ritz yet..."

Sabine found herself humming the minute she set foot on Bond Street. They peered in at the window displays. She checked their back trail with some constancy, but no one appeared.

A used bookstore presented and Sabine felt her spirits lift even more.

By and large, Sabine was not a non-fiction reader, but her father had mentioned a book to her before she'd left for Europe, an older book, but worth reading, he had said. She went scanning the racks for it in the Science section. She found it easy enough and wondered why she felt compelled to do so. But after having bought her copy of James Gleick's *Chaos*, she figured it should have been obvious. Chaos was what her so-called vacation felt like.

Ari joined her at the front of the store. The sun had come out outside and Sabine found her heart yearning to be out in it.

"What did you get?" she asked.

"A book of poetry by T.S. Elliot and a new Terry Pratchett novel!" Ari replied.

Sabine groaned. Ari had a horrible fondness for anything by Pratchett and an equally horrible fondness for reading whole sections out loud.

"It's not that bad! Besides, what did you get?"

"Um, book on chaos theory."

"And you're giving me a hard time?"

A few blocks away, they stumbled onto a small church surrounded by a garden filled with raised beds of flowers and trees. In the garden's midst, stood a statue in the Greek style, the bronze greened with age. At its feet there was a plaque that read: Peace. The raised beds were made out of concrete with a wide ledge, making convenient benches. Sabine sat at the feet of the goddess of peace. The vacant holes for eyes bothered her.

Another wave of feeling hit and Sabine reeled. Memory woke in her head with the Waking Dream hard on its heels. The next moment, the vision of a young girl who could have been Sabine's reflection. The girl sat surrounded by the black coils, which Sabine felt so often in her own dreams. No Memory this, but some Future.

The girl had no eyes.

She looked straight into Sabine's face and smiled so sweetly. Ari's hand was on Sabine's upper arm, tight in concern and a bit of panic. Stillness settled over her. Knowingness tried to assert itself, but as she reached for the knowledge the Dream had brought her, it fled.

"Omen?" Ari had to ask.

"Oh, come on," Sabine said with a sick, crooked grin. "Aren't you enjoying this vacation, Ari?"

They ended up at the Ritz, deciding against a stay in the church garden. The tea room was cream white and peach, with powder blue furniture spread here and there, low couches and chairs around Regency coffee tables. Immaculate service people wearing tuxedos and tails descended on them as they entered.

Sabine felt grubby as hell in her black jeans and turtleneck, with her scuffed and dull walking boots. Even more so when the *maitre d'* seated them towards the center of the tea room.

Tea was served with clockwork precision. Sabine didn't feel like talking much and Ari also said little, sticking to small talk. The food was wonderful, but where the Dorchester had made them feel comfortable, no matter their dress, the Ritz reminded Sabine at least of how drab their travel clothes were.

Ari stared at the table next to theirs and Sabine cocked her head, trying to lock in on what so intrigued her tablemate.

A man dressed in a blue suit with a green satin vest and a scarf around his neck in the same delicious green. Dark brown hair, verging on black, and Sabine was sure his eyes were a dark hazel with green if she knew Ari at all, but Sabine almost flinched when she saw the shadow of a black wolf pass over his form. She had forgotten about the after effects of the Waking Dream on her life. How she had to beware the visions that sometimes attended even the most casual of glances.

Sabine tried to catch her friend's eye, but Ari's attention remained focused.

"Ari...?" Sabine started to ask, when he made eye contact with Ari.

His smile blinded. Even Sabine was struck by how it lit up his face and made him seem like a wonderful boy. Before Sabine could say anything, Ari scooted over on the divan and patted the cushion next to her, smiling like a schoolgirl.

"Ari, what are you doing?" Sabine said in a low voice. She knew she hadn't imagined the wolf-shadow.

"Hmm?" Ari asked, not even hearing Sabine's question.

She didn't get a chance to ask again, because wolf-shadowed man had an attack of the nerves. His smile faltered a little and he pressed a hand to his chest, miming the universal, *you mean, me?*

Ari smiled even more brilliantly, which coming from her could be a devastating experience. Sabine had watched stronger men melt under the total wattage of the Israeli at her most charming. Ari patted the divan again and beckoned him over with her other hand. But Sabine detected a quiver in her friend's gesture.

Ari, nervous?

Sabine closed her eyes and offered up a prayer to the Gods of Hormones.

He made his tentative way to their table and for another blinding moment, Sabine felt the wolf shadow.

"Ladies?" he said upon reaching the table's edge, but he only had eyes for Ari.

"Join us. Please," Ari said, her voice like silk.

A waiter appeared out of nowhere and moved the young man's tea things to their table, without them having to even ask.

"My name is Ari. This is Sabine," Ari waved over at Sabine. The man broke the heat of Ari's gaze long enough to glance at Sabine, which earned him a wry smile. He bowed, just a slight and very precise move, and when he spoke again, it was with a light Germanic accent, but the tone and tenor were like velvet, or fur.

"My name is Ulrich Wolfjen. Ulrich to my friends."

Sabine didn't need any preternatural sight to see the way the two of them tried to resist leaning into each other, but pretty much failed. His eyes were indeed green, flecked with warm brown. She tried to find other things to put her attention on, people watching the room.

Sabine only heard part of the conversation, picking up that he was a lawyer, waiting to pass the European equivalent of the Bar there in London and was staying with a few friends. His English wasn't perfect, but it was better than Ari's German, which was to say, non-existent. She more felt than heard Ari gasp.

"What?" Even Sabine was a bit surprised at how hard and curt that one word came out of her mouth. She couldn't decide if Ari appeared scared, worried or amused.

"I see that my observation is correct," Ulrich added and Ari laughed, but even to a stranger, Sabine knew it sounded weak.

"Oh, you know. Just the usual weirdness one meets on vacation."

Sabine filled in the rest of the conversation with lightning quickness. "Fill me in." Sabine didn't even try to modulate her tone.

"I observed to your friend that you have already had an interesting time here in London, one that had not gone unnoticed."

Sabine's slow, spreading smile was not pleasant. "Truly?"

"I also said that with your, hmm, how do you say? Auras? Yes, that's it, you were probably going to experience more of the same."

"Really."

"Really," and then Ulrich's gaze went back to Ari, and Sabine saw his self-containment flowing away like water from a high place. The emotion in his face was so naked, Sabine had to look away.

"And I could not... I could not live with myself to not mention it," he continued.

"Why warn us," Sabine took a huge gamble. "...Wolflord?"

Ulrich's gaze was on her, whip-crack fast. "My reasons," his gaze dragged back to Ari, almost as if against his will. "My reasons are my own."

Sabine inclined her head in acknowledgement, knowing she would get nothing further from this spirit that chose to walk in a man's shape.

He rose from their table, tea forgotten. Sabine knew that Ari didn't even notice that her hand reached out to grasp his sleeve.

"Will I see you again?"

Sabine noted also the distinct absence of the plural in Ari's sentence. She would have felt amused if the current of power that had dropped on their table hadn't been so strong and so worrying.

He hesitated. "I will be at the café here on the corner, the one across from Green Park Station on Sunday at noon, to meet friends," he said, but then looked back at Sabine. "But I do not think you will make it. Good day, ladies."

He made his little precise bow again. "I hope, no, I am certain, we will meet again."

"As am I," Sabine said, her voice soft. Sabine bent her head, trying to give Ari privacy for her grief as the Wolflord walked away. Instead she smiled at the waiter when he refilled the teapot that Sabine had been the only one to drink from. She poured another cup and this time dropped in two sugar cubes, needing something sweet to chase out the taste of sorrow in her mouth.

She heard Ari take in a shaky breath. "Let's get out of here."

She Dreamed that night.

The fatigues were loose on her and at one time they had fit, but that was before, when food had been plenty and good. She caught her reflection in one of the mirrors lining the great hall of the temple, the red and black banners ragged and burning from the rafters. A man's face stared back at her. The name on her/his chest read Harrison. She had enough time to see the captain's bars on her collar.

"Harrison..." she whispered.

A great weight of grief crushed her. The smoke from the burning banners thickened until it obscured her vision. Icy cold stone beneath her bare feet then. Sabine expected to wake from the chill of it. Her feet shone white against the black marble. She wore the same t-shirt she had put on to go to bed in at the hotel room.

Coils of blackness floated above her, with a rainbow shine like an oil slick, covering the ceiling, the entire surface a mass of shifting ebon limbs. Sabine stared in jaw-dropped awe. It was terrifying, sinister, and horrible in the truest sense of the word, and yet, Sabine felt her heart break for the symmetry of its beauty, the sheer perfection of its hideous design.

"It is the Beloved."

A girl's voice. Sabine knew it well, for it could as well have been hers. It matched the tones she had heard on recordings. But this voice had power and resonance that Sabine had never possessed.

"The Beloved?" Sabine asked, her voice seeming tiny in the vast cavern.

The coils floated down to her, defying gravity and her own fear. They split apart and from out of the depths of that roiling mass came a cradle of steel and magick. Sabine had a visceral memory of the caress of that mass, for she had Dreamed it.

"I knew that," Sabine added in a near whisper.

The girl laughed in recognition and relief. It jarred. Sabine didn't think joy or the sound of it was something that that place ever knew.

"Oh, at last, at last," the girl cried, and Sabine saw where the girl rested in the cradle, the Beloved shifting its coils to reveal her.

Sabine's own face looked out at her, but pale, so much paler, as if no sunlight had ever darkened this girl's skin. A child, verging into a young woman. She had no eyes. Sabine felt her heart leap in terror and then the feeling was gone.

"Who are you?"

"Zoë, my name is Zoë. Oh, Sabine, I have waited so long! I have called and called."

"Why?"

"Don't you know?" Zoë's face clouded, and how she could be so expressive, with no eyes to convey her feelings, Sabine didn't know. They were black holes, not even scars, as though she had been born without them. Yet Zoë looked straight into Sabine's face and Sabine realized with a dreadful start that Zoë could see her.

Sabine would never know what prompted her to speak.

"I have seen ghosts. The fraternities move with strange design," she said, this time in a voice that was no longer a whisper, but still low in terror that someone might hear them.

She continued, not understanding what prompted her to confess to this young mirror of herself. "I am afraid. I am so afraid, Zoë."

"I know." Zoë's face clouded again, this time in grief. "But only you can help us."

"What is going on?"

"The time is upon us. Yours especially. Remember, when you wake, Sabine. Remember."

"This is real," Sabine said. She Dreamed, she knew that, but still this conversation was true, and Zoë and the Beloved existed somewhere. Zoë smiled and the power of sudden helpless hope on her face nearly broke Sabine.

"The Oracles all share one sight," Zoë said.

Her eyes opened on early morning light seeping in around the corners of the heavy hotel curtains. Sabine stared at the ceiling, the power of the dream, if it could be called just a dream, still a tight grip around her mind and heart. It didn't take much light either to see Ari sitting up in her bed.

"Who is Harrison?"

"Huh?" Sabine gurgled.

"Harrison. Who is he?"

Sabine rubbed her eyes. Her feet still felt cold as if she had just stepped off of the cold marble. "Why do you ask?"

"You were crying in your sleep and then I heard you say 'Harrison'."

Sabine looked down. Her hands were wet.

"I... Dreamed. I dreamed I was in this place. It was burning, and then I saw myself in a mirror and I was wearing those fatigues again and the name on my chest said Harrison. And I was a man."

"That's all?"

"No. It felt like something terrible had happened. Hopelessness," Sabine sighed, the last word a whisper.

"Was that all?"

"No," she said after a long pause. "But, but it's not something I feel I can talk about just yet. I don't know what it means."

"All right. But you will tell me?"

"Yes." Though how did you explain dreams that were Dreams and conversations that made no sense?

"It's seven. Do you want to go back to sleep?"

"No." The strength of that negative shocked Sabine further awake.

"Okay. Why don't you take the shower first?"

Sabine still worried over her friend's kindness an hour later. But tea, toast, eggs and Irish bacon had a way of driving away even Sabine's champion worryfest. The sorrow from the first part of her Dream failed being so easily banished though, and she found herself depressed enough to be obvious.

Ari who put her teacup down with a thump.

"Well?" asked Sabine.

"You know what you need?"

"A vacation from my vacation?"

"No," Ari said. "A change of scenery."

"What do you recommend?"

"Madame Tussaud's."

"That's avoiding weirdness?!?"

"We might as well head straight for the weirdest place in town. Besides," she paused for dramatic effect. "It's two blocks away from Baker Street." Ari was a huge Sherlock Holmes fan. She had the entire Jeremy Brett as Holmes series on DVD, all the books, all the academic stuff, you name it, she had it. She even had a photo of Irene Adler and the King of Bohemia from the Brett TV series on her fridge.

Sabine dug out her handy dandy map of the Underground and the two of them poured over it. They would have to change lines twice to get from Earl's Court to Baker's Street, but it wasn't going to be too unpleasant as far as Sabine could tell. It wasn't rush hour and they didn't have to go through Piccadilly Circus.

The Tube came to its usual squealing stop and Sabine and Ari piled out with the other passengers . Ari squealed with glee when they hit the cement. The entire station was tiled, and on every other tile was the profile of the Great Detective himself.

And then Madame Tussaud's Wax Museum turned out to the have the longest line that they had had the misfortune to meet.

"Of course. An hour and a half wait. Of course," Sabine muttered, looking up at the sign over their head.

"Hmm. Popular spot, I guess." Ari's eyes glittered with suppressed laughter.

"Go ahead. Laugh." Sabine grinned at her friend.

"Think of it this way. With this many people around, who would try anything?"

After a hot and miserable wait in line, complete with elbows in the kidneys and glaring tourists, they got inside at last. Sabine would later not be able to tell if it were the heat or the crush of people or what other force caused her to start feeling nauseated and upset. All she knew was that at one point, while she hugged a piece of wall with Ari in front of her, and tried to take a deep breath, she saw them.

The same two men she had spotted at the Victoria and Albert museum and who had followed them to Harrods.

"Heads up," Sabine said between one pant and the next, pretending to look at the wax figure next to her. Mirrors were plentiful in Tussaud's, to give the illusion of a larger space.

"Hmm," Ari said, catching their reflection. "The Malice Twins."

"Malice Twins?" Sabine chuckled in spite of herself.

"The Malice Twins. Gods, do they have only one suit apiece?" They wore the same gray Mandarin collar suits as before and the bald one wore his round black sunglasses even inside.

"What idiots."

"We're bracketed," Ari said in a cold voice.

"Where? The same suits? Makes them look like Mormons, doesn't it?" Sabine muttered, acid cutting her tone. There were four others of the Twins' ilk, though none as evil looking. The additional men didn't have the same feel about them as the Twins either. Sabine felt her nausea grow.

"I don't feel so good."

"Time to go," was all Ari said, and they headed for the exit.

A strange anger fell on the crowd, the people's faces around them distorting, and Sabine felt her blood grow cold. If she hadn't known better, she would have thought it a type of battle fetter.

"Ari..."

"Magick..." Ari hissed.

They tried to press by some people to get out, since the presentation areas narrowed to a mere hallway past the original exhibits of Tussaud's. Two touristy looking women turned on them, murderous rage on their faces, and Sabine didn't know what Ari said or did to them, but they backed down like cowed dogs.

They paused a moment by one exhibit that stopped them both in their tracks. Sleeping Beauty, the wax figure of the mistress of one of the King Louis' of France. She breathed by some unknown mechanism and Sabine felt a chill for a different reason. It was as if the soul of the woman somehow still was within the wax form. It scared the living hell out of her.

"This means something..." Sabine said.

Someone's hand gripped Sabine's elbow in a vise lock grip that was not Ari. The bald-headed Twin. He had managed to cross through the crowd without either of them noticing. Adrenaline shot through her veins like ice.

"Miss Parsons."

"Can I help you?"

"You will come with us."

"Really?" Sabine smiled. "Ari?"

Ari, who had moved behind him, sent her fist right into the man's kidney, doubling him over. Sabine's arm came free from his grip.

"Right. Running!" Sabine grabbed Ari's free hand.

They dashed through an ever angrier crowd. The strange madness increased its hold and Sabine didn't know how they emerged from the maze of Tussaud's in one piece. At one point, they careened into another group, sending half of them to the ground in the collision. On the way up, two of the other men that had been with the Twins tried to lay hands on Sabine again and this time Sabine did the smartest thing she could think of.

She screamed.

It shocked the entire crowd of people into total silence.

"Go!" Ari shouted.

Madness erupted again. They were on the sidewalk outside now, people running in every direction. A space of twenty feet opened between them and their pursuers. The lead pursuer, not one of the Twins, but a dark man with black hair, reached into his coat. Time slowed down for Sabine and she was reaching for the small of the back holster that was no longer there. A holster she had not worn in thirteen years.

"Gun!" She threw Ari to the ground, terror rising in her. Then, somewhere in her torso, in her heart and her solar plexus, she felt something...break...

And she Reached.

A sudden twisting force cracked out of her body, from her out-flung hand, but even she could tell it was weak, too weak to do anything. She struggled to plant her feet; she needed to be grounded for this to work.

The next whip of invisible energy struck the man and his reaching arm. He staggered, but did not go down. Then another whipcord of force burst from her and this time it cracked thunder. The newspaper stand right next to the man flung itself at him and his companions, felling them in a flurry of limbs and painful yells.

The men gave her looks of mingled fear and rage from the concrete. They scrambled to their feet and ran.

Sabine's head split with agony from her left eye to the opposite side of the back of her neck in the next instant. She bit back a scream from the agony.

"Sabine!" she heard from so far away.

She staggered and went down on one knee, the blinding pain squeezing her eyes shut. The light of the day cut like knives into her skull. She could feel every pulse of her heart, every beat, as if her veins were going to burst open.

A cool hand on forehead and the pain receded a bit, but only a bit. Sabine cracked open one eye and saw Ari kneeling next to her, her Game Face on.

"We have to move," Ari said.

Sabine didn't know how far they went, as the pain bent time. They stopped in the shadow of a building at one point and Sabine managed to pry her eyes open. A bank. On the wall, a bronze plaque caught her attention. She even managed a laugh around the pain.

"221B?" she offered, and Ari broke her Game Face for a quick grin.

"I figure no one will look over here," Ari said, and Sabine realized that next to the memorial plaque of the abode of the Great Detective a sign announced the Sherlock Holmes Tea House and Museum.

"Tea?" Sabine managed.

"Yes. And some pain killers for you obviously, if we can manage it."

"I'll be okay."

Ari gave her a sharp look, started to say something, and then snapped her mouth shut. "Inside," she ordered, managing a bright smile for the man dressed like a Victorian Bobbie, standing in front of the tea house.

Sabine found herself seated in a comfortable chair in no time, the pink taffeta upholstery distracting her. The pain made it so that tiny details became all she could handle. Ari ordered tea and painkillers. She then leveled the "Give-It-To-Me-Straight" face at Sabine when their server left, and Sabine felt her headache strengthen.

"I hate to ask, but what happened back there?"

"I don't know," Sabine said, careful around the pain. She had never told her friend that a vast store of knowledge lay buried in her past. Buried it, and then trained herself to forget, because if she didn't forget, she would go mad. After all, people could not move things by thinking about it, could they?

"Code breaking," Ari continued.

"What of it?"

"That wasn't all you used to do for Them."

The tea came and Sabine gave thanks to Divine Intervention. Sabine felt her headache receding. But it left room for something else.

Not again, Sabine thought. *This couldn't be happening again.* She was normal, normal, normal. Panic bubbled up from somewhere underneath her, and she watched the edges of her vision go black.

"Sabine!"

"What?" Sabine snapped back to herself.

"Are you all right?"

"Fine, fine," Sabine said, shaking even so. "I just need a few minutes. It's the headache."

"Sabine," Ari began again, voice hard.

Sabine felt the panic slip and a small anger replace it. She knew for a fact that she didn't know everything there was to know about her friend. Needless to say, best friend or not, Sabine had her own secrets and was not about to divulge this one, whether or not it had any relevance. It would mean remembering.

"All right," Ari sighed in the face of Sabine's frown.

"*Sub rosa,* Ari." It was Latin, an old spy term, but for the two of them it meant secrets they were unprepared to divulge.

Ari opened her mouth, and then shut it with a snap. She laughed, her Game Face breaking, and Sabine's friend, her dear, dear friend, once more sat at the table, replacing the cold professional.

"Oh, *sabra!*" Ari only called her a prickly pear in Hebrew when she had to give way to something that Sabine had gotten stubborn on. They finished their tea in better humor, and Sabine's headache released its claws.

If Sabine dreamed that night, she remembered nothing and was glad for it. The feeling of unease from the previous day and her restless night kept her less than talkative all through breakfast. Ari pried not at all, nor posed any questions, much to Sabine's gratitude. In her friend's shoes, she would have been eaten up with curiosity.

They got back to their hotel room and Sabine pretty much vegetated in front of BBC 1 through 4 till evening fell, when Ari threw her book on to the bed.

"What?"

"That's it! We are not doing this!"

"Doing what?"

"We are not hiding in our hotel room like Nazi fugitives waiting for a Mossad hit! We are going out!"

"Okay," Sabine drew out the word.

"Get dressed! And makeup! Must have makeup!"

Uh oh, Sabine thought.

"Move!" Ari rapped out when Sabine sat there like a lump.

"Moving!" Sabine yelped and ran into the bathroom. "May I ask where we're going?" Sabine thought to ask as she washed her face. She ducked just in time as Ari threw Sabine's leopard print dress at her.

"Dancing," Ari said and stripped, throwing her tourist clothes on the floor and dropping a black Empire-waist dress over her head. Sabine started to undress at a slower rate, picking up her dress and laying it on the counter.

"Dancing." Sabine didn't phrase it as a question.

Ari sighed, the mad-on draining out of her as suddenly as it had appeared.

"I am tired of waiting for another hammer to drop. We need to have some fun, and fun means putting on our war paint, wearing our dresses that we haven't worn since we got here, and flirting outrageously with men at some horrible nightclub with no intention of ever giving them the time of day," she said. "If the Malice Twins want to show up again, they can at least buy us a drink first before trying to drop us into a burlap sack."

Sabine tried not to choke.

"I mean, come on, what is with the fashion victim identical suits? As if that's going to intimidate us? Please!"

"So, where are we going?"

"I thought I saw a bar around the corner on Knightsbridge Road that had a sign that said dancing. Or am I hallucinating?" Ari said, smudging her foundation on with quick practiced strokes.

"Yep, I do believe you are right. If not, we can always hail a cab and have the driver take us to a likely spot. They usually know what's hot."

"Ooo! Good idea!"

A very short time later found the two women on the street in black high heels and short, short hemlines. They strode through the cool London night the two blocks to the bar and were rewarded with a neon sign that indeed advertised "Dancing Every Night!"

"Pay dirt," Sabine said for her friend's benefit, and they stepped into the welcome darkness of the club, heels ringing off the cement walls of the short corridor.

Cover ended up being five pounds per, and Sabine was glad to see, for Ari's sake at least, that the smoke wasn't too thick when they got inside. Sabine didn't mind the haze and took a deep breath, letting it ease the knot that had formed under her breastbone.

The music pounded. Ari lead the way to the tiny dance floor at the back of the bar without a backward glance. For half an hour, they danced as if they were made out of steel, and tireless. When Sabine staggered off the dance floor, the lights flashing in her eyes, the artificial smoke thick enough around her to make it hard to see for long distances, she almost didn't know where she was for a moment. Ari bumped into her from behind.

"Water!"

"Whiskey!" Sabine countered.

A booth presented and Sabine sank into the red overstuffed bench with a contented sigh.

"Any particular type of whiskey, or whatever the bartender favors?" Ari asked.

"Dealer's choice."

"Okay. Living dangerously tonight, eh?"

"What, going out in high heels didn't already give you a clue?" Sabine closed her eyes, pretending for a moment that she didn't need to pay attention to her surroundings. Ari had been right again. Getting out was what the doctor ordered.

Ari returned and set a large tumbler of amber liquid in front of Sabine who eyed it with a raised eyebrow. "That is not one shot."

"I told him to make it a stiff one," Ari said.

Sabine raised the tumbler in a toast in the general direction of the actual bar. "To the good taste of the tender, then."

Apples and oak smoke seemed to roll over Sabine's tongue. For a moment, she closed her eyes and was not in the bar. She didn't know where she was, but a light summer breeze touched her cheek and she smelled...apple blossoms. No images came with the taste. It could have been memory or the more fickle Memory that sometimes dogged her, but the smell remained until she opened her eyes.

"Is it bad?"

Sabine brought her eyes back to focus on Ari. "It is the best whiskey I have ever had in my life."

"Well, that's a relief. What's with the odd expression then?"

"I've never had whiskey that tasted of..." Sabine found she almost couldn't put the taste of it into words. Not that she didn't have the words, but there was some power in naming what she was drinking, some acknowledgement that would be irrevocable, once it was made.

Nonsense, she thought. *It's just a shot or three of whiskey.*

"Tastes like what?"

"Apples," Sabine said and felt something go, *click,* like tumblers falling in a lock of cosmic proportions, but had no time to chase the thought.

"Hello, ladies!" A boisterous voice shouted next to them, and Sabine looked up with a surprised expression. On the other side of their booth's wall, three gentlemen leaned, in various states of alcoholic contentedness.

"Hello!" Ari said, turning on the wattage of her smile. Sabine just shook her head. The suckers for the evening had arrived.

"Good evening," she chose to say instead.

"And how are ye fine ladies on this evening?" The middle-placed man was the spokesman for the three, and Sabine had to smile. The accent was obvious enough even for her to know a Scot when she heard it. The three couldn't have been more unalike if they had tried. The middle one was tall and built like a lumberjack with dark brown hair. The man on his left was willowy like a Byron-esque poet getting ready to die of consumption, black hair rumpled in all directions, and the Scot's companion on the right was blond and pale as if he'd never seen any sun. The dark interior of the club made it impossible to determine any of their eye colors.

"Very well now," Ari said.

Pleasantries were exchanged and Sabine heard Ari give their names, but for the most part, she just sat back and relaxed, not bothering to pay any attention. Ari was quite happy with having found very willing victims for a safe game of flirtation. She asked their names, but Sabine still wasn't listening until the spokesman said his name, at which point, Sabine frowned.

"Pardon?" Sabine asked.

"Stoot!" The burly man said, and Sabine grimaced, not believing that to be his name.

"What?"

"*Stoot!*"

"What?"

"His name is Stewart!" Ari leaned over and yelled in her ear.

Sabine burst out laughing. "Oh! Stewart! Got it!"

The next few moments should have been pleasant ones, but weren't. The whiskey found its way to her mouth more often, not numbing her sense of trouble. Hysterical story from Stewart notwithstanding on how he came to be in the company of an Irishman and a Welshman named Adam and Paul, she couldn't shake feeling disturbed.

An icy hand descended on her shoulder.

Sabine cursed twenty kinds of gods for not remembering. The Dream didn't give her certainties, it gave her feelings.

"Miss Parsons." The voice that accompanied the hand was just as icy. The face of the bald pair of the Malice Twins loomed into her view. Out of the corner of her eye, she saw Ari freeze.

Where's your friend?! came Sabine's next crazed thought, her skin breaking out in a cold sweat.

"Step outside with me."

Fear turned to rage. "Get your hand off of me, you fucking asshole," Sabine said as loud as possible.

Baldie grimaced. A loud Scottish voice erupted behind her.

"Here now! What's this? Are ye bothering the lass?"

Sabine grinned with shark-like fierceness.

"Mind your own business, my friend. The young lady and I are acquainted."

"Is this true, me girl?" Stewart asked.

"NO!" Ari and Sabine's voice rang out together.

"Ye heard the ladies, my friend."

"I told you to mind your own business." Sabine felt the crackle of energy, ozone building on a storm-wracked horizon. *Magick.*

"Stewart! He's hurting me!" Sabine yelped, feigning pain.

A meaty fist swung over her head and connected solidly with Baldie's jaw.

"Woohoo!" Sabine yelled and dived under the table at the exact same instant as Ari. Their heads cracked together with a bone jarring *"thunk!"*. "Shit!"

Ari expelled a pained, "Ow!"

"Time to go!" Sabine added.

"Crawl! Crawl!" Ari commanded as she shoved Sabine out from under the table.

Bodies careened into each other. Sabine forged through the free-for-all that Stewart's one punch had spawned. Ari hung on to Sabine's purse strap. Sabine ducked as a fist came at her and heard some other poor patron *"woof!"* in surprise as he was hit.

She had the door in sight when she was jerked off her feet by the pack's strap and snapped around to see Ari being manhandled by Baldie's shorter partner.

Sabine took a deep breath to scream, reaching for the power she'd thrown earlier—

—which didn't come.

She could feel the alcohol cutting her off from the tenuous strength—

Ari, calm and collected, set up to break the man's arm, her arm snaking around her attacker, his elbow suddenly hyper-flexed as she shifted her weight, and with the short scream of the frightened woman that she wasn't, she broke his arm. There was an audible crunch that made Sabine wince. Short Boy screamed.

Ari dragged Sabine for the door. They piled out on to the sidewalk with several others, all scrambling in every direction, sirens shrieking in the distance. Sabine made it about a block, when the adrenalin drained out of her and the shakes made her wobble on her heels. She clutched a short ornamental wrought iron fence and slid down to the curb, the shaking so bad she couldn't keep her teeth from chattering.

"Sabine!"

Sabine fixated on her friend's stockings. There was a large run in the right knee. Sabine thought, *what a waste, expensive stockings ruined.* She must have said it out loud.

"Screw stockings!" Ari yelled.

She's losing her English again, Sabine thought.

"All right?" Ari asked, her arm coming around Sabine's shoulders as she sat down on the curb with Sabine.

The street lamp light lay stark and cold across the concrete. Sabine teared up and clenched her eyes tight closed to make it stop. The night cold bit in to her skin, colder than when they had gone into the club. Her butt started to go numb too, sitting on the curb. Ari had to be cold too. But Sabine couldn't stop shaking.

Deep breath, she thought. Cold air filled her lungs.

"I hate this," she said, ashamed that her voice shook. "It didn't come..."

"What?"

"Nothing. What the hell is going on?"

"I don't know, *bubela.* But when I find out, someone is going to pay."

"Ari," the change of tone must have scared Ari, because her face went from rage to concern.

"What, *bubi?*"

"Cops. Controllers. Why aren't we calling in? Why aren't you calling in?"

"Two things."

"Only two?"

"Two. One, you were already flagged by the State Department. We call anyone, we're on the first plane for home, end of vacation."

"So far, this isn't what I think you had planned."

Ari ignored her. "Two..." and she didn't go on.

"Ari?"

"I contact my controllers, and it'll be worse than deportation. We'll be on a plane for Israel. Because they'll have to poke you to see why they are following us. And really, so far, this could be nothing?" The fact she had to make it a question made Sabine shake her head.

She couldn't argue with Ari's reasoning. Sent home in the equivalent of disgrace from a frikken' vacation just annoyed the crap out of her. And the alternative? Ending up in the not-so-loving arms of the Mossad?

"Right," she said instead. "Let's skip it."

CHAPTER IV – SENSITIVE DEPENDENCY

Waterloo Station, United Kingdom – Paris du Nord, France

The next morning, they stood on the platform in Paris du Nord not even an hour later from having boarded the train in London. Glancing around, Sabine felt her stomach go tight. Most of the concession stands were closed. Never mind that she spotted three Romani working the crowd, all three of whom took one look at her, and made the sign of the Evil Eye.

"May Day," she muttered.

"May Day's a national holiday?"

"Only the biggest one of the year in most European countries. Biggest Communist holiday, I might add. Workers of the world unite and all that crap," Sabine said, scanning.

"But... But... Who knew?" Ari asked the air.

"Well, actually I did, but I forgot."

"Why?"

"Because it's a big deal here. But no worries, that's why I insisted on the guidebooks. Gimmee a minute," Sabine said, positioning herself in such a way so that her back was against the wall as she dug through the outside pocket of her bag.

"Why are you scanning?"

"Roma."

"Huh?"

Sabine lead the way to the curb. Outside, a huge crowd milled and in the center of the roundabout, a curly-headed young man swung a huge red flag. Sabine shook her head a little. The sky hung gray and menacing, setting the flag off to great effect. She already felt off kilter and had a kink in her neck that made her want to rip her own head off.

Train seats, who said they were comfortable? Sabine thought.

A BMW squealed to a stop in front of them and it took Sabine a moment to realize it was indeed a taxi. She made a mental note of the fact that BMWs in Europe seemed to be the equivalent of Chevys back home. The Gallic driver got out and piled their luggage in the trunk in a manner that made her glad they had nothing breakable. He did not wait for them to get settled or state where they wanted to go before driving off like a recruit for counter-terrorism defensive driving school.

She managed to communicate where they wanted to go to their cabbie by the simple expedient of holding open the guidebook and pointing at the address. The moment where he read it off while careening down the street made her heart stop.

"Remember what I said about London cabbies?" Sabine gritted out.

"Yeah?" Ari said, serenity personified.

"I take it back. This is worse."

More windy roads and terror for Sabine later, they stood on a tiny street which had a sidewalk on only one side of the street, looking at a building that had originally been built in the 1500s and according to the guidebook's assertion, a hotel.

Inside, the polite woman behind the counter in the tiny lobby spoke terrible English. Sabine knew her French wasn't any better and they mimed their way to taking a room for the week.

Sabine followed Ari to the staircase. She had a moment's dismay generated by the sway-backed look of the red-carpeted risers. But Ari climbed them with alacrity and despite the alarming creaking, she didn't fall through a hole.

"We need to talk," Ari said, just as Sabine stuck her head in the wardrobe to check out where to hang some of her clothes. She jerked her head back out. She had thought Ari particularly quiet since the train station.

"About what?"

"Several things. Like what are we doing for the rest of the day—"

"Sleeping."

"And, the contents of your fanny pack and what you meant at the train station. Oh, yeah, and what are we doing tomorrow? My vote's the Louvre!"

"In order. What fanny pack? And, I didn't say anything at the train station."

"Ah ha, we can't pretend that the bottle in your fanny pack doesn't exist."

"Should we talk about this here?"

"If we're bugged, we've been bugged for days, because it would be in the luggage, and we might as well just kiss our butts goodbye."

"Point. Point. Okay. You're right. But unless you've got a chemical lab tucked into your back pocket that you haven't told me about, I don't see how we can do anything about said little jar of cold cream. And as for the train station..." Sabine trailed off. How could she explain the gypsies? No. One did not mention that, not until one knew what was going on.

"I'm not sure yet," Sabine finished.

"Sure about what yet?!" Ari's exasperation cut.

"Ari, please. I would tell you if I knew what the hell was going on."

"The same way you'll tell me what happened at Tussaud's? The same way you'll tell me what you've been dreaming? Or would it be better for me to call us in after all?"

Sabine just looked at her. Raised an eyebrow. It wasn't as if Sabine was the only one who'd ever withheld information in their friendship.

"I'm sorry." Ari hung her head. "I guess I'm more tired than I thought. I've dragged you to another country on a stupid holiday—"

"Stop," Sabine cut her off, closing her eyes in exhaustion. "Just stop. We are going to bed. And we will have this idiotic discussion tomorrow when we are both well enough rested to be able to give each other the appropriate amount of shit. And decide then if we need to call your controllers."

"It's still morning."

"Bite me." Sabine climbed on to one side of the king-size bed, punched the evil bolster that was there instead of the pillow that should have been, and fell immediately into a deep sleep.

"Remember..." Zoë said.

Sabine stood in the Beloved's chamber, a cavern she now knew better than any place in her waking life. The stone was icy under her feet and as always the vaulted ceiling stayed shrouded in darkness. The Beloved's coils slid as if in a dance and Zoë looked down at her, sightless sockets locking on her own living eyes. Cloying incense mixed with something fouler in the air. Sabine knew she would now see something other than Memory and other than the Future. A Possibility, a quantum fluctuation in a fluid state experiment.

"Remember what you are about to see..." Zoë whispered.

The chanting began. Sabine wanted to run. She remembered this sound from other nightmares.

"No."

"Remember!"

The chanting, Latin and guttural. Sabine knew she should know the words, but her mind rebelled. She tried to move, but found herself rooted to the spot.

She saw Him.

They brought Him before the Beloved, thirteen hooded figures in robes that were dark as old blood. They stripped him to the waist, his torso scarred and pale.

Sabine wanted to scream.

He didn't struggle. Yet, he defied them somehow. Sabine glanced up for Zoë, but she was gone, the coils of the Beloved descending to the floor, carrying Its precious cargo to Its Masters.

"Oracle." The leader of the blood-robed disciples detached from the loose circle. The Beloved parted Its coils, bringing Zoë into view. His voice was like velvet and Sabine shuddered.

"Ask." The unearthly tones of Zoë's voice were so pronounced that Sabine could feel echoes in her own soul and realized that her own mouth had also answered. What was happening to her?

"Is the time come?"

"The time has come," Sabine and Zoë spoke as one.

Another figure removed itself from the group and stepped forward. From under the blood red robes, came a bundle swathed in black cloth. The bundle moved feebly and Sabine realized with a start that it was a baby, at the exact same moment that He went still as death.

"Yes." The leader sounded amused.

What happened next happened too fast for words. The disciples fell on the Beloved and ripped Zoë from the coils.

"No!" Sabine shouted but was unheard. Zoë looked at Sabine, her grace gone, unable to even stand, as one of the disciples grabbed her by her tangled blond hair and laid a long, thin curved knife against the white of her throat.

"Remember," was all she said.

They laid a knife to His throat as well. Sabine felt, as if from far off, her sleeping body struggling. The bearer of the child removed the swaddling and Sabine sucked in air.

Demon. Glazed black eyes darted from face to shrouded face, skin leprous gray and repulsive.

Without a word, the knives were drawn across two throats, and Sabine finally screamed. Blood fountained in every direction. The disciples roared in triumph, bathing the demon child in the offering. They put the child into the Beloved. Its sleek blackness turned dull and leprous, like some nightmare disease.

Sabine's scream echoed in the hotel room. She shot out of the bed, coming awake halfway across the room, hearing her name shouted at her.

"Sabine!"

I know this voice, Sabine thought brokenly. She was in Paris. She was in a hotel. She was not in a cavern. She was not covered in blood.

"Sabine!"

"Ari," Sabine said, hoarse. "I hear you."

But she could still hear Zoë.

"Remember."

They didn't speak of it in the morning.

The room they shared was strange. The bathroom was a pre-fabricated box with all its amenities installed in what once had been a closet. Very small, all one plastic thing and a shade of brown that reminded Sabine of some unfortunate gifts her childhood cat had sometimes left her. The one light in the bathroom was also placed so as to cast very little light into the shower.

But in that shower, her forehead placed against the chill plastic of the shower wall, the thin stream of water running down the back of her head and not enough to keep her warm, she was thankful and relieved. Ari had said nothing of the night.

"Breakfast?" Ari asked, typical morning cheer when Sabine climbed out of the shower. She smiled, though it felt as if her face stretched in an odd manner.

"Breakfast sounds loverly."

Sabine ordered croissants and espresso at the café catty-corner to their hotel. She also discovered that what they called espresso in the States was an evil weak thing and that she had found the equivalent of the caffeine Holy Grail.

"Wow," she said after half of her itsy bitsy cup of caffeinated death.

"Good?" Ari asked from across their tiny table. It was too cold to sit outside yet, the sky overcast and threatening, so they were crowded in with several other people inside. She had ordered the pâté plate for breakfast and looked in seventh heaven.

"Wow."

"I'll take that as a yes."

"Wow." Sabine looked ready to park all day, but Ari got up a little while later, food put away. "Where we goin'?"

"Louvre!" Ari pronounced.

"Oh boy. Museum crawling. We have such luck with that."

Ari scowled at her.

Her first mistake was in putting her head back into the guide, after getting through the turnstiles for the Metro. Which meant that when she looked back up, she was shocked to find that she had lost Ari. Until she turned around and saw who Ari had stopped to talk to, or more accurately been apprehended by.

"Um, *pardon, madame,*" Ari began and the ancient woman looked her straight in the eye and Ari shut up, not asking for her arm back, even though the woman's fingers dug into her elbow. The woman wore unrelieved black except for a fringed shawl colored in hues painful to the eye. She wore gold coins and tiny bells from her ears and gold chains around her neck of varying sizes and lengths. Ari couldn't see her shoes, but she wouldn't have been surprised if the woman had been barefoot. She looked as if she were rooted to the very heart of the earth.

"You are in great danger. The woman you travel with is not one to be caught in the company of," the woman said in clear unaccented English.

"What?" Ari gasped, because the woman's grip was harsh and the words made no sense.

"If you do not leave her behind and look to your own safety, you will find yourself in a place where even your oaths cannot protect you."

Ari felt herself go cold and the gold *chai* pendant around her throat suddenly seemed made of lead and heavier than the moon. "Let me go," she said with a voice of steel and wrenched her arm free.

"Listen to me!" the woman said, her black eyes fierce and direct. "A dark cloud follows her and a storm races in her wake. Lightning and thunder attend her passing and you will find yourself lost if you keep her company." Their eyes locked and Ari found her volatile Israeli temper stirring.

"I'll take my chances." And she marched herself to her friend's side.

"What was that about?" Sabine asked in an oh-so-practical voice.
"Cryptic warnings."

"Cryptic warnings?"

"Yeah. Like either of us need any more. You're having nightmares, I'm not doing much better and now strange women are giving me dire warnings in Metro stations. What's next?"

"That was no strange woman." Sabine's voice was calm, but her words ratcheted Ari's attention on to Sabine like a magnet.

"What are you talking about?" Sabine stared after the dark-haired, yet ancient woman with an intensity Ari had never seen in her friend before.

"That was a Rom. That was a gypsy," Sabine said.

"So?"

"They don't talk to normals unless it's to shake them down. They especially do not hand out foretellings for no money." The two women exchanged a long glance and continued on their way to the museum.

"Next flight up. I'm certain of it." Ari said, an hour later, the two friends finally in the Louvre, in search of the Venus de Milo, and she was still cheerful in spite of all the walking. Sabine tried not to glower at her or appear as wilted as she felt, but her friend saw through her.

"Really!" Ari was right this time. They emerged at the top of the stairs into a long hall filled with Greek antiquities. There were not one, but four statues to the Goddess Athena in her many guises.

"The models weren't particularly thin, were they?" Sabine mused out loud. The Athena she stood in front of was a little larger than life sized, carved in marble with the goddess' hand upraised as if enjoining her viewer to seek something higher.

Wow, Sabine thought. Not even close to her Nike back in London, but still, there was something. Better yet, this statue wasn't missing any pieces, which was even better.

Ari nudged her. "Had enough?"

"No. You know I can stare at sculpture all day." Sabine turned her head to look down the long hall of Greek antiquities and without a word took off for the end. Ari looked up and found her at the foot of a fifteen-foot-tall statue surrounded by a piece of temple wall.

Sabine stared straight up.

The figure was of a woman bearing the mask of Tragedy. Ari racked her brain for the name of the muse, for this was a representation of one of the nine daughters of Apollo.

"Do you think this is a sign?" Sabine finally spoke, her voice subdued.

Ari craned her neck up and considered. "What do you mean?"

"That this is all fucking doomed, doomed, doomed, as in, a fucking Greek tragedy."

"What?" Ari knew she had come in on the middle of one of Sabine's convoluted thought processes.

"Ari, we don't know what they are. And we haven't been followed today as far as I can tell and I don't know whether to be joyous or damned, to badly paraphrase Gomez Addams."

"Well, here is probably as good a place as any to talk about them," Ari said.

"No bullshit, Ari, you have no idea what they are?"

"No bullshit."

Sabine cursed fluently in Russian, an old tell from her much younger days. Can we find out?"

"Do you really want to? We had this conversation."

That stopped Sabine cold. "What do you mean?"

"You know what I mean."

"As in, if we find out, we get involved, and if I won't convert and move to Israel, what in the Jews non-existent idea of Hell makes me think that it is a good idea to involve your bosses?"

That startled a laugh out of Ari. "You left out the part about, what about your insistence that you don't want to have anything to do with the fraternities anymore?"

"Yes," Sabine sighed and dropped her head into one hand and scrubbed hard.

Ari gently touched her friend's shoulder. "Are you going to be okay?"

Sabine looked up with a bright smile, shadowed by the unidentified emotion again. "Yeah, I'm great. You just know how much I hate not knowing."

"Yeah. I do. But, *sabra,* I really don't think you want to find out. Look, I have to, good conscience and all, forward our little package on to my home, but y'know, we can do that soonest and just forget this shit. Really." She patted her friend's shoulder. "Our vacation just got off to a bad start. But you said it. No sign of nothing since we've been in Paris."

"Roma."

"Do the words, "I'm an idiot" mean anything to you?" Ari said, acid-tongued.

"Ari!"

"No, really. I guess we both spoke too soon. But," Ari frowned with sudden resolve. "Who gives a shit? We weren't trained for nothing, were we?"

"Well, it's around here somewhere," Sabine said as they climbed out of the Paris Metro the next morning and into the delightful sunshine they had been seeing so little of; she looked up from deciphering the map in her hand. "Thataway, I should think." She nodded with her head towards the way they already faced.

"Wow."

The architecture was lovely on most of the older two-, and three-story apartment buildings, though Sabine couldn't identify the period or the style, and trees were planted everywhere, shading the sidewalk, leaving the wide avenues sunny. No houses or buildings faced the main drag itself and it wasn't until they had walked a block and turned on the street indicated on Sabine's map that they got to appreciate the wonderful façades and wrought iron balconies of the buildings. French doors and chiffon curtains could be glimpsed through the windows, flowers and plants hanging in every window box. It was so picturesque that Sabine clicked away with Ari's little old school film camera before they had even reached their destination.

"Don't shoot up all the film," Ari teased her.

"It's okay. I've got another six rolls in my coat."

They approached a high wall with an open wooden gate and a small window on the left side of the gate was a ticket office.

"This is the Rodin museum?" Sabine wondered out loud. "I thought it was his house where he worked."

"Got me," Ari said.

They paid for two tickets, muddling through digging out Euros and walked through the gate and into a large courtyard landscaped in the old park style. Immediately to their right stood the Thinker, Rodin's most famous and lasting work, on a seven-foot pedestal streaked on all sides in wide rivers of green where the bronze had oxidized and run down the stone. Directly to the left, against a tall white stone wall, stood The Gates of Hell in all of their blackened-bronzed glory.

"Oh. Oh," Sabine sighed. "It's..."

"Wonderful," Ari said, but she looked straight ahead at the Edwardian mansion that had for so long been the home of Rodin and his work and now its caretaker.

"Oh goodness. Where should we start?"

"Well, let's start inside and then come back outside. I want to see the inside of the house!" Ari said, heading for the glass double doors leading into the main hall.

They wandered the rooms and split up and rejoined each other several times. The house was as of much interest as the sculpture itself, though the interior of the house mostly held the studies and small models of the great sculptor's larger bronze works. Ari found Sabine again upstairs, staring at the Danaid, a woman lying coiled as if she were just melting out of the very marble.

"Done?" Ari asked.

"Sure. The garden now?"

"Uh hmm!"

Outside, the sun still shone warm and bright, verging on hot. The sky was the clearest either of them had seen in the entire trip and Sabine sighed in gratitude. *No chance for broken rainbows that were devoured by dark clouds of blackness,* she thought.

"Which way?" Ari asked.

"Gates of Hell!" Sabine announced.

"You and bloodshed," Ari laughed, following in her friend's ecstatic wake.

"It's not bloodshed! It's art appreciation!"

The glare off the white wall behind the Gates of Hell was so bright that it was almost difficult to look at the piece. In blackened bronze, it was more imposing and awe-inducing than the smaller version that Sabine had once seen back in the States. Naked bodies writhed across the surface of the doors, giving flight and movement to solid metal. A smaller version of the Thinker crowned the door, and Sabine stood mesmerized. The statues of Adam and Eve, posed as if exiled from the garden, flanked the piece, Adam on the left, Eve on the right.

She glanced around the courtyard and down the side of the house where trees started in true park fashion and tourists and natives wandered amongst the sculptures and through the well-maintained park.

She looked back at the gates.

The gates stood ajar, a blinding white blue actinic glare spilling from the crack like a flaring star.

Wide open.

Sabine blinked hard. The doors were shut. The sunshine poured down warm on her skin and shone on the blackened bronze.

"Oh shit," Sabine said, blinked again. The blinding light stayed gone. But scarlet after-images stayed on the backs of her eyelids from the intensity of the light she had seen.

"What?" Ari asked.

"Did you see that?" Sabine asked, turned her head slowly to look at her friend. "Oh shit."

"See what? Sabine?" Ari's eyebrows came down.

"The gate. The gate was open."

"No way. Vision?"

"Don't know." Sabine went back to staring at the Gates, waiting.

Nothing happened.

Ari grabbed her arm, pulling her away in a quick walk, muttering under her breath. Sabine only gained comprehension of what she was saying halfway through. "…museums. Why did it have to be museums? Is the Shekinah punishing me? Is it the ham sandwich I had when I was twelve?"

Sabine stopped, tugging Ari to a stop with her. They stood under the trees of the park, the Burghers of Calais standing watch over them.

"Ari, please. A minute." Sabine caught herself staring past the park hedges at a gold dome visible above the trees of the park. "What's that?"

"Don't know," Ari replied. "Looks cool though."

Sabine dragged the Planet Guide out of her pocket and started flipping through it. She made a silly noise and started walking, toxic gates forgotten by force of will.

"I take it we're going?"

"Les Invalides! Nappy's buried there!"

"Napoleon?"

"Now *there* was a total poseur," Sabine said when they stood in the viewing gallery above the last resting place of Napoleon Bonaparte,

Emperor of France. The great vault of the cathedral of Les Invalides arched above them and Ari found her eyes more drawn to the ornate main altar, than the incongruous tomb. The inside domes were painted with angels and clouds and the blue-stained glass created puddles of indigo light.

Then there was this hole cut in the floor and a tomb.

"Yeah," Ari replied. "But the French still want him back."

"You should talk; the Jews still want King David to come back."

"True. Wonder if he was really short too?"

Sabine wandered off, pursuing something of light and shape with Ari's camera, while Ari stayed a moment longer to gaze on the tomb of the diminutive emperor.

"החברים שלנו עם המטריות מחפשים אותך, *Arila*."

To her credit, Ari did not jump. Not at the nearness of the voice, nor in recognition of the fact that it was Hebrew that he spoke. She casually turned towards the voice.

" יהושע , זה לא מנומס להתגנב הזקנים שלך",

she answered, keeping her voice low and an eye out for Sabine. Sabine however was occupied with French architecture.

"אל תדאג . אני אשמור על הלוויה שלך",

Joshua said. He was just a hair shorter than Ari and beautiful, with olive complexion and curly brown hair, His eyes were as brown as her own.

" לא אכפת לי , שיהיה לי אכפת ? "

Ari said, neutral and cool.

" את נראית נפלא על מצלמה נסתרת . "

"אתה משקר".

" לוואי שידעתי . ניסינו למצוא את הקלטת של המוזיאונים , אך האוצרת שלנו לא מצליחזה להגיע לאן הוא נשמר . מדיניות השאלה וכל . "

Ari nearly swore.

" האם יש משהו שאני יכול להגיד Bubbi ו Zeda ? "

Joshua asked and Ari went a little still. The code was clear. *Do you require assistance, backup and/or air support*, was the translation.

" לא כרגע . תגיד להם שאני אהיה בבית בזמן לפסח . "

I require no assistance.

" זה יגרום להם שמח . "

Your funeral.

Joshua melted away. When Ari turned around, she saw Sabine staring their way with a puzzled expression. Ari smoothed her features and prayed that her friend did not suspect anything. She hated keeping secrets from Sabine, but the entire point of their trip... Well, the entire point of their trip was rather defeated, Ari decided. But she couldn't bring herself to give this new news to Sabine. She would just pray to the *Shekinah* that nothing else happened.

Like the fact that the British Museum's security net had picked them up on video as witnesses to a murder and that now, British Intelligence wanted them for questioning. Compared to gates of damnation gaping open with light that only her friend could see, it seemed almost banal. She'd just make sure they didn't pause at all in London on their way home.

But if nothing else, Joshua's visit at Les Invalides seemed to be their lucky charm, though Ari continued to not tell her friend. Two more days went by and they saw neither hide nor hair of anything weird and even Ari began to hope that maybe their troubles were over. She even justified that it gave her reason to not tell Sabine of the other agent's visit.

The next day, they emerged from their Metro ride onto the wide avenue of the Champs-Elysée to a day overcast and chill, the sunlight that had been with them having gone wherever Spring had. They walked the length of the avenue to the large oval park at the end and the triumphal arch that until then, Sabine had only seen in photographs. It must have been another holiday, for a military band performed underneath the arch and an enormous French flag waved in the breeze in huge and artistic billows.

"Picture time!" Ari announced and Sabine groaned in mock horror, but suffered Ari to take the picture. They milled about. Gawked at the architecture. Ari announced that she was hungry. Sabine glanced up and down the avenue.

"Where?"

"There." Ari pointed. One each Hard Rock Café.

"Woohoo!" Sabine cried. "Saints be praised! American food!"

A familiar meal annihilated and put away (Sabine had never missed a hamburger that much) two hours later had them on the street again, at a loss for activity.

"Look! A movie theater. Wanna catch a flick?"

One each Hong Kong action flick dubbed in English with French subtitles later, they left having killed another few hours. But the exit of the theater proved difficult. The theater didn't dump them back into the lobby, but into an empty hall. No indication that anything was out of place or worrisome in the least, but even so, Sabine felt a chill.

"This is a little spooky," she said, staring up and down the gray corridor, the pleasure of the day gone.

"Oh?"

"Nothing. Just don't like long empty halls with nobody in 'em but us."

"Well, I can't imagine why you would feel like that," Ari said, and grinned at her friend. "Paranoia isn't exactly a trait you have or anything."

"Yeah, yeah. Laugh it up," Sabine grumbled.

The corridor ended in an alley behind the theater, their conversation having carried them through the industrial puce colored hall to the exit. Ari came to a halt.

"Okay, you felt it that time, didn't you?" Sabine said softly and that was all she had time for.

They came out of nowhere. Gray coats. More of the Malice Twins' ilk. Sabine whipped around at the sudden footfalls running towards them, she thought she saw the taller one of the Twins and knew the other one couldn't be far behind. She couldn't count how many of them there were. Too many.

Ari said something, but Sabine couldn't make it out except for the urgency. She ran, not waiting. The exit of the alley was too far away for Sabine's taste. They had to reach the Champs again, get to the Metro. If they could get to the trains...

Something whistled by Sabine's ear and she ducked. She heard Ari swear in Hebrew and wondered how she could hear so clearly. Her vision was suddenly sharper. Her heart pounded in her ears, which made her irrationally angry.

They burst out of the alley and a black BMW sedan screeched to a halt right in front of Sabine, but she had no time to stop. She bounced off the hood, and spun, watching Ari make the turn with more ease, her long legs opening up distance between them as she headed for the Metro sign. Sabine moved to run just as the door to the BMW popped open and the other of the Twins appeared.

She didn't think.

She Reached.

A howling wind came out of nowhere, throwing debris and trash between her and her pursuers. Thick with grit and small stones, Sabine felt it cut her cheeks where it whipped past her. She didn't wait to see if it worked. She ran.

Ari was long out of sight, having made the Metro. She didn't worry. Sabine knew that Ari would make her way back all right. She threw herself down the stairs into the bowels of the underground transit system.

The last thing she expected to see, having thrown herself over the turnstile, not even bothering to pay, was Ari holding the doors of one of the trains. She saw Ari's mouth open, but didn't hear her screams. She could feel the urgency though. Magick aimed at her back, designed to bind and cripple.

She Reached again, this time twisting her place in space and time. She didn't know how she did it. All she knew was that she crossed the difference of space between her and Ari in the space of a heartbeat.

The train doors slammed shut and the train surged away.

Sabine fell to the train floor, wracked with dry heaves.

Ari could only stare. Sabine had vanished and then reappeared right next to her. Their pursuers had been left behind, and she watched the receding figures on the platform behind them.

They stood in place, shocked into stillness and she knew how they felt. This was more terrible than dreams and Dreams. This was now forbidden magick, at least as far as her rabbi was concerned.

She dropped to her knees to help her friend, who lay on the floor of the train, dry-heaving, and prayed that they would find some way to survive.

They emerged onto the street near their hotel. They both looked up at the sign for the Relais Odeon at the same time. It was still open. Sabine glanced at her watch. Cheap and black plastic. It was only a digital watch nothing special, nothing...magick. It wasn't even midnight yet.

"Hungry?" Sabine asked.

"I could eat a whole cow," Ari said in a voice drained of all emotion.

"We'll make them serve you one."

The Relais was bright and cheery and loud. Mandolin music played in the background. Sabine felt weary to her bones. Did these people know what was out in the night? Yet the Relais was packed with people laughing and talking and drinking red wine.

"Blind. They're all blind."

"What?" Ari asked, as they sat down at a little booth.

"Nothing," Sabine replied, climbing out of her coat, every muscle groaning in protest. She felt creaky and old. Whatever she had done, and her mind shied away from examining her recent actions too closely, had drained her in a way she had never felt before. It just felt like she had tried to stuff her body through a sieve and then put it back together on the other side. With gum.

"It's almost midnight," Ari said after the waiter left, meaning, *why are you ordering caffeine at this time of night?*

Espresso had figured prominently in Sabine's order; Sabine just looked at her.

"Never mind."

They ate in silence, or as close to it as they could. The noise around them in any other situation would have made Sabine feel more relaxed. She was just too rattled. All she knew was that it made her teeth grit together and she ate with alacrity and drank her espresso with less enjoyment than total focus.

"Do we just have bad luck or is there something you want to tell me, Ari?" Sabine asked. "I mean, is it like spy season and we just don't know it? I know it was tax day when we left, but this is ridiculous!" Sabine waved the waiter down and ordered another espresso.

"You sure you want more caffeine?" Ari asked, watching with growing concern as Sabine drank the last half of her first little cup.

"Why not? It can't make me feel any worse."

"Point. You have a point."

"Yes, I do."

They said nothing, while the voices went on around them, Men and women laughing and living. Sabine felt like they were all living on borrowed time.

Ah yes, her little voice whispered. *Magick and malice walk the night openly and care not for who sees it.* Some days, Sabine hated that her little voice had a penchant for the sarcastic.

"Maybe..." Sabine started.

"Maybe what?"

"Do we call in?"

Ari froze over her tea. "I don't know. My gut..."

"I know." Sabine didn't wait for her to finish. "It doesn't feel right."

"We're probably fools."

"Yes, but we'll be fools together."

Chapter V – The Stuttgart Experiment

Paris du Nord, France – Stuttgart, Germany

They couldn't get out of Paris fast enough.

The next morning, Sabine started packing and Ari had to help her. It was getting to be a bit of a puzzle. One whole pocket of Sabine's bag now held nothing but shot rolls of film. They hadn't found a photo place in Paris, so Sabine was lugging the rolls around.

"Need to ship these home," she muttered.

"We will. Eventually," Ari laughed. "It'd be easier if you shot digital."

Sabine made a face in disdain followed by a response that might have been a smile. She'd managed to go to sleep after sitting by the window for hours once they'd gotten back to their hotel room, but not until she had made the decision to get out of Paris.

Things turned comedic when they went to go pay the reckoning on their room, for the nice lady who spoke no English was mystified by their sudden desire to leave. Sabine never did quite understand what the lady's protests were about, beyond that they had something to do with, how could or why would anyone want to leave Paris?

They were lucky and got a cab on St. Germain des Pres almost the instant they stepped outside. Straight to Paris du Nord he drove like a madman. They piled out in front of the immense façade of Paris du Nord in short order. Sabine looked both ways for pickpockets and led the way into the concourse.

"Hey, how about Stuttgart?" Ari burst out.

"Stuttgart?"

"Look, whatever horrible coincidence or curse is following us, it wouldn't go to Germany. It especially wouldn't go to Stuttgart."

"Stuttgart?"

"Sabine, you are repeating yourself…"

"Stuttgart?"

"…Bad!"

"I can't help that!" Sabine yelped. "Ari! Stuttgart!"

"If it's bad, we'll leave."

"Damn straight we will."

"Sabine, come on. Where's your sense of adventure?"

"Oh, don't even go there." Sabine cocked her head back to look up at the Departures board again. "Stuttgart," she muttered.

"Stuttgart," Ari said brightly.

"Fine. Just fine."

As they boarded the train for Stuttgart, Sabine realized something unpleasant.

Paris had grown on her.

The train raced out of the station, leaving the Paris suburbs behind in a flash. The train ran through rolling hills and fields turning golden in the early afternoon light, Paris a beautiful skyline behind them as they curved away from the City of Lights. The train rocked and surged under Sabine and she felt more than heard as the steel wheels hit the seams in the iron road.

The train stopped when they hit the German border. When Sabine looked out the window, it wasn't modern Germany. The ground was torn and muddy. She blinked hard. It hadn't been any part of her imagination either that she had felt she wore a uniform again, and had a foot taller of height while sitting.

Captain Harrison.

Her Past.

"Why's the train stopping?" Ari asked, looking up from her Terry Pratchett novel.

"Well, that answers one question," Sabine muttered.

"What?"

"Never been to Germany, have you, Ari?"

"What does that have to do with anything?"

Two men in uniforms, H&K MP5's on slings under their arms and a very burly German Sheppard dog boarded the train. Sabine started digging her passport out. They were an obvious training pair, for the younger man, who was quite handsome, checked the passengers' papers, while the older, who had a very handsome mustache to go with his dark good looks, looked over his shoulder and corrected him every so often.

"Border patrol," she said, keeping her calm. Ari went for her own passport.

The guards got to them and Sabine made herself smile and hand over her passport and their train tickets. Ari also handed over her passport. The young man started to ask them something in German and the older man, smiled and coughed.

"Americans," he said clear as day, and the poor boy flushed.

Sabine just smiled at him. The boy was very new to the circuit if he couldn't remember to ask in English his questions when he held two American passports. It didn't change the fact that she felt that if he had asked his questions in German, she would have been able to answer him in kind. She also wanted to go for the sidearm that she knew she had never carried in a regulation US Army holster on her hip.

"Border patrol." Ari looked at her.

"The Germans take their security very seriously."

"Oh dear."

The rest of the ride into Stuttgart was more subdued, though not to complete silence. They traveled through farmland at which point, Ari glued herself to the windows, pointing out the local livestock, while Sabine tried to continue to read her Clive Barker book.

With every mile they covered, Sabine felt an encroaching dread. She blinked and sat on a troop train, dirty and exhausted and tired, pain in every muscle and bone. Fear under all of that. She blinked again and she rode a modern train with Ari.

Blink.

She, no, *he* looked at his hand-picked squad and prayed that they would get through their mission alive. Four young and exhausted men. Talented and driven. But what they faced was not in any Army training manual.

Blink.

Sabine dug her fingernails into her hand with a sudden fierceness. *I am Sabine Parsons, American woman, itinerant writer and struggling artist,* she thought fiercely. *I am not a Captain in the United States Army. I am not an analyst. I am not a member of the intelligence community. Not...*

Not anymore.

"Sweetie?" Ari broke in on her inner struggle. "Are you all right?"

Sabine blinked a couple times and this time stayed in the present. So she lied. "I think I'm getting train sick."

"I think I've got some crackers in my bag."

Sabine smiled. "That might help."

Close on to 7:30 in the evening, the train pulled into the station at Stuttgart. They climbed off, trusty black bags wheeling behind them, and walked into a beautiful, high vaulted hall of a station. Sabine still felt a chill and the dread returned. She felt the breath of Captain Harrison on the back of her neck, the breath of his memories, a life she had lived and which now pressed in on her present as hard as deep water tries to crush a diving bell.

Her eyes hurt from the dry air and fatigue. They had left what little warmth behind them in Paris. Cold penetrated even into the station and she shrugged deeper into her trench. Ari looked around and smiled as they traveled deeper into the station. She led the way to a clear spot by some deep wooden benches.

"Well, guidebook time, I should think," Ari said.

"Way ahead of you," Sabine responded, having already bent down to get it out. It took her only a moment to find what she sought and her stomach sank.

"We gotta book."

"What?"

"Tourist Board closes in," Sabine whipped a look at her watch. "Twenty minutes."

Sabine was right on the state of the weather as well, when they dog trotted outside. They emerged into a gray world. Gray buildings and a sky that looked like a ceiling of slate. Sabine felt like her soul became heavier with every step they rushed.

A pedestrian tunnel opened from the small mall that adjoined the station. Everything for the most part was already closed. They emerged once more back under the clay sky and for a brief moment the sun broke through the cloud cover.

The hit the Tourist Board not quite at a run, but at least before it closed. The nice ladies there, thick accents aside, spoke flawless English. There was, however, only one place left with rooms and that was a little guesthouse. It was also extremely expensive. Sabine translated marks into dollars in her head and winced when the lady told her how much.

"How long?" Sabine asked Ari, meaning for how long would their stay be. Ari must have started to feel whatever dread had been stalking Sabine because she jumped when spoken to.

"Um, two nights, I think will be fine," Ari said. The nice lady made their reservation and locked the door after them when they stepped outside. The dread really liked the sound of the *"snik snik"* of the lock turning closed. It sounded like they were stuck out in the Cold.

But she wasn't a spy.

Not anymore.

"What next?" Sabine asked.

"Food?"

Sabine laughed, the dread pushed back by force of will. "Oh, all right, oh appetite that walks as a woman."

"Is that my new Indian name?"

They ended up finding a smorgasbord across from the tourist board and ran into the first of their problems.

"Where do you want to go to after here?" Sabine asked, putting away the last of a roll.

"Well, I have relatives in Hungary and I would like to see Budapest," Ari started.

"I would not suggest it." They both, to their credit, did not jump out of their skins, but Sabine would have liked to.

"Ulrich!" Ari breathed out.

And indeed it was, which had Sabine looking past him to see who else was with him. She had heard about this kind of phenomenon from a friend of her stepmother's who was also a world traveler. He had mentioned how he often ran into the same people while traveling.

But that wasn't what Sabine felt was going on.

"What are you ladies doing in Stuttgart?" he asked and Ari gestured for him to have a seat with them. He was dressed in his understated, elegant way in a beautiful black suit, with a dark blue shirt and tie, his black hair combed back. Sabine did have to admire his poise and fashion sense, even if she was suspicious beyond measure at finding him in the same restaurant with them.

"Not much so far," Ari said as Ulrich took his seat. "How are you?"

"I am well. And you?" He remembered Sabine. "You as well?"

"Wonderful now," Ari said.

"Fine," Sabine said.

"You're here. You're really here," Ari said for the non-sequitur.

Sabine tried not to groan. *Oh, great. Just what I need,* she thought. *Love sick spies and werewolves.*

"Why not Budapesht?" Sabine pronounced it in the Russian manner. She got his attention and wished she hadn't. One glance and she realized that *he* was afraid.

Of her.

"It is not safe or wise to travel much further east." But his attention was drawn back to Ari.

"Why?" Ari had enough remaining intelligence to ask.

"There is the obvious fact of the after effects of unrest in the Balkans," he said, gentle, if matter-of-fact.

"Duh! Refugees."

"Yes," he said, but did not elaborate.

"And?" Ari saw something more that Sabine did not. His skin rippled and Sabine watched in momentary fascination. Human skin was incapable of such motion. But wolf, that was a different matter. A profound tell of discomfort.

"It is just not safe for you." He then remembered Sabine again. "For you both. Americans." The last was so blatantly tacked on that Sabine and Ari both gave him the hairy eyeball.

"Where are you staying here in Stuttgart?" He changed subjects.

Sabine reached into her fanny pack and handed him the sheet, without even waiting for Ari to ask her.

"Ah! May I call while you are here?"

"We'd love that!" Ari blurted.

"Better than a root canal," Sabine added *sotto voce* and Ari kicked her under the table. "Ow!" He gave her a puzzled look, but Ari once more claimed his attention.

"I'd love it."

"Then I shall call without fail." His smile melted Ari into a pile of goo. Even Sabine felt herself thaw a little. For a Wolflord, he was damn charming.

"I'm afraid I can't stay," he continued.

"What a shame," Sabine commented and that earned her a glare from Ari.

"Well, we'll see you soon, won't we?" Ari put in.

"Yes. Till later, ladies," he said, rising and making them a small bow. Ari stared after him until he was long gone out of sight.

"Well." It was all Sabine said.

"What?"

"Nothing."

"You don't mean that."

"It's not worth going into yet."

"Why not?"

"Lack of data." That got Ari's attention. Analyst-speak out of Sabine. "Where are we going after this then?" Sabine asked again.

"Well, it sounds like Hungary and the rest is right out."

"Yes. But."

"Well. Wait. But?" Ari's face creased a little.

"Let's just go to the hotel tonight and talk tomorrow."

They finished their meal in relative silence, but Ari was still cranky and feeling the full effects of dairy on her system from the meal. She looked pale and mulish at the same time and Sabine knew she was in for it. There was no reasoning with Ari when she had a milk reaction. It made her emotionally unreasonable and cranky. It was like Ulrich's visit had never occurred. Instead, Sabine gritted her teeth and tried to find a cab as fast as she could as soon as they stepped out of the restaurant.

A tan Mercedes Benz sedan stopped for them eventually. She piled Ari into it and then had to put up with her grumbling as she tried to make herself understood by the cabbie. Again, the simple expedience of handing the man their destination paper solved the problem for them. Then they drove by the first of the anti-Judaic graffiti scribbled on one of the walls illuminated by the headlights of the car as they sped on their way.

Ari went silent.

The lady who ran the establishment, a nice enough woman with a smiling face and short cropped white hair, looked like a lost extra from The Sound of Music, and spoke no English. Sabine wondered for a brief moment if she were trapped in a mime film. Or a permanent game of Charades.

Mime completed, their room was nice enough, of a grayed blue interior with white comforters on the beds and real pillows. They unpacked a little, in the where-are-our-toothbrushes manner, and Sabine took the twin bed nearest the weird little bathroom and pulled the comforter over her head.

"Good night?" Ari asked in a subdued manner.

"Goodnight," Sabine said and tried to mean it. "I'm fine. Just let me sleep."

"All right. Sweet dreams, Sabine."

They weren't.

Sabine fell into sleep and the Dream waited in force and terror, swallowing her like a medieval dragon swallows knights whole. She crouched in Captain Arthur Harrison's skin. They had lost half the squad between coming through the last minefield and running into an over-strength squad of SS. Harrison turned his head to take in the last two of his handpicked men.

Rodriguez, all wiry thin and exhausted looking, stared back at Harrison. He gave him a cocky grin and Harrison felt a little ease, but not much. The wound in the boy's shoulder had stopped bleeding. Harrison glanced at his other squad man. Locksley, one shade of brown from all the mud, was fast asleep. Harrison almost laughed.

He cocked a head over the edge of the building they crouched behind. Below them, in the heart of a bombed out Stuttgart, was the building they had come to infiltrate. With only two men now, it wasn't the fate of the war that rested on his thin shoulders at that moment.

It was the fate of the entire world.

Harrison felt the fear again. Without meaning to, his hand went again to one of the three satchels strapped to his body. His squad mates carried the same number and the same contents. Experimental and high yield explosives.

What is in that building? Sabine tried to ask, but before she could find the answer in her Past's memory, she stood again in the cavern of black stone. The coils of the Beloved were already in motion. The cold black stone again cut straight into her feet with their chill.

"Sabine!" Zoë cried as the coils parted between them, her face white and frightened.

"Zoë. What's wrong?"

"You must get out of Stuttgart! You must get out of Stuttgart now before they find you!"

"Before who finds what?" Sabine couldn't understand. The haze and weight of Harrison's memories half remembered, mired her down.

"Oh, you must—" Zoë broke off and they both jerked their heads at the sound of footsteps—

She woke.

She lay in the tiny bed and waited for her eyes to adjust to the dim light leaking from around the curtains. Ari snored soft in the other bed. She had not cried out in her sleep, but this dream had not frightened her as much as it had confused her.

She knew there was something strange and wrong about these dreams. Sabine stared at the ceiling, half-seen and ghost-like in the thin light. She wanted and did not want to talk to Ari about her dreams. They made no sense to her. She knew that they were somehow...true. But she couldn't prove it and even though she knew Ari would believe her without question if she told her the contents of her dreams, Sabine just couldn't bring herself to do it. It didn't matter how certain she felt, it didn't matter that somehow she knew her dreams were connected to what was happening to her, to them both. She didn't want to allow that what she Dreamed were true.

Sabine closed her eyes.

I will sleep without dreams, Sabine vowed.

She thought she never would, which was why she was so surprised to find her eyes opening hours later.

Sabine had to give the guesthouse some points. The curtains blocked out so much light, she was certain they were left over from World War II and the bombings or it was grayer outside than she thought.

Ari stumbled about the room and pulled the curtains open.

"So much for sunshine," Sabine croaked.

"It could burn off."

The little bathroom was still strange to Sabine's eyes in the morning light. Her cursory examination the night before had revealed only the sink with its hose faucet and the towels piled behind the toilet on its tank. No towel bar, and the tile was the same gray blue as the carpet in the hotel room.

"Wow. Color coordinated," Sabine managed to get out without sounding too froggy. Stuttgart was not agreeing with her allergies.

When they both emerged from their room, heading for what they thought was the front door and outside, they were stopped by their hostess. She babbled something at them in German. Sabine tried to focus through the fog that was no coffee yet in her system.

"Oh. Breakfast. Something about breakfast," Sabine said, and the woman smiled and made broad gestures for them to follow her upstairs.

"*Danke, mein frau,*" Sabine tried in her pidgin German and was rewarded with another beaming smile.

"American?" a voice said and they both turned to face the other inhabitant of the dining room, a stout gentleman in a tan suit, with a plain face and a nice smile. Brown eyes regarded them with friendly inquisitiveness.

"English!" they both said in unison.

"A surprise, eh?"

"But very welcome. I'm Sabine." Sabine followed her name with an offered hand.

"I'm Ari," Ari supplied for herself.

"Jake," he said and went back to buttering a roll. "What brings you to Stuttgart?"

"Would you believe stupidity?" Sabine got out.

"We just got on the first train that was leaving Paris. We're on vacation and exploring Europe," Ari said instead. He smiled.

"Oh, that's wonderful. I remember being in college and doing the very same thing."

"So what about you? Business?" Sabine asked, as she heaped a plate for herself with meat and cheese.

"How'd you guess?" he asked.

"Wild guess from the suit."

"Yes. I'm a heavy equipment salesman back in the States. Some of our presses are made here in Stuttgart, so I'm here for the obvious reasons."

"That's not the typical salesman job," Sabine laughed. "Do you like it?"

"Very much. I actually get to travel quite a bit because of it, which I've always enjoyed. But enough about me. Do you have any ideas what you're going to do here?"

"We don't even know what's here," Sabine offered. Ari was busy stuffing her mouth with bread and tea.

"Well, there's a museum downtown. There's a Porsche museum also."

"Oh boy."

"Yeah, but other than that, it's really the architecture that's worth a gander. I can find out what bus you need to take to get you downtown, if you'd like."

Sabine brightened at that. "Actually, that would be wonderful. But even better, do you think you could ask her where we could find a map?"

"You and maps," Ari said with a little laugh. Sabine stuck out her tongue.

Jake, their new friend, spoke to the hostess in rapid fire German and she responded in kind. Before they knew it, they had directions to the nearest bus stop, the correct bus information, but no map.

"There you go, girls. Have a great time," Jake said, finishing up his own breakfast and handing them a slip of paper. He'd scribbled down the directions they needed and slipped his little leather notepad back inside his jacket.

"Thank you so much, Jake," Sabine said in return.

"See you girls later."

"Sure thing," Sabine said, and Ari just smiled, still eating bread and tea, though some of the roast beef had managed to make it to her plate too.

"Well, cool. Something to do and maybe we'll be able to find a map," Sabine said.

"Why do you have to have maps?"

"I told you. I don't like being lost."

"You said that before."

"Well, I really don't like being lost."

"Yeah, well, no one will be able to find us while we're in Stuttgart." Sabine didn't know why she twigged to that statement. It was delivered innocently enough. There wasn't anything suspicious in its content. But she knew just as she knew the backs of her hands, that Ari kept something from her.

"Who?"

"What?"

"Why would anyone want to find us? The entire point of this trip I thought was that no one would be able to find us. Leaving behind all our troubles for a while in America, yackety smackety," Sabine elaborated.

"Right." Except Ari's body language had changed.

"What's wrong? Is someone trying to find us?"

"What makes you say that?"

"Because you're keeping something from me."

"No, I'm not," Ari tried with a smile.

"Don't Game Face me." It came out like ice. They sat there for a full minute, neither saying a word. When Ari did speak, it was to say the one thing that Sabine did not expect.

"British Intelligence wants our heads on pikes."

"What?!" she yelped.

"I ran into one of my brothers." Ari didn't continue.

"What? When? Where?" Sabine modulated her tone when she saw that their hostess was becoming concerned from the sound of their voices, even if she didn't know what the funny Americans were saying.

"In Paris."

"Where?"

"Les Invalides."

"Shit!"

"Sabine—"

"Don't Sabine me! Jesus fucking Christ!" Sabine sucked in a breath. "What did he say?"

"The British Museum."

"What about—" It hit Sabine like a ton of bricks. "Oh, motherfucker." She sucked in another breath. "How?"

"On tape."

"Witnesses."

"Yes. We are."

"Shit." She sucked in one more breath for good measure and then started swearing monotonously and steadily. In Russian.

"Sabine—"

She didn't stop.

"Sabine!"

She stopped. Without a word, Sabine stood up, put on her trench, put on her pack and headed for the door.

"We're leaving?" Ari asked and then got up in a scramble as Sabine disappeared out the door.

Outside, Sabine snatched out the piece of paper Jake had given her and got her bearings from the sign in front of her, then took off for the stated bus stop.

"Wait!" Ari said, coming out the door. Sabine paused a half second and started walking.

"Damn it, Sabine, wait!" Sabine stopped. "What's wrong?"

"When were you going to tell me?" Sabine bit out.

Ari chewed air.

"God damn it, Ari. No maps, no hotel reservations, we've got fraternities on our ass and fucking dire portents from people who moonlight as wolves!"

"Hey, no reservations makes it harder to find us!"

"No reservations, also means that if we fucking disappear, no one will fucking know it either!"

"Sabine—"

Sabine started walking again.

"God damn it, Sabine!"

She didn't stop this time. Ari kept up. There were advantages to having long legs.

"I'm sorry! I didn't know how to tell you! I brought you here and all that's happened is that everything's gone to shit. And I didn't know you needed maps."

"Yes, well," Sabine conceded. "How could you? Most people have Thomas guides or GPS units in their cars and it's never come up before."

"No, it hasn't!"

"But your own fraternity sent someone to find you, Ari."

"We don't need maps, Sabine. It'll work out. They won't find us."

"I need a map, Ari. And your brother found you. And so did Ulrich."

"Leave him out of it."

"How the fuck can I?"

"Sabine—"

"I don't want to talk about this anymore."

"Sabine!"

"No."

Bitter silence fell between them. They emerged out on to a main road, tree-lined and green in the overcast. Sabine saw the bus stop and went to cross the street, but Ari saw something else. A small café on the corner.

"I'm hungry."

"Fine."

"I'm going into the café."

"Fine."

"Fine."

Ari stalked off.

Sabine dug in her fanny pack till she found her Silk Cuts. She dug around in her trench coat's pockets till she found her matches and lit up her first cigarette. A disgusted little voice in her head muttered something about the fact that she hadn't felt like smoking in days. Sabine silenced it with a fierce urge for it to drop dead.

She stood on the street, under the beautiful green tree in front of the cafe, under a solidly gray sky, and began to chain smoke. And pace. And scan.

Ari came out of the café after a half an hour.

"I bought you an espresso and a bear claw. They're waiting inside," she said in a frosty voice.

"Fine."

She dropped and then ground out her cigarette with the ball of her foot and walked into the café. On the little counter in the front window where one could stand and eat, sat a perfect little white espresso cup and a familiar pastry on a perfect white plate.

Sabine felt a twinge of hurt guilt.

Even mad, Ari had bought her something to eat and something to drink.

She stood and ate and drank. Out the window, she could see Ari pacing now, though not smoking, never having picked up the filthy habit.

She also began to see Ari's side of the argument and didn't want to, but couldn't help it. She was fundamentally as fair a person as she knew how to be and still be human. She didn't know how she would have told her what had happened either, put in Ari's position. This vacation got worse with every day and at the rate it continued to progress, Sabine didn't want to consider what else could go wrong. British Intelligence wanted them for questioning. She knew that Ari's fellow spook had to have had other information as well.

She just wanted to go home.

Ari stopped in her pacing.

Her head came up and the next thing that Sabine knew, Ari marched into the café.

"This is stupid," she said.

Sabine opened her mouth.

And laughed.

It hurt, but it helped.

"I'm sorry," Sabine said.

"I am too. I am so sorry, Sabine. I just didn't know how to tell you."

"I know. I was just thinking that I wouldn't have known how to bring it up either if it had been me." She stared into her espresso cup. "What are we going to do, Ari?"

"I don't know. But we'll figure it out."

Things weren't at complete peace between them. Sabine could feel the lingering awkwardness. They didn't have long to wait for a bus to come along. It was very clean and white and gray. Sabine felt oppressed by all the utilitarian gray that seemed plastered everywhere and to everything. However, there were bus maps in a pocket on the way into the bus and Sabine snatched one up. Ari thought to say something, but took one look at Sabine's face and thought better of it.

Sabine stared out the bus window as it pulled away from the stop. She had to admit, it was the smoothest riding bus she'd ever been in.

And fast. They rolled along and the gray and green of Stuttgart slipped past in a blur.

Including more of the previous night's graffiti.

"I'm Catholic," Ari declared in a low voice out of the blue.

"*Fiat lux,*" Sabine said, dry as the Sahara.

Ari saw their stop coming up and laid a light hand on Sabine's arm to let her know before pulling the wire to signal they wanted the next step. Too soon, they stood on the sidewalk in downtown Stuttgart. As far as Sabine was concerned, she couldn't tell the difference between the street where they had gotten on the bus and the place they now stood.

She consulted her bus map.

"Hmm. It looks like there's a pedestrian tunnel over there that leads to the museum." Sabine pointed across the street where a dark archway stood surrounded by dark green shrubs and taller spreading limbed trees.

"Lead on."

Which Sabine did, looking both ways before crossing the street. They drove way faster in Germany, hell, in Europe, than they did in America. She had already felt close to death of the automotive kind ever since London. The last thing she needed to do was get pasted by a car when there was so much else to choose from. Like spies. Like werewolves. It was a practical cornucopia of self-destruction.

Even before they stepped through the opening into the stairs for the underground pedway, Sabine didn't like it. It was too dark and too confined.

Perfect place for an ambush, she thought. They took the long flight of concrete steps into the tunnel and Sabine grew more nervous by the second. The tunnel they emerged into was low ceiling and claustrophobic. Unpleasant.

But not as unpleasant as the graffiti.

"I see our artist has been here."

"Why, Sabine?" Ari asked in a small voice.

Sabine made herself stop and consider the graffiti when all she wanted to do was get out of the tunnel as fast as possible. She gave her full attention to the walls and the explicit images of rape and torture and death. The images were raw and bright in their colors. The Jews were depicted as faceless, which told the analyst part of her a great deal. The subject in question had never met a real Jew ever in his life. This was a taught prejudice.

The human in Sabine cowered behind the analyst and kept her distance.

"I don't know," Sabine said after her consideration. An analysis wasn't going to help her friend. It wasn't her friend, Ari the Spook, asking this question. It was Ari, the Devout Jew.

She had no answer, because, she, Sabine, fundamentally had no real faith in anything. Not anymore.

So she had no answer and ached at her friend's fear and pain.

"You never worked anti or counter terror, did you?"

"They said they needed me more in Foreign Service. Uncle David suggested I do Foreign over it."

Sabine wondered what Ari's psych profile looked like for a brief moment then made stopped her train of thought, now even more frightened. Her friend was not a subject to be analyzed. But the analyst was where she reacted from more and more. She didn't like it.

Even so, she had a guess why Ari had been sent to Foreign Services. She knew her friend's passionate nature. There was no place for it in counter terror where coolness of mind and heart were needed against the irrationalities of the zealot.

It was the only way to deal with it.

The other option would drive a person insane.

After, all, she'd seen what it had done to those she had known.

But that was years ago.

They went on and emerged into weak and fitful sun. By reflex, Sabine looked up.

To watch the beginnings of a pale rainbow swallowed by an enormous slate cloud.

It had to be the worst museum in the world, Sabine decided after fifteen minutes of being inside the Stuttgart Museum of Art. As far as she could tell, it was the home of all the art that the Third Reich had stolen during the War, but no one wanted back afterwards.

For instance, the hall of supposed Dutch Masters, was, in fact, a lot of bad oils of overweight and overly red-faced German merchants from various periods of time. And then, the piece de resistance as far as Sabine was concerned, a Magritte, which she didn't like.

"Well," Sabine ventured to say. "It's nice to know that even the great painters were capable of making art that just plain sucks."

"Boy, ain't that the truth," Ari replied and continued to frown at the paintings on the walls.

Which was sad. The building itself was a beauty, dating from the Bauhaus movement in Germany. The upstairs gallery they stood in was large, with high ceilings and had several areas where one could stand outside and enjoy what little view there was. Ari and Sabine stepped out on to the balcony nearest them and looked down to see a beautiful modern courtyard hung with small ivy, tall and slender birch trees planted for shade.

Sabine searched the sky.

The cloud cover was total. No sign of her lost rainbow.

"Well. Now what?" Sabine asked the sky as much as Ari.

"I'm hungry."

"Let's find the cafeteria or whatever it is that they've got around here." Sabine offered and offered her arm as well.

They walked outside after lunch, the leaden sky a low, oppressive canopy, and Sabine forgot swallowed rainbows and feelings of earlier uneasiness. The morning's tension was gone and all that remained, bad museums aside, was the warmth of being with her dearest companion.

They stepped out on to the path heading back for the pedestrian tunnel and Sabine knew that even she did not have luck this bad.

The Malice Twins.

"Back for a rematch, assholes?" Sabine spat out.

"Sabine!"

"I'm sick of this! What do you want with us? Leave us alone!" Sabine shouted.

"Come with us and find out," the shorter of the Twins said with a malicious smile.

"As if, asshole."

"We merely wish to speak to you."

"You're speaking. Get on with it."

"Sabine…" Ari said the warning, but she didn't have to bother. Sabine felt it, the gathering energies in her gut. She knew what to call it at last. The Twins were beginning to Cast.

She saw their linked hands.

"Takes the two of you, eh?" she muttered and then louder, "Don't try it."

"You will come with us now."

"I think we will not and you two can go to hell."

"Sabine—!" This time the tone was, don't goad them.

They threw the Casting.

Wind, like the last time, but more powerful and shrieking in its violence. Sabine felt herself go cold all over in sheer animal terror. This was force primeval. This was power. She felt her own Reaching, Reaching to counter, but...

The Casting hit.

They were too powerful. Sabine rocked on her feet, near ground down by the sheer percussive force of their combined wills, barely having raised a shield in time. As it was, she slid two feet, just keeping her feet. But she had not been fast enough to include Ari in the shield. She only had enough time to see Ari cry out in surprise as the force hit them. A brief flash of glaring light erupted from Ari's throat. Ari flew through the air. Sabine didn't even have time to wonder how she could see the energies that she saw. She'd never been able to see them before.

"Ari!" Sabine screamed.

With a horrible crunch, Ari landed on the path.

The Malice Twins stood next to each other and Sabine watched their auras flare as they went to Cast again. Even as she reached for another Defense, a small part of her brain even then wondering how she even knew to do what she was doing.

She wasn't strong enough to stand against them combined and Ari was only just struggling to her feet.

Gray shapes exploded out of the surrounding bushes.

Sabine screamed.

Enormous wolves poured in the gap and stood between her and their attackers. Their auras flared and Sabine took a step back. Their size alone told her they weren't normal wolves, besides the fact that they were in downtown Stuttgart.

Then the most enormous wolf of all came to the front of the pack and Sabine knew.

Black as pitch and larger than his compatriots.

Ulrich.

The Wolflord.

The pack growled as one.

The Twins wavered in their Cast, thinking for a moment to go against the combined might of the Were Pack in front of them. Sabine felt cold again. Whatever drove these two terrified them enough that they thought to fight a united Hunting Pack. It was insanity.

They gestured in sync, twisting the Cast to another use and between one eye blink and the next, they vanished.

She shook her head, which was stupid, because it made her ill.

The combined attack of the Malice Twins couldn't drive her to her knees. But the aftermath of fear and adrenaline could, and the terror as she felt more and more like she was changing. Into someone she didn't and did know.

She fell to her knees and retched.

Someone stood next to her, but Sabine didn't look up from her dry heaves.

"I don't think the bush is a hungry cub," A thick German accent said. The words didn't quite register, but they were said with kindness and a touch of worry.

Sabine craned her head up to look. A young man, blond hair so fair as to be gray white, crouched next to her, his eyes the same color as a Siberian Husky dog, pale enough blue to pass for silver. He was of a color, but no albino, and she knew he had to have been one of the wolves. He wore a loose white sweater and tan slacks and loafers. Behind him, she saw other men and women walking in different directions, all apparent humans, except for the telltale flickers of auras.

"Neat trick," she croaked.

"Trick? *Was ist?*" he asked, his forehead crinkling in confusion.

"Clothes. Where do you keep your clothes?"

He smiled and laughed a little.

"Magick. *Ja?*"

"Of course."

Her eyes searched for Ari and found what she had half expected to see. Ulrich helping Ari to her feet, their auras merging into each other, hers with black jags in it from trauma, his dark blue with fear and worry.

"A frightened wolfie. Funny."

"*Was?*" Her companion asked and Sabine just shook her head. She felt like five miles of bad road. She shook her head with less violence this time, to clear it, hoping not to be sick again. But when she opened her eyes again, the auras were gone.

Something terrible was happening to her. And that's when she felt it.

There was nothing left inside of her.

She Reached.

Nothing responded. She felt nothing. She Reached again, harder and felt the nausea return in force. Sabine felt herself go cold again and stopped.

"Are you all right now, *hen?*" the young man asked.

Sabine shook her head in the affirmative.

"I will be." But her voice sounded hollow with fear. She made herself master it.

"What's your name?"

"Fen," he said with a smile and Sabine was certain if he had still been in wolf form, would have wagged his tail too.

Ulrich helped Ari all the way to her feet and came over to Sabine and Fen. Sabine sat on her calves, the gravel of the path cutting into her shins.

"I have a car. Can I drive you back to the guesthouse?" Ulrich offered.

Sabine started to get up. Fen offered a hand, but she waved him off.

"That would be really nice," Ari said.

"This way." He gestured towards the museum's parking lot.

Ulrich ended up having a sleek black Mercedes waiting in the lot with another young wolf, a young woman, matching companion to Fen, dressed in a chauffeur's uniform. She opened the back door at the sight of them. Fen, on the other hand, veered off to a BMW motorcycle of an interesting shade of blue-green and climbed on it.

Sabine just crawled in the back seat of the car and closed her eyes.

"Sabine?" Ari tried.

"Just leave me alone," she said and turned away from Ari.

She opened her eyes when she felt the car well in motion and then to stare out the window at the failing light.

She got out of the car as soon as they reached the guesthouse and went inside, leaving Ari and Ulrich on the steps of the guesthouse with his lieutenants.

Ari did not follow.

"Why— How—" She couldn't seem to figure out how to start her sentence. "No. First, how did you know we were there? Second, how did you know they would be there?"

Ulrich looked uncomfortable, but to his credit, did not flinch.

"It was a suspicion only."

"Do you know who they are?" She lowered her voice. "Who they are associated with?"

"Not exactly."

"That's not exactly help."

"I—" He looked pained. "I would do anything to keep you from harm."

He looked away at the same time Ari stepped back. Intensity crackled between them. Ulrich looked like he couldn't believe he'd just said what he had.

"I would help you. I do not know who they are or who they are...associated with. Honestly," he said, once more the master of his features and emotions. "What I do know is little and probably as much as you yourself know, *madame*."

"Ari," she corrected. To have this man defer to her, she just couldn't have it.

"Ari," he said it like a caress.

Ari gave herself a mental shake. This was no time to be making time with a werewolf.

"Tell me anyway."

"They are magicians—"

"Duh," she cut in.

"—Which you already know. Dark, and in service to something darker. We know not what."

"Who are you associated with?" She felt cat paws of fear trip up her spine.

He looked more uncomfortable.

"At times, I have been known to help BND."

German Intelligence. Truth. She knew it the moment he said it. She also knew what he left unsaid.

"Freelance."

"It is difficult to employ my kind," he said with a sudden wolfish smile.

"Well, yes, I guess so."

"We suspect them in a multitude of crimes and terrorism, but know nothing definite. I would tell you more if I knew more," he said and held a hand out, diffident, as if he expected her to smack him with a rolled up newspaper.

She started to take it and stopped.

"I know." She also knew that if she touched him, they would be out there all day and all night. "But you will tell me if you discover more."

"My word on it," he smiled. "*Rachel.*"

Ari froze.

"Been checking up on me, eh?"

"*Nein*, no. I met a young man in Paris. He called himself Joshua."

"That idiot."

"*Nein*, I and mine have helped your parents and grandparents before."

Ari felt another tickle of fear. He knew the codes to give.

"Well, if you see him again, smack him for me," Ari said, trying to metabolize this sudden and unexpected shift in allies and information.

"Smack?"

"Hit him."

"Why?"

"Never mind." Ari sighed. She allowed herself to touch him lightly on the arm.

"I need to go and check on my friend."

"Yes. You must."

Ari felt it. She was in direct contact with him. Fear.

"Yes. Will I see you tomorrow?"

"I shall come for breakfast if it is acceptable?"

"Yes," Ari said with a forced smile.

She had to force the smile, because she couldn't figure out why Ulrich, someone she knew to be powerful, lived in a terror of her best friend. Who to the best of her knowledge had some extraordinary abilities, but...

They weren't frightening.

So what did he know that she didn't?

Ari found Sabine standing on unsteady feet next to her bed.

"Are you okay?"

Sabine moved her head to look at her friend, but it looked like it took every ounce of her remaining energy to do so.

"Sabine?"

"Where are we going tomorrow?"

This non-sequitur derailed the information Ari had meant to give her companion.

"I hadn't really thought of about it yet—"

"I have to get out of here."

"Right now?" Ari felt a spike of panic.

"No. Tomorrow. Out of Stuttgart."

"Okay," Ari said, trying to sound placating, but not managing to keep the hurt out of her voice either.

"Ari, please."

"Sabine, what's wrong?"

"I'll be in the bathroom."

"Sabine?"

Sabine locked the bathroom door behind her. Another stab of pain lanced through her stomach. She stifled a pained bleat and stumbled her way to the sink. She leaned hard on the porcelain basin as she waited for the water to heat up. She didn't look in the mirror. She had never been so out of control of herself before ever in her life. Not even when He had died.

She bathed her face and felt her world rock as her hands shook.

"I don't shake," she whispered.

A knife stabbed into her guts, pain so sharp that she wondered how she could not be bleeding. She gasped and crumpled to her knees, hanging on to the sink in a death grip.

"No!" she gasped and felt her eyes prick with unwanted tears. "No!"

The entire situation collapsed in on her.

She was in Stuttgart. Over six thousand miles away from home. Only one other person knew where she was and that person was with her. If anything happened to Ari...

No one else knew their whereabouts, except two crazy magicians with minions who wanted them dead or captured or worse.

Cold sweat trickled down between her shoulder blades and another knife blade of pain went through her and this time crashing pain came in on her temples as well. She felt as if her skin were too large, like she were trying to shrink into nothingness and couldn't stop it.

"No!"

She couldn't keep herself from collapsing to the floor, her sweating hands slipping off the slick porcelain. Unable to do anything but be with the pain, Sabine curled into a fetal ball.

No one knew where they were. Only Wolflords and dark magicians. If they disappeared tomorrow, no one would know. She'd never get home. She didn't know where she'd be tomorrow. She didn't even know if she'd have a place to sleep. She was turning into a monster. No maps. Trapped in the labyrinth. Lost, they were lost.

She lay on the floor and keened.

In the morning, Sabine opened her eyes on to a world that bore no resemblance to the one she had fallen asleep in the night before.

The pain was gone. She didn't know how and she didn't know why. All she did was close her eyes and gave thanks. She opened her eyes again. They were blurry and a bit gritty, but blinking cleared her sight of the dim room. Morning again, she could feel it, but still gray. She didn't need to open the curtains to see that. She could feel the weather on her skin.

A moment's fear traced a finger across her skin.

She suppressed it with a violent thought.

She'd always had a knack for weather prediction. It didn't mean anything. She would hold it together, she thought, angry.

Ari still slept in her bed and Sabine got up, not bothering to wake her. She began to pack. She didn't bother to get a shower. She just packed.

"Are you all right?" The little voice that spoke from the other bed didn't sound like Ari. Sabine stopped and came to sit on her friend's bed.

"I'm fine," she said, too calm.

Ari regarded her with a steady non-expression looking for who knew what. Whatever she searched for, she didn't find.

"All right," she yawned fit to crack her head open. "Ulrich is going to join us for breakfast. Is that okay?"

"Oh! That's fine!" Sabine said with a little of her old brightness. "Maybe he can give us a ride to the station."

"Oh, yeah. Yeah. That would be nice."

Sabine just smiled, because she could tell that Ari's thoughts weren't on the relative safety of Ulrich taking them to the station. They were on the concept that that meant she would have more time to be with him.

"Do I have time for a shower?"

"Make it fast," Sabine said, folding her dirty clothing and making a mental note that she needed to find a Laundromat soon.

A sharp knock sounded on their door.

Sabine felt her shoulders tighten until she heard Ulrich's voice call a cheery good morning through the door.

"I don't think you are going to get that shower," she said and went to answer the door.

Ari just squeaked and flew out of bed to get dressed.

"Hello, Ulrich," Sabine said with a smile, opening the door a crack. "We'll be up in a minute. Just go up to the breakfast room. We'll meet you there."

Out in the hall, Ulrich looked fresh as a daisy, in brown slacks and a tan sweater, his matching dark brown loafers polished to a perfect shine.

"*Zer gut, liebchen*," he said.

"*Liebchen*, eh?" she teased. "Ari better not find out."

They broke their fast in a relaxed manner, for which Sabine was grateful. Both Ulrich and Ari acted as if nothing untoward had occurred the day before and that was how Sabine wanted it. She was six thousand miles from home, true. But it didn't mean she didn't know how to take care of herself.

"Are you ready to go?" Ulrich asked.

"We need to finish packing."

Packing took no time and they piled into Ulrich's car, the blond girl once more driving. But this time she smiled at them and Sabine cocked her head at Ulrich.

"Who's she?"

"Oh! Freja, Fen's sister," Ulrich said and said something to Freja that was far more complicated German than Sabine knew. Freja smiled and waved.

"Hello," Sabine and Ari said in unison and she laughed. It made Sabine feel better to have a name. Too much paranoia, she thought to herself. Need a vacation. Oh wait, I'm on one.

Back at the train station, they piled out and Freja drove off to park the car, leaving Ulrich and the two companions on the sidewalk, struggling with their bags. Sabine argued with her computer bag, getting it to sit on the back of her suitcase, when she saw the first gray suit.

"No," she said in so even a voice that if Ari hadn't known her, and Ulrich had guessed, no one else would have thought anything was untoward.

Both their heads came up like hounds hunting for scent.

"Where?" Ari asked, her voice matter of fact, but she spotted the watcher for herself. He was on his phone and the distance between them too great for them to stop him in the most direct and violent of manners.

"Leaving," Sabine said and took off for the station at a fast trot.

"Right," Ari answered and Ulrich just fell in with them.

The train station was held against them. Gray-suited men and women were scattered through the crowds going to and from the trains. Ari searched for the Departures board anyway.

"We've got a train to Milan in one minute," she said.

"Let's go," Sabine said, her voice tight and controlled.

But Sabine didn't have eyes in the back of her head and the only thing that saved Ari was Ulrich tackling her from behind. Sabine knew she was too late to do much but react, the minute she felt the rising Cast vibrate through the world and twist the weather she felt along her skin.

The Casting hit her square in the back.

Sabine found herself flying and somehow, twisting and Reaching with all her might, pulled her legs before her and landed on her feet, her bags spilling at her feet. Without even looking, she Reached and Cast, screaming at the top of her lungs.

"BASTARDS!"

They staggered and wolves again exploded out of everywhere around them. Human only a second before, skins warped in the blink of an eye and the Hunting Pack attacked.

Ulrich alone stayed in human form and tossed Ari to her feet, staying by his side.

"Get on the train! *Schnell*!!!" Ulrich yelled.

"Ulrich!" Ari yelled, her gun in her hand.

"No! We go! Now!" Sabine yelled, just as Ulrich shouted as well.

"*Mach schnell*! We will hold them here. Go!"

The train started into motion and Sabine threw her bags up, jumped, turned, wrapping her arm through a handgrip, and held out a hand for Ari. Stronger and longer-limbed, Ari grabbed her arm and swung up, bag and all, wrenching Sabine's arm in its socket, but Sabine held on and pulled right back.

"Yikes!" Ari squeaked at the answering strength in her friend.

Sabine felt her breath come back to her as she settled into a train seat a moment later.

"Adventure, eh?" Sabine said darkly. "Where is it, eh? Wouldn't go to Stuttgart, eh?"

"Sabine…"

"What were you smoking and why aren't you sharing?"

"There was—!"

"No way of knowing," Sabine cut her off. "I know. I'm sorry."

Sabine leaned forward and put her head between her knees and took a deep breath.

"Bomb scares. Shooting at us. All of it," she continued.

"And we are now on a train going as far away from Germany as we feel like going." Ari tried to sound comforting.

"Yes. Yes, we are," Sabine responded.

But there was an echo to her voice that hadn't been there before.

CHAPTER VI – TRANSFORMATION OF FORMS

Stuttgart, Germany - Milan, Italy

The train beat a quick retreat from Germany, but not quickly enough. Sabine decided it had to feel that way. After all, with every second they stayed in Germany, she waited for the train to blow up around their ears. She'd never been so glad to see a border sign in her life.

It took Ari an hour to recover.

"I'm sure he's fine," Sabine said.

Ari snapped out of staring out the window, the frown vanishing from her brow. "I know."

Sabine dug out her book to pass the time.

"Sheepie!" Ari declared and Sabine closed her eyes, stifling a sigh. *It begins,* she thought, and humor warred with paranoia.

Every little sheepie, the black mountains, the brilliant white snow and the dark waters of the lakes like so many polished obsidian mirrors required an exclamation of appreciation. Little houses sat perched against the sheer mountain rock faces as if kept up by sheer defiance of the laws of gravity. Ari was irrepressible. Nothing could keep her down for long.

Sabine tried to read. Clive Barker's words, even interrupted, washed over her like soothing water. Yes, it was horror. But considering the way things had been going, it seemed more like non-fiction than fiction. But more, the beauty of his words soothed her and she struggled to stay in the fantasy he built with those words, because she just didn't want to think. If she thought, her heart started to thud in her chest again and she couldn't breathe.

Her bones still hurt from dark magick striking her back. The skin on her back had to be burned to a crisp. It no longer burned at that moment, but her bones, oh, how they ached.

Clive Barker. Damnation and salvation. Much easier to deal with, she thought in a fractured manner.

"Heidi house!"

Sabine put her book aside and looked out at the unrelieved gray of the sky.

Dear Gods, she prayed. *How about some sun? Where is the sun? Doesn't She love us anymore?*

The train began its descent in that exact instant. The clouds cracked open to spill golden light over the mountains. Sabine closed her eyes and mouthed the words, thank you. The warmth seeped into her skin and she felt some of the primal fear let go.

The rest of the trip was so uneventful that later, Sabine couldn't even remember it until their arrival in Milan. Weary to the bone and feeling the trauma of the aftereffects of their flight from Stuttgart, they tottered off the train like a pair of decrepit old ladies. Sabine, for herself, had to stop once on the tarmac and blink in the spilling sunlight that fell from the glass-roofed train barn that arched above them.

"This is an improvement," she remarked.

Religious icons were everywhere.

Kiosk after kiosk sold plastic statues of the Virgin Mary of every description, including in snow globes. They came to a stop for the now-routine search for the tourist guidebook and Sabine pointed out the modern attempt at relics.

"You've never seen the Church of the Holy Sepulcher," Ari said.

"Hmm?"

"Nothing can be removed from the site, because once there, it is holy. You've not lived until you've seen several hundred dusty plastic rosy flaming hearts. Or the holy stepladder."

"I gotta see it."

Sabine cracked the guide as Ari kept the look out.

"Tourist Board dead ahead," she said, sucking the info into her brain.

"Cool. Let's get you a map."

Milano from minute one couldn't have been more different from Stuttgart.

Their arrangements were made in minutes from the cheery open Tourist Board at the center of the mall. They stepped outside five minutes later, under a cloudy sky that had signs of clearing, into an empty grand square in front of the most imposing train station Sabine had ever seen. Heroic figures were carved in deep relief in panels on the sides of the building, all bravely pointing towards a future that had not come. The end of the war had found a defeated Italy. Grotesque statuary with gaping mouths sat as fountainheads for the bottoms of the panels, empty at that moment, water gone to other climes and sunnier skies.

"Woohoo! Fascist architecture at its finest!" Sabine commented. "But did I fail to mention that the muggings all happen in this square, according to the guide?"

"Right," Ari said with a sigh. "So where are we going?"

They stopped in front of one of the ubiquitous McDonald's that seemed to dot the countryside of Europe and Great Britain.

"Well, according to the wonderful and helpful map the nice Tourist Board gave us, there is only one main drag in all of Milan."

"One?"

"One. So, we head down two blocks, make a left and it should be another short block down. The Hotel Marguerite." Sabine lifted her head. "Ooo."

"What?"

"McDonald's."

Ari hung her head and sighed.

Sabine and Ari fell through the door at the Hotel Marguerite a half hour later. It took some doing, since the hotel sat on a tiny industrial street that at first, Sabine was certain they had gotten lost on. But a very unimposing façade did present itself as their chosen hotel by declaring itself through a tiny sign and a tiny lobby with a tiny hotel desk, the floor done in beautiful, old, black and white marble tile. They marched up, grateful and weary, and had less trouble making themselves understood than they had in Paris or Germany combined. Sabine found more and more reasons to like Italy.

They took possession of two large and unwieldy keys and were made to understand in broken English that their keys were to be dropped off in the morning before they went out or the maid could not straighten up. Or at least, that's what Sabine hoped the young man in the white shirt meant. If not, it was just to make it easier for them to toss the room.

They embarked on the last leg of that day's journey, heading towards the back of the hotel and an elevator that Ari distrusted, since she was certain it would collapse the instant they stepped on.

"Oh, don't like this."

"I know. It's a closet on pulleys."

The poor thing did manage to land them on their floor, the third, and disgorge them without its cable snapping.

It wasn't the smallest room they'd been in so far, or the largest, but it was the most run down. The building, while not as ancient as the one in Paris, had not had the same renovations, but even so, held its own charm. A pale blue coverlet draped the king size bed (they couldn't get a room with two beds) and to the left of the door, a large if narrow, rectangular, and long bathroom opened up. The same black and white marble tiled the bathroom. The floor in the room was planked in warm golden oak. Across the way, closed French doors indicated the only window. The only light that fell into the room came from the window in the bathroom as far as Sabine could tell.

It was a dive, but lived in and loved, and Sabine didn't care. Someone had mended the coverlet, painted in the grout to hide a broken out piece of black tile.

"Cozy."

"Yeah."

"Sleep."

"Right now?" Ari questioned, surprised at Sabine's one word vehemence.

"Now."

Sabine didn't mean to be short, but everything had collapsed in on her between one breath and the next. She had a room for the next five days. She had a bed and she had a head that ached so bad that if she didn't lay down in the next five minutes, she would fall down.

Moments later, Sabine was out and unresponsive as a stone.

Fourteen hours later, Sabine rose from her self-induced coma. In the right hand corner from the bed, Ari looked up from her laptop as Sabine sat up, still groggy.

"I was wondering if you'd ever wake up again."

"I could eat a horse."

Ari looked like she had just won the Lottery.

"Oh, I'm so glad you said that. I've been sitting here for the last hour trying to keep myself from waking you. I'm starving."

"Dummy. Should have woke my ass up."

"I tried. You flailed an arm at me and called me something that I'm sure was unkind, but wasn't intelligible."

Sabine closed her eyes in embarrassment.

"Sorry."

"It's all right. Can you be ready soon?"

"Give me five."

Face scrubbed, since a bath was out of the question (there was no shower stall for a quick shower), Sabine rummaged through her suitcase and came to a horrible realization.

"Okay. I need a Laundromat."

"Ditto in spades."

"Do you have anything left that's clean?"

"Black skirt?"

"I'll take it."

They stood on the corner of their hotel's street and main drag. The sky persisted in returning to gray, but the temperature was warm.

Everything was closed.

"Oh dear."

Ari mewled. Desperation fueled Sabine's scan. Must feed the Ari, must feed the Ari, she repeated to herself.

"Look! Some place is open!"

A red door across the street and a sandwich board listed specials, but no restaurant name.

Stepping in a moment later to the dim interior, the gray suited maitre d' spotted them first. Sabine had a bad moment when she saw the color of the suit until the petite, silver-haired gentleman stepped out from behind his podium with a huge smile.

"Bonjourno, signoras!"

They managed to convince Antony, (that much they understood), the

maitre d', that no, really, they didn't want five courses after five minutes of arguing in laughable pidgin Italian-English. Sabine suspected he spoke better English than he let on, because a couple of times, he responded to her very clear English asides to Ari.

Even so...

Someone started to whistle in the kitchen.

It was the theme to The Godfather.

Ari and Sabine just looked at each other.

"No."

"No one will ever believe us," Ari said with a nervous giggle.

Antony returned with their lunch/breakfast with alacrity and again fussed over them. He was solicitous of Sabine and made much of her in Italian that sounded beautiful, though incomprehensible.

Sabine didn't figure it out till halfway through lunch.

"They think I'm a widow."

Ari gave her the up and down once over with her eyes. And followed it up with more giggling.

"Well…"

Sabine looked down and sighed.

"I'm just batting a thousand, aren't I? Trench at the Dorchester and young widow's weeds here in Milan. Oh well, could be worse."

"I don't even want to know what your definition of worse is."

Sabine started to reply and stopped. She wasn't going to speak the thought that had crossed her mind as clear as day. Besides, she was certain there had to be worse things than being dead.

"So, what's on today's agenda?" Ari asked as Sabine struggled with the bill.

"I was thinking we could pretend to be tourists," she answered, the reckoning settled.

"Oh, what a refreshing idea."

"Because it's either that or cower in our hotel room."

"No, no, no!"

Sabine materialized the small guide she had gotten from the Tourist Board with her map, out of her pack and began flipping through the pages.

"Here we go." She stopped on a listing of sites, all of one page. "Well, there ain't much, except, oh, this sounds cool, a great basilica downtown. Not only that, but according to our handy dandy guide, the Duomo as it is referred to, is topped by a nine foot gold statue of the Virgin Mary. Begins to explain all the plastic idols."

"Nine foot?"

"Nine foot."

"Well, then we have to go."

Not only was there only one main drag down the center of town, there was also only one metro line. It ran the length of the Boulevard and had one branching.

Fifteen minutes deposited them at the Duomo station. They emerged into the skies that Renaissance artists had painted to portray the Ascension of Mary. Against that sky stood a soaring romance of a building.

For the first time in her life, Sabine felt her breath taken away. She stood in awe. The feather touch of something glanced across her soul.

In the breaking, glorious clouds behind the cathedral, the sunlight shone on the Virgin like a prayer and Sabine felt her eyes prick with tears. Such beauty. There was nothing like it back home. Nothing that communicated the feeling of the sacred, that before even walking into this temple, one was moved by the Presence of Eternity. People crossed the square in front of the church in constant motion and flock after flock of pigeons would startle and wheel into the sky over the spires of the basilica. Miniature angels against a tower of a faith's heaven.

Crossing the square themselves, both Sabine and Ari were even more awestruck by the sheer size of the building. The intricacies of the architectural features were so involved that it resembled a confection of lace or an elaborate wedding cake, more than a building. Set into the center of the front of the basilica were two enormous doors, each door depicting a different scene with accompanying panels. One, the Ascension of Mary, the other, the Pieta, the carrying of her Divine Son from the Hill.

Once upon a time it had been bronze, but age and time had turned the metal verdigris. Until Ari pointed out where everyone kept walking up to the doors. There were three separate spots on the doors that were worn through the bronze to the iron beneath.

"What's that?" Sabine wanted to know.

"There are relics in the door, I would guess. The faithful touch the doors for luck and answered prayers. Just like home," Ari said, her tone wistful. Sabine was reminded that Ari was not an American. For her, Israel was and would always be home, and especially Jerusalem, the golden city of her birth.

They stepped in the side door with several of the faithful. Men and women, regardless of age, went to the two large founts at the back of the pews, crossed themselves with holy water, and knelt, before stepping further in. Ari and Sabine followed their example, pagan and Jew they might be, but respectful of this house of a beloved God and Virgin.

"Isn't lightning supposed to strike you dead?" Ari asked in a low voice, just as Sabine crossed herself.

"No. Only Jews."

"Ooo."

There was a momentary sensation though as Ari teased her. Sabine stopped. Had someone laughed?

Looking up the great exalted height to the ceiling, Sabine saw her first one. A dove, carved into the top of the pillars that supported the great roof. She thought to point it out to Ari, but stopped. It wasn't that uncommon a motif. She looked down. But everywhere? The dove returned in the corners of every great square of tile, carrying the olive branch and Sabine began to search for it in earnest. Sure enough, it repeated in endless, subtle detail.

Ari wandered off, entranced and staring up at the arching elegance of the ceiling. Sabine gave a quick glance to make sure Ari was well on her way. Sabine surreptitiously made her own way then to the shrine of Mary Magdalene amongst all the others with its own bank of offered fire. She even managed to move in a lull of the crowd, no one standing at that moment in front of this place sacred to an ancient world's whore who had washed the feet of a messiah with oil and her hair, known as the Apostle to the Apostles.

She dug out two lira and deposited them in the offering slot and took up her two tapers. Lighting off the nearest candle, she nestled her two offerings in empty slots and kneeled.

Here she would speak His name and pagan as she was, Sabine bowed her head and gave up her offered heart.

For my dreams. For Edward, wherever he may be, alive or dead. Help me, she prayed, and felt another feather of the Presence.

But grief replaced the sensation.

Had she ever admitted how much she missed him? These dreams that plagued her now, where as often as not, she dreamt of him as clear as if she saw his face only the day before. Her heart ached. It was a difficult history. As far as Sabine knew, Ari knew next to nothing of her time in the intelligence community and for a moment, she regretted it. But she knew as little about Ari in relation to her masters in Jerusalem. One didn't ask and one didn't tell. It was one of the many reasons why they were able to call each other best friends.

But it also meant that in all the past years, Sabine had not told anyone about this pain, not even in her brief foray into therapy when she had been sixteen and had been a nerve-wracked wreck out in the Cold, unable to function in or out of the fraternities.

Edward.

Make the dreams stop, she prayed, her eyes beginning to sting. I don't want to dream anymore. I don't want to remember how much I miss him.

And the Voice spoke.

Oh, dearest, why do you weep? the Voice cried and Sabine broke down and sobbed in silence. Her heart cracked open and more than ten years of grief poured out of her in silence, unable to be given full voice. Sabine went still, the feeling coming again, the sense of wings and feathers and it enveloped her as if she were one of the Faithful.

I am not of your flock, she thought, projecting as clear as she could.

Are you not, Beloved? came a whisper in her heart.

Sabine felt herself become glad. This was the Spirit. This was the true Spirit of the Numinous. But still she wept. For everything. For Edward, for wolves in Stuttgart, and dreams and Dreams that she could not stop nor understand.

Sabine opened her soul to the Presence. Feathered light seemed to touch and turn over each pain in her heart and after that touch, the pain eased. Not gone, but healed somehow and put in some strange perspective.

Why do this for me? Sabine asked, her tears drying, her heart now filling with a gratitude so intense as to rival the pain of only a moment before.

The Touch eased even that intensity, so Sabine could breathe for the first time with relief.

Why not?

Sabine asked no more.

She dried her eyes on her sleeve, hoping her eyes were not too puffy or red. She didn't want to have to explain to her friend. Instead, she crossed herself and took the image and the light of the two candles and put them in her heart as permanent prayer and memory, for this gift of unseen and unasked for Grace.

Beware of Greeks and their gifts.

It was barely a whisper, but Sabine heard it even so.

"Why?" she whispered.

Remember, and for a moment, the Voice sounded a little even of Zoë. But Sabine felt no fear. Only understanding of the warning. The feathered light still protected her heart.

She rejoined Ari, only after she had found enough strength to regain her composure and found her friend behind the altar, looking at the seals of many saints. One, Ari grinned at like a fool till Sabine gave it her full attention.

"Albertus Magnus?! Is that right?" Sabine exclaimed.

"No wonder I love it here!" Ari said with a giggle. "My favorite saint!"

"Can you have a favorite saint? Jew and all?"

"Why not?"

Sabine did not dispute the point. After all, she had just been granted dispensation from pain because this temple's Presence did not require her following belief to intervene.

They moved on, finding stairs under the area of the altar. Getting to the bottom with several other people, they discovered it was the vault. Several signs in several languages explained that the church's specific relics were displayed in the chambers, but the crowd was thick and they found themselves against the wall, more than once.

They did manage to see the relics, but the small sacristy under the altar was barred and gated, leaving them to stare through the bars. The relics were interesting and beautiful, but Sabine found the mummy of the cardinal in the glass coffin, highly disturbing.

"Shouldn't they put him away?" she said, shuddering.

"But he's one of their favorites!" Ari replied, tongue in cheek.

They headed back the way they had come, finished after an hour of gawking and drinking in the Duomo. On the way out, Sabine saw two doorways, but no identifying signs.

The one dove at the right corner of the nearest arched and narrow doorway was what riveted Sabine's attention.

"What's that?"

"I don't know."

"Let's go."

"Uh…"

"There's no sign that says, 'Keep Out'." Sabine said with an undertone of, don't-be-a-'fraidy-cat.

The doorway opened into a narrow and steep stone staircase, the walls so close that anyone of extensive girth would have had trouble negotiating the passage. They descended for some depth, Sabine feeling the weight of the stone around her, but here, there was no claustrophobia. Only stone and the Presence.

They stepped out into a crypt with a low ceiling and cordoned off from the few remaining crypts, further excavation showed an ancient well, deeper under that, another foundation, all the way down to a third.

"Whoa," Ari breathed and lit up. Archeology was her passion and here in the roots of the Duomo, sat a finished dig.

"Cool," Sabine agreed, almost overpowered by the strength of the Presence here.

Raised catwalks let tourists pass over the excavations, protecting the dig from harm, and they wandered, staring at what had to be early Roman foundation in one spot, to be pre-dated in another spot by something far older. On the way out, three display cases contained the findings of the dig, including the shards of brilliant blue tiny mosaic tile that could still be seen in some places intact on the bottommost layer, but was destroyed most everywhere else.

Then Sabine saw Her.

She was an early, early Goddess figure of plain stone, weathered and beaten, but recognizable to Sabine no matter how destroyed.

"Of course," she breathed.

Different faces. Different names. Does it matter? The Eternal endures. Without Love, we would be lost, Sophia whispered and Sabine nodded. The Goddess lived and took on the likeness of a dove.

How am I to face this alone? Sabine prayed in sudden response, the past three weeks immediate and heavy in her memory.

We are always with you.

They didn't stay much longer and, once more, just as Sabine put her foot on the stair, she heard the Voice again.

Remember...

They stood for a long moment outside. The sun came and went through the majestic clouds, but it held no portent for Sabine. The weather she felt across her skin was only the passing of wind and rain, winter's grip loosening. They watched the pigeons wheel and circle, come to ground for a moment and bread, another moment, back to winging across the sky. If Ari had heard Voices as well, she made no indication and Sabine didn't ask. Either way, Ari seemed content to watch the sky and the birds and take a moment before returning to the mortal Earth.

"That was wonderful," Ari sighed.

"Yes, it was."

"So what's next?"

"According, once again, to our handy dandy guidebook, the street directly behind the Duomo here is where all the fashion boutiques live."

"Shopping!" Ari squealed.

They chose the Benetton boutique, based on the strength of the window display.

Sabine bought white clothes. White mini skirt, white sleeveless shirt with silver buttons.

But her last purchase was the most difficult for her. A bikini, the first she had even thought to acquire, black and silver rainbow-ed metallic, flashy like what she thought a mythical fire salamander's scales would have to be. Armed with her purchases, she regrouped with Ari, who had already seen her stuff and had her own bag of goodies.

"Coffee," Sabine announced.

"Right. Espresso?"

They found an outdoor café on the avenue only a block up from the Benetton boutique. White-clothed tables scattered across the cobblestones, with servers wearing immaculate white aprons who danced amongst the tables and the patrons.

They sat down and the clouds scudded by on a wind that was warm and rain-scented. The occasional shaft of sunlight broke through and illuminated the pavement and the passers-by. Sabine felt drunk on the day. Her heart still warm in her chest from her time in the Duomo and clothes sat in a bag at her feet that she would never have bought at home.

When her espresso arrived, it came in a perfect white cup with gilt around the edges of the saucer and lip of the cup.

Perfect.

"Let's stay," Sabine sighed.

"Yeah," Ari agreed. "Get a little apartment and come here every day for espresso and tea and people watching."

"Uh huh."

A woman in immaculate green and gold Versace walked by and Sabine and Ari stared after her.

"Wow," Sabine gaped.

"Ditto!" Ari breathed right after.

"Now that's what I call coordinated."

"Yeah. Wish we had enough money to go shop at the Versace boutique."

They sat for an hour and Sabine felt no urge to move. Ari, though, had murdered her tea while people-watching, her toes tapping to some inner music. Sabine stared at the clouds and let the warmth chase the cold of Stuttgart out of her body.

"Feel up to wandering?"

"Nah."

"Do you mind if I do?"

"No! Just don't get picked up."

Ari laughed.

"Never happen."

Ari was gone only five minutes.

Sabine stared at the sky, daydreaming.

"May I join you?"

The voice that broke in on her dreaming was beautiful. Tenor and rich, flavored with something that wasn't Italian or French, just cultured European, a voice that spoke many languages, and found its home in many places. Resonant, it rippled across Sabine's hearing like velvet.

The man who stood next to her table was as beautiful as his voice. Olive-skinned and black-haired, green eyes drank her in with a totality that in anyone else would have been far too provocative. He was tall and dressed in a beautiful cream suit that complimented his coloring to perfection. Sabine was convinced his stylist had to be five feet behind him and fussing over how the wind ruined his charge's hair.

"I'm waiting for a friend," Sabine said with a struggle, resisting the overwhelming urge to invite him to stay. A warning feathered on her skin.

"Then I shall not keep you long." He sat down with the grace of a panther. Sabine admired his form without disguising her regard, which was quite unlike her. The broad forehead and beautiful green eyes against his pale skin were so striking, and his black hair fell forward from time to time, requiring him to sweep it back. His hands were as beautiful as the rest of him, long-fingered like a pianist's, and unscarred.

Not a laborer, Sabine thought in a detached part of her mind.

"What brings you to Milano?" The Italian name for the city, so similar to the English, but rolling off of his tongue.

"Tourism," Sabine said with a smile.

"I am lucky then."

"Oh?"

"Such beauty is not often seen even in this city."

Sabine laughed.

"Flattery should at least be moderately sincere."

"Ah! I cannot believe it! Such a rebuff!" he said with this incredible smile. She smiled back.

"Believe it."

"Clearly, you do not own a mirror."

"Now, you really are going too far."

"Then I will not discuss the fact of your beauty if you refuse to acknowledge the truth. Are you long for the city?"

"A few days," Sabine hesitated to admit.

"I am Allejandro Corsico." He held out his hand and Sabine took it. A jolt of sexual heat went through her body the minute his skin connected with hers.

"Sabine Parsons," she managed to say only a little out of breath.

"Do you know anyone here? It is much better to see Milano with a guide. Her beauties are many and hidden."

"No. Just passing through."

"You must come to my villa here in the city," he remarked as if it just occurred to him. "I would love to be your guide."

All of a sudden, Sabine found herself thinking of her last dream of Zoë. Sabine couldn't chase it out of her head. She kept hearing the warning and overlaid over that, the Voice.

Sabine wanted to say yes, but the warning rang loud in her ears. The wanting to say yes was as strange as the feeling of fear.

"I'm afraid I'm otherwise engaged," she managed, her Game Face up and on with sudden reaction.

"I am disconsolate!"

"I doubt it," Sabine said with a laugh.

"Ah, you mock me now, but I shall prove it to you one day," he replied. "However, I promised to keep you only a moment."

Again, panther grace as he took to his feet.

"*Signorina.*"

He kissed her hand and faded into the crowd, just as Ari walked up, leaving a tingle of such heat on the back of Sabine's hand, that she rubbed the spot, trying to rub out the feeling.

"Who was that?"

"Corsico. Allejandro Corsico."

"Ooo! Exotic!"

"Yeah. Exotic."

"Hellooo! Earth to Sabine!"

Sabine shook out of it, stopping the full on stare after Corsico.

The sun westered when Sabine and Ari emerged from the Metro on to the street near their hotel.

"Hungry," Ari announced, already staring at the Red Door across the street.

"I think I can be convinced," Sabine said.

They finished their meal two hours later and Sabine sighed in full repletion. Michael (their adorable server, since Antony had too many people to seat), cleared their plates and they both sat back, all set for the check when Antony returned with a plate of biscotti and two dainty glasses of an amber liquor that looked like molten gold.

"No, no, no!" Sabine said and he laughed, putting the plate and drinks on the table.

"Mange! Mange!" he said and they both groaned, but took cookies anyway. Satisfied they would eat, Antony returned to his podium to escort other guests into eat.

"I'm gonna explode."

"Ditto," Sabine agreed.

"You've got to drink this."

"I know. Can't be rude."

Sabine took a tentative sip from her glass. It was the sweetest fire to have ever touched her tongue.

"Hoo!" she gasped.

Ari laughed and nearly choked on a crumb.

"Good stuff, eh?"

"Smooth!" Sabine choked out and had another sip. Her lips went numb after sip three.

When they got back to their room, Sabine was half drunk and so, had forgotten everything. The Duomo. Voices. Strange, yet beautiful men on the Via Spiga. But forgotten or not, a strange feeling gripped her belly. Without thinking, she unhooked her pack and unzipped it.

"What's up?" Ari asked, still smiling, but a little concerned at Sabine's sudden concerted action from only a minute before being drunk.

"Nothing. It's just been one hell of a long day." She dug out her cigs and lighter.

"Is that all?"

"Feel weird."

"Going to be okay?"

"Yeah. Need to smoke."

Sabine opened the wooden French doors on to a tiny balcony with a wrought iron railing. The view consisted of the backs of several buildings and a small service courtyard three stories below her. All of the buildings were beige stone or golden beige paint, except for the gray concrete of the courtyard. Not interesting by any remote consideration, but in the small square above her there was nothing but blue sky, darkening to the kind of indigo that the Milanese dye makers would have killed to reproduce in their silk. The smell of oregano and basil wafted towards her on the warm breeze. She stepped out and lit her first cigarette.

One star came out, then another and Sabine crouched, the glowing tip of her cigarette just one more star in the firmament around her.

They didn't go out the next day, except to eat and sort their laundry. Sabine pored over the guide till she found a Laundromat near their hotel and after an early dinner, they piled out on to the street to go and wash their clothes.

"When did we pick up another tail?"

"Where?"

"Across the street. Male pair, blond and brunet."

"I see 'em." Ari's brow furrowed and then she smiled like she wasn't doing anything that resembled staring at the two men. "Huh."

"I know. They're not our idiots in gray." Sabine went back to folding her laundry from the first load. "Any ideas?"

"Clueless."

"Joy." Then it hit her. "Huh. I've got an idea."

She started out the door.

"Sabine, what are you doing?" Ari called after her, trying to keep smiling and not panic out of her mind.

"Nothing. I'm going to see if they have change," Sabine called back, loud and bright, with her patented plastic smile. "Pardon? *Excusez*? Do you have any change? Do you speak English?" Sabine asked, Game Face on, making her way across the narrow street.

"Oh, *sì*! Yes! Laundry change?" the blond of the pair answered.

"Yes! Oh, thank you! You are so helpful!"

"You are welcome. Students?"

"Tourists. You?"

"Mmm, how do you say? Natives?"

"Yes, native."

She flirted for a few minutes longer.

Long enough to make out the guns fitted for right hand draw. Not the Malice Twins' get. The Twins and their cohorts had neither carried guns nor as far as Sabine could tell, did they need them. In a way, it was almost comforting to see guns printing under the jackets. It meant no other hidden talents. She hoped.

She tossed her hair as she headed back to Ari and her fixed smile, where she folded laundry mechanically.

"Well?" Ari asked.

"Well. New players."

"Joy."

"Wonder when and why we picked them up."

"Honey, if we knew that, we wouldn't be having these problems."

"Well, yes, isn't that the fucking truth."

They finished their laundry and went back to their hotel room. They didn't spot their new tail. But that didn't mean anything.

The next day dawned dark and fog bound. Sabine for once deliberately Reached out to taste the wind with her skin. Nothing read out of place. Only low pressure and moisture from the ground. The way wind and weather were supposed to behave, and she felt her back uncoil, from where she had tensed.

The entire morning went by without event or comment until they sat over the remains of their antipasto breakfast and Antony had retreated after serving Sabine more of the espresso she so loved. She already had the guidebook open.

"Find anything interesting?" Ari asked.

The book flipped open to a picture of an enormous fortress. Sabine breathed out in raw appreciation.

"Oh yeah!"

Ari craned a glance over and rolled her eyes.

"Oh. Bloodshed."

"Bloodshed!"

The Sforza of Milan turned out to be a short trip by Metro. They emerged in a continuing gray day to reddish-brown stone surrounding them and the overgrown greenery looking vibrant against the overcast.

Not as ancient as the Tower of London, Sabine allowed herself a smile as the small hope that since it wasn't as old, meant that she wouldn't have to fear for her Memory. It was only fantastic architecture. They wandered under wall and into courtyard after courtyard, staring up and down at this testament to an age of empire building and war.

They made their way into the main body of the fortress, to emerge into an inner murder court, complete with catwalk and arrow slits, the chains for where the cauldrons of boiling oil would have sat still intact on the upper wall.

They followed the other tourists up the stairs to the catwalk, following signs that indicated that there were several museums (free!) further in the interior of the fortress.

Sabine set one foot on the catwalk after a German couple in matching green sweaters and staggered as an explosion went off in her ears and behind her eyes.

The catwalk swayed under her feet as another blast rocked the foundations of the fortress, and she was in Memory.

She really should be used to it by now, but she wasn't. Her skin felt icy and she strangled her scream, choking instead.

Flames surrounded her. Her men, armored and wounded, screamed and yelled as the attackers rushed the catwalk. A cauldron of boiling oil burst next to her and the spray scalded her armor, scarring the devouring dragon on her chest.

The attackers broke through the first rank of defenders.

She felt the rising battle tide in her blood, preparing to scream the counter attack.

The catwalk collapsed under them and Sabine staggered—

She fell in flames and boiling rain...

"Sabine!"

"Died here," she choked out.

Ari just nodded, grim response, and helped her off the walk.

"I felt it that time," Ari admitted.

They leaned against the wall on the opposite side. Sabine didn't know how Ari had gotten her there. No one seemed to notice either of their distress and she allowed herself a moment to close her eyes. A short Memory, but violent in its intensity.

Sabine did everything in her power to pretend that it hadn't happened.

After all, why not? She had no fucking explanation for what was happening to her. She had past life flashes that made no sense to her and the theme or thing in common with any of the Memories were wars or violence or death by violence.

In the end, she didn't think she wanted to know what they meant. She just wanted them to stop and her time at the Duomo seemed a million years ago.

"Are you going to be okay?"

Sabine opened her eyes and gave her friend a face that wasn't a smile, but wasn't a grimace either.

"I'll be okay if it kills me."

"That's what frightens me."

"I meant figuratively."

"Just as long as we're clear on that."

"Clear as mud."

Ari harrumphed and Sabine laughed. She had to. She was losing her mind and her friend was worried. As if she wasn't worried herself.

"Oh, gods, Ari, what's happening to me? To us?"

"I don't know and I don't care. But when I find the people responsible, they're going to be cat food."

"Are you ready?"

"Oh, let's go look at things we can never afford or own."

"Good."

So they did and if Sabine staggered from time to time, because a flash of Memory staggered her bones, Ari pretended not to notice, because Sabine refused to verbalize and walked on, pointing out different pieces of art or antiquity, all while her soul felt itself fraying at the edges.

They were walking back out of the fortress, heading back for their hotel, when Sabine heard a voice she recognized.

"Mr. Corsico!" Sabine responded.

Corsico strolled towards them, resplendent in cream suit and open necked shirt in black.

"Please. Call me Allejandro," he said as soon as he was close enough to be heard in comfort.

"Allejandro," Sabine conceded.

"Please introduce me to your lovely companion."

"Ari Doran, you already know all about Allejandro."

"So my fame proceeds me?" he asked with a laugh. "Your friend did not believe me when I called her beautiful."

"She's been known to do that," Ari said.

"So how are the two most beautiful women in all of Milano today?"

They both laughed. From anyone else, the flattery would have sounded false.

"Not so good actually," Ari said before Sabine could answer. "Sabine, I'm not feeling so good."

"Do we need to go back?" Sabine asked.

"If you don't mind."

"No worries." Sabine turned to Corsico who also looked concerned. "I'm sorry, Allejandro."

"Not at all. Signorina, feel better soon."

Before Sabine could move, he had her hand and kissed the back of it again.

It was like a knife through her arm, into her body.

It was the quickest escape Sabine had ever made from anyone in her life. She waited till they were out of earshot and around a corner before looking at Ari's pale face. She buried very real concern in the same spot that she'd been burying her fears.

"What's wrong?"

"There's something...wrong with him."

Sabine kept herself from looking over her shoulder.

Yes, there was something wrong about Allejandro Corsico, but Sabine couldn't figure out what it was. No aura showed up around him for her, but until Stuttgart, she'd never seen auras before anyway.

Then why did she feel this liquid heat at her core? His touch seemed to still be on the surface of her skin, the back of her hand where his lips had touched. She desired him.

And feared him.

"You're right. There is something. But are we just jumping at shadows because of all that's been going on?"

"More than likely, but, he just gives me the willies! Sexy willies, but still the willies!"

Sabine laughed.

"Well, I'm glad to see I'm not the only one who feels it."

"Yeah, he is kind of raw sex on wheels, isn't he?"

They had a fantastic dinner at the Red Door. They went back to their hotel. Sabine closed her eyes, and opened them in the Dream.

Zoë and the Beloved floated uncoiled before her in the great chamber.

"You've met him," Zoë said, her voice for the first time sounding like a little girl's. Frightened.

"Huh?" The dreams always seemed to leave Sabine stupid.

"It doesn't matter. I saw it, no matter what future I looked into."

Sabine looked a wordless question, no longer surprised that Zoë could read her face, even without eyes.

"You are leaving tomorrow?"

"Yes. For Nice."

"Good. Good," Zoë whispered, the coils of the Beloved enveloping her.

Sabine's sight grew black and filled with stars. She dreamt of doves for the rest of the night. When she woke in the morning, it was with a full and rested heart. The Dream of Zoë for the first time felt just like that. A dream, too weak and frail to stand in the morning light.

CHAPTER VII – INITIAL CONDITIONS

Milan, Italy - Nice, France – Monte Carlo, Principality of Monaco

"So where to—"

"Cannes."

Ari was startled at her friend's sudden vehemence. Sabine didn't notice. She stared at the Departures board, her expression rapt. They stood in the Milan train station, crowd milling around them.

"Cannes?"

"Nice."

Ari saw Nice on the board.

"Nice?"

"It's right between Monte Carlo and Cannes. And if I remember right, the Cannes Film Festival is going on right now."

"Wow."

"I know I haven't asked for any city in particular up till now, but Ari…"

"Say no more! Cute men in Speedos! South of France! Let's go!"

For the first time, it was Sabine's turn to be glued to the train windows.

In the deepening twilight, the Mediterranean appeared like an expanse of cerulean velvet. The beginning lights of the mansions dotted along the coast looked like multi-colored jewels, reflecting in the water. When Monte Carlo first appeared around the bend, it came into view like a queen out of the rosy sunset.

Sabine's heart felt full in her chest. For that train ride, Sabine felt all right with the world.

They found a little hostel by virtue of Sabine and her guidebook again. It was a two story walk up on the square of the Palais du Justice. They'd seen very little of the outside, it being dark and the streets narrow and ill lit. Sabine still couldn't figure out how their cab driver had gotten his BMW down the alleys in the first place.

Negotiations completed, Sabine and Ari followed their temporary landlord down a long dark narrow hallway. He opened a door as crooked as he was. The landlord gave the word weasel a whole new meaning.

The room made the one they'd left in Milan look like the Four Seasons.

"Oh. Dear." Sabine said. "I'm sorry, Ari."

Ari gave it the visual once over. Two beds. One queen size bed, one twin size bed, a kitchenette with a sad looking hot plate, a half size refrigerator. At the right, a narrow hall pretended to be a bathroom with a tiny shower stall and a pedestal sink. All of it painted an unfortunate shade of mustard yellow.

"Oh well. Can't be helped. Besides, I've stayed in worse places."

"Where?"

"The Gaza Strip."

Sabine took the twin bed by the rickety closed French doors. The blankets smelled musty and old, but Sabine didn't care. It was a bed. It wasn't swaying with a train.

The next morning, one cup of espresso, an Earl Grey tea, and several croissants later, found the two women in the market around the corner from their room. Sabine had insisted on going to the beach afterward and bringing a picnic as well.

The morning sun found a golden city in the clear, warm sunlight, the buildings a butter yellow more often than not. Cobblestone streets ran in every direction and Sabine had her map as a permanent fixture, open in her hand once they left the square in front of their hotel. The square of the Palais du Justice was a bustling thoroughfare during daylight hours, consisting of tourists, lawyers and those who employed them, traveling back and forth to the imposing façade of the courthouse or to the café set up across from the Palais. It served a mean cup of espresso.

Around the corner from the hotel, the market was a tiny hole in the wall that back home Sabine would have called a Mom and Pop. She guessed it would be *Mère* and *Père* here in the South of France. They bought groceries for their little kitchenette and both of them were transported into gourmet raptures when they discovered homemade pâté made by the lady of the establishment.

They made a quick trip back to the room, dropped off the regular groceries (eggs, tea bags, the important things in life), packed the shopping bag back up with their picnic fixings, changed into their new bikinis, and flew right back out on to the street

They stepped out.

On to rocks.

"They weren't kidding," Sabine said in surprise, the echo of her Dream strong with her. "It's covered in little rocks!"

She meant the description of the beaches from her guidebook, since so far, the guide had been full of entertaining wrong facts when they weren't just plain weird. But in this case, the rocks turned out to be super comfortable and held in the heat of the sun.

Standing in the shallow water off the shale beach, Sabine let the sun bake her, and once and for all, gave up the last three weeks of fear and adrenaline. The sky and ocean were picture-perfect shades of blue with not a cloud in sight. Little waves rolled to the shore. The world fell away and Sabine felt only clear weather across her skin. No storm on the horizon. No clouds. No rainbows.

"Thank you," she whispered to the limitless blue.

After a half hour of this idyll, Ari spoke up, muffled a little since she was on her tummy.

"I hate to bring up a horrible subject on this most perfect of days, but—"

"But we need to debrief," Sabine finished, lying flat on her back. "Where do you want to start?"

"The pills."

"Gods, I'd completely forgotten about them! Shit. Well, what is there to say? We have them and I'm certain that we are not the people that man meant to give them to."

"Maybe we were," Ari said, her tone contemplative.

"Excuse me?"

"The Duomo."

Sabine had nothing to say to that.

"Something else is at work here," Ari continued, tilting her head to look at Sabine.

"I don't like that."

"Me neither." The sun no longer seemed as warm or as comforting as it had been only a moment before. "What else?"

"Stuttgart."

"Current definition of hell."

"Besides that."

"Um, see above. Not enough data."

"Pills?"

"Fuck if I know. I submit Paris."

"Hmm."

Sabine closed her eyes and struggled to feel the serenity of the sunlight and wind.

"Posit..." she trailed off.

"Yes?"

"...a major operation currently being implemented in the European Union by freelancers."

"I'm with you so far."

"Add one ex-analyst and one not so ex-spook."

"And?"

"'Cry havoc and let loose the dogs of war.'"

"Why?"

"It has something to do with these dreams..."

"You're still dreaming."

It was statement and Sabine tilted her head to consider her friend. Ari looked neither worried nor scared, lying on her stomach, her skin pink from the sun.

"Yes," she replied.

"We really just know very little, don't we?"

"No." Sabine drew the word out. "We know that a higher force moving through this wants us involved."

"And?"

"This is fucking up the operation."

"What makes you say that?"

"Why grab us?"

"Ah. I see your point." Ari stared back inland.

"We're the unknown variable from their point of view. We know there are at least three players at work here; Ulrich and his cubs, the Malice Twins and then whoever the fuck all has been tailing us since Milan, if not sooner." Sabine ticked them off on the fingers of her right hand. "If we were only a minor annoyance, they'd ignore us. But whatever wants us involved has somehow not hidden well enough to not be detected by the Opposition."

"Continue."

"Whoever our bozo players are, they know enough that somehow we're important enough to grab. Interrogate. Whatever."

"Joy. Wish we knew why we were so damn important."

"Yes, well, that is the most important of lost bits of datum. Without it, I could be totally stoned here."

"No, no. It's a good analysis based on what little we've got." Ari gave her a sly grin. "Are you sure I can't convince you to join the Mossad?"

"Ari!" Sabine laughed with mock outrage.

"Joke! Joke! Laugh?" Ari said through giggles. "Think we'll get home without being shot?"

"Oh, I sure hope so." Sabine stared out to sea. "Even if we haven't even scratched the surface."

"No. We sure haven't. *Kinohora.*"

"Kino what?"

"'God forbid'."

"Oh." A beat as it sank in. "Yeah. Oh dear, oh my."

The next morning, going through her suitcase, Sabine made a unilateral decision.

"We need to ship half this shit home," she announced.

Ari saw the pile of film rolls Sabine was making on the tiny table in the middle of the room.

"Oh dear."

"Like, today."

They found a file box in a stationery store and bought packing tape to go with. When they got back to the room, Sabine started to unpack the rolls of film she wanted to ship home.

"Well, at least our trip to hell is well documented."

"Hey, we may need these pictures in court."

The rolls went into the box, along with two shirts that were too warm for the south of France. Packed and sealed, they marched around the corner to mail it and spent what Sabine was sure was far too much for boat delivery. Afterwards, they stood on the sidewalk for a minute, neither saying a word.

"Well, now what the hell?" Sabine asked.

"Dunno."

"I feel amazingly directionless."

"Well, you know what my vote is…"

"Yes, oh hungry one. We can go eat."

They walked out into the square and turned around in a circle. Sabine spotted the sign first.

"Chez Wayne? What kind of name is that?"

"Let's find out!"

Who knew it would turn out to be an English ex-patriot's pub? Ari decided Sabine needed a drink after dinner. Which turned out to translate out as three or four.

The pub closed at 2 AM. They stood in the square, no people, only the warm evening breeze for company. Sabine swayed with the wind, warmer than she had been in weeks and more relaxed than she had been in weeks.

In the morning, they sat in the square, in the perfect Nice sunshine, and Sabine took deep breaths. The air smelled like Heaven. Warm and spiced with things she could not name and heavy with the sensual emotions of everyone around her. The weather itself seemed to smile in delight and Sabine sank further in her chair. The weather she felt across her skin communicated everyone's emotional state. She knew she should have been alarmed by this new turn of events, but couldn't seem to muster the energy.

Which is why when she felt Him, it felt like being doused with ice water.

"No," she whispered, stiffening.

"What?" Ari looked up from her lunch.

"Nothing," Sabine forced out a neutral reply.

But couldn't force away the feeling that said that He had only been standing five feet away. Sabine looked in the direction of their hotel. A group of men in well-tailored suits were just stepping inside, but that was nothing of note. The court was in session in the Palais.

No, she thought this time. *No.*

He's dead.

Through the gray, the train sailed more like a ship through a sea of cloud. Sabine had hoped for better weather to see her first view of Monte Carlo, but there was a part of her that didn't mind.

The morning had dawned gray, but before she'd even opened her eyes, Sabine knew that they were going to Monte Carlo. She hadn't dragged Ari to the South of France to have cloud cover keep her from seeing the one city in Europe she'd been mad about since she'd seen her first James Bond film.

Short train ride, she thought when they got off only a half hour later. Both of them were subdued and had spoken little, neither over breakfast nor on the train. It was like they had taken a strange vow of silence for the day that while not enforced, was for once, the companionship of two who had now been so much in the other's company that they no longer needed words.

They ended up walking with no destination in mind, down the twisting streets, few people around, only to come out on a view of the city.

The city was a jewel.

Buildings nestled in the flanks of the mountain and in front of them, a great rise of rock, and a fortress. Sabine headed for the old Roman road that lead to the top of the rock, instead of heading for the indicated, shorter route.

It took an hour to walk the incline and they passed through several gates. A fortress that could be held for an indefinite length of time. They emerged at the top of the rock to step into a courtyard in front of a small palace and a collection of buildings that would have been a village, except that no village had homes as beautiful as these.

They followed a path that lead away from the Prince's palace that crawled along the edge of the rock and overlooked the sea, giving a view of the rest of the City that was a Country.

The path ended and Sabine led the way back into the center of the fortress city. A choice of three different streets opened before them, all going in different directions. Figuring moderation in all things, Sabine chose the middle road.

The streets, designed for pedestrians and no cars, baffled Sabine's usual implacable sense of direction. After only five minutes, she had to admit to being lost. But for the first time on that trip, in fact, for the first time in her life, Sabine didn't care.

Ari was with her. She was in Europe. She was surrounded by beautiful buildings, and sculptured gardens. It was a monument to the highest impulses of Man's yearning. Beauty and ease and even if it was bought at great expense. She felt…safe.

But her stomach grumbled.

A small sign presented itself. A café. They stepped in and Sabine felt herself transported back to California.

Surfing photos covered the walls. A surfboard leaned against the wall. Out of the back kitchen, a young bleached blond man stepped out and smiled at them. He wore tie-dye and his jeans were torn. It could have been Santa Cruz.

They sat and had tea at one of the scarred wooden tables with a set of mismatched chairs. Sabine had tea as well, for once espresso-ed out.

She was waiting. Not happy or in fear, just waiting. Like something fine was going to end. Sabine shook her head. She was getting weird even for her. She was just sick of the overcast.

The vise was back around her heart.

"Sabine?"

"Chest…" she wheezed.

The sky outside felt heavy against her skin and her eye sight tunneled, then cleared as everything took a sickening lurch to the left. She felt the waiting no more.

Something had happened.

"Sabine!" She heard Zoë shout and pain and all, tried to get up.

"Zoë?" she whispered, unable to shout back.

"Sabine?" Ari's hand on her arm.

"Ari."

"Who's Zoë?"

When Sabine rolled over in the bed the next morning, Ari was already sitting up, waiting.

"What today?"

"Back to Monte Carlo."

"All right. Plan?"

"Beach." Sabine pulled out her new clothes just as more rolls of film fell out of the bag. "Dress the part. Oh, bloody hell and the post office again. These rolls of film are breeding."

An hour later, they stepped off the train into the most perfect of Monte Carlo days. They paid the fee at the private beach behind the Casino and headed out on the teak walkway for a spot near the water. Ordered drinks from the gorgeous waiter. Tried to get comfortable, in the old age dance of looking for the perfect way to recline to get sun, be relaxed and yet, look sexy at the same time. Then the drinks showed up, Sabine paid for them and they both had to start over.

She lay back on the chaise, her Diet Coke in her hand, her top already on the pebbles next to her and sighed.

"Now this is the life."

"Do you think he can be had for love or money?" Ari was on her stomach and staring after the scrumptious waiter.

"In Monte Carlo? Anything for a price."

A little while later, Sabine stood in the water, watching little gray fish nibble at her knees and considered her comment. The sun beat on her shoulders and the water flashing in the light would have been blinding if not for her sunglasses.

"Anything for a price..." she murmured to the fish.

Their next stop after two hours of blissful baking in the sun was the Casino proper. Sabine didn't have to argue at all to convince Ari to stop and have a gander. Stepping into the coolness of the Casino's interior was also a blessing.

The Casino was a work of art and worth the fee. Green flocked wallpaper, beautiful carpets, but most of all, the exquisite Belle Époque paintings and murals that adorned the ceilings.

Late afternoon also meant there were few people in the Casino, so no one to neither get in their way nor comment on their lack of gambling. The slot machines were tastefully installed, but as far as Sabine was concerned, if you'd been to Vegas, you'd seen all casinos.

Until they walked to the roulette pit.

Sabine had to stop and smile. Five die-hards sat a table in the middle and played for medium money, but it was clearly a game for the love of it, not the winning of it.

"What's that?" Ari asked suddenly.

"What?"

"That." Ari pointed out the roulette game.

"Roulette? You know roulette."

"Not really. Can't say that I've ever gambled."

"Why would you? You do it for a profession."

"Yeah."

"Well, let's get closer," and she lead the way to one of the benches that lined the walls.

Sabine explained. After all, it was all Game Theory. Any good codebreaker or analyst knew Game Theory backwards and forwards. How numbers ran in series and that luck had little to do with it. That with a wooden roulette wheel it could be fooled, because factors such as weather and humidity could also affect how it spun and what numbers came up. That a serious player knew this and never sat down to a roulette table to play until he had watched it for some time to see what runs the table favored, what colors, and if it had a repeating number that it favored.

She didn't think about it. It was Game Theory. Once upon a time, she'd been very good at it. For a brief time, she smiled, once more in her element. Codes and the probability of the Universe.

One of the serious men left the table. The pit boss looked up. He gestured to the now open seat.

Sabine laughed in true delight.

"Oh! No, thank you! Non, merci."

He smiled and the game went on, but he did continue to look at her and the empty seat from then on. Sabine just laughed again and waved a hand weakly.

"Go play!" Ari suggested.

"What? You crazy? And lose all our money?" Sabine laughed.

"I don't have a feeling that you would lose."

"No, no. That's okay. Maybe another time and when I have a few thousand francs to burn for no other reason than to just play to play."

"I'll hold you to that."

Sabine glanced at her friend. She'd sounded so serious.

They wandered out from the main salon. Time to head back for the little hole in the wall they currently called home, though by route of wandering and walking and staring at the city.

At first, Sabine thought the sudden outdoor brightness had blinded her when they stepped out.

No.

He was there.

She turned around wildly, scanning like mad, not caring what Ari thought.

"Sabine?"

"I felt him. I felt Him! He's here!"

"Who?"

She stopped dead in her tracks.

Opened and closed her mouth. Could neither speak nor actually voice her truth.

He wasn't alive. She was going mad. That was all.

"Sabine?"

"Losing my mind," she said, her voice sounding odd. Frightened.

"Ah, what a day!" Ari laughed, leading the way back into their hotel and Sabine followed, laughing as well.

The smile stayed with her, until she felt a presence behind her a bare half-second before she felt the barrel of a gun pressed between her shoulder blades. She tried to keep herself from stiffening. She succeeded and didn't slow her pace.

"You're going up to your room," a warm male baritone said and propelled her forward with a light push with the barrel.

Sabine stepped forward, wondering why she felt that she recognized the voice.

Sabine watched Ari, still laughing, bounce into the elevator, spin around and shock paint itself white across her face. Ari looked from the one behind her to Sabine's face and back again, the expression just feeding the suspicion Sabine already had.

"You first. Get your key out," Sabine's Presence said, and Ari stepped out of the elevator first.

Sabine turned, careful not to look at the one behind her and stepped out then before being prompted.

Ari wasn't smiling or laughing anymore. Ari got the door to their room open and walked inside without a backward glance, Sabine continuing to play Follow the Leader, even if she was the one in the middle.

He shut the door behind them and three men stood up from the little, rickety table, each one of them armed, the holsters obvious under their suit coats. Sabine came to a stop in the middle of the room and waited. Her Presence did her a favor and walked around to face her.

Pure rage crossed Sabine's face and then vanished, replaced with an expression of amused resignation.

Alive, was all Sabine thought. *The bastard really was alive.*

"Edward," Sabine said.

"Sabine," her Presence responded.

"So you're Edward Quintaine," Ari said, more statement than question.

"Yes. What are you doing in Europe?"

"Vacation?"

"Cut the crap."

"Who says I'm lying?" Sabine bristled. "We—" she indicated Ari and herself. "Are on vacation. Last I checked that wasn't a crime. Or did I miss something?"

Edward re-holstered his pistol and gave Sabine a considering look.

"No. You didn't. But your timing for a vacation to Monte Carlo could have been better."

"I knew it," Ari said, sitting down on the bed. "We really just do have a knack for this."

Edward gave her a quick glance but returned his gaze to Sabine.

"Which is why I have trouble believing it."

"I swear to Crom, Edward, we are here on vacation. I've always wanted to come to Monte Carlo, Ari needed someone to come to Europe with her and is indulging me. If we are raining on your parade, I give you my word it is entirely unintentional."

"I'd rather penta the truth out of you, but it will have to do."

"I am telling the truth, Edward."

"Let's go." He gestured to the men.

"No."

They all halted right where they were and Edward turned back around to face Sabine.

"No?"

"No. You're not leaving me behind this time," Sabine said.

"I don't recall that I offered an invitation."

"If you leave without me, I will find you. No matter where you go, I will find you. You are not leaving me behind this time, Edward."

Ari saw real anger print on Edward's face as he advanced on Sabine, stopping when he had well and truly invaded her space.

"This is not a game, Sabine. And what makes you think I'm taking my eye off of you?"

"I never said it was. I never thought you were."

"Then you have no idea what it is you're asking."

"You're not leaving me behind."

Their eyes locked on each other, each looking for a weak point.

"Kill her," Edward said, not taking his eyes off of Sabine's and pointing at Ari, who squeaked.

"Forget it."

"The answer is still no, Sabine," Edward said and turned on his heel.

"Edward, please. I am begging you," Sabine said, strain in her voice.

He spoke without turning around. "I didn't think I'd ever live to see the day that you'd beg for anything."

"Edward."

"All right," Edward said, his tone mild, which sent warning bells sounding off in Sabine's head. "If it's that important to you, you come with me right now."

"Okay," she said without any hesitation.

The answer seemed to startle Edward. It wasn't apparent on his face but he gave her the strangest look.

"You're very different from what you were like when you were sixteen," he said, his tone considering.

"People change, Edward."

"Apparently." He held her gaze for a long time. "Get your things." She went.

And just shook her head when Edward lead the way to a suite in the same hotel and one floor above the one that she and Ari had been staying on. Edward's entourage peeled off inside the door to one of the rooms, the steel gray-haired of the set flashing a grin at her before retiring for the evening. Edward crossed to the sitting room and pushed open the door to another of the rooms.

He was still beautiful. The thought was jarring in her head.

Thirteen years had only made him more so, not less.

"You can sleep in here."

Pushing herself forward, Sabine peered into the room and found it not inhabited in any way.

"If you need anything, I'm next door," Edward continued and indicated the connecting door. "Good night, Sabine."

Sabine watched him go in and raised an eyebrow. Well, if it were a test, it was a damn good one, she thought. Minutes later found her lying in a different bed than the one she'd woken up in that morning, staring at the ceiling.

Sabine woke in a room that left her more disoriented than normal.
Where was Ari?
Where was she?
She sat straight up in bed with a bolt of returning memory.
Edward.
If she went out the bedroom door, there was a good chance she'd see Him.

Alive.

She put her head in her hands.

What next? she thought.

When she stepped out, dressed in the previous day's clothes, she found only him, sitting at the small table in the suite's living room, a coffee cup by his elbow, reading the local paper.

He looked up. No expression.

"Pack."

She stood there for a long moment and then nodded. She wouldn't want her around either.

As she packed, it hit her.

No Dreams.

Shouldn't she have dreamed?

CHAPTER VIII – ENTROPY FELT

Nice - Port City of Marseille, France

Ari waited in the lobby with the rest of Edward's companions. Ari was packed. They all looked rumpled. Sabine fought the urge to laugh. Whoever had started the fight and for whatever reason, détente had been reached.

"I'm coming with you," Ari announced.

"No, you are not," Edward said.

"Yes. She is," Sabine said. "Or do you want her running straight to her masters in Tel Aviv?"

Edward said nothing. Just looked at Sabine.

"Actually, I do need to call my Bubbi."

"You do not need to call your controller," Edward cut in. "She comes with."

This last said to the tense men who all relaxed.

"Yes, I do!" Ari insisted.

"No. You don't. Out."

Outside, two black Mercedes sedans waited. The men loaded the luggage and Ari and Edward argued. Sabine watched the sky.

She felt nothing against her skin.

Marseilles, France

They got off the train an hour later in Marseilles and Sabine buttonholed Edward.

"We need to make a stop."

"Whatever for?"

"Laundry."

He only nodded. Inclined his head at the Sofitel they were headed towards.

"Don't get lost."

Why did she felt he meant the opposite?

The Laundromat that they found with help from the guidebook sat down by the harbor. Marseille had been built on an older Greek city and the remains of a Greek harbor. They saw none of it.

The Laundromat had no change machine. Sabine marched across the street. She'd spotted a magazine store. She haggled with the owner who didn't want to give her any change. But she was in no mood to put up with any of it.

Back at the Laundromat, Ari had already sorted out the clothes. Black and black filled three washing machines. No one else loitered. Sabine thought it strange. Every Laundromat they had been to in their entire trip had been empty.

She handed over the change and parked her butt on a spindly-legged chair, pulling the guide to France out from the outside pocket of the suitcase they had brought the laundry in.

"Christ on a crutch with a side of fries," Sabine sighed; it was only then she noticed that her friend looked more than a little depressed. "Hey."

Ari poured detergent in the machines.

"Hey, what's the matter?"

Ari paused. When she spoke, her voice stayed subdued.

"This isn't going as I had planned."

"I don't think it's going as anyone had planned."

"Fuck Edward and his plans." Ari's voice was distant. That disturbed Sabine more than if her friend had spoken with her customary passion.

"What's wrong?"

"You're going to go with him."

"Yeah," Sabine replied slowly.

"Our trip is going to hell."

Sabine kept her mouth shut. To point out that their trip had gone to hell from the outset didn't seem like a very politic statement at that moment.

"I know I've ruined everything, but I had hoped. We've never had time like this together." Ari fixed Sabine with an expression that struck Sabine to the bone. "You are my best friend."

"And you, mine," Sabine said.

"But...oh fuck it!"

"But to be the friend of a spy is to be half in that world and it has no regard for love or life or the petty concerns of mortals. It cares only for the lives of nations."

Sabine snapped her mouth shut. Where had that come from?

Ari nodded.

"Yes," she said. "Yes."

"How did he know about the British Museum?" Sabine asked out of nowhere.

Ari paused in the act of pouring fabric softener into the last machine.

"Good question."

"And if he knows about that, who else does?"

"Even better question."

"I really fucking hate this."

"What's to like?" Ari asked and Sabine went back to her guidebook.

"This is amazing," Sabine burst out.

"What?"

"According to the handy dandy guidebook, Marseille used to be the capital of white slavery and crime." She looked up. "Trust Edward to bring us to the Chicago of France."

"Yes, for a dead man, he's remarkably..." Ari trailed off.

"Alive?" Sabine offered.

Apparently she failed to hide her bitterness.

"Sabine..."

"Don't want to talk about it."

"Where has he been?" Ari insisted. "Why now?"

"Do. Not. Want. To talk about it."

They headed back to the hotel. Sabine knew nothing and she hated it. For all she knew, Edward had already changed his mind and they were going to get back to the hotel to find him and his men long gone. She hated that thought even more, but couldn't keep herself from thinking it.

Edward.

Alive.

Hadn't her dreams been telling her that fact for weeks now? The real mystery wasn't that he was alive when she'd believed him dead. The real mystery was, where the hell had he been all these years? And why the fuck did had the rest of the intelligence community wanted her and everyone else to believe him dead?

"You're going to leave me behind, aren't you?" Ari said out of nowhere.

"No." Sabine was furious; she couldn't help it. "Not if I have any say in the matter."

"What if you don't?" Ari's voice was flat.

Sabine had no answer for a moment. But she did have one if she thought it through and the answer cut her to the bone. She closed her eyes in silent agony, but neither could she deny the truth of it.

Edward Quintaine was only the figure of her sleeping and waking nightmare.

Ari Doran was the only friend that had stood between her and a personal hell.

It might kill her to never see Edward again and to be left with no answers to her questions, but it would kill her more to lose the only friend that she knew loved her without question or reservation.

"Then I go with you."

"That wasn't the answer I was expecting." Ari didn't stammer, but she still sounded choked up.

"You're my best friend, Ari." Sabine could say nothing further. Words were too small.

Edward Quintaine waited for them. He gave them a room key and they reached their room in short order. Ari collapsed on one of the beds. Sabine went to make more coffee. And pawed for her cigarettes. She had only two left.

"We leave tomorrow. If you have to go out, eat here," Edward continued. "Don't go out after dark."

"We'd figured that out," Ari replied.

"Good," he paused. "You won't be coming with us, Ms. Doran."

Ari was off the bed in a heartbeat. But before she could say a word, Sabine found her voice.

"Then I won't be going with you."

"What's this?" he asked.

Sabine hung her head. She kept herself from sighing or crying.

"That's not the point either," Ari interjected before Sabine could answer. "Don't make her choose, Mr. Quintaine. Besides, that would be an extraordinarily foolish thing to do, leaving me behind."

"Are you threatening me, Ms. Doran?" Edward made it sound so polite.

Ari smiled winningly.

"I would never do that." She turned hard in a second. "But ditch us and I will make sure that every fraternity on the face of creation knows that you are still alive."

"You would, wouldn't you?" he said. "I choose not to call your bluff. But I think you'll be the one who wishes they were left behind by the end of this."

He went no further with that cryptic comment. Sabine burned with curiosity. What the hell did he mean by that?

"Please stay in your room. We leave early tomorrow."

Edward closed the door behind him and managed to do it without Ari or Sabine having the last word.

"It's really happening, isn't it?" Ari said into the silence he left behind.

"What is?"

"All of it. Your dreams. The attacks. All of it."

"Let's not talk about it."

"Why not?"

"Because, you're right," Sabine said and turned to face her friend. "And as far as I can tell, we're stuck."

"Are you sure?"

"No."

Ari punched the bed.

Sabine fell into a reverie that was as much fugue state as thought process, watching the light cross her skin. Don't set, she thought. Sun, don't set. She so desperately did not want the light to fail, even though of course, it would. Every day ended. Pure physics.

CHAPTER IX – OF CATS AND DEAD PHYSICISTS

Port City of Marseille – Paris du Sud and Paris du Nord, France

Sabine blinked her eyes in the early morning light floating in through the train window. They were on an express to Paris. She didn't know the time. If coffee didn't appear in her future and soon, she was going to go murderously psychotic.

Edward sat across from her, staring out the window. His team, whose names Sabine had still not managed to acquire, were around somewhere, but she didn't know where. Ari sat next to Sabine, another damn morning person, glaring at Edward.

"Coffee and or espresso and no one gets hurt," Sabine announced.

"Ooo! Tea!" Ari stopped glaring at Edward.

"Yes, caffeine. You want anything?"

Edward gave her an appraising look.

"Coffee would be nice."

Civility. Sabine decided to not look shocked. Well, no point in being an asshole, if he was stuck with them, she guessed.

The dining car stood packed to capacity.

After five minutes of trying to get to the take out bar with no success, Sabine wandered back to the seats. She hadn't even been able to get a Coke, and either her migraine was returning in force or the closeness of all the people in the dining car was getting to her, but the end result managed the same effect. She felt feverish.

Edward looked up at her return without Ari and Sabine just shrugged. Dug out her laptop, turned it on, and started to write. She didn't know why she bothered to keep an account of their trip, but old habits died hard. She'd been writing for herself for so long that the idea of stopping now just didn't make any sense.

So she wrote, ignored Edward, and wished for caffeine.

Why am I so angry? she typed. I have nightmares of this man's existence still being here on Earth and when I find out that he is indeed alive, I'm bent as all hell.

Because it meant that all she had thought she knew about that time in her life was a lie. Her stomach knotted. Her fingers stilled on the keyboard. To not know the truth from the lie... That was the entire trip to Europe right there in a nutshell. For the first time ever in her life, Sabine wished that she didn't know the truth of Edward's existence. She immediately felt the pain of that thought, because she knew that she didn't mean it.

He was alive.

So what else wasn't true about her life?

Her head still hurt. The sleep she had failed to get the night before prompted her to turn off the laptop. She stared out the window for a time and rubbed her temples.

"You're taking this all rather well." Edward's voice was a surprise.

"Define rather well," Sabine replied. The rocking of the carriage and the sun coming in through the window were eroding the last of her willpower to stay awake.

"Me."

One word. A wealth of meaning. That alone kept Sabine awake. How the hell did she answer him?

"Oh, let's just say that I'm not surprised by anything anymore," Sabine said.

"Let's not."

"You wouldn't believe me if I told you, Edward."

"You might be surprised."

"Yes." It was her turn to respond slowly. "I might, mightn't I? Either way, it doesn't surprise me that you are alive. Beyond that, what else is there to say?"

"Why?"

"Why, what?"

"Why aren't you surprised?"

Sabine stopped again. She couldn't tell him. He wouldn't believe her.

"I'm just not."

"An inferior answer for an analyst."

"I'm not an analyst anymore," Sabine said, cold and hard.

"No. I guess you're right."

Sabine missed nothing. His tone said it all. She wasn't fooling anyone.

The conversation didn't continue. Sabine found her eyes slipping closed more and more. She couldn't help it. Her head slipped down against the window and came to rest on the vent. Cool air breathed against her cheek, but she didn't care. The world started to slip away. Sabine's fears could not keep her awake any longer.

She Dreamed.

Sabine stood on the beach again, the shale stones hard against her bare feet. Storm clouds massed on the ocean and growled with thunder that shook her to the bone. The cold air tried to steal her warmth.

She stood next in a room in a small, unfamiliar house, her belongings everywhere. More wondrous still, in the sunset light falling through one of the room's windows, a million brilliant blue butterflies spun around her.

And in the next moment were consumed in flame.

Her breath choked in her throat.

The butterflies burned.

They were gone in an instant and again, she stood somewhere else, but took in none of her surroundings, only the sky above her. A terrible and great rainbow arched over her. Right before her eyes greater and more terrible clouds, blacker than midnight, devoured the many-colored light.

She couldn't wake. Sabine screamed.

A coil then. Darkness and oil rainbows, warmth and protection. Zoë there and it was all that Sabine could do to not weep with relief.

"Wake up, Sabine!" Zoë commanded and Sabine's eyes flew open.

The train decelerated. Sabine sat up. In the seat next to her, Ari dozed. Across from her, Edward still stared out the window. Her screams had been unheard in the waking world. Edward gave her an unreadable glance as she sat up. At her movement, Ari also woke up and took in the slowing train.

Sabine felt a momentary stab of fear.

Paris overcast, but even as she scanned the sky, she felt the fear recede. There were no rainbows. She rubbed her nose. The sleep hadn't helped her head. She still felt her headache and her sinuses felt stuffed with wool and cotton. She dug around in her fanny pack and found her last allergy medicine. Ari's cold tea was all that there was to take the pills with, but Sabine managed it with a grimace.

They needed to get across town to Paris du Nord. The older gentleman, dressed today in gray flannel, was the one to flag down two taxis for the whole party of them. Edward separated her from Ari without a word and escorted her into the lead cab by her elbow, just as Ari was shepherded into the second cab. Sabine tried to read nothing into Edward's actions.

The madcap driving of the cabbie chased the last of the wooly sleepies out of Sabine's head. Out the car's window, she drank in her last sights of Paris.

Her stomach dropped in tension. The Dream on the train had not let its grip loosen. If she closed her eyes at all, she could still see the brilliant rainbow devoured by the clouds. Her eyes scanned the sky. It hadn't happened yet.

Devoured rainbows didn't mean the end of the world. Burning butterflies didn't mean the death of hope.

Did they?

She shoved the thought out of her mind.

Sabine felt the weariness for the first time. She wanted to go home. Sabine found herself staring at Edward. Even as she felt the urge to be home, she knew it wasn't going to be possible. The man sitting next to her had made that impossible.

Paris du Nord came too soon. Sabine breathed a sigh of relief to see Ari getting out of the cab behind, even as Edward had her by the elbow again. He only left her side when the group sat ensconced in the Eurostar waiting area.

"He wasn't kidding about getting us back to London, was he?" Ari sounded a trifle out of breath, sitting down next to her.

"Apparently not."

"What do you think the big damn rush is?"

"Gods, Ari, if I knew that, I'd be a millionaire. All I know is that we must have been right about one thing."

"Which one thing?"

"We stumbled into some huge operation."

"Yeah," Ari sighed, her breath coming more even now. "Still no idea what it might be?"

"If you mean, did I get any new information out of him on the train while you were fighting with the Dairy Police, no. Nothing new."

"Drat."

Edward returned, new tickets in his hands.

"We're on the next Chunnel."

"How'd you manage that?" Ari wanted to know.

Edward just smiled. Ari snorted.

"When is the next Chunnel?" Sabine asked.

"Within the hour."

"Yikes." Sabine just stared at him. "Why do you want us out of Europe?"

The words were out of her mouth before she even thought about it. The question was far too direct and she knew it.

Edward didn't answer.

"Hmm," Ari murmured. Edward gave her a sharp glance and Sabine needed no supernatural powers to read his mind. He knew as well as they did that at this point in the situation, Ari had to contact her controllers. But they also knew that Edward would allow that about as soon as Hell froze over.

"Well, you two can glare at each other. I'm going to the Ladies." Sabine got up in one smooth, sharp move.

Edward started to get up again from where he had taken a seat across from her, when Ari snorted again.

"I don't think she needs your help going to the bathroom, Edward. Besides, she's not going to ditch you, duh! As if..."

Sabine drifted out of earshot before she could hear more of Ari's tongue lashing. It was shaping up to be a doozy.

She was washing her hands when the small woman in the tan suit bumped into her.

"Oh, excuse me," Sabine said on automatic, until she realized that the little woman with the curly brunet hair and hook nose wasn't getting out of her way. The woman smiled, brief and blinding with good humor.

"Tell Arila that her Bubbi and Zeda are watching," the woman said. "And we are watching you as well."

The next instant, the woman was gone, a practiced fade into the meager bathroom crowd.

Sabine dallied on her way back, arriving in time to see them gathering the bags. By the time she sat on the train, she still had no answer to her question.

CHAPTER X – APERIODICITY OF HEARTBEATS

Paris du Nord, France - Waterloo Station, London, United Kingdom

It was a Bank Holiday.

That much Sabine ascertained from the conversation that Ari conducted with the Tourist Board reservation desk, a move Edward had insisted on. Made sense, Sabine thought. Altered identity or no, Edward clearly wanted no one else to see his passport unless completely necessary.

Either way, not a single room could be had in all of downtown London.

"No room at the inn," Sabine said under her breath.

"Does that make me the ass?" Edward inquired.

"You should only be so lucky," she managed as a response.

One thing Sabine did know though. If Edward made jokes, he was about ready to tear his hair out. She couldn't believe that that much about him had changed. The waiting for Ari to finalize their arrangements wore on Sabine as well, but she again had to wonder why Edward kept scanning the concourse.

For a brief mad moment, Sabine wished for a sniper to just liven up the waiting and then shook her head. She'd already had enough excitement on this damn trip.

Ari turned away from the counter, with a slip of paper in her hand.

"All right," she sighed. "I've managed to get us a place."

She didn't continue. Sabine felt her heart sink.

"It's in Outer London."

"Outer London. What does that mean?"

"London's London, isn't it?" Ari tried.

"Let's go," Edward said.

It turned out that they required British Rail, not the Underground, to get out to Surbiton. As they climbed aboard, Sabine felt a sudden attack of the stubborns.

"Before we go any further, Edward," Sabine started and Edward halted halfway down to sitting in one of the many empty benches on the train car. "If you don't introduce us to your god damn Boy Scout troop, I swear to Crom, I'm going to find some Penta on this benighted island and get it out of them myself."

Edward had the good grace to look startled and embarrassed.

"I haven't introduced them?"

Ari and Sabine shook their heads in the negative.

"Ah."

The gray-haired gentleman gave a blinding smile and held out a hand.

"Philip Dougherty." Sabine shook it with a bemused smile. He gestured to the other two who walked up and down the car, looking for whoever knew what threat they thought they could assess.

"Those two are Andrew and Tony."

"Last names?" Sabine inquired.

"Can't tell you everything." Philip smiled again. A likable guy. She bet that he could break her in half with one hand, of which both looked like they were the size of her head. A big man, now that she had a chance to look him over. He'd been very successful in staying in the background. Only being close showed that plenty of sandy brown still held sway amongst the gray hairs and his blue eyes twinkled with mischief. She'd hate to play poker against him.

"Well, nice to finally know who the fuck you are, Philip."

"Not a problem." However, he vanished for a seat at the stern look Edward shot him.

"What's the matter, Edward? Don't want us getting acquainted?"

"If I thought it would make a difference, no, I don't."

"Where is our god damn room!?" Sabine demanded an hour later.

Ari gave her a tired grin.

"Antarctica?" she replied.

"Damn it!"

The B&B (turned out it wasn't a hotel Ari had acquired for them) was laid out like another warren, reminding Sabine of their first hotel stay a million years ago and half a city away. Right when she was getting ready to just sleep in the hall and damn the torpedoes, Ari gave a jubilant yelp. Sabine didn't say a word to Edward, she just barged in right after Ari and slammed the door in his face.

A cozy room, done in oranges and browns, two twin beds against the wall and a TV mounted high on the wall to the left of the beds. Sabine poked her head in the bathroom. Large tub. She nodded to herself in satisfaction. Dropped her luggage.

On a small table next to the room door sat an electric tea pot and a small basket filled with tea bags. Two white teacups sat overturned on two matching saucers and Sabine wanted to weep in relief.

"Civilization at last."

Fortified by tea and silence, Sabine looked at Ari and voiced the question on her mind.

"Where in God's green Earth are we?"

"Surbiton."

"And that means?"

"New definition of hell."

Sabine choked on a laugh and got to her feet to unpack a few things. Found a t-shirt to sleep in. She kept digging for her traveling kit of toothpaste and other items when she heard Ari swear in Hebrew.

"What's wrong?"

Ari started running around the room, looking in her own trench coat, her bags and came to rest in the center of the room.

"My passport is gone."

"Oh. Shit." Sabine could think of nothing else to say. Then she started to swear. Steadily and creatively. She stopped after a minute.

"Where did you last see it?"

"The Eurostar office," Ari replied. "I definitely had it there."

Sabine sighed a little with relief.

"It'll be there. They'll have saved it, I'm sure."

"I hope so," Ari said in a small voice.

"How are we going to tell Edward?"

Ari swore again in Hebrew.

"You really are going to have to tell me what that means."

Sabine found the strength to finish unpacking, even though her head spun over this new wrinkle. Christ, and she'd been stupid enough to wish for some excitement. She wanted to slap herself.

Sabine dumped out her fanny pack on the side table next to her bed and the cold cream jar hit the table with a loud clack.

Oh, damn, she thought and closed her eyes.

Sabine decided to drop the tac nuke in the morning. It ended up being over kippers and toast.

"Speaking of things you don't know, we've got a couple problems."

Ari and Edward stopped mid-chew. Philip, who had joined them for a change, just shook his head with a rueful smile and poured himself more coffee.

"I really don't like the sound of that."

"Me either," Ari chimed in.

"Well, you don't have to like it. These are the facts," Sabine speared one of the sausages on her plate. "We've got to go back to the Eurostar office today."

"Why?" Philip wanted to know.

"I don't have my passport," Ari supplied.

"Oh—" Philip cut himself off without even a look from Edward. Sabine's guess was that he restrained himself from indulging in a creative swearing fit, the way that she had the night before.

"That's not all," Sabine added.

Edward closed his eyes.

"There's this."

Upon later reflection, Sabine decided she might have found a better way of doing it, but it was the only way she could think of. She set the cold cream jar on the table.

She had not expected both Philip and Edward to dive on it.

"Son of a bitch," Edward swore, even as the two men ended up slapping each other's hands very hard in the initial rush to cover the small jar on the table. Philip retreated and poured himself more coffee with shaking hands, until he realized that he was overflowing the cup and running into his saucer.

"Hello," Sabine sighed. "What's this then?"

"This changes everything," Edward said.

"Yes, yes. What, your mother wasn't a female dog? What?" Sabine said testily. "How about explaining for the rest of us in the audience who are a bit on the slow side?"

Philip looked like he was trying not to choke, while Edward looked at his kippers and toast in his hand, put them back down on his plate and frowned. The jar was now in his other hand.

"No," Edward said.

"No what?"

"My mother was many things, but a bitch was not one of them."

"Thank you for sharing," Sabine's face was doing a good imitation of a thundercloud. "And that's all very well, but what the fuck are they?"

Edward stared at the jar in his hand for a long moment before answering.

"Mind control drugs. Very advanced." He handed the jar back to her.

She didn't take it.

"Where did you get them?" Edward's voice was strange.

"The Dorchester."

"Oh, now come on! I know the Dorchester isn't handing these out as after tea mints!" Philip exclaimed.

"They aren't. This man, normal enough, Brit, dropped them on our table at tea four, five weeks ago."

"You've had these for five weeks!" Phillip stared.

"Well, that explains it," Edward said.

"Explains what? How 'bout you guys start being a bit forthcoming with an explanation or two?" Ari took her turn to exclaim.

"I was right. Bad drop," Sabine said. "He was there to meet one of yours, wasn't he?"

Edward didn't answer her question.

He pulled a cell phone out of his inside coat pocket. Today's suit was a silvered blue in color and had shown no indication that he had anything in his pockets, much less the gun that was holstered under his left arm. Sabine had to commend his tailors.

"Quintus, check me," he said into his phone.

He listened, his brow furrowing in a frown, before saying, "Surbiton."

Even Sabine could hear someone asking something in disbelieving tones on the other end.

"In Surbiton. Yes, Surbiton, the middle of nowhere. Yes, it's in Surrey. Look it up on the map. I don't want to explain," Edward finished.

"So," Sabine began. "We need to go back to the Eurostar office. I'm sure that they have Ari's passport."

"Why?"

"Last place I remember having it," Ari filled in.

"All right. Be ready to go in fifteen minutes," Edward announced.

"Right," Sabine said and coughed. Edward gave her a sharp look, and left for parts unknown. Phillip just sat and stared at his coffee cup. It took him a moment to realize that Edward was gone.

"Well," he said for no particular reason. "He told me that you were entertaining company, but I had no idea that this was what he meant."

It took less time to get back to the Eurostar office than it had to leave it the first time. The two ladies behind the counter were both helpful and started to look for Ari's passport, while another clerk continued to man the desk.

"I'm afraid we cannot find hide nor hair of it," the lead one said.

"Then what are we to do?" Ari asked, her face white.

"Well, first, you'll need to report it stolen. The Bobbies are right across the way there." The clerk pointed at the Police sign across the concourse of Waterloo. "Then, I guess your best bet is to get to your embassy."

"Will they be able to get me a new one today?" Ari asked.

"Oh surely. They're just over Grosvenor Square way."

"Wherever that is," Sabine muttered and turned to say something to Edward, but he was gone. Preparing to panic in earnest, he came back into view, having lost all three of his entourage.

A remote part of her brain tried to point out to her that she had not been ecstatic that he had disappeared for a moment; that her reaction had been fear. She squashed the thought with the mental equivalent of a large croquet mallet.

"But in the meantime, you must let us pay for your cab fare," the clerk continued to Ari.

"Oh, that would be lovely," Ari said. They tidied up their conversation and the three of them stepped out onto the concourse. Before Sabine could ask where Edward's three musketeers had gone, he spoke.

"I've sent Philip and the team to make other arrangements. What's our status?"

"First item is to make a stolen property report to the police, then we've been offered a cab to the embassy to get Ari a replacement. The staff here seems to think it shouldn't be much of a difficulty to get her one."

"Duly noted." Edward nodded and led the way across the concourse.

They walked into a secure waiting room that had no windows and an outer door and an inner door. It was only a moment before a very large and very polite British police officer by the name of Mac ushered Ari into whatever inner sanctum that existed. Sabine thought to talk to Edward, but he didn't even bother to take a seat as Sabine had, instead making for the door.

"Hey! Where are you going?" Sabine exclaimed. This time she didn't care if she sounded frightened or not.

"Relax." His voice had the awful tone of being soothing; Sabine wanted to cringe. "I'll be right back. I want to see if Philip's turned up yet."

"Oh." Sabine forced herself to relax. "All right."

He was gone as soon as the words were out of her mouth.

She sneezed. Looked for a magazine to read. None to be had. Ari and then Edward, with entourage in tow, returned within the space of moments of each other. Philip gave her a quick grin, which she returned. Edward seemed bent on staying expressionless. Sabine waited for them all to get back out on the concourse before asking any questions.

"So, how are we doing?"

"Actually, not so bad and not so good. The nice policemen don't think there's much of anything that they can do to get my passport back. Apparently, this has been quite the problem with the Chunnel and they've had a rash of passport thefts lately," she shrugged. "I also didn't bring any passport with me other than my U.S."

"I had hoped," was all Edward said.

"No dice," Ari said.

"Drat," Sabine said. "Off to the embassy then."

"Not so fast," Edward said.

"Why not? We've gotta get her a passport if you want us out of the damn country."

"I agree. I just want to make sure that we are going about this with some sort of plan, not just by the seat of our pants, which appears to be you two's idea of a normal operating procedure."

"Bite me."

"Now or later?" said so urbane, it took Sabine a moment to realize that Edward was yanking her chain.

"Get a taxi," she decided on a safe reply instead.

Philip disappeared. Andrew and Tony scanned the concourse and they all tried to not look like a rock star's entourage. Philip, as Sabine had hoped, already had a taxi, the door wide open. Before Sabine could wonder, all five of them managed to pile into the large black vehicle.

Sabine found herself wedged between Andrew and Tony.

"Hi," she said with a weak grin. "How ya doin'?"

The drive over to Grosvenor Square, which turned out to be in Leicestershire, was short and sweet. Sabine climbed out first, climbing over Philip and Ari.

To look at the ugliest building on the face of the planet.

"Tell me," Sabine began. "That is not a gigantic gold eagle shitting out a gigantic gold nest up there."

"Okay," Ari snickered. "I won't. But it won't change reality."

"God almighty, no wonder the rest of the world thinks we're idiots!"

"We give them other reasons as well," Edward commented.

The United States of America Embassy, as it could be nothing other with a giant gold eagle on top of it, was a shade of institutional gray that Sabine thought was a relic of the Cold War. Upon instant reflection, she realized it *was* a relic of the Cold War. The building was exactly square, had darkened windows, no ornamentation except for the horrible and truly enormous eagle and nest on the roof and took up an entire city block.

It was also closed.

"What?!" Sabine shouted. "This is the end of enough! What fucking embassy is closed on a Monday!?"

"This one," Ari and Edward said in sync.

"Joy. Joy, joy, frabjous fucking joy," Sabine said and sat straight down on the cement.

She more felt than saw Ari walk to the Embassy door and knock on it. Sabine stared at the cement. Ari returned a few minutes later, having gotten the attention of a security guard.

"Apparently," Ari began to the top of Sabine's head. "Embassy is open only on Tuesdays and Thursdays. He says I can definitely get a replacement passport. I just need to go and get some pictures taken so that they will have them to put in the thingy."

What happened next was not something that Sabine was ever clear on later. All she knew was that one moment, she was sitting on the sidewalk, staring at her walking boots, now dusty and worn from several weeks of walking in Europe, the next... Six men in precise suits that couldn't have screamed MI6 louder than if they had been wearing signs, surrounded them. Sabine never saw them coming.

They'd stepped out of two black unremarkable cars, she realized when she looked down the street. But they'd managed to enclose them in under a minute. To Edward's credit, neither he nor his men moved in any way that could be construed as a threat.

One of the precise gentlemen stepped forward. He was balding, his once black hair salt and peppered prematurely, what little of it that there was left and had a face that had seen better days. It clearly at one time had made far too well the acquaintance of a broken bottle or two and his black eyebrows were full and bushy. The kind that people used to describe the expression, beetling. She was sure they must beetle beautifully when he wanted them to. His tweed suit was lovely, Sabine thought, but he was missing the bowler hat. She really felt he needed a bowler. He gave a little bow that only registered from his shoulders up.

"Good afternoon, Miss Parsons, Miss Doran." He flipped open a very official looking passbook with equally official documentation. "My name is Nigel Lovejoy. We'd appreciate it if you and your companions would come with us."

He gave a pointed glance at Edward.

"And refrained from making any sudden moves."

Edward only smiled. Sabine got to her feet before anyone could do anything stupid.

"We'd love to," she blurted out and tried not to fall flat on her face. No mistaking it. She really felt sick. She hoped no one noticed.

They ended up somewhere near the Tower of London. Three large black cars had taken them away and she hadn't been able to see much out of the windows. Ari had been separated from her. Sabine didn't feel like speaking to Edward. When they did finally reach their destination, it was to get out in an underground parking lot that was only gray in Sabine's memory later. Oh, yes, and filled with many other black cars.

After a short walk they were ushered into a small room with a television and a DVR. Mr. Lovejoy accepted a DVD from one of his men who left right after and inserted it without much preamble.

It was security footage. From the British Museum.

Sabine watched herself leap on top of the Nike Athena and thought very slowly and distinctly that they were all going straight to hell.

"Let's get down to brass tacks as you Americans like to say," Mr. Lovejoy said. "We received this footage approximately four and a half weeks ago. Is there anything you'd like to tell me about this incident?"

Stunned silence was the only answer that he received. He opened his mouth to ask another question, when a slight young woman in a khaki skirt suit walked in. The other man who had come in with him also left, leaving them all alone. Philip, Andrew and Tony converged on the DVR and began running the DVD back and forth. Edward took turns from staring first at Sabine, then at Ari.

"You were where?"

"We went museum crawling. It's not our fault."

"You just managed to be there. Right then. Less than a day in the country."

"Oh come on, Edward. You already know that this trip was ill-conceived and doom ridden," Ari said.

"Of course," he gritted out. "But now you have managed to get us entangled in the Brits security net."

"Oh, not so badly, Mr. Quintaine," Mr. Lovejoy said, coming into the room again. "Though I must say, I am greatly honored to be in the presence of such an august and deceased personage."

"I am sure that the honor is all mine," Edward replied.

"Where were we?" Mr. Lovejoy began. Sabine didn't wait for him to continue.

"We were in the midst of being interrogated," Sabine said. "And no matter what I tell you or Ari tells you, Mr. Lovejoy, I honestly do not think that you are going to believe any answer that we give you."

"Try me. I might surprise you."

Sabine paused a moment. Either his smile was genuine or he was a better player than she had ever gone up against.

"We went to sightsee at the museums. Those two men came in shortly after we did. We did not hear their conversation. All we heard was the ugly one shoot the scholarly one and then we left. Quickly. Which yes, does mean that we left the scene of a crime. We have no excuse for that one.

"Why?"

Sabine narrowed her eyes at him.

"I should think that I wouldn't have to explain, Mr. Lovejoy."

"Ah, yes. You refer to your past and Miss Doran's present." His grin was very amused. Sabine didn't know if she were beginning to like him or hate him.

"What I find fascinating is that I have in my custody one dead spy, one retired analyst and one very active spy, all connected to the murder of one of our own in the British Museum," he continued.

"Spy is such a dirty word," Edward commented from the corner.

"Yes, but accurate."

"I don't know what to tell you, Mr. Lovejoy. Mr. Quintaine might know more, but I doubt he'd tell you."

"Oh, on that score I'm sure you are most correct, Miss Parsons. But you have to understand my position. You are my only witnesses to a murder of a key defense analyst. Am I to just let you go?"

"You will if you know what's best, Mr. Lovejoy." It was Edward's turn to speak. "We cannot stay in this country for long."

"Why not, Mr. Quintaine?"

"I suggest you talk to your government."

"Threats already, Mr. Quintaine?"

"If that's what it takes to get us out of here."

"Knock it off, Edward." Sabine cut in. "I swear to God, Mr. Lovejoy, we don't know anything more than that. If I did or Ari did, we really would tell you.

"I truly wish to believe you, Miss Parsons, but the facts remain."

Sabine scrubbed her face, one handed and mostly between her eyes. Which didn't explain her next actions. In reality, she didn't have a clue what prompted her to blow their op sec to Kingdom Come.

"Show him." Sabine glared at Edward. Edward merely raised an eyebrow.

"Show him," she repeated and with a shrug he put the cold cream jar on the table.

Mr. Lovejoy considered the jar with polite interest.

She frowned.

"Are you perhaps suggesting I need to look into skin care, Miss Parsons?"

"No." Sabine swallowed and hid any surprise she was feeling. "It's not what it appears."

Even though she felt Edward tensing behind her, Sabine opened the small jar and dumped out the silver pills.

"Advanced cold cream?"

"No again." Sabine took a deep breath. "But on too little data and too much assumption, if I had to guess, I think your man was killed for these."

That finally appeared to hit Mr. Lovejoy between the eyeballs. His stillness in face and body would have been a credit, if it weren't for the fact that his left cheek pulled into a tic. Sabine idly considered informing him that he had a significant tell. She filed it in the back of her head of things to remember.

"What are they then?"

"From what I've been told by my sources, mind control drugs. And I do not think that I was meant to get them."

"Assuredly not." Mr. Lovejoy sat back, hard. Why tell me this?"

"Because I had intended on taking them back to the States to find out what exactly they were and to turn them over to the appropriate authorities. But with a dead body on the floor and us in your custody, it behooves me to let you in on what I've got, don't you think?"

Sabine tensed, waiting for his decision. From where she sat, he had only two to make. Hold them till the cows came home or let them go.

"Mr. Quintaine."

"Yes?" Edward gave no indication of his opinion.

"Is Miss Parsons telling me the truth?"

"Unfortunately, yes."

"Do you have anything further to add?"

"Nothing that I could say that wouldn't be divulging intelligence in areas that would imperil lives."

"Ah. Not even a little hint."

"Without sounding melodramatic, those pills are a threat not just to U.S. security."

"And when were we going to hear about this?"

"Not to put too fine a point on it, Mr. Lovejoy, but I think that the guy who was going to tell you is now in a morgue," Sabine interrupted, not really wishing to watch Edward and the British get into a pissing contest.

Mr. Lovejoy paused.

"I am surprised that you are no longer an analyst, Miss Parsons."

"I quit." And the voice that came out of Sabine's mouth surprised even her. No one should sound that harsh or that angry.

"My apologies."

"Accepted." It was Sabine's turn to straighten in her chair. "So, this is my suggestion. Take half the pills and get them analyzed. I keep half, because I do think I need to get them back home, and you let us go."

"Just like that? Why should I not keep both you and the pills?"

"Because if you don't, Mr. Quintaine will get our embassy involved, Miss Doran will get her embassy involved and then you'll be in shit creek."

She didn't need to look to know that Edward had to already have his cell phone out in his hand. Mr. Lovejoy's quick glanced over her shoulder only confirmed it.

"Modern technology," he said and it was an imprecation.

"Yeah. Ain't it a bitch?"

Mr. Lovejoy was gracious, even in defeat.

"Is there anywhere that we can drop you then?"

"Yeah." and Sabine allowed herself an evil little smile. "The Dorchester."

Which left them once more having tea at the Dorchester, but this time, Sabine knew that a couple of girls, if there had been a couple of girls there, could have played the game Ari and she had played only a few weeks before with their table. Though she did wonder in a small way what card they would have had to lay on their table. United States Intelligence? Or Freelance?

Because the one thing that Edward had so not come out with was who he now worked for.

She ate a scone instead of asking.

Ari conversed with Philip. Edward did a good impression of a starving man as he plowed his way through tea. Neatly. But it was plowing all the same. The other two, Tony and Andrew, had been sent on errands again. Sabine wondered if she would ever get to know more than their faces and their names.

She reviewed the day's events. One, no new passport for Ari. Upsetting. Two, picked up by the Brits. She winced internally. Why couldn't she have a boring life, like other people? Oh, right. She'd asked for some excitement. Once more she felt like slapping herself.

Her head still hurt too. In fact, sitting in the comfort of the Dorchester, Sabine finally realized how wretched she felt. Adrenaline had been keeping her going for so long, that she'd been able to ignore how her body ached, her head split and how stuffed her sinuses were.

"Crap," she muttered.

"What?" Her three table companions chorused.

"I think I'm getting sick.

"Oh, is that all?" Ari laughed. Edward and Philip didn't.

"Just out of curiosity," Sabine tried to change the subject. "Did anyone think to ask the Brits if they were the ones responsible for stealing Ari's passport? Stupid me didn't think of it till just now."

Philip brightened at that.

"Actually, Tony managed to go after that one. They swear it wasn't them."

"Well, duh, but it was worth a try."

"We need to get you back to the hotel," Edward said.

"I'll be fine, Edward."

"You'll be fine at the hotel."

"After we finish tea!" Ari interrupted and there was no arguing with her tone. Sabine gave her a grateful smile. Right then, she was more grateful for having Ari as a friend than she had ever been in her life. So, their lives were going to hell in a hand basket. There were times in one's life where a quiet afternoon's tea was more important than all the weighty matters of kings, queens or the fate of the world.

Sabine was grateful for the afternoon, but by the time they crawled back into Surbiton, she felt like the walking dead. She heard none of the conversations that Ari had with their keepers/captors.

No. All she cared about was falling on her bed of pain and dying.

The first part she accomplished with alacrity, until rolling over, she realized that it was not Ari in the room with her.

It was Edward. His hands that lay a cool, damp cloth on her brow and his voice that asked her, "Would you like a cup of tea?"

Must be hallucinating, she thought.

"Yes. Thank you," she croaked. Post-nasal drip was making her sound like a screen star from the '30s.

"Where's Ari?" she asked.

"I sent her to dinner."

He stayed with her until she fell asleep. Her fever made her woozy and confused, but even so, Sabine wondered how much of that really was due to her fever. Because she could feel her heart lay tight in her chest and not with illness.

Edward was alive.

His hands changing the cloth on her forehead. His voice in her ears.

He really was alive.

It's all been a lie, was a fevered thought. All that she had believed for the last thirteen years had been the lies of the people in power in the community she had left behind.

"What day is it?" Sabine asked woozily over tea and toast, she hoped only a day later.

"Tuesday," Edward replied. "Are you sure you're feeling all right?"

"I'll feel better if you'd knock it the fuck off and quit fussing."

Ari smiled.

"She's feeling better."

"What's the plan for today?" Sabine bludgeoned on.

"Back to the embassy!" Ari replied in heroic tones. "And hopefully without incident."

"Amen," Edward said.

"Great." Sabine poked at her toast. "Just as long as we go really slowly. The world keeps going sideways."

So the United States of America Embassy was closed for lunch as a result. The ridiculous building was closed again and now she knew there was a conspiracy to keep them from going home.

"I say we blow it up until they give Ari a passport," Sabine growled.

"I think that might defeat the purpose a bit, honey," Ari said and took her friend by the elbow. "Come on. I saw a Richoux tea house around the corner."

"Trust you to be more concerned with your stomach than your passport."

"I merely have my priorities straight."

"That could be argued."

"Yeah! Over tea!"

Sabine gave up.

Edward did not.

"It's not safe."

Ari blew up. Without warning.

"Stuff it!" she yelled.

Edward had the good grace to look a trifle surprised.

"I'm sick of your damn security fetish! If we were going to get whacked or picked up, which we already have I might point out! It would have happened by now. I want tea! And Sabine is coming with me! And you are shutting up and shoving it up your ass!"

"Fine," Edward said. Sabine guessed that even Edward knew when retreat was the better part of valor.

Sabine spotted a Times newspaper dispenser on the way and wobbled over to it while digging 75 pence out of her pocket.

"What are you doing?" Edward followed.

"Getting a newspaper."

"Why?"

"Because I want to be reminded that there are people in the world having a worse time of it than me."

Tea would have been a quiet affair too, except for one small hiccup. Just as the scones and sandwiches were served, Nigel Lovejoy entered the red and brown interior of the Richoux. Sabine, glancing over his shoulder, saw that two of his men stood on the street in poses that were meant to be casual, but failed utterly. Mr. Lovejoy wore a gray suit that would have done Edward proud, and also carried a London Times under his arm, as well as the requisite bowler hat in the other hand, his black umbrella draped over his arm.

"May I join you?"

"I swear to God, I just wanted a paper!" Sabine blurted out.

He gave her a quizzical expression than glanced down at his own paper. He then laughed and Sabine couldn't figure out why that irritated and relieved her simultaneously.

"As did I. You did not compromise a drop, Miss Parsons."

"Thank god for small favors. Scone?" And she passed the plate of scones while everyone else at the table glared at her. Well, not entirely true. Philip seemed to be having a choking fit with his tea. Sabine would never credit the snorting to be anything else. Tony and Andrew both appeared to be chewing on their bottom lips.

"I owe you an apology, Miss Parsons," Mr. Lovejoy said, taking the proffered scone and passing the plate to Andrew, who merely smiled stiffly. The table was very crowded now and he struggled to find a place for the plate when one of the overly attentive staff appeared with a small side table.

"Apology? Exsqueeze me?" Sabine burbled.

"Pardon?"

"Never mind. Apology?"

"Yes." He unfolded his paper and took out a sheaf of papers and handed them to her.

Mr. Lovejoy waited.

"Holy shit," Sabine muttered.

"I see that the formulae are not so much gobbledy-gook to you as they were to me."

Sabine uttered a few confused mono syllables before finding the English language again.

"Probably not much better than you, Mr. Lovejoy."

"Nigel, please."

"Sabine," she said and continued her thought. "But I remember enough of my high school chemistry to know that one of these chains is common to lysergic acid diethylamide."

"Yes."

"Is that bad?" Ari asked.

"More commonly known as acid, sweetie," Sabine said in an aside and completely pre-occupied by other thoughts. "Why share this with us?"

"Because you were absolutely right, Miss Parsons. Our man was most assuredly killed for these pills. We went back and had our forensics team do another sweep through his clothes and his fingernails. Traces of that chemical were found in one pocket and underneath two of the nails of his right hand."

"Shit."

"Profane, but accurate."

"It's still not much of an answer, Mr.— Nigel."

"Let's just say that I am following up a hunch of mine, Sabine. I have a feeling that it would be fortunate to have you owe me a favor or two."

Sabine found herself truly liking Mr. Lovejoy.

"You know, that's the first honest thing I've heard from one of you people so far. Shoot, Nigel. Consider the favor owed."

Edward made a strangled sound. Sabine ignored him. His three henchmen were making the same noise. Mr. Lovejoy smiled and helped himself to more tea.

"We've had unusual activity for the last five weeks." Sabine suppressed a shudder, but Mr. Lovejoy spotted it anyway. "Yes. The same amount of time you've been in Europe. Your timing is suspect."

"Color me stupid," Sabine said.

"Yes, well," he paused. "Upon further consideration by our analysts, we decided that as with all operations and what one of my analysts insists is a perfect example of chaos in an ordered system, you and your friend just happen to have bloody rotten timing."

"I could have told you that," Ari commented.

"Hmm. Yes. So we've had to exclude you from our calculations. However. Opportunity. You gave me key data, Sabine. And I don't believe in coincidence."

"Neither do I." Edward's turn to add two cents.

"Not surprising, Mr. Quintaine." No first names there, Sabine thought.

Mr. Lovejoy reached into his newspaper again and put two small pictures in front of Ari and Sabine. He didn't go on, because both young women had gone white as sheets.

"Ah." He tucked them back into his paper. "You know them."

"Yeah! The Malice Twins!" Ari exclaimed.

"No. We don't know them," Sabine groped for words. "We only know that they've tried to kill us a couple of times."

"Their names are Otho Buonocore and Lazarus Genge. To the best of our knowledge, they are freelance terrorists. This is the first time that we have tracked their movements so far north of their area of operation."

"Great," Sabine sighed. "Who are they working for?"

"Last information had them affiliated with some remnants of the Red Army in Germany and Austria."

"That explains the BND," Ari said. Sabine knew what Ari was thinking and also was keeping her mouth shut.

"Pardon? What do you know of German foreign intelligence in this matter?" Mr. Lovejoy asked, but Ari just shook her head; he went forward with a pointed frown. "We know precious little more. But, even with what we do now have, it takes no great genius to know that in the wrong hands, this chemical would be far too valuable to certain terrorist factions. I have been instructed by my superiors to ask and give as much aid to you and yours as possible."

"We will do what we can, Mr. Lovejoy," Edward said.

"I am surprised. And grateful, Mr. Quintaine."

Weirdly enough, they finished tea talking of other matters, such as the other sights the women had gone to in London and the weather.

Sabine forgave him a little of it later. Whatever documentation he had in the inside pocket of his suit, when they got back to the embassy, Edward managed to skip them past the preliminaries and straight to the people who could get Ari a new passport.

Two hours later, even though they had a temporary passport for Ari, Sabine was ready to collapse again. Andrew and Tony actually hovered over her and Edward kept glancing over at her, his expression unreadable. As a result, as soon as Ari had her passport, they were outside in the twinkling of an eye and Edward was hailing a cab.

Another half hour of travel found them back in Surbiton. Sabine felt a great deal better, but also felt compelled to head for her computer, put her head in some pages and not come out until dinner.

Sabine and Ari got to their room, shut the men out, and Ari began to pace, while Sabine went looking for her computer. She had a bad moment where she thought that Edward had walked off with it, but discovered it under the bed where some security-minded person had hidden it.

"Let's ditch the boys and go get some grub. I found out where the pub is in town from the nice ladies at the desk the other night," Ari announced.

"I don't know..." Sabine said, being focused on booting up her computer.

"Let me put it this way. If we don't lose them, I'm going to go postal."

It was pathetically easy to get out of the hotel. Sabine almost felt offended. Then decided she liked the mild exhilaration of ditching their keepers with all the ease that the warren allowed, as opposed to the real exhilaration it would have required, i.e. sheer adrenalin, if there had been real opposition to their leaving.

In fact, a depressing thought presented that Edward and company might have been waiting for them to ditch, so *they* could ditch.

Sabine pushed the thought away. If only knowing that Edward was alive was all that came out of this trip, she'd have to be content.

The walk to the center of Surbiton also turned out to be a real joy. Surbiton might have had nothing of real interest to see, but Sabine loved small cottage gardens and there were plenty of those. Downtown turned out to be all of three streets and one pub, The Firken and Financier.

Sabine took this as a good sign, followed by what she saw was the special for the day.

"Gimmee a Mad Cow burger and put everything on it. If I'm lucky, it will kill me."

Food served, devoured at speed, and empty plates were pushed away. The burger did not slay Sabine, so she ordered another cup of tea, (no lemon), and leaned back in the hard wooden chair, preparing to relax. Ari seemed to be doing the same, but her forehead creased in a frown.

"What's wrong?"

"Edward knows who the Malice Twins are," Ari said with no preamble.

"Duh. So you caught that too."

"Duh twice. Do I look blind?"

"Don't go Jewish on me. What about it?"

"Why didn't he say anything?"

"Got me. Don't even have the first clue. Either doesn't have clearance to have spilled it in front of the Brits or I just don't know." She took another sip of tea. "It's not like he's been very forthcoming anyway. Ever."

"Could you possibly paint 'Non-Disclosing' in bigger red letters on his forehead?"

"Ahem. No, I don't think I could. What do you want to do about it?"

"I don't know."

"Didn't think so." Sabine considered. "We can still ditch them completely."

"No," Ari said. "I just don't like not knowing what's going on and I don't like it that Edward knows so much and yet feels that it's somehow safer to keep us in the dark. It's never safer."

"You know that. I know that. I also have the terrible feeling that Edward is going to learn that for himself, or already knows it and is ignoring his better judgment."

"I know I've said it before."

"Said what?"

"We're in it deep now. Aren't we?"

"Yes. But it bears repeating."

Edward walked into the pub.

"So much for ditching them," Sabine said. "Or them waiting to ditch us."

Edward went to the bar and joined them when he had a tall glass of Guinness in his hand. He sat down without invitation and without a word of recrimination.

"Why, by all means. Sit down," Ari said.

"Don't mind if I do. The burger any good?"

"Not lethal," Sabine said. "Unfortunately."

"Too bad. Maybe I'll get one in a minute." He took a sip of his drink. "I've gotten our plane tickets changed."

"Excuse me?" Sabine asked, her forehead creased in confusion.

"Tickets. Changed. We leave tomorrow."

"Uh, okay. Why?"

He just looked at her.

"Okay, never mind."

They walked back to the hotel as slowly as they could as the sun slipped down behind the horizon.

It was over.

That was Sabine's first thought when she woke up the next morning in her hotel bed, seeing even in the dim morning light their packed bags. No more London. No more Europe.

No more strangers trying to kill them either.

She sat up, slowly.

Sabine realized that she felt glad. Exhaustion filled her. Being at the end of the trip, while she wouldn't have traded the experience for anything in the world, Sabine found she was more than ready to go home.

She put a hand to her chest. She could feel it all the way to the bone. Changed.

Sabine almost laughed out loud. To think, that the original intent of the trip had been to get her to forget about her troubles. She sobered. The Dreams. That had been the intent too. Too bad they had not been forgotten as easily as her troubles. And now, one of her Dreams was even made flesh.

Outside and two hours after breakfast, two gray BMWs waited to take them to the airport. They didn't get a chance to even load the luggage. Sabine's sight seemed to hone to a crystal fineness when she saw them.

The Malice Twins.

It was unlike her and not in keeping with her character, but she did it anyway.

She screamed.

They Cast, and the cars exploded in twin eruptions of gasoline fueled fire that threw them to the ground with the force of a giant's fist.

They shouldn't have dawdled over breakfast. The thought was so crystal clear in her head that Sabine was amazed that everyone couldn't read her mind. Even half stunned on the ground, the psychic maelstrom that was the rising tide of the Twins' powers screamed inside of her. Sabine could still think. The food sat in her stomach like a lead weight. Adrenalin coursed through her system, making her sick. She stared at the wreckage of their cars and did the only thing that she could think of as she staggered to her feet.

She Reached.

It came, the power more terrible and terrifying than it had ever been. Sabine felt another scream bubble in her breast and fought it to silence. She would never scream for these bastards ever again.

Her sight cleared. She could see the energies around the Twins. She had no time to attack. Their Cast fell on her, but this time, Sabine was ready. Her right hand flashed out and down and a silver dome flashed into existence, rebounding the Cast in their face. The blow of the spell almost drove her to her knees, but this time, this time, she thought, she'd protected her friends.

The Twins staggered, their shield a hasty thing that only just averted the force of their rebounded spell.

Sabine didn't wait. She Reached again and...

Someone else Cast.

Sabine spun around to see Edward Quintaine, spy for his government, his white shirt torn and stained with soot, standing in a circle of brilliant golden light, preparing to Cast.

She didn't wait to ask. She still had the Casting of her own. She waited for the tide of his to reach its crescendo and as one they Cast together.

The Twins' shield held strong. The short one even had the gall to laugh, though he sweated like a pig. Sabine felt herself go hot and cold, and found herself thrown into the street, unharmed, for somehow they moved her shield and her with it.

Their attacks were focused only on her. She looked up to see a truck heading straight for her, driven by a gray-suited minion and had a ridiculous moment to think, oh right, they're called lorries in England.

Only to be tackled and thrown out of the way by a man who felt like a wall of iron. She rolled on to her back in shock.

"Here you go, lassie!"

"Stewart?!"

"The same, me girl."

"What are you doing here?"

"Lending a hand, I should think?"

"I can see that! Why?"

"No one tells Stewart McMillan to ignore a lady in distress, lassie. No one."

Sabine felt the rising of two competing Casts. She knew Edward didn't have enough to save her or Stewart. She scrambled to her feet, to meet whatever came, standing.

"Get behind me, Stewart!"

She Reached further down than she thought she could. The muscles in her body strained to the point of tearing.

She Cast.

Wind howled, dragging everything and everyone into a sudden vortex. As sudden as its appearance, it was gone, leaving Edward and his men to stand in confusion, and Sabine to stare at the empty spot where the Twins had been a second before. She didn't even need to stretch her senses. She knew part of her spell had hit.

But the bastards had escaped.

Again.

Strange silence, she thought, the fighting over. Her eyes slid over the wreckage of the smoking hulks of cars that had been moved into the center of the street by the rampant exchange of energies. Edward helped Philip up from the ground, now with no sign of any eldritch energy or power to be found.

"The cat's out of the bag now," she muttered, realizing that she had just wielded her denied power in front of a huge audience.

Her eyes searched and found her friend. For a brief moment, she thought she saw a flash of golden light from Ari's throat. She blinked.

Terror snuck up with the silence. Her power. Stronger. Who cared about dreams and Dreams? She knew. Nothing was that powerful. *She* was not that powerful.

Her eyes and Ari's met. If she were getting stronger, it was because she would need it. In that one look with Ari, she realized Ari knew it too.

She also knew that Ari Doran was going to shoot first and ask questions later of the next obstacle or person who tried to hurt them. Sabine felt a knot ease in her chest. No matter what dreadful events waited for her, Sabine knew she was not going to be alone as long as Ari drew breath.

Sabine remembered the man standing silent next to her. No one needed words. The train, Sabine thought, and turned to the chance met friend met in a bar so long ago.

"Stewart, how did you find me? Us?"

Stewart looked uncomfortable, his clothes torn and stained. Sabine's heart hurt for him.

"You're nae gonna believe me."

"Try me!"

"Och, I believe ya. I saw a ghost on the Underground."

"An old woman," Sabine said. Her memory seemed to be as fast as the speed of light. Her first train ride into London.

"Aye, how did ye— No. I can guess. Aye. An old woman. She told me where ye were and said ye would need my help."

"You religious, Stewart?"

"Aye?" His face crinkled in confusion.

"Then go to the church and light a candle for me for that woman. Tell her I said thank you." Sabine stood on her toes and kissed him on the cheek. "Thank you, Stewart."

CHAPTER XI – CHRYSALIS OF STATES

San Francisco International Airport, United States of America

As the plane taxied, Sabine realized she didn't know what to do. She wasn't even off the plane yet and her worries were back with a vengeance. So much for vacation.

Everything she owned sat in storage. Granted, the storage unit had ended up only half filled, an exercise Sabine had conducted with sick rage and grief. She couldn't even fill a whole storage unit with all of her belongings, even when it was the smallest unit available.

She took a deep breath. It would all work out somehow.

Sabine smiled a little. Apparently the trip had helped. For her, consummate worry wort, to be content with staying at a friend's until she could get on her feet…

It was a substantial change for the better.

The 777 came to a shuddering stop and Sabine, still slightly tipsy, got to her feet to meet her new world. The confusion of deplaning and gathering luggage meant that not much of anything was said, until Sabine found herself standing in the concourse of San Francisco International Airport and realized that she had yet to ask Ari if crashing on her couch were an option.

"We'll drive," Edward said.

Sabine opened and closed her mouth before getting a chance to say anything.

"Someone will take you home as well, Ari," Edward continued

"Huh?" Sabine found enough intelligence speak.

"Where are you taking Sabine?" Ari's asked, low and dangerous.

"Safe house. Her things are already there," Edward replied.

This time, Sabine wasn't even capable of monosyllables.

"Excuse me?" Ari blurted out. "Moved her things?! That was a little bit presumptuous, don't you think?"

Edward gave Ari a look that Sabine didn't even know how to decipher.

"It's fine," Sabine said.

"How can you say that?" Ari demanded.

"It's either this or your couch, Ari."

Sabine tried to communicate through her expression everything that she feared to say. That this was also the only way that she might have a remote chance of keeping in contact with Edward. Of finding out what had happened to him. Why she continued to dream about him.

Ari somehow managed to grasp all of it and more. Sabine didn't like that Ari saw deeper than Sabine wanted.

"All right."

Albany, California

Ari let herself into her little house, a city and a bay away, and with
the next breath, restrained the urge to reach for her gun.

One of her "brothers" sat at her dining room table, reading her
paper, and petting her most irritable of cats, George. Dark-haired and
dark eyed like all her brothers, he had a paratrooper's physique and an
utterly charming smile that he turned on her now.

"The cats needed feeding," he said.

Ari decided she'd shoot him after all.

"Why did you let her go with him?" Joshua asked.

"Joshua, you idiot, 'let'?"

He put the paper down. Ari dropped her luggage and went to the
long galley kitchen behind him to put the kettle on.

"I wondered."

"Wonder no more."

"So what are you going to do?"

"Wait."

"Wait? You were supposed to stay in contact with her."

"She's my friend! Screw politics and screw them!"

Joshua said nothing.

"I'm going to wait."

"For what?"

"For her to call."

"Will she?"

Ari just gave him a look that spoke volumes.

"Don't you, Bubbi or Zeda, worry. She'll call." Ari began to make
tea. "Now make yourself useful and tell me if my rental properties are
still standing or do I need to go play landlady?"

Joshua laughed.

San Francisco, California

Sabine woke in strange surroundings.

It was her own queen-sized futon on its slightly too small frame
that creaked whenever she turned over. But the small room with the
vanilla walls and white trim it lay in was a complete mystery in her half-
awake state.

Memory came back.

The room was so tiny it hurt. She hadn't closed the curtains the night before. Actually, she didn't remember much of the day before. She looked out the window. She could see the ocean. The tiny house stood near the top of a hill in the outer Sunset district near the Stonestown Mall. No fog either, leaving the ocean cool and blue, meeting the horizon.

Sabine lurched up out of bed to take a better look at the little house Edward and his men had decided was her new home.

It was tiny. A shoebox. She found her desk and her computer in the only other room, equally tiny as the so-called bedroom. A front room with overstuffed pillows to sit on. Her stereo and CD collection sitting on the floor. She didn't own any furniture. A tiny kitchen that didn't have anything in it and that she bet she could reach the fridge from the stove without even reaching hard.

But there was a tiny back door in the kitchen. It opened on a deck over an enormous backyard with an untamed, overgrown garden and a clear view of the ocean. Sabine stood there and looked at the infinite blues that she could just see over the trees and houses. She turned around and went inside to find her cigarettes.

Clear weather, she thought as she lit up, just as at the same time, the feel of a body larger than her own, settled over hers. Harrison, was her next thought.

She stared at the cigarette between her fingers.

How much of this was her? How much was him, her Past, now so strong in her memory and Memory?

She finished the cigarette and went back inside to sit on one of the two cushions and stare at the walls. Her reverie didn't last long. She could never sit still. She needed to eat. Her bag sat by the front door, answering one question by its presence. She wasn't a prisoner.

Sabine pawed through her bag and dug out her car keys. Dumped her cigarettes in. She wondered what the chances were of finding her much-abused silver Acura Integra outside. Sure enough, it was parked in the driveway.

Sabine headed for the mall.

The day ran together. She ate at the food court. Window-shopped. Went grocery shopping. Went back to the postage stamp, only finally having it sink in that the little house's exterior was painted an unfortunate shade of pink.

When the time came, she cooked a small dinner and ate a bag of potato chips after. Wished for a TV. Smoked another cigarette on the back patio, staring out into the darkness at the ocean she couldn't see. Felt the jet lag hit.

The day had gone too quickly for nothing happening. Even so, the minute her head hit the pillow, she fell into a deep and dreamless sleep.

The next morning after twelve hours straight of sleep, Sabine finally felt rested. She got up to do housework but discovered that her unknown movers had unpacked her with far too much competency.

She sat down the front room. Wondered what music she'd listen to. Considered getting up, getting in the car.

Someone knocked.

Sabine opened the door, and decided that staying in was certainly not on the agenda.

"May I come in?" Edward Quintaine asked.

Sabine stepped aside, thinking in sudden clarity, 'ah, so this is what a sucking chest wound feels like.'

An hour later, the fluttering in Sabine's stomach came in waves, butterflies upon butterflies. She followed Edward's white Astin Martin. A current model blue Chrysler Plymouth stayed on her tail. She was sure that if she tried to lose Edward, they would make sure that she got to the intended destination with no mishaps. Except with maybe a little discussion if she were so inclined. Which she wasn't.

She looked at it from their probable perspective. She was, after all, the woman who, once upon a time, had turfed her own self out into the Cold. She had been sixteen.

Edward's car turned into an underground parking garage off of Beale Street.

Financial District, Sabine thought. She had a moment of coldness sweep over her. How long had he been in the district, when she'd been living in San Francisco for the last eight years?

She parked and there was no discussion as they waited for an elevator. The elevator arrived and Edward pulled out a security card. Had to insert it before the elevator would even move. Sabine caught the name on the card.

International Filmworks.

"Could you possibly have picked a more unimaginative name?"

"It's not meant to be remembered," Edward said.

The elevator doors opened on a security check point. Edward greeted the guard on duty by name. Mel. Indicated Sabine, but didn't introduce her.

The hallways were basic office, corporate. Nothing out of the ordinary, except that in this case, whoever had furnished the area had the good taste to not indulge in motivational pictures and posters. No people wandered the halls, but she could hear the murmur of voices through open doors and it was…comforting.

She felt another chill of fear. Comforting? It felt comforting?

She brought her attention around, because Edward had stopped, opening one of the many faux dark wooden doors, revealing an empty office. The office windows stared at the San Francisco/Oakland Bay Bridge. Early cubicle furniture with overhead cabinets, a few file drawers and anachronistically enough, a large oak desk shoved under the window, were the only furnishings. A very large office. All of it industrial gray, which was an interesting choice with the beige industrial carpet.

"Your office. Someone will be by later with your security access cards," Edward said, standing aside.

"I get security cards? Oh boy," Sabine commented.

"I'll see you later then," he finished and walked off down the corridor.

"Hey!" she tried to call after him. "What am I supposed to do?"

No one answered her.

The hours dragged.

Sabine got hungry.

It was easy to retrace her steps. Her forehead creased in confusion for a moment when she saw the security check point, but Mel, the guard, a portly man with no hair and bristly black eyebrows, looked up and smiled at her.

"Miss Parsons! Oh good. I have your security cards." He held out a card like Edward's.

"Thank you," she said awkwardly. "Um, lunch?"

"Yes?" he asked with a kind smile.

"Where can I get some?"

"Oh, well there's a nice place where you can get a burger not far from here…" and he proceeded to give her directions.

She went home around five in the evening. She'd seen no one. She'd done nothing except rattle around her supposed office or go outside and mill in the wasteland on the sidewalk that California law relegated smokers to.

At least I'm not being held against my will, she thought, before she went to bed that night.

It left only the one question. What did Edward want?

Sabine went back the next day anyway. A blue Geo followed her this time. She went up to her so-called office. Spun around in the office chair. Went to lunch. Smoked. Opened her last pack of Silk Cuts from London.

After lunch and a few paper airplanes that now littered the office, Sabine daydreamed about Europe and especially the café in Paris and the one in Milan. So many of her new memories, good and bad, now seemed to be found at white linen-covered tables and sun in her Memory's halls, with perfect white cups of black espresso before her.

One day had stretched into four days. Monday rolled around again and still no sign of anything on the green blotter of the big old oak desk. At first, Sabine wondered if Edward had forgotten her. But the more she thought of it, the more she knew better.

It was a test.

She just couldn't for the life of her figure out what kind. She stared at the ceiling and sighed in annoyance. If she could figure that out, she'd know how to deal with it. She knew that he didn't trust her. Sabine knew distrust when she saw it. She saw it on her own face in the mirror every morning when she asked herself why she continued to go occupy an office that held no work.

Which didn't change the fact that she was also still bored.

A happy little tickle of a thought inch-wormed into her mind.

"What a lovely idea!"

Mel called after her in a startled voice, when she passed his checkpoint.

"Miss Parsons, where are you going?"

"Out. I'll be right back," she grinned.

Mel tried to call her back, but Sabine knew he had no orders to detain her. He only ever asked her destination. Edward continued to have her followed on her way to and from work, but it remained at low-level surveillance.

She toyed with losing the followers and giving them a wild goose chase, just for a lark, but her destination lay around the block. Her plan, when discerned, would give them enough of the heebie jeebies.

Sabine marched into a tiny art store.

She bought stationary. Lots of it. If she had to be bored, she might as well write Ari lots and lots of letters.

The next day's unscheduled trip was to go in search of something to read. Mel didn't panic quite as much at her departure. She almost felt bad for him. She knew she was making his life very difficult and he seemed like a nice enough gentleman. Granted, he was a spook. A lot of them cultivated such an air.

Sabine stood in the little newsstand shop next door and tried to figure out what the hell she wanted to read. Nothing appealed. She'd read all she could think to read in the past week, looked at Vogue and all the entertainment magazines, she'd even bought a National Enquirer in desperation. She toyed with the idea of writing a story , but decided that even they wouldn't believe the things that had happened to her.

She zipped up her leather jacket, before stepping back outside, though the day was warm and sunny. She felt cold. No amount of sun or warmth seemed to do a thing to warm her. Probably just that time of month, she thought.

It wasn't. She figured that out after checking her office calendar. Her biological clock was punctual to a fault.

She sighed. Time to write another letter.

"*Dear Ari,*" she began on hideously rose-flowered paper.

All is the same. Read boring as shit.

No sign of anyone. About ready to commit suicide. Or murder. Can't decide. Any suggestions?

As for Him, don't even ask. I don't see him except in the hall. I still haven't figured out what this stupid Test is about. I'll find out. I'm sure. I don't know what the deal is, but I will figure it out.

She wrote for hours, stopped for tea and to look out the window. At the end, Sabine wrote concerns she didn't know she had until that moment.

I've seen no more broken rainbows, but I'm worried. I'm so cold today, Ari. I've had no dreams either, good or bad. But I have a feeling they're coming back and they're going to be worse.

She stuffed all eighteen pages into an envelope never designed for such quantity. She took it out to drop in the US Mail bin in the hall. She looked to see how full the bin was and saw the letter she'd posted to Ari from the day before.

Her guts went cold. She reached down for the other letter. She turned it over in her hands. No matter how careful one was, if you knew what to look for, steaming always left marks.

She smiled. She should have been angry. The quick coldness left as quickly as it had come. She dropped both letters in the bin and went back to her office, but not until she had propped open the door enough to see who would come by.

Andrew showed up. Looked both ways down the hall.

Fished out her latest letter.

He was good at scanning, she had to give him that. But the idiot didn't think to look for her office door.

Sabine laughed under breath. As if! Smuggling out secrets to the Mossad on Victorian stationary. Well, paranoia was a good trait, she guessed.

"Losers," she said out loud and hoped that the office was both bugged and had a video tap.

The next day, Sabine stood at the photocopier around the corner from her office, waiting for it to finish. Her letter fed into the top feeder very easily.

If they wanted to know what she was writing, they could damn well not steam open the letter.

The copier finished, she stuffed the original in its envelope, and paper clipped the copy to the envelope. Went and dropped it in the bin. Went to her office, and cracked the door.

Tony for a change wandered by the mail drop and he stared a long time into the bin. He started laughing. Detached her copy of her letter from the envelope and went off down the hall, still laughing.

But he left her original letter in the bin and Sabine closed her door with a smile. She figured she'd take a nap.

Edward stood in the doorway a half an hour later, and Philip peered over his shoulder. They stood for a moment more before withdrawing into the hall, Edward closing the door. He had time enough to take in every detail of Sabine's sleeping face. The stray mussed hair falling to obscure her features, the sweetness and lack of stress. He felt something, but didn't stop to identify the feeling.

"Why don't you give her something to do?" Philip asked.

"I'm waiting."

"Waiting for what? For her to expire from boredom?"

"No."

"Hello? What then?"

Edward turned away.

"Edward?"

"I'm just waiting."

Sabine woke to the sun. Looked at her watch. Four o'clock. Stretched. Heard her back crack in too many places. Sleeping in her chair was not a good idea, but either she slept in the chair or on the floor.

Her stomach grumbled at the memory of tea at the Dorchester. Scones. Sandwiches. Someone else doing the dishes.

She wanted tea. And a cigarette.

It was possible to get afternoon tea in San Francisco. Smoking would be more of a challenge and probably done while walking. Sabine bitterly missed the pub and smoking inside.

A half an hour later, Sabine sat down in an overstuffed chair in the Compass Rose, in the St. Francis Hotel right on Union Square, surrounded by décor more appropriate to the height of the British Empire. Sabine ordered high tea from one of the waiters dressed as an Indian ghurka.

Only one problem, besides being unable to smoke.

It made her miss Ari all the more.

But Sabine hadn't called her. She didn't want to give Edward an excuse to put her out in the Cold.

She had put the return address on her letters to Ari, specifically the little pink safe house on Ashton. That was all she dared.

They kept the building too cold. She acquired a space heater, even though outside, it was the height of summer. But summer in San Francisco meant that the fog rolled in till noon, rolled out for four hours, and then rolled back in like clockwork for the ride home. The only upside to fog, Sabine decided, was that it was neither cloud nor rain and therefore, could not create nor devour rainbows.

Sabine futilely warmed her hands on her umpteenth cup of Earl Grey tea. She'd succumbed and brought in a book to read and one of her notebooks to write in. She'd found her old CD player boom box. She'd yet to use any of them. She just stared out the window.

It was quite ridiculous. She saw Edward in brief flashes. He said nothing beyond the pleasantries. She wandered back and forth on any given day. Stared out the window. Argued with herself over and over about why she didn't call Ari or leave the building or do something.

The last time she'd run into Edward, she tried to buttonhole him.

"Why are you keeping me here?"

He had held her gaze for a long moment, stone-faced and unyielding.

"So I can keep an eye on you," he said.

She requisitioned an armchair one day and had moved the oak desk. The desk had the mass of a small truck, and Sabine was sure she had given herself a hernia. She fell on her butt a few times, trying to drag it. The desk now hugged the right hand wall, leaving the window clear. Her armchair, when and if it came, would sit before the window. If she had to be bored, she would do it in comfort, specifically by hanging in the chair upside down.

She'd have her back to the door whenever she sat at the desk, a minor downside. But if she were lucky, someone would shoot her and put her out of her misery.

In the meantime, the window beckoned with its view of the bridge and the fog. And as long as the fog remained, Sabine remained happy.

Then it hit her.

Fog.

She was in a fog. You couldn't see the landscape in fog. Only your hand in front of your face, if even that. She gripped her cup harder, her knuckles showing white. Maybe fog wasn't such a good thing after all.

The next day dawned clear with the sky an impossible shade of robin's egg blue, the kind of blue that photographers used in their postcards to lure unwary tourists to San Francisco to freeze.

Sabine stayed in her office long enough to rearrange her desk accessories again. Mel asked feebly where she was going when he saw her.

"The Japanese Tea Garden, Mel," Sabine answered. "It's too nice a day to stay inside."

"Ain't that the truth," Mel said.

"Ah, Mel! Cabin fever?"

The warm air was a tonic. Sabine's boredom left her on the drive across town. The cigarette she smoked while driving drove the jitters out of her body. No traffic moved on Fell Street, a rarity for the city, like the blue of the sky. In record time, Sabine pulled up to Stow Lake. Not many people outside of natives of the city even knew of the lake's existence inside of San Francisco. Nor did they know that a small path lead from the lake to the Japanese Tea Garden.

Meanwhile, her permanent tail, Tony and Andrew from the looks of it, desperately tried to look like tourists, with no cover or crowd to blend into. Sabine ignored them.

In the garden proper, the wisteria trailed down the tea house bloomed in full riotous lavender color, the magnolia trees competing with the abundance of blossom, dropping their ivory leaves on the manicured moss covering the toes of the trees. Through it all, the garden's waterfall laughed down the rocks.

Sabine didn't go into the teahouse.

She knew what she needed.

In the back of the garden hid a place Sabine called the Maple Walk. Down an easy-to-miss small winding path, lay a small grove of Japanese maples. Tourists rarely found their way there.

In that grove under a hedge, a bench nestled in the green where one could think.

Sabine sought the further solitude that the sheltered bench would give her. True, she had solitude at the office, but a watched solitude wasn't much of one.

She hoped Tony and Andrew would amuse themselves at the tea house. From there, they'd have a good view of the entrance and the exits. Granted, they probably didn't know of the third exit right off of the Maple Walk.

Sunlight fell through the maple leaves in a green that looked like hope. Sabine fell more than sat down in that shade, staring at the sky peeping through the leaves. She wished she could light up another cigarette, but that would get her kicked out of the park.

Edward couldn't have it all his own way. She'd had enough. Waited for him. Waited for something. Anything. Lie to her with complete deniability. She didn't care.

But the silence. She cared about that. Playing this game... He could just go to hell and kiss her ass.

Her heart clenched in her chest.

He could vanish, she decided. But she wasn't going to be the fool for anyone.

No. She'd go on and live her life. Chalk up Europe and all the strangeness to just being Europe. Go look for a job. Find a place of her own.

Hell, maybe she'd try to get back into radio broadcasting. She had loved radio.

She looked up into the green of the leaves and the sunlight and knew she was kidding herself. But her resolve settled further in her bones. She was done. She missed Ari. She missed her life, what little of it she'd lead before. She had no need for Dreams or power or broken rainbows.

It was as simple as that.

Now she just had to figure out how.

She dreamed and knew she Dreamed. She stood in the great echoing cavern, the elegant blackness of the Beloved like some poetry of darkness arching above and away from her.

Zoë in the coils of the Beloved then, its oily sheen reflecting black rainbows along its sensuous length in the leprous pale blue light that came from everywhere and nowhere. She knew Zoë did not dream, that she was awake. Sabine knew how dangerous it was for Zoë to do this thing. If she were discovered, there would be some terrible ramification for the child, even if Zoë's keepers could not detect whose dreams she had intruded into. All this Sabine knew in her Dreaming logic.

"Butterflies are transformation," Zoë's voice echoed in the great stone chamber, soft and beautiful.

"I don't understand," Sabine responded.

Always the same stone chamber. The dreams terrified her far more than any other. Sabine wore just a t-shirt, the one she'd gone to bed in, a plain black over-sized one. Her sweat stuck the shirt to the space between her shoulders.

"Butterflies have the ultimate power, the most basic of powers. They can transform themselves into something so different from what they began as."

"But they are fragile," Sabine said, feeling an uncoiling fear in her belly. She feared for this reflection of herself, feared that she would not be able to save herself or the girl. She scanned the temple, certain that the child would be discovered.

"Don't be afraid," Zoë smiled, the vacant black holes of her eyes staring at Sabine. "Butterflies have been known to cause storms."

Zoë's hand emerged from the coils of the Beloved. A butterfly winged from her hand. But even as it flew around Sabine's head, causing her to follow it with her eyes. The Dream began to fade, and Zoë spoke again.

Sabine woke with her ears ringing with the words.

Her open hand lay on the covers and in it, nestled a brilliant blue butterfly the size of her palm. Early dawn light came through her window painting everything ghostly. The butterfly winged out of hand as Sabine took in a breath. Flew around the room clockwise three times and landed like a prayer on the top of the curtains.

Sabine stared; Zoë's words echoing in the waking world, terrifying by the simple fact that Sabine didn't know what they meant.

"Beware the Preserver. He looks for you even now."

Sabine stared at the gray overhead cupboards in her office a few hours later, not seeing them in the slightest, and thought about butterflies.

Zoë warning her, that much needed no interpretation. The symbol of the butterfly… Zoë meant something specific. Sabine closed her eyes tight in frustration. What she could figure out, though Zoë hadn't come straight out and said, was her chance to go back out into the Cold had just vanished.

She wanted to scream. Everything was a bloody riddle! Edward, butterflies, all of it.

And never mind the clincher.

Who the hell was the Preserver?

A rarity occurred as she stepped out of her office. Edward. They exchanged pleasantries. She thought about strangling him as an alternative to screaming. But then a little inspiration occurred to her.

"What do I need to feed a butterfly?" Sabine remarked.

"Pardon me?" Edward said. "Flower nectar I would think. Why do you ask?"

"No reason. Think Research could find out for me?"

"Yes. Why?"

"No reason. Just curious."

"Sure," Edward said.

Sabine kept her smile to herself but felt it on the inside, turning to get her tea, for once leaving a befuddled Edward in the hall. Whether or not he'd meant to, she'd just gotten permission to wander around.

"Off we go to Research," she muttered.

Sabine got home, well content with life, having gotten to poke her nose around Edward's little club house, having found Research through virtue of Mel.

Walking up to the porch of the pink house, Sabine spied a large package and mail. Sorting it on her way in, knocking the door open with her hip, she noted most of the mail consisted of bills for the little house, which some thoughtful asshole had already put in her name. Nestled amongst the bills though, appeared a large purple envelope addressed to her old post office box, without a forwarding label, which meant someone had to have ransacked her POB.

Yet more consideration from Edward's little minions, the bastards. The letter bulged at its glued seams, bearing a return address that Sabine knew and loved.

"Ari!" Sabine cried.

The large rectangular package covered in brown paper bore no return address. Sabine chalked it up as yet another test of Edward's.

She took the letter outside to read and get a much needed cigarette.

The combination of letter and her dream, turned her day to complete ash, the cigarette forgotten on the railing of the balcony to burn to nothing.

Dearest Sabine, The letter began. *I have no way of telling this to you but straight out. While we were in Europe, your mother died. People apparently have been trying to get a hold of you for the last three weeks...*

The letter went on, but Sabine barely understood it. She still hung on the first statement.

Her mother.

Dead?

Eleanor Teresa Parsons.

Sabine sat on one of the heavy cushions in her front room and stopped reading.

Her mother was dead.

She didn't doubt the veracity of her friend's information. She began to read again. Assorted information trickled past her forebrain, but not to her heart. Her mother found dead in her state-supported apartment in Kent, in Washington State. Mysterious circumstances. That penetrated a little. Legal matters Sabine needed to deal with. A question if Sabine wanted Ari to notify Sabine's father, Mark Parsons.

Her parents had been divorced for years. Had in fact divorced when she was fourteen. Her father remarried, but her mother never had.

There were reasons for that.

Her mother had been diagnosed with a form of schizophrenia when Sabine had turned 18. The diagnoses had pointed out that Eleanor had suffered from the disease for years.

It had nearly destroyed Sabine's world.

Until that time, she had always thought that her mother, her family, all of it, were just normal. Thought her problems with Eleanor were due to her being a terrible daughter.

Never that her mother was mad.

Treatment and lithium had changed everything. Times had been hard, but they had built a fragile relationship. Not close, but it had been there.

Now Eleanor was gone.

Sabine could find no tears in her.

Sabine laid a hand against the large package, brown paper rough against her palm. Found a corner and tore the paper just to do something.

There was no note.

But there was a black guitar case.

Her mother's guitar.

She'd brought the guitar to work, trying to work through to some emotion. She'd named the guitar, Aya, not knowing why, only knowing, holding the mellowed wood instrument in her arms, that the instrument was older than she was. One of the few things that her mother had owned longer than Sabine had been alive. She sat tuning Aya when something made her raise her head from her task.

A little girl peered into her office, only face and shoulder leaning around Sabine's door frame.

They stared at each other. The girl so solemn, Sabine wondered if she would speak. She also wondered what a child was doing in a building full of spies.

Long blond, almost white hair framed a perfect heart-shaped face, and blue eyes the size of saucers stared in clear curiosity. Sabine made a face at her, crossing her eyes, mouth gaping open. The girl jumped, giggled. Ran off.

CHAPTER XII – STRANGE ATTRACTORS

It was a pregnant butterfly.

Sabine watched Zoë's gift. It fed on the plant Research insisted was the correct source of food for that particular butterfly, identified as a Ulysses Swallowtail, indigenous to Australia. She watched in wonder as the jeweled insect laid hundreds and hundreds of tiny little green eggs on the leaves. It took breaks to fly around the room, landing on Sabine's hair, or brushing her face with its wings or landing on the curtains.

What was the meaning of this gift?

Magick, Sabine thought, knowing nothing impossible. She also knew a message lay in the sending. Now all she had to do was figure out what it meant.

She needed to buy more plants. There were going to be hungry mouths to feed soon.

Another day. Sabine went for a walk, up the Embarcadero to Coit Tower, around noon, figuring the exercise would be good for her, even if the cigarette in her hand defeated the purpose. She'd gotten into such a habit of walking (and smoking too) in Europe, that it didn't seem like such a bad idea.

On the way back she met the last person she expected to see, in front of the Ferry Building. The Via Spiga in Milan, Italy, flooded back into Sabine's forebrain, almost brighter than memory, bringing with it more the tinge of Memory.

"Mr. Corsico! My goodness, small world!" Sabine said, dropping her cigarette and grinding the stub out, all as cover for her surprise.

"Sabine! What a delight to see you, *bellisima mia*!" Allejandro Corsico greeted her in turn. She hadn't had much of a choice in greeting him. He'd stared straight at her as she made her way back on the Embarcadero.

Again, impossible physical attraction. Sex appeal exuded off of him in waves, like heat. Sabine decided he just had to have the most overdeveloped set of pheromones of any man she'd ever met. But...

Under the sexual attraction, Sabine felt her heart race. A cold sweat that had nothing to do with exercise fell across her skin.

"What brings you to San Francisco?"

"I come visiting friends. And you?"

"Oh, I work around here," Sabine said. "I'm only out for my lunch break."

"Shall I walk you back then?"

"Oh no, no, you don't have to," Sabine laughed. "How long are you in the city for?"

"Ah, you know how it is. I am lucky to have a vast inheritance and I can live the life I desire. I stay as long as the city delights me," he said with a laugh.

"Lucky man," Sabine said and went sick with unexplainable dread.

"I am blessed, *sì*. So, may I call on you while I am in your fair city?"

"I don't think so," Sabine said, forcing a smile to reach her eyes. "I am horribly busy with deadlines for the next month or so."

"Oh, that is too bad! All work and no play make for dullness, no?"

"I love my work," Sabine lied. "I guess you can say that I'm married to it."

"Such a pity."

Corsico looked like he would have liked to talk longer, but Sabine decided she needed to make her escape.

"I really must be getting back."

"I am sure that I will see you again then." He made to reach for her hand, but Sabine walked away, waving in retreat.

She remembered too well what his touch had felt like on her skin.

She confused herself further, by taking a different route back, an unusual precaution for her, hearkening to old and recently dusted off and practiced tradecraft. She walked up Market. Turned right on Beale, making for one of the large Pacific Gas and Electric buildings. Even went so far as to walk into the Beale Street building. Hung out in their lobby for over half an hour, scanning the foot traffic. She felt safe after that. She scanned the whole way back.

But she couldn't shake the strangest feeling.

She felt that Allejandro Corsico knew exactly what building she had come from, where she was going and that it amused him to pretend that he didn't know a damn thing.

All the while, the skin on the back of her right hand, tingled with the memory of his touch.

The next day, Sabine stayed close to home, if IFHQ counted as her new home. She did venture out after a while to the Starbucks that lived

on the bottom floor of another Pacific Gas and Electric Company
building, which turned out to be the favorite coffee joint for everyone
else at International Filmworks . It was closet tiny, but had tables
squeezed in. She retreated to this place with her stationery and a café
mocha. It wasn't Europe, by any stretch of the imagination, but it was
San Francisco, and Sabine did love her hometown. The people alone
made it worth living in.

She waved at Tony and Andrew who came in fifteen minutes after
her and not just because they were tailing her. They didn't join her,
seeing her with her writing implements out. But she recognized several
other people that she knew by appearance from the bowels of her
building. The only person who didn't show up for a caffeine infusion
was Mel, and she was sure that if she sat there long enough, she'd see
even him. She dubbed the place, Spook Central, and noted the name in
the letter.

She finished five pages. Folded them and stuffed them in their
envelope, even though it wasn't finished by a long shot. Her mocha had
gone cold some time before which she forgot, took a sip and regretted
the impulse. She disposed of the last of her cigarette, tossed the paper
cup, and took in the day.

It had turned beautiful. Fog slipped down the streets far off in the
distance in the direction of the Outer Sunset, falling down the sides of
Twin Peaks. She knew that the little pink safe house would be fogged in,
but from her vantage point, it just looked like immaculate gray lace
falling across the hills. Where she stood, warm, sweet air surrounded
and the smell of the Bay didn't overpower.

She got back to the building and her floor. Was on her way to her
office when she saw the little girl again. They stared at each other.
Sabine made another face. The little girl giggled again and ran away.
Sabine got a better look at her this time.

The urchin wore blue denim overalls and a flowered t-shirt that
day. White and pink sneakers. Couldn't be more than eight or nine years
old, Sabine decided, and today, the girl's hair fell in braided pigtails
down her back. Still young enough to run around screaming and not old
enough to want too terribly to be an adult. Sabine didn't know the kid's
name and yet, already knew that she liked what she had seen.

She continued into her office. All thoughts of cute little girls went
right out of her head the minute she did.

A ten foot high by ten foot wide tablet, easily a foot thick,
apparently made from solid gold leaned against the near wall, propped

on an immense easel that somebody had built quickly from the looks of
it, next to the door. The entire surface of the golden tablet lay covered
in dense inscription that at immediate glance, Sabine knew was no
language that she had ever seen before. Probably had never been seen
by anyone else either.

She had enough time to stare at it, realize that it seemed to fill half
the office, feel her stomach drop through her body and through all the
floors of the building to begin tunneling to China. Turned to leave her
office.

But Edward already stood behind her.

She opened her mouth.

He spoke first.

"Come with me."

It broke the spell.

"What the hell is that?!" Sabine had not expected to yell, but that's
what came out, as her arm shot out to point at the immense tablet.

"Come with me," Edward repeated. She didn't know if the
repetition or the calmness of his tone made her fear and anger flow
away like water. Well, maybe not the fear. But the anger left and Sabine
felt goose bumps crawl along her skin.

Well, she'd asked to find out why she was there.

She followed him.

He took her around the corner from her office, down another long
hall in the opposite direction from the kitchen and the photocopier.
Opened another of the featureless doors, inside of which was an air lock
for a secure lead-lined room. No chances being taken here. Someone
wanted no electronic snooping of any kind.

She followed him into a beehive of activity.

At least twenty people were packed into a massive conference
room with every wall covered in photos, maps and charts. Several white
boards were set up throughout the room on easels, next to large tables
with more data, all of them radiating out from an even larger conference
table set in the center of the room. Which was clean, as opposed to the
other tables. A set of electronic surveillance monitors and other
equipment lined the right hand wall, Tony and Andrew working the
machinery, which didn't surprise Sabine at all. Today they had either
advertently or inadvertently dressed in matching white t-shirts and jeans
with work boots, which made her smile.

All activity stopped the minute she walked in.

"Team," Edward said in the ensuing silence. "Sabine will be joining us. Let's give her an update."

Sabine tried to not feel like a bug under glass and stopped smiling.

The men and women converged on the center table, some carrying files, others carrying tablets of paper. Sabine followed Edward to the table and before anyone could speak, she held up a hand.

"Before you inundate me with too much data, I only have one question."

Mouths snapped closed all around and the mean temperature in the room had to have physically dropped, Sabine was sure.

"What is that monstrosity of a tablet in my office?"

The temperature came back. She wondered what they all thought she had been going to ask.

"Oh, that's easy," Tony said, standing up and going to his section, coming back with a folder, which he handed her. "One of our ground teams finally hit pay dirt. We think it may be one of the major tablets that our opposition is using in their plans. Major coup."

Sabine nodded and didn't open the file.

"Plans?" She said and Edward filled in.

"The monstrosity of a tablet, as you so succinctly put it, is a prophecy tablet, according to our research," he began.

"Out of solid gold," Sabine interjected.

"It's not gold."

"We don't know what it is," a small, balding and bespectacled man said from further down the table. "If it were gold, we would never have been able to move it. But four men can move it easily and it doesn't scratch."

"Yes." Edward gave a quelling glance and continued. "Marcus, our metallurgist. The tablet is also impossible to carbon date, but research surmises that it has to be pre-Babylonian. Language unknown. Code unknown."

Sabine felt herself go cold at the last sentence.

"What we do know is legend, not pure research. Myth around the three tablets, and we don't even know which one we've found, says that they recount the means for releasing the Elder or the Elders, depending on the translation that you look at."

"The elder," Sabine said.

"Yes. There's more, but that's it in a nutshell. The team will give you the pertinent data whenever you ask for it, if you'd like the raw data."

"Actually, I would," Sabine said, her brain beginning to function in spite of herself. "Let me just make a shot in the dark."

Edward nodded.

"Our idiots in Europe. The Malice Twins. They work for the people who had this tablet."

Edward nodded again.

"And just a wild guess, if they had this tablet, this, let me guess, mystical tablet, and if they have the other two tablets that would be..." she searched for an appropriate term and found none. "Bad."

One nod. That was all he gave her.

Sabine wished she had never gone to Europe.

"Do we know if they have the other two tablets?"

"We're pretty sure that they don't," Edward said, but Sabine saw a tell.

"Pretty sure?" Her voice was acid.

"We're not certain."

"Great. But we have this one." She dropped the file on the table, and gripped the back of the chair that she had never sat in. "Next you're going to tell me you've got a copy of the Smaragdine Tablet around here somewhere."

"Hermes Trimegistres' Emerald Tablet? No, but we're looking for it," Andrew said distractedly, pouring through the photographs on the table in front of him.

Sabine just stared at the top of his head.

"So? What are we? Intelligence's answer to mystical espionage?" she asked. She got no answer. She scrubbed her face with the palms of her hands.

"Correct me if I'm wrong, but the government is funding your pretty little black bag to do this, right?"

Edward nodded.

"Why? Why fund mystical counter-fucking-intelligence?"

"They don't," Tony replied.

Sabine stared at him. It was getting to be habit.

"We are who we are, Sabine," Edward said, his face impassive. "I'd like to say we are and have the power we have because of global cooperation, but the truth is, we have what we have because we've got enough blackmail material to ransom the world and keep busy acquiring more every day. We have a brief and shallow charter from several world governments to pursue our field of intelligence. But no one takes us particularly seriously."

"No surprise there."

"Yes. But there are other forces at play than the ones you played, Sabine. The Malice Twins, all of them, are the fruits of Special Projects."

Sabine sat down.

Special Projects.

Why was she surprised? Edward was alive.

"Then there's you. Ex-SpecProj. In Europe. In Stuttgart—"

"Wait. What's Stuttgart got to do with anything but bad museums and were—" She almost didn't cut herself off in time.

"Pardon?"

"Bad art!"

"The tablet," Andrew cleared his throat and looked up. "We recovered it in Stuttgart."

"Oh—" For once, profanity failed Sabine. Nothing bad enough existed to say.

"Exactly," Edward said instead.

"Criminy," she finished her breath and sentence. "The gods hate me."

"No. Only us," Tony said cheerfully.

Sabine sat and a type of waiting silence filled the room.

Too many bombs of information had been dropped on her head. She needed time to think. She looked at Edward and knew she would have no time to do so.

Spec Proj. Also Known As Special Projects.

Her past.

All of it.

"So brief me already."

"Tony and Amanda are our two resident research magicians," Edward began the introductions, and indicated a tall, willowy, black-haired woman wearing a long flowing black dress, at the end of the table.

After that, Sabine let the words flow through her. She never did pay attention to briefings. Or more accurately, she never had in the past. She knew that her back brain would hear it all. Besides, in her experience, briefings were for the person giving them, not for the ones receiving them. She'd done enough in her time. Instead, she stared at her fingers where they were laced in her lap and let the words go.

But the end of the briefing brought her full attention up.

"So what's her code name going to be for purposes of Comm?" Tony asked, as everyone started clearing up their papers to go back to their tasks.

"She already has a code name," Edward said and silence fell as heavy as stone, bringing up Sabine's head like it was attached to wires. "Has for some time."

"No kidding?"

"No."

"All rightie." He picked up a pad to scribble it down. "Shoot."

"'Oracle'," Edward said and Sabine felt not just cold, but as if she had been dropped in a lake of ice.

She stayed in that place, as she followed Edward back to her office. She found her voice with difficulty as they walked up to her door.

"Why tell me all this, Edward? What's my place in this?"

Edward held open her office door. He gave her only three words. "Break the code."

She went inside, shut the door in his face and as soon as the door stood safely shut behind her, did the one thing that she didn't expect. She burst into tears. Not code. She had sworn she would never break a crypt ever again.

And here also lay the truth, an ugly truth, holding no more of her evasions. She had hoped for something that never existed.

What else would Edward want her back for? What was she thinking? What was she doing there? Nothing else lived there in his head or heart. Nothing ever would.

Sabine wept, her stomach tied in knots, tearing her apart. The pain hurt, but tears were not what doubled her over. It felt like a burning coal sat against the inside of her stomach. She tried not to choke as her nose ran. She looked around for some Kleenex through half-blinded eyes, but saw none. She ended up wiping her eyes with her shirt sleeve and blowing her nose on a piece of 20 pound bond paper. It didn't feel good, but it did the job.

She sank down to the floor.

Memory flowed around her. Too many surprises jogged it loose. She didn't stop herself from turning over the barbed thing, this memory.

She remembered when she put herself out in the cold thirteen years ago.

She'd had her own office then too. Child prodigy code breaker and something more for Special Projects. It had been a monitored office too. Edward had come to her then too. But to sit in her office.

Her heart beat so hard and hurt and ached in her chest, as she remembered him holding her hand. Telling her he just wanted to spend time with her, pained by something he could not, would not speak of, but said he just wanted to spend a little time with her. Just a little time, just for a little bit longer, because who knew when he'd get a chance to just be with her again, just wanted to enjoy her company for a little while. And they talked and he stared at her with an intensity she had never suffered from him before, as if he memorized her face. Then he would go back to being easy and normal.

But whenever he thought she wasn't looking, he stared with an expression so unreadable, so un-understandable to her, that it would haunt her for the rest of her life.

He was dead the next day.

Sabine wouldn't know until a week passed, when the so-called report came in. And it would all be over.

Sabine would go home and never look at a piece of code again. She would go to college in some other field, get her degree doing something that had nothing to do with computers or cryptography.

She looked at the folders on the desk. Some considerate soul had brought them in while she was at the briefing. The file names were printed in the upper left corner in Arial ten point letters. She stared at the tablet, the massive tablet that owned her room now.

She turned around to take in the large phosphorous eye of her computer screen. Someone had turned it on, logged her into a UNIX mainframe from the looks of it. She sat down at the desk.

She sat there for a long time, staring at the screen.

A half hour later, she had the mainframe running her first series of solutions.

It had gotten dark outside when Sabine turned away from the computer to look at the files on her desk. Her solutions had all been duds so far, but she wasn't surprised. First solutions rarely worked. They were there to whittle down the things that she knew wouldn't solve the problem.

She had been gratified with the processing speed of the servers. She had given it a couple algorithms that back in the day used to crash the old frames she'd used and it hadn't slowed down appreciably. Impressive.

She went to make herself coffee, after piling the files on the floor next to her armchair. She wanted a cigarette, but the files called.

She came back, settled herself in for a long read, and started to flip pages, coffee now in hand.

The usual crap, she decided. Everything from climate and agriculture from countries where activity had been tracked, to mission reports. Backgrounds on assorted organizations were also included, the weirdest group being a think tank of paramilitary, parapsychologists and anthropologists whose stated mission was to capture and study… A zombie.

She couldn't scoff. A huge gold tablet sat in her office. Written in some unknown code. Zombies were mundane by comparison. After all, she'd read Wade Davis, though she had a feeling that the zombie hunters meant the actual decaying dead, not the nerve toxin-ed, buried alive poor souls of Davis' book. She was somewhat surprised at all the intel, but guessed that Edward had decided that if he were going to let her in on everything, no half measures would suffice.

She skimmed. Something would stick, she knew, and she'd read in more detail later.

Which didn't take long.

Dates.

At first, Sabine just felt a niggle. Her forehead creased. She went back for the mission histories. Began to catalog by date, putting them in order in her lap.

And then she stared.

Thirteen years.

She began to tear open files, looking for locations, especially for indications of what, who and where the controllers for the missions were located. Facts began to wash through her. They had been fighting people like the Malice Twins in engagements that ranged from data steals to full out terminations of each other's agents.

A lot of people had died.

She felt no horror. Not yet. Not even the photos bothered her. No.

She had other fish to fry.

San Francisco kept coming up. Control always in San Francisco. She saw code names, didn't know who they meant, except for one.

Quintus.

Quintus always came back to San Francisco. Control always in San Francisco.

Ari Doran picked up the receiver for her outraged telephone at an hour that she was sure was too ridiculous for words.

"What were the chances of him always having been in San Francisco, Ari? What were the fucking chances?" Sabine raged on the other end of the line. Ari woke up fast.

"Zero. Zip. Nada. What's your point?"

"So how did he manage to hide? This fucking peninsula isn't that big!"

"It's amazing how easy it is to hide when you're thought to be dead," Ari commented. Sabine shut up for a brief moment.

"There is that."

"Yes. There is that."

Another silence.

"I feel stupid, Ari."

"Why? For believing what you thought to be the truth? How were you to know that the idiot wasn't dead?"

"I don't know. But I should have known." Her voice was grim. "I just should have known."

"I don't see how you could have. But that's not what makes me think."

"Want to elucidate that one, oh spook-like one?"

"Why did he stay so close?"

Ari dropped the phone into its cradle a few minutes after that. She glanced at the device next to the phone. Two in the morning, but she wasn't looking at the clock.

She had the trace.

Yes, she had the return address on Sabine's letters. Had even driven by the pink house in San Francisco. But Sabine had not called, and letters were not what Ari had waited for. She trusted her friend, even as it had hurt to let her go it alone for even this brief period of time.

Yes, she'd done all these things in respect for her friend.

Tomorrow, she'd know where that idiot of a man, Quintaine, had taken Sabine.

Three hours into her next day, Sabine sat, elbows leaning on her knees, staring at the gold tablet. The computer's hard disc hummed as it ran more solutions.

The characters alone were not of any known language in the database. Which left one of many problems, namely that she kept getting the niggling feeling that she should have recognized the character set even so. Yet, no amount of racking her brain kicked loose the necessary memory. So she just stared.

Marcus, the metallurgist, came to mind though. Sabine went up to the tablet and laid a hand on it. No reaction. The surface felt cool to the touch. Metal. Soft feeling the way that gold was, yet, a difference. This close to it, she could tell. It colored too rich a yellow in some ways and too solid seeming. It looked more real than the office it stood in, like a slice of ultimate reality taking a break on an easel for her amusement.

She scratched a fingernail across the surface.

Nothing.

She went down to the mission room that Edward had taken her to the day before. Asked for a Petri dish and a sharp dental tool, or something with a diamond cutting head, to Tony's confusion.

She sat down cross-legged by the easel, once back in her office, and tried scratching the underside of the tablet.

Nothing.

She scratched harder.

She crunched at the damn thing for ten minutes. Tony had assured her the tool was a diamond head. She didn't have a high pressure water drill, though she was getting to the point where she wanted one, mystical and rare fucking tablet or not.

"I just want to know what you are made of," Sabine said.

Flakes fell into the waiting lab dish in her hand.

Sabine did not drop it.

"Thank you," she said and clambered to her feet, trying not to shake in reaction.

She headed back to the mission room, walking carefully with her hand over the Petri dish. Went up to Marcus, bent over some device she didn't recognize. Tapped him on the shoulder.

"Oh, hello," he said owlishly, looking up at her. She almost made a comment about his shirt. He had had spaghetti for lunch. The red stain clashed with the green shirt he wore. But so did the orange tie, so she decided to just say nothing to someone so obviously color blind.

Instead, she held out the dish.

"What's this?" he asked, frowning at it.

"Flakes off the tablet."

He almost screamed. Choked instead. Sabine almost dropped the dish.

"WHAT?!"

"Dude, chill!"

"Oh my god!!!" He staggered and groped for the table. "How? How did you get a sample? Is the tablet damaged? Have you destroyed it? What—" He was well and truly panicked and would have rushed out of the room if Sabine hadn't set the dish down to grab him. Even so, Tony and Andrew made a beeline straight for them.

"Calm down! The tablet is perfectly fine."

"Then, then, then how?!" Stuttering seemed to be phase two of his shock.

"First, breathe."

He gasped like a fish. When she thought he wasn't going to pass out, Sabine answered.

"I asked."

"What?"

"I asked. I think you all failed to remember that the damn thing is mystical."

"So?"

"Which often means that there's a certain degree of..." she struggled to find the right explanation, because the knowledge came from no knowledge base she actually had, just pure gut and sidewalk intuition. "Sentience."

"What's going on?" Tony asked.

"I got a metal sample off the tablet," Sabine said and watched both Tony and Andrew go white. "What?"

"Holy shit."

"What?"

"Nothing. Nothing. But you got it."

"Yeah." She turned her attention back to Marcus. "Now do you think you can analyze it?"

His head turned to the dish the way a compass needle turns to true North.

"I'll find a way," he breathed.

"Good. Because I think its composition may be one of the keys to the code."

"Yes," Sabine said and left.

She meant to go straight back to crunching on the tablet, though this time in code breaking mode, except Philip stood in her office, staring at the tablet.

"Hello," she said, not quite sure what else to say. This man, so close to Edward, had not been alone in her presence once. Now here he stood, unannounced and at his ease.

"Good afternoon, Sabine," he said. He wore what she now thought of as his ubiquitous dark gray suit, though with a striped blue and white shirt that would have done a banker proud. He also wore a rather lovely blue tie that set off the twinkle and color of his eyes. Eyes that now appraised her over the rims of his glasses.

"Afternoon."

"I've been sent to collect you for hand to hand training."

"Erk?" Sabine managed.

"Didn't check your e-mail, did you?"

"I have e-mail?"

"Threw you in the deep end, didn't we? Yes, you have e-mail. You also have a schedule and you didn't show up for your unarmed training class with me. So here I am. Can you break from this?" He waved at the tablet.

"Sure." Sabine set the dental tool down on her desk and followed Philip out.

They took the elevator down a couple floors and stepped out into a floor that was all workout room, but with a fitness club vibe. Wall to wall windows let in a great deal of sunlight, illuminating the equipment against the left wall, reflecting in the mirrors behind them, making the floor look immense. In the center lay a large collection of blue mats, stretching in vast expansiveness, padding and gloves dropped in profusion by the edge.

"Showers and locker room are over there." Philip gestured to the right. "You've got locker 9 and should find a *gi* in it. I'll see you in a couple of minutes."

"Erk. I mean, right," Sabine said, feeling more and more out of her depth.

"Edward tells me that you have some previous training. So we'll just skip the basics," Philip called after her. He'd gone into the men's locker room before she could squeak a protest.

"Erk!" she said instead and went to change.

A few minutes later, Sabine stepped on to the mat.

They bowed to each other. Sabine knew one thing when she looked in his eyes, his glasses stowed somewhere. She knew she was in for one hell of a trouncing.

In fact, Sabine thought with amazing clarity, she was learning to fly.

The ground, padded or not, slammed into her with the kind of force that only gravity and cement, aided by human muscle for velocity, could produce.

"OOOOF!"

Only problem with learning to fly, she thought. *Landings are a fucking bitch.*

Philip moved into her line of sight, upside down, grinning like a loon. "Perhaps a break?"

"…erk…" Sabine managed.

Philip vanished out of her vision and returned a moment later with a bottle. He helped her to right her orientation to the rest of the world. Handed her the bottle, materialized a towel and sat down next to where she sprawled, since sitting was not something she felt capable of doing.

She gulped the water and mopped her face. She couldn't remember sweating this much. Ever. In her entire life. It ran off her body in a continuous stream, between her breasts, down her back. The *gi* felt like a hundred pounds of wool.

Philip, the bastard, didn't even look winded.

"You bastard," she had to share.

She was beginning to hate his laugh and yet it held no mockery. Philip was just a happy fucking guy. Yep. She hated him.

"You're not the first to say so, but I can assure you, my parents were and are still married."

"Makes—" She gulped water. "—no difference."

"Exactly." He mopped his own face, but Sabine didn't feel that he needed to.

"What is the fucking purpose of this brutality?" Sabine managed.

"Edward wants you safe."

Sabine was certain that he had hit her too hard. She couldn't have heard what she heard.

"Speed. Strength. Technique. These are all good things to have in hand to hand, in martial arts, as I'm sure you well know," Philip said. "But fundamentally, they are not what win fights."

"What does?"

"Well, ultimately and ideally, to use the cliché, he who runs away, lives to run away another day. Especially someone like you. You are not meant to get into stand up fights. But we can't always pick and choose when someone wants to clean our clocks. That's why I'm here. But that's not what I meant."

"I like the running away part."

"Yeah. Too bad you don't seem very good at it," Philip laughed. "Actually, you already instinctively know what I aim to teach you."

"Oh?"

"Yes. Intent."

Sabine's lips went sideways in an expression that made Philip laugh again.

"Huh?"

"The person who gets away or wins the fight is often not the person with the best skill. The person who gets away is the one who is the clearest in his or her intent that they want to survive."

"Oh, I'm clear on that."

"Exactly. But there's one more step to intent that you do not have mastered."

"Enlighten me, oh great one." Sabine managed a laugh.

"When you did get in that fight before we left London, you were not clear in your intent."

"What are you talking about?" Sabine bristled.

"I'm talking about you. You were not clear on one thing," he paused for effect. "Your intent was not to destroy them."

It stopped her cold.

There had been one thought on her mind. Making them go away, but even without him spelling it out in plain English, Sabine knew that the thought of killing the Malice Twins, of destroying them...

She had been, no, still was, an analyst. The last few weeks had proved that to her. She and her kind recommended the taking of human life rarely and when they did… It was up to others with their special training and their years of experience to carry out such plans.

"You think I'll need to."

"I know you'll need to."

"Why?"

"Because you, my dear, appear to be cursed with what we call the bomb magnet. And if you are, you need to train twice as hard and be twice as clear as anyone else."

"It's not me," Sabine said.

Philip's face was kind when he spoke.

"I know. And if I am good at what I do, you will never have to become such a person as has the kind of intent that I am speaking of." He got to his feet and began to do some stretches. "But, if by some gross mischance, you should find yourself in the wrong situation, you will be prepared."

"Oh, I will, will I?" Sabine struggled to lighten the mood.

"Oh, yes."

He came straight at her with another attack.

Hours later, or so it felt, Sabine dragged herself to the showers. She turned one of them on as hot as she could stand, crawled in and sat crumpled on the white tile. Muscles that she was certain had never existed until that moment, fulfilled their new purpose. They all told her she was going to die.

She felt like rubber. No, rubber had some sort of consistency. She felt like runny Jell-O. That was it. And she was going to die. She pressed the side of her head against the cool tile wall, the hot water running over her body and shook.

Philip had forced her to stretch before packing it into the showers. He had also made her swear that she would stretch before bed. She was going to do more than that. She was going to find a bottle of vodka and drink herself sick. Okay, maybe not sick, but she was going to drink. Lots. And smoke the cigarette she'd been wanting for the last four hours.

Sabine had no idea how she got out of bed the next day. Or managed to drive into work, stagger to her office and collapse in her wing chair. Granted once she got there, she knew she was never going to move again.

She gave a quick check at the computer. Decided she might as well try to work on her solutions. Which made her glance at the ever-present monolith dominating her office. Its presence began to take on the aspect of comedy. She needed to bring in a boom box and play Thus Spake Zarathustra. She had a feeling that Edward would throttle her for it. Which would neatly put her out of her misery.

She snickered again. Except it hurt to laugh. A huge heave of effort got her out of the comfy chair and over to the computer. She thought about checking her e-mail, now that she knew that she had an account. She decided ignoring it hadn't hurt her so far.

Push your luck! she thought and turned her attention instead to one of her appropriated yellow legal pads. She scribbled symbols, glancing at the tablet from time to time. She then reached for a spiral notebook, her beginning record of the code.

She fell into the space in her head that twisted code out of shape into sense and didn't notice the passage of the hours.

Nor did she notice how easy it came. Because if she had, it would have frightened her.

"Hello."

Sabine looked up from her notebook. She had moved back to the big desk. Her ideas for her second pass at the encryption were not shaping up well and she knew she frowned.

The little girl stood in the center of her office. Sabine had neither seen nor heard her entry. The child's hair lay in two braids again, tied off with purple ribbons. She wore a purple dress with big blue flowers which hung one size too big on her slight frame. She also wore no shoes, which made Sabine's lips twitch.

"Hello. My name's Sabine. What's yours?"

"Michelle." The little girl smiled back and bounced up to seat herself in Sabine's overstuffed chair. "Whatcha doin'?"

"I'm trying to figure out what that says." She pointed at the gold tablet. Michelle looked at the huge tablet and blinked.

"Why?"

"Because it may tell us something important."

"Oh. Daddy must want it."

"Daddy?"

"You don't work in the Big Room."

Sabine paused, lost at this non-sequitur.

"Big Room?"

"You know. Where Uncle Tony and Uncle Andrew won't let me go." Michelle frowned. "It's not fair."

Sabine bit her lip to keep from laughing.

"Well, there are reasons for that. It's probably not for little girls."

"So why don't you work in there? Everybody else does."

"I don't like it in there. Other people distract me," Sabine said.

"Oh." Michelle seemed content to sit and say nothing more.

"Who's your Daddy?" Sabine managed to ask, remembering her earlier question.

"He's the boss!" Michelle replied. "You know!"

"Edward?" Sabine just managed to keep from squeaking.

"Only Uncle Philip calls him Edward. Everyone else calls him Mr. Quintaine," Michelle explained, then had to backtrack, as only a young person could. "Well, no, Uncle Tony and Uncle Andrew call him Edward too. Except when they're in trouble, which is lots!"

Sabine laughed. It was either that or cry.

"So. Edward, I mean, your Daddy, he brings you to work often?"

"Only when school's out and Mommy doesn't want us around anymore," Michelle said, a haunted look in her eyes for a brief second that broke through Sabine's earlier shock. But the look stayed too brief for Sabine to read.

"Wait. Us?"

Before Sabine could get an answer from Michelle, the answer materialized. A boy, a year or two older than Michelle appeared, in the doorway, hair as tow as Michelle's and eyes as blue. He wore an adult Los Angeles Lakers jersey with a number 24, and a pair of very neat and clean jeans. They were a matched set, Sabine thought, but where Michelle was fey and smiling, he was serious faced and solemn.

"Michelle, what are you doing in here?" the boy asked, in stern tones.

It amused her and saddened her at the same time. He was used to being in charge of his little sister. Which meant there had to be a reason he felt responsible for her. Those reasons were never good.

"I'm making a new friend."

Sabine smiled at Michelle's statement.

"You shouldn't bother the lady," The boy said.

"I'm not bothering her! She's talking to me!"

"Michelle…"

"Don't Michelle me! You're not Daddy! You can't tell me what to do!"

"Dad told me to watch out for you."

Sabine decided she better step in before sibling warfare broke out in earnest.

"It's okay. I like Michelle's company," she offered.

"See?" Michelle shot back at her brother in triumph.

"And who are you, young man?" Sabine decided she better ask.

"Jacob, ma'am."

"Hello, Jacob. My name's Sabine. You call me ma'am, you make me feel old."

"You're not old!" Michelle jumped to Sabine's imagined defense.

"Thank you, Michelle."

They visited a little longer. Sabine found out little. It was weather talk, as her poor dead mother would have called it. They left a little while later by Jacob's decision, hand in hand, Sabine saw with a wistful amusement. They gifted her with a solemn (from Jacob) and happy (from Michelle) promise that they would come by again another day. Jacob may have been solemn, but he loved his sister and Michelle loved him, clear as crystal.

Sabine's office seemed very large and very empty after.

Married.

Sabine sat back in shock that she now allowed herself to feel.

He was married.

Had children. Two. Two intelligent, beautiful children.

She could not doubt that he must have an intelligent and beautiful wife.

Sabine closed her eyes and tried to understand why she wanted to cry.

She came up with no answer. Decided code was easier to understand and break, than trying to decipher emotions or pain that held her heart in its grip.

The next day, Sabine succeeded in driving out of her brain the fact that Edward was married. Focus on the tablet's encryption had helped. But that focus left her with a nagging suspicion that she was going at the code breaking completely, utterly and catastrophically from the wrong end.

It made her cranky.

The halls were empty on the way to the Big Room, Michelle's comment being far too accurate. She restrained the urge to knock first before stepping through the last of the doors in the airlock.

A quick scan at all the little worker bees, the other analysts that Sabine did not feel included with, turned up two facts. Tony was not in residence, but Andrew was. Marcus also bore down on her at first sight with an expression that gave new meaning to the word, intense.

"Andrew," Sabine said, heading for him before Marcus could capture her entire attention.

"Sabine. How are you?"

"Cranky as hell. I'm here to make you share my pain. Tell me there's a fucking research library in this benighted hell of a place and that it will have copies of historical codes."

"How historical?" Andrew asked, even as Marcus made a strangled noise by Sabine's elbow.

"Like ancient. Um, a copy of the translation of the Polygraphia, all six volumes, stuff like that."

"No shit, ancient history. What do you think we are, the NSA Rare Book Collection?" Andrew joked.

Sabine just gave him a look. He stopped laughing.

"Okay. No sense of humor, eh?"

"None," Sabine answered; Marcus sounded like he was going to have a hairball. "I know I'm asking you to have stuff that the Cryptologic Museum would have, but I gotta have it."

Andrew nodded, placating.

"Okay. Release your sphincter. We've got it. Or if not, we've got stuff like it. I'll take you—"

"Ms. Parsons!" Marcus choked out. Andrew grinned.

"—Later," Andrew finished.

Sabine flashed him a quick grin and turned to the apoplectic metallurgist.

"Yes, Marcus?"

"I've got the analysis of the tablet! I must discuss this with you!" he burst out. Sabine wondered how he'd manage to keep from exploding.

"Ooo! Fantastic! Show me!" she said, even as he ran off to his station.

He handed her a sheaf of papers. The sample from the tablet sat in a different Petri dish, this dish heavily scratched and worn looking, several graphs and photos off of an oscilloscope next to it. Sabine began to flip through the report, glancing at the photos and graphs from time to time. And started to frown.

"Is this right?" Sabine asked, almost too soft for Marcus to hear, since she was mumbling into the paper. "I mean, I am by no means a metallurgist, but is this right?"

"Exactly! You see it right away! I knew you would!" Marcus almost jumped up and down.

"Is this saying what I think it's saying?" she mumbled again.

"Yes! Yes!"

She dropped the report and pinned Marcus with an intent expression.

"If I'm not brain dead, it's still composition unknown, but molecularly it's perfect? Like diamond, but somehow better?"

"Yes!"

"Is this possible?"

"No! But it's sitting right there! It exists!"

"But then, by rights, it should have a ridiculous amount weight to go with all that mass. You shouldn't be able to move it at all, right?"

"Yes! Yes, yes, yes."

"Calm down, Marcus."

"Yes, Ms. Parsons."

"Okay. First, Sabine. Not Ms. Parsons. Enlighten me on this one. What does it mean for this to be molecularly perfect? Super light? Impossible to reproduce?"

"I talked it over with Andrew," Marcus said, his excitement bubbling up again. "His theory is that it's not man made."

"Oh Christ, Astarte and Ifni!" Sabine burst out. "Not little green men!"

"No, oh no!" Marcus began to grin. "God."

Sabine felt her mouth drop open and then grinned in a fixed manner.

"God."

"Yeah! Or some equally supernatural force with a capability to reorder matter on a fundamental scale."

"Well, technically, magick does that," Sabine interjected.

"Not like this, according to Tony," Marcus warmed up to his subject. "He says the power cost would be far too much. We're talking about manipulating matter on the molecular level. Also control that's ridiculous! You're talking about lining up all the chains of atoms and molecules into a perfect chain spiral of matter. No one has that kind of mental ability! Well, not anyone human!"

Sabine frowned harder.

"God."

"God."

"Right." She scrubbed her face hard. "You know what, I'm going to pretend that I didn't hear any of this and I'm going to go do my research."

"Why?" Marcus asked.

"Because, I refuse to accept that a god! Any god! Would have time to personally screw up my fucking life!" she responded. "But I'm taking this with me. Hope you have a copy." She grabbed the analysis.

"Yes, I do," Marcus stuttered in reply, but it was delivered to Sabine's retreating back.

"Andrew." Sabine's return to Andrew's corner of the Big Room found him once more involved with his security monitors.

"Sabine!" Andrew said, but without looking away from his monitors. Sabine gave a cursory glance and realized that he had most of the satellite direct news services on the monitors. The usual intelligence, she thought. It depressed her that more analysts and intelligence services used journalists by remote control, especially CNN, rather than depending on their own HumInt. She didn't care how wonderful Ted Turner's news service was. There was and never would be any good replacement for the man on the ground.

"Ready?" she asked instead.

"Yeah." Andrew broke away and dropped into an easy stride next to her.

The library, it turned out, lived closer to Sabine's office, than the Big Room. In fact, it was two doors down from what she called her home away from home, behind another of the ubiquitous doors that had no signs. Andrew pushed held open the door for Sabine to walk in first. Which she did with alacrity only to come to a slow stop in the middle of an immense room.

Someone had bothered to do a good job in putting in shelving. All the way to the top of the eleven foot ceilings were archival quality bookcases, many with glassed in doors lining the walls and then several freestanding stacks that went to the ceiling. A handy library ladder stood ready and waiting by the door. She made a slow circle to take in the collection.

She gave a low whistle.

"Impressive."

"Edward insists that it is pathetic, puerile, philistine, and poorly indexed, but I've never had a problem with it," Andrew said. "Can I leave you on your own? I got a stack of shit still to do."

"I'll be fine. Get back to work, you."

"Great. Come and hit me over the head if you need anything further."

"Careful. I may do that literally."

Another chuckle escaped Andrew and he left her, surrounded by the smell of old paper, leather and binding glue. She began to wander, not even looking for the index yet, just scanning titles.

A half an hour of cruising the stacks and Sabine found her attention being drawn to a set of very old books that were on one of the main shelves. It looked like an Encyclopedia Britannica almost, but older and more worn. She lifted out a volume and read the spine.

It was the Hermetica.

Sabine counted, shock making her jerk in her motions.

All 42 volumes.

It had to have been transcribed from somewhere, but she had no idea from where. She'd have to ask Edward. It was an unusual find and unusual to find in his library, actually, to find it in any library.

She replaced the book reverently.

Well. She was sure it would be good for research. Hell, like if she felt like summoning Metatron, the Voice of God, for shits and giggles. She shook her head with an almost inaudible sigh. She went back to searching the stacks for the books she did need.

Huge volumes of occult lore. She shouldn't be surprised. She had a fucking mythical tablet hanging about her office.

Edward had a visitor a day later. He walked into his office at eight in the morning to find Sabine already standing there, wearing the clothes from the day before, her hair escaping in a million directions.

"I need to see the photos of the site," Sabine began without preamble.

Edward continued his motions and set his briefcase down. His office held no difference from Sabine's, except that well-cared for potted plants sat under the large window, a fichus tree on the floor and a few African violets on the ledge, to be exact. One of the violets was in a pot that could only have been made by a five year old, painted a shocking yellow.

"Good morning, Sabine," Edward said instead.

"Oh. It is morning, isn't it?" she commented.

"Have you been home?"

"Screw home! I need to see the photos of the site and Tony and Andrew won't give them to me!" Sabine cracked.

"Ah. The recovery site of the tablet." Edward understood without her help. "Why?"

Sabine stepped up to the edge of his desk and rested her hands on it, her head coming down, and her eyes closing in sudden weariness.

"I don't know why. I just know I need to see them."

"That's not good enough, Sabine. They're not pretty."

"Screw pretty," she said, weariness in her voice. "I just know that there's some clue to the encryption in where the tablet was found. Something I'm missing and I need more data."

"That is a better reason."

"Fuck if I know if it is a better reason. I just know I have to see them. Hell, if I could, I'd really like to physically see the site, but I'm sure that's not possible now." She collapsed into one of the wide chairs in front of his desk. "The composition of the tablet, the lack of any clear pattern, the symbol choice, I mean, yes, there's some pattern! But it's not mathematical as far as I can tell, or it's some new fucking algorithm that is so far fucking out there…" Her head dropped against the chair back.

"Whatever it is, I am grasping at straws and I know it," she finished.

"You'll get the photographs," Edward said and Sabine got to her feet to go. "On one condition."

She raised an eyebrow at him.

"Go home. Get some sleep, a couple of hours at least and a shower."

She started to say something, but closed her mouth and nodded.

"Good. The survey of the site will be in your office when you get back."

She nodded again and made her way to the door, but stopped just shy of leaving.

"By the by," she said over her shoulder. "Where'd you get the Hermetica?"

Edward smiled.

"My secret."

"Sweet. Very nice," she said.

But that left Edward to sit and stare out his own window, puzzling over the interchange, the smile fading from his lips.

Sabine had come to him.

When and what had changed?

Sabine stretched in her chair and her neck cracked like a zipper. It helped somewhat, but she still ached and the stiffness from having sat in one position for far too long didn't go. Her eyes ached from staring at the computer screen.

No amount of work was worth this much physical discomfort, she decided. She was never going to make any more sense out of the text in front of her without an infusion of strong caffeinated beverage.

She frowned into her coffee cup. Empty.

"Well, we can't have that..." Sabine said out loud and pushed herself out of the chair. It didn't help that the arthritis in her hands crunched them into claws if she didn't will them to lay flat. Past time to acquire a new cup of coffee.

She let her mind drift as she waited for another pot to brew in the tiny break room. Unlike other places that Sabine had worked, coffee did not sit around all day hoping for someone to drink it. It very much appeared that the second anyone made a pot, it evaporated into everyone's mouths. Which was fine in Sabine's opinion. Waiting for a pot to brew meant she didn't have to think about the big gold thing in her office.

She flexed her hands and grimaced in pain. Yes, a very bad day for her arthritis. She loved San Francisco, but the fog and the wet played havoc with her joints.

She sighed.

I know I'm not old, Sabine thought. I've just lived a life that most people would have lived in two or three lives. I'm not even done with this one either.

She flexed her hands again, but this time grinned with the pain. It didn't help that Philip trained her hard. He had started her on the heavy bag. As if the arthritis weren't enough. If it hadn't been for visualizing Philip's face as the bag half the time, she would have given up on the striking and punching drills. He was a nice enough man, but a sadistic trainer. She hoped she never had to be thankful for that fact.

Her thoughts continued to wander, making no sense. Fatigue dogged her brain. She wanted a cigarette, but didn't want it enough to make the trek outside to the smoking area.

The trip home for the catnap and shower had helped, but Sabine could tell it left her short on paying back her sleep deprivation account. On the one hand, she'd agreed to head for the safe house to appease Edward, on the other, she had done it, because bloody tired analysts were stupid analysts.

But that wasn't the problem.

She'd hit the obsessive phase of a code-breaking binge for her. At this point, she'd work till she dropped. No inanimate fucking piece of metal was going to defy her with incomprehension. She'd crack that damn code if she had to use a hammer, a chisel and several pounds of dynamite.

Third pass on her encryption solutions. Sabine felt a tickle of despair. She'd never had a solution take this long before. She could eliminate everything within the first pass on a normal encryption. And this was over three days since she started.

"Must have lost my touch," Sabine whispered to herself and jumped out of her skin when Edward spoke up from the doorway.

"You haven't lost your touch."

"How long have you been standing there?" She kept her voice even.

"Long enough. You need to take a break."

"I just had one."

"I do not call a cup of coffee and a Reese's Peanut Butter Cup a break."

Sabine stared at the floor, considering her response.

"I'll get something in a minute."

"Yes, you will. Right now. Because I'm taking you to get something to eat. Grab your coat."

Sabine was too surprised at the command to do anything other than comply. She put her jacket as she followed him out of her office.

She wondered, if I can't get a decryption, can I get an explanation?

He took her to Mel's Diner, out near Japan Town. A short drive, but still a drive. They took a booth near the back, ordered milk shakes and chili fries. For a brief moment, Sabine realized that she could almost pretend that no time had passed. That they were as they had been, out for a friendly time. But then she looked across the table and saw an older Edward Quintaine. Knew that if she looked in a mirror, she would see a much older face than the teenager she had once been who had sat in this same diner with a much younger Edward.

She hid none of her thoughts from her face. Or at least her discomfort was not hidden.

"What's bothering you?" he asked.

"The truth?"

"The truth."

"You. To be honest."

"Me."

"Yes. You."

"We share symptoms then."

"Pardon?"

"You bother me too."

Sabine digested that remark. The shakes were delivered and her coffee arrived, warm and black, unending in its cup.

"Isn't that more revealing than you wish to be?"

"Is it?"

"Don't get all damn obscure on me or I'll make you wear this coffee and then I'll be damn upset."

He laughed. He actually laughed. Sabine began to think the day full of wonders.

"If it is more revealing than I wish, well, what's done is done then. Isn't it?" he answered, the laugh still on his lips, softening lines in his face.

"I guess so," Sabine offered.

Silence on the table. She didn't even wait to crack.

"What did you want to talk about?"

"Direct as always."

"Is that a failing?"

"No. Just an observation. I wanted to talk. Yes. About Europe."

Sabine sighed.

"Could we skip it?"

He smiled again. Sabine frowned.

"Sabine! I'd think you didn't have a good time on your vacation."

"Did you have a good time?"

He sobered.

"It had its moments."

"Yeah, well, if you count moments of unremitting terror, than yeah, I had a blast. Thanks so much for asking."

"Well, in some ways, I don't have much sympathy."

Sabine considered that with a raised eyebrow.

"Excuse me?"

"Well, for two young women who insisted that they were only on vacation, you sure had a knack for hitting every single place that we had an operation or agents running."

"Excuse me?"

"You're repeating yourself."

"Yeah? So?!" Sabine's voice rose. "Explain already!"

"London."

"What about it?"

"The British Museum."

The mental arrow hit home and Sabine felt herself go numb with shock.

"That analyst was yours."

"Stuttgart you ran into one of our agents and nearly gave him heart failure."

"What? Who? We didn't—"

"The guesthouse?"

Sabine's jaw dropped. She knew without asking that he meant the helpful American they'd met over breakfast.

"Then you hit our drop in Nice…"

"Your drop? What are you talking about?" Sabine spluttered.

"The post."

"Oh, just shoot me. Fucking just kill me and get it over with." Sabine buried her face in hands and dropped to hit the table.

"Don't think I didn't think about it."

She sat up like she'd been electrocuted.

"Excuse me?"

"Why? Do I need to excuse you for something?"

"You thought about it?"

His smile vanished.

"I thought about it."

Silence again. This time, Sabine left it between them, knowing that if Edward Quintaine had seriously considered killing her; killing her *and* Ari, he'd…

"I changed my mind." His turn to not leave the silence on the table.

"Why?"

"I had to know for sure."

"Know what?"

"If you were working for the Opposition. If I had misjudged you."

Sabine's voice stayed gone again for a long moment. Too many thoughts raced through her head.

"But I hadn't," he said.

"What convinced you?"

"London the second time around. The tablet. A lot of things."

"Oh?"

"I think something…" he couldn't finish. Sabine realized it with a small shock, knowing how to finish the thought for him.

"Brought us to you. Brought me…to you. Got us involved."

"Yes."

Silences were prolific at this table, Sabine thought. Food arrived in the middle of this one. The waitress, a tall brunette, curls pulled back in a ponytail, gave the two silent booth occupants a puzzled glance when they didn't even acknowledge her when she set their fries down.

They stared at each other as the fries ran the risk of getting cold and the shakes warmed to goo.

"So."

"So," she said back just as soft. She reached for a fry and began to eat with determination.

He laughed. Short and even sweet.

"So indeed. And I decided if I'm to have you back, involved that is…" He had problems finding words, Sabine saw with another shock. "I needed to know what happened to you."

"In Europe?" She found it easier to focus on the immediate subject.

"No." He seemed to struggle a little. "In the last thirteen years."

A fry paused on a way to her mouth. Chili dripped on the table and stayed there. The fry continued its journey.

"Ah."

"So?"

"I put myself Out." Even he could hear the capital "O". "Went to school."

"College?"

"Yes. Eventually. It took some doing. My grades weren't good out of high school for some strange reason. I never did get my homework done." Edward didn't rise to the bait of this comment. They both knew why she had nearly failed high school. She hadn't been there. She'd been in small rooms in secret locations, decoding the impossible for means and ends that she knew very little about at the time.

"What did you decide to major in?"

Sabine found a detached part of her mind wondering at this whole exchange. A part of her thinking, that for anyone passing by, they'd think they were two old friends catching up.

"I was going into Radio."

"You would have been good at it."

"You say that..." Sabine couldn't finish the rest of the sentence.

"So what happened?"

"I quit."

"Why?"

"My ex basically told me to."

"Told you to." A statement, no question in tone. Sabine realized with that tone that Edward already knew all about her past. A considerable tell for him to let slip. She knew that he had done it on purpose. This was no interrogation. It was verification. Even now, no matter that he said he was convinced of, how did she describe it? She didn't know what to call it. Harmlessness? No such thing. Decent intent? Same thing.

"Yeah." The fries had no answer.. "I thought it would save us. Our relationship."

"It didn't work."

"No. It didn't. I found out giving up on your heart or your dreams, doesn't make people love you."

Silence for too long this time.

Edward was white and staring out the window.

"Edward?"

"No. It wouldn't, would it?" His color came back. "Doesn't sound like it was lucky for you."

"Yeah, well, I'm always winning the booby prize."

"The booby prize."

"Yeah." She took another bite of the fries. "What about you? Besides being married and having two kids, you had to have done something else while you've been dead."

"To be honest, not much really." Edward shifted a little. "Being dead should have been more restful though."

"You don't say."

"Yes. I do," he paused, a small frown, coming and going. "An impertinent question."

"Is that a statement or a question?"

"I have a question."

"So shoot already. I mean, ask already," Sabine corrected herself. Edward laughed, a short bark this time.

"Why did you agree to come out to eat?"

"Free food."

"That's not what I'm asking. Why have you changed your mind?"

"About what?"

"You're not glaring at me anymore."

Sabine stopped eating. At least one thing hadn't changed, she thought. He still could change subjects like turning on a dime. She frowned at the table.

"I'm too tired to be angry anymore, Edward."

"So why stay? Why work on the encryption? I know you vowed to never code break ever again. I know this is the life that you have done everything in your power to get away from. Yet here you sit. Why?"

"Don't have anything better to do," she shrugged.

"That can't be true."

"Believe it or don't, Edward. It's better than doing nothing and I don't exactly have any place or anything better to do."

"Really."

"Really. Take it or leave it."

"That's sad."

"Well, you're not exactly the Hope and Joy Patrol, yourself," Sabine snorted. "Why the third degree?"

"Unbearable curiosity," he said.

Sabine laughed well and truly for the first time.

But it was short lived.

"I'm sorry about your mother."

There was the subject change again. The laughter died on her lips. Sabine sat, cold again. Until the words had left his mouth, she realized she had forgotten about her mother. Forgotten about her death. It hit her like a punch in the chest that nearly undid her.

"What happened?" she asked.

"I don't know. I know only as much as you do."

"Can you find out?"

"You're asking me?"

"Yes."

"All right."

The waitress took the picked-over food. Sabine ordered a warm up on her coffee. She stirred it in fitful starts and stops as she had picked at the earlier food.

"I need a favor."

Sabine swallowed her coffee and did not breathe in surprise.

"Depends."

"Would you mind babysitting Jacob and Michelle?"

Sabine made a small noise.

"You want me to baby sit."

"Yes."

"Where's their usual sitter?"

"I have to send Tony out."

"That way, is it?" she asked.

"You made a request of me."

"My mother…"

"No." Whatever Edward wanted to tell her, it was again having trouble finding its way out. "The photos."

Sabine racked her brain. What the hell was he talking about?

"Oh!" she burst out. "The monstrosity!"

"Yes. The… monstrosity. They should be waiting for you when we get back."

"Oh. Oh. Good."

"Ready to go?" He was already on his feet.

"Yeah." She followed far slower.

CHAPTER XIII – BUTTERFLY AND HURRICANE

Sabine didn't see the photographs until the next day. She returned from lunch, only to have Philip drag her off for more training. At the end of that, she just went home. No matter how important the photos might be to her research, she was in no shape to give them any amount of correct attention.

Even then, she didn't see them until the afternoon. She walked in the door of her office and found Philip already there, ready and waiting, far too cheery. A morning person, she thought and shot him a venomous look. Her only plan that morning had been to find the coffee maker and to marry it.

"Good morning, Sabine!"

"Why?"

"Excuse me?"

"Why does it have to be good? And what evil have you got planned, you horrid man?" she asked, dropping her black bag on the ground next to her desk.

He laughed again and it broke through a little of Sabine's non-morning-ness.

"Shooting."

"Oh." She sat down. "Is that all?"

"Is that all? Come one, let's go!" He made a motion for the door with his head.

She stared at him.

"Right now?"

"Right now."

"But I know how to shoot."

"That remains to be seen."

Sabine opened her mouth. Thought about saying something. And then just gave him a slow, evil grin.

"Okay."

His own smile faltered a little.

"This way then."

She thought about asking him how they managed to hide a shooting range inside San Francisco city limits, a city notorious for its gun control laws, when all became clear. Philip lead her to the elevator again and a floor below the training floor. An armory waited behind a chain link cage to the left of the elevator, taking up that half of the floor (obviously not on the city's watch list) and a video shooting range taking up the other half, behind its own fence, but without the locked door. No live bullets for this range. Just blanks and noise, she figured, and a good way around the city's ordinances. She bet they even told the city that it was a "video arcade".

She let Philip gear her up. Hand her shooting headphones. Safety glasses. Just because they were blanks, didn't mean there wasn't going to be ejecting hot brass. He gave her a quizzical look from time to time when she asked no questions and merely took all he handed her. He took her to the small case (a mere five foot by five foot rack mounted on the wall just inside the fence of the range) with a sign that indicated in large red letters, "Not Live Ammunition Weapons". He pulled down a modified H&K P7 Mark XIII 9 mm pistol. Handed it to her.

Sabine had plenty of time to watch his jaw drop. She pulled the slide, dropped the magazine, checked the throat, slammed the magazine back into the grip, squeezed the grip safety and sent the slide home with a "thunk!" that brought a smile to her lips. She knew he'd been expecting her to flub the safety on the H&K. It was a quirky safety specific to that exact model of pistol, a very heavy squeeze grip, built into the front of the pistol grip. No other safety existed on the weapon. She looked down long enough to make sure the ready light on the IR sensor underneath the barrel of the pistol lit on and steady red.

But she didn't say a word.

Let him hand her the blank ammunition. Let him pop up a simple standard ring target on one of the video screens. She dropped the magazine again, loaded in thirteen rounds.

She stepped up to the firing bench and her brain emptied out.

The pistol rested in her left hand, her right hand cradling it, the barrel resting on the bench.

Years had passed since she had fired a weapon, practice or otherwise. Fear made old muscles tighten and others loosen. Felt her breathing slow. Felt her heartbeat slow as she counted the beats. Felt a part of herself watching when she breathed in. Breathed out. Felt the time dilation that always occurred when she shot a pistol. Breathed in again and...

Proceeded to fire.

The slide locked back. Empty. She put the pistol down. Stepped away from the firing bench.

Philip stared at the target.

Sabine burst out laughing.

"I told you I could shoot."

"You didn't say that you shot expert!" Philip burst out.

Sabine's smile faded. Her glance slid off him sideways to come to rest on the pistol lying on the bench.

"I thought Edward would have told you."

"Who taught you?" he burst out again, wonder and a huge smile lighting up his face.

"No one."

He saw her face. His smile leaked away like water out of a broken glass. Her face was bleak and stone.

"I've never had a lesson."

He just stared at her, so she went on, taking off her headphones and glasses, her voice dropping in volume as he followed suit.

"One day, Edward took me to the range. Put a gun in my hand. A Colt Officers Mark VII .45."

Her eyes were back on the P7 again, as if drawn by a magnet.

"He said I was an instinctive natural."

Back in her office.

Feeling cold and sick and seeing the target as clear as day in her mind's eye.

Flipped open the top file folder that had been set out for her.

And sat down. Hard.

Bodies. So many bodies, she thought dispassionately.

Started flipping through the photographs paper-clipped to the inside of the folder. Counted. It was either stay cold or get angry. Or weep. Or both. She glanced at the other side of the file. Counted names. Counted bodies in the photos. Most of the dead were not the team sent in.

So.

This was where they had recovered the tablet. Some site in Normandy, France. A bunker left over from World War II, but on entry, the team had found an SS temple, worshippers, and a guardian. A guardian that slaughtered half the team.

She dug through the file. First slowly, then with more and more intent. There were no other photos. There was no report. There was nothing on what had killed half the team. No after action report. No debrief.

Nothing.

Sabine sat back hard in her chair.

Okay, she thought in the same cold place she lived in for that moment. He had handed over the report. Why suppress this? Why keep this from her?

She was up and out of her chair before she even realized it or before conscious thought caught up with her.

She at least had conscious questions to ask when she stepped through the door of Edward's office.

"What killed them?"

Her voice sounded calm and distant even to her ears. Edward didn't look up at her in alarm. Just set his pen down and pushed his papers away. Gave her an even stare. Somehow, even though she'd given him nowhere near enough information, he answered her question.

"We don't know."

"What do you mean, you don't know?" Sabine took a seat without invitation. Crossed her ankles and prepared to wait.

"Exactly what I said. We don't know."

Sabine studied his face. Remembered things about him that she thought long forgotten. Tells that she had learned and been taught. Thought, screw it, and launched what she saw in his face.

"They don't know. But you do."

He didn't answer her.

"It killed five people. Screwed over the ones left living. Yet— There's no after action report. No debrief by the mission shrink and no first persons from the team itself. Why suppress this, Edward? Why leave me in the dark?"

"You asked to see the site. Nothing more."

She opened her mouth. Closed it.

"You're right. I did," she said and regrouped her thoughts. "You really wish to protect me that badly from this information?"

Oh, there was a break, she thought, as his face cracked. It was fast, but she saw it.

"Yes."

Oh, wow twice! she thought. *He's even telling me the truth.*

"I won't press you."

It was his turn for surprise and he leaned back in his chair, a sudden tension leaving his body.

"Thank you."

"Don't thank me. I don't know for certain that it isn't the very clue I need to crack the damn tablet. But if you think it's going to send me into the screaming heebie jeebies to know what did kill them..." She gave him a hard look before continuing. "Let's just say I think you are forgetting who I am."

She got up.

"I'm getting back to work."

Halfway down the hall, she realized that she'd just threatened him. Had to stop. Shook a little.

"Well, when the hell did that happen?" she said to no one in particular and moved on to her office.

She first spread the file photos out over the desk. Old, old habit, but she knew that she needed them out as she read.

The reading was difficult. Dry mission report on the front end and then horrifying on the back end. The forensic information alone pointed to Something, (she refused to think it a Someone), with some form of sharp something about five feet long. It had gone through the team like a thresher through wheat. At a certain point, she put the forensic data aside and just went for the atmospherics on the actual site. Threat to the contrary, even the little information that was in the file held enough to turn her stomach. Disemboweling, beheadings,... Even with the missing information, it was a little too much. She didn't think she'd be sleeping well that night.

The report referenced a bit of ancient history as spies considered such things. The recovery team had not been the first visitors. She saw a note about an operation staged in the late days of World War II.

She felt cold again.

She knew a little bit about Hitler's obsession with the occult. The site had been one of the many SS temples that he had caused to be built. But this one had been special, aside from it being on French soil and not in Germany proper like the others. The temple had been built on the site of a previous and far older pagan temple. No data on actual age of the site, because for one, they hadn't had reliable carbon dating in the 1940s and for two, no one on the cleanup crew thought to grab samples. They were spies. Not archeologists.

Sabine shook her head in dismay, because a hard, fast date on the tablet was exactly what she needed.

She needed to go bug Marcus again. And get a million books on Hitler and the occult connection. She hoped something would slap her in the face. Her algorithms went nowhere.

She glanced over at the computer. Today's algorithm, one of her own, used numbers that pushed the limits of the computational power on the mainframe. She couldn't use the truly large numbers she would have liked, because she flat out didn't have access to that kind of computer. The NSA and the NRO had that kind of access, but she didn't and paid for the lack.

But, she had a sinking suspicion that she was going about it all wrong.

A suspicion that said the tablet wasn't in code at all.

Her gaze slowed, drawn as always to the Monstrosity as permanently described in her head.

No. Her beginning suspicion was that it was in plain...something. Language.

But what language?

Because when she'd gone for a symbol match, running a basic comparison program against the database, it had come up negative. And the computer had every symbol set known to man in its archives. She'd checked. She'd asked Tony and the others.

If it were language...

It wasn't known to Man.

She closed her eyes. She was not going to give into Marcus' and Andrew's insane idea.

No Gods. No Gods, lesser or greater. She refused to even entertain the idea. Someone's made up language then. Worse and worse.

So. The Tablet remained un-cracked.

Her head hurt. She needed painkillers, more coffee and a vacation.

Oh, wait, she thought. I just got home from a vacation. Vacations are a bad idea. Fuck it.

She looked at the Monstrosity again to get her thoughts in order. It didn't help. She turned back to the desk. Saw another set of folders buried under the various photos and the reports. She fished one out.

Had a moment of déjà vu as she flipped open the cover.

Sabine stared at the photos on the inside flap. Her skin went stone cold.

Rodriguez.

Locksley.

Flores.

Hartman.

She knew these men.

Her Dreams.

And for the first time ever, Sabine saw a picture of herself. Himself. Whatever.

Captain Arthur Bredon Harrison.

She didn't have to look at the accompanying text to identify the man. The face that looked out at her from the old black and white photograph could have passed for a relative of hers. The similarity of feature stood out glaring in the image. But that wasn't what made her cold.

The same soul looked out from the eyes. Sabine knew she looked at herself. A Past.

The Dreams were true. She hadn't imagined him. She didn't want to know what it meant to find her Past in a file.

She read for hours. Stared at the earlier photos, even though they turned her stomach. She read and stared for so long that the computer had time to initialize her next algorithmic sequence. She eased her neck up and back, wondering why her eyes burned and hurt, when she finally noted that the sun had long since gone down. Thick fog had rolled in. She couldn't see the bridge.

She pushed everything out of the way on her desk, making a little spot to rest her forehead. She meant to rest her eyes for a minute.

Just a minute.

In less than a minute, Sabine Parsons fell sound asleep, dead to the world.

She almost felt used to it, the sense of reality and unreality that stood attendance with the Dream.

As always, she stood in the Beloved's presence. Zoë was nowhere in sight, tucked somewhere high in the Beloved's embrace, somewhere near the ceiling she could never see.

How strange, she thought. Zoë? Asleep?

She looked down. She wore the clothes she'd been wearing at work. Also as always, she did not question her basic acceptance of all that she saw. It merely was. She Dreamed and the Dream was.

She stepped back.

Into someone.

She spun around.

Edward.

Sabine curled into Edward's arms without thought, an impulse that in her waking world she would have denied. She buried her face into his chest. Edward wrapped his arms around her…

…then shifted into a blackened shriveled corpse, claw-like hands digging into her shoulder blades.

Sabine tried to jump away, adrenaline flooding her veins. The arms held her fast even as she struggled. Neither she nor the corpse made a sound, even though her mind screamed.

She twisted in the revenant's grasp. Gasped for air and her denied scream. Slammed her eyes closed in denial of the sight before her.

And the next instant wasn't there.

Sabine stumbled on ground in a place that looked to be as much a temple as the Beloved's. But here, grace was refused, even dark grace, in return for pomposity, if old and tattered now. She looked up and saw banners that had once been new when a house painter in Berlin decided he needed to rule the world. Now they hung torn and shredded, fire-blackened and dingy in the gray. Light came from the entrance, no other. Overcast outside of this place, Sabine determined.

In the poor light, she saw wreckage. She stood on top of a pile of rubble, great stones cracked and collapsed beneath her feet. Either time or disaster had laid low this place, and she could not tell which reason to be the cause of the destruction.

She looked to the entrance of this once grand temple done in Grecian heroic style, modeled so clearly on the Parthenon, her ear drawn by a falling stone. Saw the recovery team cross in, pause before the altar, all in good order. Each with their own line of fire.

Her head snapped back to the altar behind her. The altar that still stood intact in this place of destruction.

The Golden Tablet hung over the altar, suspended by no means that she could perceive.

And behind the altar, rose…

Her mind rebelled.

Snakes?

No.

Demons?

There are no such things, Sabine's mind insisted.

Its claws.

Then gunfire.

Sabine jerked away to someplace else.

She was taller and she wanted to vomit, because she knew who she was. Who he was.

Captain Harrison's skin hung as her own and he stood in the same temple, but new as bright morning. Brass gleamed like gold at the ends of the swastika banners, the eagles defiant and evil in their regard.

The Lodge surrounded him.

His squad was gone. Only he remained. The Tablet hung before him, unattainable, unreachable, and he knew. They had failed.

"Goodbye, Edina," Captain Arthur Bredon Harrison said, and released the detonator in his hand.

Stone came to bury him alive with the sound of thunder.

Sabine woke screaming.

Edward was there.

His hands on her shoulders.

Sabine had a horrible moment of disconnect, when she looked around and couldn't figure out her location. She started to thrash.

He held her down.

"It's all right. You're all right. You're in my office."

Sabine gasped, the scream long gone out of her, but the Dream clung to her. She could still feel the stone, dust choking her, the crushing...

She closed her eyes tight and shuddered. Threw his hands off of her shoulders with a violent wave of her hands and got to her feet so quick as to be more jump than stand. It would have been graceful too, if the blanket hadn't tangled in her legs and she nearly tumbled to her knees. Instead, she did an awkward jump and dance to disentangle herself. Stumbled to the center of the room.

"Are you all right?"

Her eyes stayed on the floor as she struggled to bring her breathing back in line.

"I'm fine."

A ludicrous lie. He didn't call her on it.

"What did you dream?"

The images came like knives. Sabine squeezed her eyes shut, then snapped them back open, refusing to give in.

"Nothing." But it came out as a gasp. "Nothing at all."

She walked out as fast as she could.

She should never have gone outside.

It was ridiculous. All she knew was she had to get out, out, out, out! The next minute, she froze on the street, not sure how she had gotten there, nor having any clear memory of walking, because now here she stood on the corner of Market and Beale. The fog hung all around, the street lights pale and febrile in its tendrils and it was the bloody middle of the night.

She wanted to kick herself.

She'd forgotten her coat. Gods, she was an idiot.

She started to turn back. She didn't give a shit if Edward were there or not, revenant from her dream or not. The cold cut too deep into her barely covered skin.

"Miss Parsons!"

That melodious voice. At this time of night? Sabine stopped in her tracks. Turned to look up Market, away from the Ferry building, and found Allejandro Corsico walking towards her, dressed impeccably in a black tuxedo, a white scarf draped around his neck.

"Mr. Corsico?"

"Sabine," he chided.

"I'm sorry. Allejandro."

"What are you doing out so late?"

"I could ask you the same question," Sabine said with a stilted laugh. "I'm an idiot and working late and I had to get a breath of fresh air, only I have just discovered that the stupid day has totally gotten away from me and it is the middle of the damn night."

"Perhaps it is time to go home then?" he suggested.

"Perhaps. I have to finish up a few things first and then get home."

"Well, if it is fresh air that you require, perhaps I can entice you to come and get a cup of coffee with me?"

Sabine was about to say yes, screw Edward and the world, when her entire skin went cold. But not the cold of fear or the cold of the night that had just been biting into her. No. This cold gave her the definition of eldritch. As in, say Yes, and Bad Things Will Happen. The words died in her throat.

"I would love to." The lies came smoother to her lips it seemed. "But you are right about me needing to get home. I'm going to get back and finish my stuff up so I can do that. Another time?" She tried a smile on him and boy, howdy, did it work.

He swept her an elegant bow with a charming smile of his own.

"I await your pleasure." There were whole depths given to that sentence in that silken voice.

She made her escape. She did go around the block three times to make sure no one followed her. The fog had turned her hair to sodden tendrils by then and had her convinced she would never be warm again.

When she got home she realized Corsico had never answered her question. He hadn't said what he was doing out at that time of night.

The question didn't linger or plague her thoughts though. If anything, the next days were a blur for Sabine. All she did was read. And forget that she had seen Corsico.

She pounded her head against the Tablet. Started ordering out for pesto pizza with all the meat in the world piled on it. Diet Coke cans began to fill her waste basket on a level that the cleaning lady began to come in twice a day.

She didn't know the day when the idea to hit up the San Francisco State archeology department for help. She just acted on it. It turned out to not pan out, but her impulse did yield her some useful information. Like, what day of the week it was.

Saturdays were not good days to find other people at work.

"It's Saturday?" Sabine blurted, not finding Marcus in the big room. Tony stood duty with a small crew.

"Some people do have lives, Sabine." he chided.

"No! No! That's not what I meant! I meant, if it's Saturday, what the hell am I doing here?" She waved her hands in front of her, trying to negate the silliness of her previous blurt.

"I've been wondering that myself."

"Oh, gods, Tony. Slap me. I'm going home. It can wait."

"Now if only the rest of the world felt the way you feel right now," Tony said and turned back to his monitors.

She knew what he meant. Intelligence matters didn't take the weekend off.

So she went home.

Stared at the ceiling in the little pink house.

She stared because, all of a sudden, she realized how bloody exhausted she felt. She had gotten to the point where she didn't want to go into IFHQ, keeping close to Edward (not really) or not, because the damn translation just wasn't coming. No algorithm. No instinct. No key.

Just miles and miles of fucking enigmatic tablet.

Her back brain started thinking again. Brought things up to the forebrain.

About her situation. About how she felt.

About her mother being dead.

The thought snuck up on her. There was no pain. Just the fact.

Her mother was dead.

She closed her eyes.

Shouldn't I feel sad? she thought. Shouldn't I be in grief? What is wrong with me? Why am I such a fucking unnatural daughter? Your best friend tells you that your mother is gone and all you have to say about it, is, oh.

Her eyes opened again, but did not see the ceiling now.

How can I feel sad? All Ari told me is that my childhood tormentor is gone.

Which led to Ari.

What was she going to tell Ari? Had told Ari already and knew wasn't the entire truth? Nothing had changed from her continuation of contact with Edward.

The Dreams had not stopped.

She had discovered nothing in any way to tell her what any of it meant.

Just like the tablet. Incomprehensible data. If she could find the key, she knew it would all decrypt into total and clear information, explanation. The why of her Dreaming. The why of Edward's continued living. Even, the why of the Illuminated Brotherhood and an explanation of their plans.

But she remained no closer to that than decrypting the damn tablet.

Ari picked up her phone's handset on the third ring, having run from the bath tub to answer it.

"Hello?"

"Am I really a butthead or am I just imagining that I am a butthead?"

Ari laughed. Sabine on her phone at last.

"You're really a butthead. But I don't hold it against you."

"You don't?"

"Nope. What's up?"

"Nothing. It's Saturday. What are you doing?"

"I was taking a bath."

"I got you out of the tub? I'm sorry."

"Don't you dare. I knew it was important, that's why I got out. Besides, four hours should be long enough for a bath," Ari said.

Sabine's turn to laugh.

"You and your impossibly long baths."

Silence fell on the line for a moment. Neither of them could find words. Or, too much wanted to be said and neither of them could figure out where to start.

"So," Ari started.

"Yeah. So. Album by Peter Gabriel."

A small laugh from both of them but then, another awkward silence.

"I just wanted to hear your voice."

"Me too," Ari offered.

"That's all. I should go."

"Okay."

Ari let her friend hang up the phone after a stilted goodbye. Looked at the silent telephone for five minutes. Resisted the urge to get in her car, dressed only in a towel, drive over to the house she had scouted out and pound on the door.

Monday came and found Sabine sitting in her office. Staring at the tablet. It felt not like much change from staring at her ceiling.

Edward found her that way. Sabine allowed him to distract her attention, which wasn't hard, because his expression read less than the metal before her.

"Sabine," Edward said, but did not continue.

Sabine sat back in her chair. She'd been leaning forward, her elbows on her knees, her chin in her hands when he'd come in. She chose open body language. Didn't even cross her legs. Just kept both feet planted on the floor and looked at him.

"Edward. What can I do for you?"

"Do you remember my request from a week or so ago?"

Sabine's forehead creased in a frown.

"I'm sorry," she said. "I'm blanking."

"Baby-sitting my children."

"Right! Right. Kids. Baby sit. Yes. I remember. What about it?"

"I had been planning on asking you to do it this weekend, while Tony and Andrew follow a lead out of town." He didn't continue.

It was starting to become a habit, Sabine thought.

"I hear a 'but' in there somewhere." Sabine filled in.

"My wife," There were undertones to that word that Sabine could not catch to comprehend. "Wishes to meet you before she allows you to baby sit the children."

"Understandable. I could be an axe wielding maniac."

"Yes, but Michelle would enjoy that."

It took Sabine a minute to realize that Edward had made a joke. She blinked in surprise.

"Okay."

"There's a small cocktail party at the house tonight. Could you please attend?"

Such formal language. It scared her. A little.

"Sure," she answered.

Only later, when she had the address in her hand and thought about what she was going to wear that evening, did several things click.

She was going to meet his wife.

She was going to find out where he lived.

It turned out to be a beautiful white house in the Seacliff neighborhood of the city. Columns, but not neo Greek or Southern architecture. The kind of building that only seemed to show up in San Francisco and screamed, money! Unlike other neighborhoods in the city, she'd even found parking less than a block away. What little yard it had was sculpted green bushes. No flowers.

A long and wide hall lead up to the massive black double doors of the building and Sabine paused before she stepped into the light of the entryway. Smoothed her black sheath of a dress. It was plain and near dowdy, but when she'd ransacked her closet, she'd discovered that she owned no evening wear, except for the leopard print that had seen so much fun and a brawl in London. She just knew it wasn't appropriate. So she'd dragged out the dowdy black.

She straightened the dress again. Wondered why she was so nervous. What the hell was she doing lurking in the shadows?

"Sabine?"

"Phillip?" Sabine squeaked and hated herself for squeaking.

The man in question stepped out of an alcove she hadn't spotted, wearing a blue suit, a small ear bug in his ear that Sabine spotted right away.

Oh yes, IFHQ hadn't rubbed off on her or woken up any old habits, oh no, she thought and calmed the butterflies in her stomach.

"You look…nice." He gave her a smile. She wondered over the hesitation that he had before the word, "nice".

"Thank you." No squeak this time.

"They're expecting you."

"Joy."

Phillip called after her.

"What?" She turned, not having heard his words.

"Don't let her rattle you." He stepped back into the alcove.

Sabine turned again for the door, frowning again. Warnings. She didn't like it one bit.

Which meant that she still frowned when the door opened. It left her cursing mentally for the damn lapse at not having her damn Game Face on.

The house was Spartan, if expensive in its furnishings. Neutral oak furniture. White cushions seen through the arch of the entry hall. She stepped into the formal front room. A group of black suited individuals milled around, polite chit-chat filling the air. No one even turned to look at her entry. A quick scan spotted embassy people of various countries. She hadn't been out of the game so long that she couldn't spot politicos when she saw them.

"Sabine."

She didn't jump. She realized she'd been expecting Edward to sneak up on her.

"Edward." She didn't turn around.

"Thank you for coming."

She kept herself from frowning by force of will.

"You're welcome."

"Come with me."

She followed him through the throng to the opposite side of the room. Someone held court in the center of a group of polite people. The queen of this court was a cool blonde, her hair done in an up do only achieved through professional hair styling. Diamond studs in the ears and a simple black dress that by its very simplicity made Sabine's look like a sack. Blue eyes the color of dark sapphires and flawless skin. Perfect black satin pumps on her feet. Small feet.

Sabine closed her eyes a brief second. Why didn't it surprise her that this woman was perfect?

A lull in the conversation and the group broke apart as the blonde spotted Sabine and Edward. She advanced towards them and stopped a distance close enough for private conversation, but not receptive.

Sabine kept herself from shaking her head in irritation. She did not need her damn spook senses coming back from retirement in such fucking force. She was here to baby sit, for Crom's sake!

"Miss…Parsons, is it?" The cool blonde held out an immaculate manicured hand.

Sabine felt her mouth want to curl into a snarl and had to work to keep anything from showing on her face.

Like that, was it?

"Sabine, please." Sabine kept her tone professional.

"Sabine." Another slight in there somewhere, in that tone.

Sabine had never heard her name pronounced in such a way that she felt you could rhyme it with swine.

There was conversation. No content. Sabine found herself out on the sidewalk not even an hour later, her trench back on and trying for the life of her to figure out what the hell Phoebe Quintaine had wanted from her.

"So."

Much later that night, if Sabine could have known, she would have gotten an answer to her confusion.

"That's your precious code breaker."

Phoebe Quintaine stood , still elegant in the civilized mess of a done party.

"Someone's been talking out of turn again, I see," Edward said with no inflection.

"By all means. Have her baby-sit." She turned to go to the main staircase curving up from the back of the front room. "Too bad she's so plain."

Which left Edward in the front room with the dead party.

Edward looked toward the front hall and the door.

"Plain?" he said and a small curve of a smile touched his lips.

But of course, to Phoebe, Sabine would seem plain, he thought. Just a trace of makeup. Just the clean lines of that face, the strength of her eyes... He cut short the thought. Didn't think how a cheap dress, old and unfashionable, had clung to the athletic form of someone used to walking and running outside, not in some hamster wheel of a physical fitness gym somewhere.

No, thinking of sun touched skin would not do at all.

He went up to his own room to shut the door, and sleep alone, once he finished turning off all the lights.

ㄱＦＶㄱﾄㄱ

In her own bed, Sabine barely set her head on her pillow when the Dream surfaced from the bottom of the lake of sleep. It pulled her in and under.

For a change, she sat on the floor of the great chamber, her knees drawn up to her chest, her arms resting on the top of the knees. Her back away from the Beloved's sanctuary, she looked out over the great hall, taking in the great columns. Her legs chilled in the great vastness of it all, since she wore only the black t-shirt she'd gone to bed in.

My feet are always cold when I am here, wandered through her head.

The Beloved. Coils uncurling from the silk sound of it.

Sabine turned her head to see Zoë lowered to her level, the Beloved as always so gentle in its handling of this child.

"Hello, Zoë," Sabine said, as always knowing that somehow, her Dreaming self, endangered Zoë somehow.

"Hello." Zoë's voice was soft and tentative. Not the voice of another Oracle with dire warnings. A child's voice.

Sabine frowned both in Dream and in sleep.

"What are they like?"

Too late, the frown returned, but this was not the frown from earlier in the evening. Confusion this time, not anger.

"Who they?"

Zoë made such a child sound that Sabine almost couldn't connect it with this naked woman child held in the coils of the beautiful monstrosity she knew as the Beloved.

"Michelle. Jacob."

Understanding flowed into Sabine. With it came a pain that she knew to be sorrow.

So much sorrow lately. Her mother's death and now… A child, who owned no childhood, asked after other children. Except that Sabine had a suspicion based on no real information, that the children in question had no more of a normal childhood than Zoë's. Though Zoë's childhood, lack of a childhood, whatever you called it, could not be compared to anyone's. Not even Sabine's own lack of a childhood.

"Michelle and Jacob are…" Sabine groped for the words. "I don't know them real well, Zoë."

"You know them." Zoë's whisper voice cut in.

Sabine stopped. She nodded, acknowledging that from the first time Michelle had come in her office, yes… There had been some kind of recognition, recognition of kindred souls, no matter the difference in age.

"They are lonely. Like you," Sabine paused. "Like me. Their father loves them, but their mother…"

"You know what you know," Zoë said the words Sabine found she could not say, but thought; said them again. "You know what you know."

"Yes. I do. Their mother does not love them at all. I know how they feel."

"But they have a father…"

"Yes. They do at that."

Zoë broke the silence that fell for a long moment.

"I don't know who my parents are."

Sabine's face remained impassive not from lack of emotion, but from feeling too much, all at once. No room for all of it on her face.

"I would say that is a sad thing, except for the fact that I think it might be better not to know."

"But I don't know who I am!"

Such a cry. It could have come from a dying bird.

Sabine was on her feet before she could even think. Her body invading the coils, till her arms held Zoë, coils of the Beloved or not.

And the coils did not repel her. The Beloved wrapped around Sabine, where she clutched Zoë to her chest.

She spoke to the top of Zoë's head.

"I know all I need to know about you and about me," she said, fierce and steady.

Zoë's arms wrapped around her, tight, yet Sabine found the breath to speak.

"You and I..." she couldn't go on. Just clutched Zoë harder.

"You and I," she started again. "We are different, yes. No one can see this and not at least think different. But I do know what I know, Zoë. You are a part of me and I am a part of you. I know this as certain as I know things when I am here with you. I don't know how that relates us. It doesn't matter."

She pulled back enough to look into Zoë's eyeless face that even so stared unerringly back into Sabine's own.

"Remember this, Zoë. Family in the end is not who you are related to, who gave you genetic birth," she paused to see if she were understood. "You choose your family, Zoë. The way I choose you now."

Sabine stood like that for a long time, her arms cradling Zoë, the Beloved cradling them both.

Time took her, with no perception of passing, till the day that she had promised to baby-sit Jacob and Michelle rolled around.

At the safe house, she packed her black bag with a few books, including a book of fairy tales. She didn't know if the children felt they were too old for stories or not, but she'd always found them better at entertaining children than any videotape or DVD. She had baby-sat five boys once at the age of fifteen, where the parents had thought that renting The Last Unicorn, which since it was animated, made it a children's movie. Only they had not ever heard of Peter S. Beagle, the original writer of the story. Sabine had ended up having to remove the two oldest boys from beating on the youngest and had in the end, resorted to her book of fairy tales, young boys being not at all interested in a story of love and regret meant for older minds.

But Hansel and Gretel always found a willing audience. Especially the versions that Sabine had.

It had been handed down to her from her grandmother, a woman she had never met, an original book of the Brothers Grimm from the turn of the century. All the stories. But not the ones that made it into cheery books with red covers and gilt binding.

This had the old nightmares. The darks and shadows that lived in the Black Forest. The tales that had grown from the terrors of the 100 Years War. Where a wicked step mother danced in shoes heated red hot by the forge at the wedding of the rightful princess. Where Death played his part and birds were always the messengers of the gods.

Where most of all, the true of heart and steadfast of spirit found a way through the darkest of nights.

These stories had given Sabine hope, even in the days when she had been enclosed in the monastic fastness of the intelligence community of her youth. She had turned to them again and again over the years. The message never failed to move her.

They always started the same.

They all, in a way, had the same message.

Not all is what it seems, and even the unlikeliest and ugliest of creatures, could hold the greatest gift of all.

Hope.

And a future worth having.

Just as Sabine stepped up to the house in San Francisco and the expectation of two children, a half world away, Andrew Wenton and Tony Ramirez sat in a rented BMW sedan the color of the leaden sky above them. They both stared through the windscreen at a castle straight out of fairy tale. Or nightmare.

Forest nestled against the great gray blocks, the castle stone a darker tone of the prevailing gray of the sky. The dark green of the trees in the fading day gave it the look of a place under a shroud.

Andrew dropped the binoculars in his lap.

"Yes."

Tony, who sat the driver's seat, had asked a question over half an hour before. The question had been prompted by them tailing a black sedan that had led them to this medieval pile.

"Well," Tony sighed. "Now we know where they live."

"Yeah."

"Edward's going to be thrilled."

Andrew went back to watching through the binoculars.

"Oh, he is."

Because they'd finally found the Malice Twins...

...And one of the home bases for the Lodge of the Midnight Sun.

The Malice Twins were found in between the time it took Sabine to step up one step from the street and too soon to stand at Edward Quintaine's front door. Where the man himself met her in the foyer of the great house and took her coat and hung it in the hall closet then asked to take her bag.

"No. That's fine," Sabine answered. "It stays with me."

"I hope you didn't bring work with you?" Edward asked, his hand dropping to his side as if he had never offered it.

"No, no. Nothing like that. Books. Whoever you had unpack my stuff was kind enough to unpack it all in alphabetical order, the way it had been on the shelves at the old place."

"Glad we could be of help."

Sabine knew she would have thought of some kind of snappy retort at that point, except that Phoebe walked up. Her arrival cut short any witty comeback Sabine could have generated.

"Ah... Sabine." The unspoken, but so clearly heard condescension.

Sabine gritted her teeth and then forced herself to stop.

"So glad you could make it. Truly, you're a life saver, I'm sure." Phoebe continued.

"I doubt it. Sabine replied with a closed smile. "It's only a small thing to baby-sit."

"Well, you say that now. The children are upstairs in the family room watching TV." Phoebe waved a hand behind her. "They're relatively self-sufficient. I don't know why Edward insists on them still having a sitter at their age."

Sabine did not know how she kept her eyebrows for jumping for her hairline. In her shock, her memory supplied her own father's voice, saying she didn't need a sitter anymore.

After all...

She was six.

Sabine went ahead and indulged in grinding her teeth for a moment.

"I'm sure I don't know," she managed to say instead, her smile brittle.

Sabine stayed in the hall until Edward and Phoebe left. Edward's parting gift was a list. Contact numbers for everyone and everything. Hospital. Children's doctor. 24 hour pharmacy. Edward planned it like any op.

On the one hand, Sabine found it a comfort and on the other, found it a sadness.

She dropped the list in the hall on a waiting credenza, along with her bag but she gently pulled out her grandmother's book.

"Hello, Sabine!" Michelle chirped from behind her.

Sabine did not spin around. She finished taking out the book. Gave Michelle a lopsided grin when she did turn around.

"Hello, moppet." It popped out before she could stop it.

Michelle loved it, her face splitting into a huge grin as she bounced up.

"You're here!"

"So I am. Where's Jacob?"

"He's watching something on the Discovery channel." Michelle made a face. "It's boring."

"Why's it boring?" she asked instead.

"It's about mummies."

"Ah."

"Come on!" Michelle grabbed Sabine's free hand and dragged her upstairs.

Sabine thought the quick pass through the house would have given her more of an insight into Edward's life. No dice. All the doors in the upstairs hall were shut, except for two. The hall itself opened up further down into the so-called family room, a different design, not being on the ground floor. There, indeed, Jacob sat glued to the large screen television and some archeology show with all the intentness of a graduate student at a Ph.D. lecture.

"Sabine's here!"

"I know," Jacob said and looked up apologetically. "It's mummies."

Sabine knew the whole of it right there. A boy's apology consisted of never saying the words I'm sorry, but did consist of explaining why they couldn't do something polite, like stand up and say hello.

"Mad for them, eh?" Sabine gave him one of her ready grins. "Michelle and I will be right as rain. Enjoy your mummies."

Sabine had never seen him smile till that moment.

Michelle dragged Sabine off to a bedroom, through the door that opened off the right hand side of the hall. Whoever had decorated the room had believed that girls, all girls, liked pink. And lots of it. Sabine hoped she wouldn't be permanently blinded by the brightness of it all.

"What's that?" Michelle pointed at the ancient book cradled in Sabine's other arm.

"A book."

"I see that!" Michelle protested to Sabine's amusement. "What's in it?"

"Old stories. Know the Brothers Grimm?"

Michelle shook her head.

"What? No? What about Hansel and Gretel?"

Another no.

"Didn't anyone ever read to you?"

A final shake.

Sabine kept the sadness from her face with iron resolve.

"Well, no time like the present." This time she took Michelle's hand and together they climbed on to the pink draped canopy bed.

Sabine pulled Michelle up half on to her lap and opened the book. It fell open to her favorite.

"All the best stories start only one way…" she began, hearing even so an echo to her own voice that she ignored.

"How?"

"Once upon a time…"

She stepped out of Michelle's room much, much later. One story had turned into many. Her grandmother's book had once more found a believer.

And apparently two.

She stopped one step out, the door half shut behind her where she had just tucked in Michelle who had fallen asleep somewhere in the middle of "The Brave Little Tailor".

Jacob sat on the floor in his PJs. Asleep.

She put the book on the floor.

He was large, but she managed to carry him to bed in the room across the hall, done in shades of blue for the same reason that Michelle's was done in pink. Tucked him in.

When she came back, the book lay open.

"Zoë?" Sabine whispered.

Only a feeling against her skin.

She looked down.

It lay open to her favorite story again, the one that she had loved above all others from the first time her mother had read them to her, when her mother had been... almost sane.

Godfather Death.

CHAPTER XIV – SABINE'S THEOREM

I really, really, really hate his wife.

Another letter to Ari. The words flowed out of her pen without thought, but staring at them in black and white, Sabine sighed at the inherent truth of the statement.

"Fuck," she said.

All it would take was one photocopy of the letter and Edward would be all over her.

After a moment's more thought, she bent back to writing, her left elbow propped on the great oak desk, the rest of her bent double over the page. She didn't need her nose six inches from the page, but it was how she wrote long hand.

The words began to spool out again. A part of her brain noted how loopy and messy her handwriting had become, when once upon a time, it had been regimental in its neatness.

And then her attention was once more captured by her writing.

She's a bitch, the words continued. *An unfeeling cow that clearly has had children for the status they confer, not for the desire, the human desire for immortality and progeny. I mean, Michelle's room is pink. Pink! Not by choice!*

When she finished, she topped out at eighteen pages of letter. Postage was going to excessive. Luckily, she didn't have to pay for it.

She made her usual pilgrimage to the photocopier. Folded up the one for Ari and took the copy. But instead of heading for the postal drop box, she headed for Philip's office.

Luck went her way. He was in his office. She rapped once on the open door and waited for him to acknowledge her. Which he did, a huge smile stretching his face. His glasses had slid to the end of his nose, from staring at the papers in front of him.

Sabine took a moment to take in the Spartan neatness and organization of his office. A few commemorative plaques hung on the walls for service to his country and one, exactly one, spider plant sat on the bookshelves under the window behind him in an unadorned terra cotta pot. She thought about getting him more, in the way her mind tried to distract her when she had something difficult to accomplish.

"What do you think of Phoebe Quintaine?" Sabine asked, figuring a direct assault the only solution.

Philip's smile didn't disappear, but it did freeze. He put down his pen and neatened his papers.

Buying time, Sabine thought, but waited. She was learning a lot of patience with this job.

"Why do you ask?"

She tossed the copy of her letter on his desk. "This can't get to Edward."

"What's this?" he asked with that still open smile and pretended lack of comprehension.

"My usual letter to Ari Doran. Don't even go there with me," she said, finding a laugh in her somehow. "I'm serious. This one can't get to Edward."

"Why?" His smile left, full attention and seriousness brought to her.

"It's my unadulterated opinion of the woman and I see no reason how it affects what I'm doing here. More importantly, it can only hurt Edward. He doesn't need to know."

"And I do?"

"I know you won't let me ship one piece of scrap paper to Ari without forensics combing it with an electron microscope, tweezers and a huge jar of paranoia."

He laughed.

"True," he paused. "But what do you care? So it hurts him. What of it?"

She'd seen this one coming. Planned on it, even.

"I don't need him on my case when I'm trying to crack code. I'm asking a favor, Philip. I'm offering to owe you big time."

This was old, old stuff in the fraternities, the owing of favors and the exchange of information. Sabine knew this game from long ago. She might have been rusty at it, but she knew Philip wasn't. She didn't know if her owing him a favor was worth shit or not, but it was her only card to play. And the truth was...

She didn't know why she cared if it hurt Edward or not. Okay, besides the obvious one that she felt more for the man than she thought or wanted to, but there was more to it than that. It was important he not know this thing. She felt it in her bones. It crept on her skin and it was Sabine's turn to freeze inside.

Shit, she thought cold and clear. It was like the weather. She felt, she fucking *felt* and knew that this one thing was bad for Edward to know.

The way she had known the things she'd known in Europe.

It shook her. She hadn't felt anything in weeks. And now, here it was, over a letter. A stupid letter, written on floral paper that was just the ramblings of one pissed off analyst.

But apparently there was more to it than that after all.

Philip saw something in her face. He pushed his glasses up and took the copy.

"Deal."

"What? No negotiation?" Sabine joked.

He grinned back at her, folding the letter and dropping it in his middle desk drawer.

"Nope. I think owning a favor from you is just fine."

"Well, we'll see," Sabine said with a grin and then followed it in dead seriousness. "Thank you, Philip."

"You're welcome, Sabine."

And that was that.

Sabine went back to her office. Dropped Air's letter in the box on the way there. Sat down. Continued to stare at the Monstrosity.

She didn't stay late. Left while the sun still rode the sky and stepped out on to the sidewalk outside International Filmworks nondescript gray concrete building. Looked up for the first time in ages and stopped in her tracks.

A flash of iridescent light disappeared into a hungering darkness.

The fog rolled in over Twin Peaks. Dark, ugly, gray fog and above her, with no explanation for its being there, a rainbow. A fragmented rainbow being devoured before her eyes.

She could not move.

First the letter.

Now this rainbow.

It's all going to go to shit now, isn't it? She thought from a great distance away.

That night, laying down for sleep, the Dream waited. She was not surprised.

Nor could anything prepare her for it.

She flew.

The ground, a patchwork beneath her, and neither plane nor animal wings surrounded her to give her this benefit of flight. She merely flew. In that place that she now called the Dream, she questioned nothing. The wind blew warm on her face. The sun warmed her back. She soared above clouds and land and in the blink of an eye, out over a great ocean.

She did not know if this were the so-called real world or not. She knew that she flew. Her heart soared, as it had never done in her entire life. She felt so free.

She began to weep.

She flew what seemed for hours. Soared above the grass lands of a veldt, skimmed the waves of a great ocean and went so high to a mountain's peak that she gasped for breath in the thin air.

When her eyes opened the next morning, they were sticky with tears. Tears from a grief that her flesh found itself bound to the Earth once more by gravity's chains.

It made no sense. She blinked in the early morning light as she turned off her little radio alarm clock, shutting off the strains of Rachmaninov's Variation on a Theme by Paganini, this morning's choice of the Classical station. She put her bare feet on the dark brown carpet of her bedroom and just sat a moment on the edge of the bed.

Broken rainbows had meant warning before, hadn't they? The Dreams that followed them always terrible.

Until now, when all she had dreamt was flight.

She rubbed her eyes, the tears not yet dry.

Was it not a terrible dream? A dry voice in her mind questioned. Was not being robbed of flight a terrible thing?

Days passed. The Monstrosity remained un-cracked. Philip continued to train Sabine every other day in unarmed combat, though no repeat at the range.

When she brought it up he muttered that he only needed to be humiliated twice. Why his comment of, twice, she'd been unable to fathom.

Another day dawned. She went into work. Sat at the desk. Wrote in her log book. Stared at the Monstrosity.

But this day had plans for her. It had plans to be Different.

Different turned out to be a hysterical Michelle.

One minute, Sabine sat in her own impersonation of a Tibetan monk contemplating a deep and difficult mandala, in this case the tablet, sitting with her knees drawn up in the big leather chair in her office.

The next minute, Michelle hurtled in, hiccupping with sobs.

Sabine didn't think. She merely opened her arms and Michelle threw herself into them in a straight run. She hit Sabine with all her fifty pound frame. Sabine suppressed a "woof" as all the air was forced out of her lungs.

"What's wrong?" Sabine cried, as the little girl shook with sobs.

No answer.

"Honey, sweetie, what's wrong?" Sabine's own distress rose as Michelle continued to not answer.

Sabine did a mental inventory. Edward? No. Jacob? Too nice a sibling. Phoebe? Her mind stalled, not wanting to consider the fact.

"Ma– ma— mommy doesn't love – me!" Michelle hiccupped out.

That confirmed that, Sabine thought and squeezed tighter.

"What happened, Michelle?"

"Na— na— nothing." The sobs were starting to space out, but Sabine didn't let go.

"Honey, something happened."

Michelle, trying to hold in her sobs, turned a tear-streaked face up to Sabine and choked a little.

"It was Jacob." This came out without any hiccups interrupting it, for which Sabine was grateful.

"What about Jacob?"

"Mommy's just mean! She's so mean to him! And I'm too small to stop her! I can't!" The hysteria ramped up again.

Sabine knew she had to do something, quick.

"Hon, honey! Honey!" That seemed to get through and hysteria was averted. "It's not your job to stop anyone. What did your mother do?"

Michelle shook her head, tangled blond hair flying everywhere.

"She was mean! So mean!"

It went on like that for another half an hour. Sabine couldn't get a straight answer. She thought of calling for Edward or even finding Jacob, but in the end, she did neither.

For once, she did the only thing that she could think of which was what Ari would have done.

She made a pot of tea.

Took Michelle by the hand and unearthed the teapot that Ari had sent what seemed like forever and a day ago.

The appearance of the teapot turned into the smartest thing Sabine did all day. Michelle loved the purple and blue roses painted on the teapot and cups. She very carefully carried the pot to the kitchen to warm it for the tea.

Sabine carried it back, since a ten cup teapot is a heavy thing indeed when fully laden. Michelle took the sugar packs and found spoons. By the time all got laid on the floor of Sabine's office (paper towels pretending as picnic blanket), Sabine had even coaxed out Michelle's usual sunny smile.

But Sabine wasn't fooled.

Broken rainbows plagued her mind for the rest of the week. It kept her company while as she stared at the Monstrosity for yet another day in a row.

When Edward came into her office, she didn't even acknowledge him. Rainbows and children with childhood hurts occupied too much of her attention. To shut them out, she focused all her intensity on the Monstrosity, as if her eyes could bore the code's answer out.

"Busy?"

"Y'know, if you sit here long enough and stare at it, it's like looking at clouds. You start to see pictures."

He cocked an eyebrow.

"See anything interesting?"

"Nope. Just images of me pounding my forehead into it till my brains leak out my nose." She leaned back and gave him her attention. "What can I do for you, Edward?"

"I need another favor."

Sabine didn't know if she liked the way he smiled. It made her insides knot up. Hard. And Michelle immediately sprang back in her mind. She didn't know if she should or could say anything.

"Okay," she said slowly. "As always, the caveat is, what kind of favor?"

"You were a huge success with Michelle and Jacob. Think you can handle another dangerous operation babysitting them?"

"Hmm. I don't know," she frowned. "Terribly high risk there."

He actually bought it. His smile faltered.

Sabine couldn't help it. She laughed. So much for my Game Face, she thought.

"I'll do it!" she said between giggles. "Oh, I can't believe you bought it."

"You would believe that I bought it if you had any idea what the two of them have done to their five previous babysitters who were not Andrew or Tony," he said with obvious relief.

"Oh?"

"I believe the worst one was when they had a poor 18 year old college student convinced that the house had been exposed to radioactive bacteria and they had to be evacuated. To the movie theater."

"Oh ho!" Sabine giggled. "Well, that doesn't entirely surprise me. Jacob is smart as a whip."

"Yes, but he can't do the large innocent eyes trick."

"Michelle?"

"I worry about the young men in her future."

"I suggest a padlock on the front door and a shotgun."

"I already have the shotgun picked out." This time his deadpan look was better than hers.

"Well, no worries in the meantime. I'd be delighted. They're wonderful kids."

"I…" he faltered again; a day of firsts as far as Sabine could tell. "I am glad you think so."

He turned for the door abruptly and just as abruptly turned back.

"It's a party. We're hosting some embassy types for meet, greet and drinks. I don't know if you have any evening clothes or not. If you need a credit chit, pull one from Philip. He'll set you up and give you date and time."

And he was gone, leaving Sabine to have that last fact sink in like a stone. A full five minutes passed before the import of his words struck home. Sabine was out of her chair before she'd even realized it.

Sabine stared into her empty-ish closet an hour later. A pile of clothes lay at her feet. She threw one more shirt off of a hanger onto the pile.

She kept throwing clothing on the pile. The search for a dress or slacks and blouse that would pass muster for an embassy party had turned into a Spring cleaning, minus the Spring.

The task guaranteed to make her sick to her stomach.

By the time she finished, she kept a few silk shirts. That was it.

Sabine stared at the pile.

Her stomach knotted again, this time in anger.

When had she let herself go?

Karma, Ari would say. Sabine agreed at a certain level, but it made it no more comprehensible. In some ways, less. She usually avoided annoying karma.

The closet looked decidedly bare, but Sabine felt better. She could not appear at any of the events or gatherings that Edward clearly expected her to attend with what remained though.

She needed to go shopping and bad. A stop at Philip's office on her way out in a mad dash for home had informed her that these shindigs were often. Sabine had panicked.

No clothing.

Multiple parties on the horizon.

Which meant she absolutely had to call Ari.

Five hours later and two malls, Sabine and Ari sat outside a cafe, sipping their respective espresso and tea. Sabine smoking and ignoring the glares of the non-smokers at the other tables. She was running out of her Silk Cuts. She'd have to find a smoke shop. There were no vending machines with British cigarettes in San Francisco.

"Thank you for coming out to play with me," Sabine said around a deep lungful of smoke.

"What? And miss a chance to spend lots of money? " Ari grinned. "Besides I got to spend money on you too and you know how much I love to buy presents."

"True, true."

"So why the mad spending spree?"

Sabine didn't answer at first.

It was enough for her that not once had Ari asked why. Not why the phone call out of the blue or any other question, related to Edward or not. And everything related to Edward. The very fact that Ari had asked no questions till that moment was a gift. Well, she couldn't avoid it.

"Let me get another espresso first."

"Okay."

Sabine returned with another espresso with alacrity and lit up another cigarette.

"Well, there's the obvious answer of that I didn't have a thing to wear after I cleaned out my closet," Sabine replied after taking her first sip from round two of caffeine death.

"And the not so obvious answer?"

"I'll be damned if I look like white trash next to Phoebe Quintaine," Sabine said with a straight face.

"Ah, jealousy!" Ari said with a grin.

"Worse. I want the bitch dead."

"Any reason other than the previous ones given?"

"No. Well, yes. Edward I can understand why she treats like shit. But…" Sabine trailed off.

"What happened?"

"I had Michelle come running into my office the other day, in tears. She was crying so hard she had the hiccups."

"Why?" Ari was aghast.

"I didn't entirely understand, to be honest," Sabine replied with a crease between her eyebrows, the forced emotions replaced by clear pain. "You know how it is. Kids can be so direct, but leave out 90% of what's going on because to them, it's self-evident. What I gathered is that Phoebe said something really cutting and demeaning about Jacob and when Michelle defended him, after all, he is her brother, Phoebe cut into her somehow too. I don't know what about. I just kept getting the, she's mean, she's mean, kind of thing. Oh yeah, and doesn't love her. That kind of thing."

Ari paled through Sabine's answer. Only a very little of her color had returned when Sabine came to the end.

"I see why you would be upset. But I don't see what this has to do with shopping."

"I know. Doesn't seem to be a connection, does there? But there is," Sabine finished but did not elaborate.

"Are we going to have to play twenty questions?" Ari asked, her color back along with a little of her humor. "It can't be that bad."

"Yeah, it can," Sabine answered firmly. "Edward's acting like I'm the answer to his friggin' prayers in relation to his children, the children in question apparently think I'm the best thing since sliced bread and the wife… Well, the wife apparently thinks I'm a frump and yet…"

Sabine struggled with the next words, hating herself for having to admit this, but to Ari, there were no lies. There had to be one place in the world that she told the truth, and that place was wherever Ari Doran stood.

"I won't get between a woman and her children, Ari."

"No matter how much you might hate her."

"Okay, I hate her. But you know what I mean. Kids are impressionable. I don't want to give them ideas or influence them against their parents! That would be wrong!"

"Kids can't be that easily influenced," Ari pointed out. "Neither of us were."

"You're right. They're not. I guess I'm just scared," Sabine acknowledged.

"Yeah. Well, you have every right to be."

"You're not making me feel better."

Ari shrugged in frustration, letting out a short burst of air in a cut off sigh.

"Honey, I don't mean to make it any worse. But I still don't see what this has to do with shopping."

"Pride. Stupid prideful vanity," Sabine answered. "I'm expected to be at all these parties. Half of the work is being done undercover at these entertainment parties. The kids are there a lot too because they're usually held at the house. I guess, I guess, I just want to look my best for them. It feels like I'd be letting them down somehow if I don't look as good as their mother."

"That's not real smart to be competing with Phoebe on something like that. Shouldn't you just be yourself?"

"Well, if you noticed, everything I bought was distinctly me. I'm not trying to compete. I guess it's just an image thing. I want to live up to their image of me. Hell, of my image of me. As someone they can look up to. So when I looked in my closet to try to find something to wear to the big shindig nonsense, I realized there wasn't a single nice thing in my closet that portrayed who I really am. I didn't have any money for so long, I just hadn't bought anything new or that wasn't regular clothes. "

Ari scowled briefly at that, nodding. But then Ari's expression softened.

"Well, there's nothing wrong with being a child's champion. I know how much it meant to me to have Uncle David."

"Yeah. I figured you would, if anyone would."

"It's okay, Sabine," Ari finally said, answering the question that Sabine held unspoken. "It's okay to be yourself."

"I'll take you word for that," Sabine growled and stubbed out her cigarette, having forgotten to smoke the rest of it, ash hanging long off the stub.

"Now come on, don't be a grouch just because some kids have chosen you to be their champion."

"But I don't even like kids!" Sabine protested.

Ari just laughed harder.

Sabine threw up her hands and finished her espresso. Ari subsided into occasional giggles.

"Though, y'know, sweetie, you probably shouldn't be telling me where all the work gets done. I may have to crash," she said coquettishly, rubbing her hands together with accompanying melodrama.

"Why do you think I'm telling you?" Sabine asked. "I want you to crash!"

"You do?" Confusion gripped Ari.

"Yes! You don't think I want to go in there without backup, do you? I do not call an eight and six year old, back up, do you?" Sabine asked.

"But, ahem, my affiliations as it were…" Ari gestured emptily, nonplussed.

"What of it? If Edward doesn't like your fraternity getting involved, he can just kiss my ass! Personally I don't think it's such a bad idea to have things spread out. Share the misery and all that. But most of all, I want back up that no one can control, not even him. That means you, sweet cheeks," Sabine said.

"Well, if you put it that way."

"I do. I want you there, Ari. Please say you'll come."

Ari thought about it for all of a nanosecond.

"Okay! But I haven't a thing to wear!" she announced in her best Jewish American Princess voice.

"Oh well, there's only one thing to fix that," Sabine returned deadpan and then broke into a huge grin. "More shopping!"

They both burst into giggles.

More shopping finished with a trip to their favorite occult shop in the Lower Haight district of San Francisco. Curios had been part of the San Franciscan pagan scene for as long as Sabine could remember, a

Voodoun botanica, not just a bookstore that happened to sell too many candles.

Sabine loved it, because when one walked in, the first thing you passed by was a jar of bat wings which always cracked her up.

She also loved the candles and the incense along with the smell that hit the minute one walked through the poorly hinged glass doors, ringing the front bell. Bookcases lined every wall. Behind the glass counters to the left of the entrance were jars upon jars filled with every herb or root under the sun. A large goat skull also hung over the cash register.

Ari made a beeline for the books. Sabine did her usual ramble through the store. Grabbed some lavender and a few other herbs, just for the smell. A Wiccan friend had given her the best cure for headaches with nothing more than a pillow stuffed with lavender, rosemary and clove oil. An incense burner and some incense joined the pile she started on the counter. The two black clad girls behind the counter knew Sabine from before. They just nodded as she started her to-be-purchased pile.

It seemed like a lovely way to end the day. Even better, a way to distract herself from parties, enormous gold tablets and other people's fucked up family lives.

Sabine paused in the middle of the store, gazing at the candles stored underneath one of the bookcases. She needed to buy some candles and a candlestick or two for the safe house. She didn't know what she believed in entirely, even if she did hear Voices with a capital V, but she did know that candlelight, and the smell of warm beeswax, always cheered her heart. She had very little of that lately.

The book dropped on Sabine's head with a loud thunk! and she yelped, reflex sending up her hand to check for a dent in her skull that had to be there. The book continued its tumble. She barely saved it from crashing to the floor, her other hand flashing out to catch it.

"What the hell?" Symbols on the cover of the book. An author's name that did not register.

She went cold. She went hot. She went cold again. Her skin broke out in sweat. She had the key.

The code was hers to break.

"I have to go."

"Hmm?"

Sabine was already heading for the door.

"Whoa! Sabine! What's going on?"

Ari grabbed Sabine before she could walk out the door.

"Wait up! What's going on?"

"I have to go."

Ari saw the book in her friend's hand.

"Well, you might want to buy that first then."

Sabine snapped back to reality.

"Shit! Yes, yes." She went to the cashier and paid for the book and everything else. Took the bag. Headed for the door again, but this time, Ari right behind her, having managed to cash out her purchases as well with the other sales girl who had said nothing, but had raised a quizzical eyebrow.

"Where are you going?"

Sabine turned to speak, then shut her mouth with a snap.

"No. No. Because if I'm wrong, I'll feel like a fool. I need you to drop me at IFHQ. Now."

"Me? You want me to drop you off there?" Ari's eyebrows climbed for the sky.

"Yes, you! And now!" Sabine couldn't hold on to her impatience anymore. "I gotta go!"

Sabine ran from the elevator at IFHQ twenty minutes later, blowing by Mel without a word, almost starting a shout out of him. He didn't when he saw her face.

She ran.

Slammed into her office, scattering her packages in a million directions. Located the bag from Curios and ripped out the book.

All speed drained from her body.

It seemed to take a million years to get to her feet.

She had ended up facing away from the tablet. Sabine found herself unable to turn around. She stared at the book in her hands. She gripped it so hard, the trade paperback bent and warped between her white knuckles.

She made herself turn, still staring at the book in her hands. It took all her will to gaze up at the tablet.

The symbols matched.

Sabine bent violently at the waist, clutching the book to her sternum, her eyes snapping shut as a pain spiked her gut.

If she did this... Her mind spun.

"It'll all be over. All over," she whispered, even as she sank to her knees.

But she couldn't tell if she were praying or crying, rejoicing or grieving.

A thought wormed its way into her consciousness. She owed Marcus money or a donut. She also felt so stupid, it went beyond words. She couldn't believe that she'd missed it. No, she wasn't a Hermetic magician, but this!

"The tablet is not in code."

The Monstrosity was written in Enochian.

The language mystics insisted was the language of angels.

The algorithm took no time to write.

Just straight symbol to symbol correlation to input. Though she had to make corrections for the fact that Enochian had no W or V character and used a weird placeholder diacritical for them. But other than, she just input the translation for each term and letter, correlating as fast as she could go. It was not elegant. She would never call it her most perfect of equations or sublime of codes. But it worked.

She wrote the final line. Scanned one last time. Set the frame to run.

All told, it ended up being only fifteen lines of code, not counting symbols and correlates.

She turned to the files on her desk.

It would take some time for the frame to decode what she had scanned off the tablet. She was glad that in all the previous boredom, she'd taken the time to scan the entire tablet with a hand scanner, inputting lines. It only waited for the algorithm to run over the dense inscription.

She had to cram fast and hard. When the frame finished, she wanted to be ready.

Files had piled up on her desk over the weeks since she had bullied her way into Edward's operational purview. But she had only glanced through most of them, not counting the eventful ones that had told her of Edward's alive presence in San Francisco for so many years.

She thought to dig through them, but then a different thought hit her.

What the hell did she actually know about any of this?

Her log book hit the desk, her pen running across the lines as fast as she could write.

Tablet. Check. Mystical. Check. Germany. Check. Memories of World War II. Check.

Her hand stopped on the page.

Germany. World War II. Hitler's obsession with the occult.

"Oh, you've got to be kidding me."

She ripped the files open, madly looking for the file where she'd seen her previous male and military self.

"Come on, Captain Harrison. Where are you?" Files were opened and discarded on the floor, the oak desk, the gray counter of her computer's domain.

She glanced at the screen. If she wanted, she could read the first lines of the Tablet. She restrained herself. Research first. Then to find out if she were smoking crack or had managed to crack her own personal Enigma.

She found the file. Background on where the tablet's finding and the previous mentions of it in intel. There was Harrison. His squad, looking young, yet older than the ages. Her eyes read, even as a part of her flinched away. Harrison, Locksley, Flores and Hartman listed as MIA/KIA, their bodies never recovered. But Sabine knew their fates. They had died on the road to the tablet and Harrison himself had fallen, buried under the rubble of a Nazi temple, all fulfilling their duty.

Except for one.

Of Rodriguez, no sign. Harrison's fifth man, his radio man. She dug further.

Nothing.

She went to the Big Room, and scanned. No sign of Tony or Andrew. Apparently they weren't back from their little trip. She spotted Marcus and made a bee-line straight for the short, frazzled looking metallurgist.

"I have a laundry list, Marcus."

"Sabine! Ah! Lovely! It would be my pleasure," he exclaimed, lighting up with a smile.

"You say that now. Wait till you've heard my demands."

She rattled off the list of things she needed some poor hapless assistant to dig up. Marcus looked more and more bemused, but his smile did not fade.

"Got it?" she finished.

"Okay. May I ask what you need ancient history for?" She knew he referred to her insistence on a million books on the Third Reich.

"You may ask."

She didn't continue and Marcus blinked. She laughed in delight at his confusion.

"I didn't say I'd answer."

"Edward says things like that. I'll make sure someone gets you your research." He turned away leaving Sabine blinking this time.

Hours later, Sabine curled in her overstuffed chair, holding her forehead in one hand, the elbow braced on the chair arm. She frowned at her reading material. The staff of the Big Room had outdone themselves. She had a stack of books at her feet on the Nazi Party and Hitler's search for all things occult that stood nearly three feet tall. Some of it sensational crap of the worst variety, but mixed in with the pulp were dissertations on economics of the period and political science treatises.

Best of all, whatever research assistant had been sent to the library with her laundry list, had also had the presence of mind to pull more than books. An entire library of Discovery Channel DVDs had been deposited in her office too. Various documentaries on World War II, as well as archival tape transfer of old war film footage, news reels and obscure propaganda. Even a copy of Showa, a documentary that Sabine would not be watching. She had seen it once. It had been enough for a lifetime.

The DVDs waited by a TV/DVD combo on a cart.

So Sabine read. Did everything in her power to not look at her computer. The translation neared completion. She could peek. But she wasn't ready.

Marcus came in hours later to check in on Sabine. He found her watching the television. She didn't acknowledge his presence. He opened his mouth, but the screen stopped him cold.

She took notes and watched. Marcus rushed from the room.

Even in black and white, human experimentation was not for the faint of heart.

His exit managed to penetrate slightly into Sabine's scope-locked state. A part of her brain considered his expression, yet continued to listen to the dry commentator's delivery of information. How the eugenics program of the Nazis had included a great deal of experimentation on live subjects.

Vultures have more integrity, Sabine thought, but no emotional attachment held to the thought. It was just cold. If she let herself feel, the weight of data, the horror of the tapes and the books, well… It wouldn't crush her. It took far more than historical atrocity to crush her.

She stalled out in her research.

Further reading got her nowhere. The blinking cursor on her screen told her the frame had completed her algorithm.

Rather than beat her head against the wall, finished translation or no, Sabine decided to do something eminently sensible for a change. She'd have lunch. Eat something. If she could. Her stomach tied a small knot. She rubbed it.

She checked her wallet.

Money had been showing up in her account regularly. Apparently, IFHQ didn't believe in paychecks but did believe in direct deposit allowances.

She had twenty dollars in her wallet.

She headed for the deli.

Outside settled on her like a blessing.

She was somewhat in synch with the rest of the world. Early afternoon fell on the street, the sky blue, the sun shining with no trace of fog to mar the San Francisco skyline. Armed with a brown bag lunch, she walked, a most wanted cigarette lit and perched in the corner of her mouth.

Two buildings down, one of the PG&E buildings had a garden. It was more concrete than planted, but it tried. For this strange little green haven, Sabine headed, though a part of her wished for Golden Gate Park and the tea garden.

The garden was arranged in a series of four terraces, each reached by a steep flight of stairs. The terraces were an extension of the building planted with plain green bushes and green trees. No flowers. But it was still green.

Sabine climbed for the fourth and highest terrace. She'd noticed that hardly anyone ever felt like climbing four flights of stairs to achieve a degree of solitude. She, on the other hand, felt the climb a small price to pay for a clear view of the Bay Bridge and a chance to eat lunch undisturbed.

The climb left her winded. Smoking didn't help, she was sure and she didn't care. It helped her think. The sun beat on the back of her head. But the top terrace lay clear. She found a seat under some shade and settled.

Only to discover that she wasn't hungry.

She unpacked her lunch anyway. Placed the sandwich with care on the bag. Opened the bag of chips. Sipped her Coke. Finished her cigarette. Lit another while Memory of other cigarettes and other moments of rest flashed across her skin.

Sabine picked. The nausea from the morning refused to dissipate. The severity had gone down from the morning, but not enough for her to make short work of her lunch.

She picked some more. Shredded the bread, crumbs piling up before her on the white deli paper. Occasionally a shred made it to her mouth. It tasted like ash.

Walking back into IFHQ, warmed through, if not fed, her nicotine fixed, she reached her office in time to see Edward leaving. He looked up, his black sweater and slacks making him look far too pale.

"Anything I can do for you?" Sabine asked, not caring why he lurked outside her office.

"The last file you wanted turned up. It's on your desk," he said.

"Oh. Great," she frowned.

Last file? She'd asked for a last file?

"Will you have an update for me soon?"

Sabine snapped out of racking her brain for what the hell file he meant.

"Um, oh. Yeah. Soon," she replied.

Yet another manila folder lay on her desk. Sabine dropped into her overstuffed chair. Flipped open the cover and had evidence hit her like a physical pole arm though the head.

She took MUNI out to the far end of Church Street, far past the Castro, and into a cheaper rent/higher crime rate neighborhood. Looking around the street in the early afternoon sun that still baked her head, she found her cross street. Sighed when faced with the prospective walk up the stereotypical steep San Francisco hill, counting numbers on the houses as she went.

She had lost her usual tail the minute she'd gotten on MUNI by dropping through three different trains. Tony and Andrew they weren't. They hadn't expected her to ditch them.

She didn't want them seeing her make a complete and utter ass of herself. She lit up a cigarette on the way, if only to steady her nerves, cupping the lighter against the wind.

She found the house.

If she hadn't known any better, she would have thought that she was expected. The house was one of the San Francisco ubiquitous Victorians, painted in cheery yellow, with orange and red trim. Its upkeep superior to the other houses on the street told the story of simple house pride. The same pride of ownership was leaking into the neighbors. The patches of gardens on either side showed fresh plantings. The companion Victorian on the right showed fresh paint on the molding in a vibrant neon purple. A neighborhood on the way up, due to old fashioned care exhibited by one person in their surroundings.

She went up the steps, approaching an old Latino man sitting on the porch. He looked at her with curiosity and Sabine paused in the act of getting ready to flick her cigarette into the gutter. Because he did an even more curious thing.

He rose and straightened to attention.

"Captain," he said.

Sabine felt her eyes sting and continued her motion, the cigarette flying unerringly into the gutter with practice that was none of hers and all of a long dead soldier's.

Words failed her as a feeling swept her that she could never describe, would never describe to another, not even Ari. The feeling that she had found, not a stranger, but a long lost brother, one thought lost in a war that was history to everyone except this man and a Life that Sabine had once lived.

"Rodriguez," she managed. She knew she wouldn't have to explain a thing.

"They're back."

"Yes."

"I'll go make coffee."

"You do that."

"It is good to see you again, sir."

"Yes, well…"

"Even if you are shorter."

She couldn't help it. She laughed.

Apparently, she wasn't a fool after all.

Inside, Sabine followed the old man down a short hall decorated in true bachelor fashion. Plain white walls, and several framed photographs of people clearly gone from this man's life hung with care. No artwork to be seen. Just memories. They emerged in a small, homey kitchen that while not recently remodeled had seen new paint in the year before. Clean white cabinets and black and white tile floor gleamed in the afternoon light, even as the fog rolled down on top of them, a gray fleecy blanket seen through the kitchen window.

Like many San Francisco properties, the house shared a ramble of a backyard, also visible through the kitchen window that spanned the entire block. A sliver of a view of Twin Peaks and the radio towers hung over it all, a view that vanished as Sabine watched, obscured by the fog. The red flashing lights flashed on, even as she looked.

But no broken rainbows. No swallowing dark.

She took a breath just in general. She didn't know she'd been holding it all in.

Rodriguez futzed with an old Mr. Coffee. He gestured for her to take a seat at the 1950s chrome and Formica breakfast set situated in the center of the room. Unlike some other houses, Sabine guessed that the yellow Formica and chrome set were original to this owner, not a throwback to some retro nostalgia.

They spoke not at all, until the coffee finished perking. Rodriguez poured the black steaming liquid into two large white mugs, the kind that Sabine always thought of as fisherman mugs. She only ever seemed to see them at restaurants down at the wharf.

She wrapped her too cold hands around the mug and pulled it towards her chest.

"Captain," Rodriguez said.

"I'm not a captain anymore," Sabine said lamely, knowing the minute the words were out of her mouth that he would laugh. Which he did, but not out of unkindness.

"Old habits die hard. Be glad that I'm restraining myself to call you sir."

"Yes, well, that would be a trifle embarrassing, wouldn't it?"

"What can I do for you?"

The directness of his question robbed Sabine of any idea of what to say.

How did she say, well, there's this enormous gold tablet in my office, I work for a bunch of spies, I guess that makes me a spy too, I've got memories of a past life as an Army captain in World War II and you're in them, I'm possibly turning into some kind of supernatural freak and I just found out that you were still alive and not dead like everyone else in my Dreams?

It didn't work.

He saved her the trouble. "You must feel pretty lost right about now."

"That obvious?"

"Only to someone who knows you. Or I should say, knew you. Regardless of the obvious changes, you've not changed much."

"I haven't?" Sabine found it hard to believe.

He had an easy laugh. It didn't mock, a fact which Sabine found she didn't know how to handle, but liked.

"You haven't. It's the look in the eyes." But he didn't elaborate. "There's only one reason that you would be on my doorstep again and it would be because the Lodge is not destroyed."

Trotted out in the open, Sabine could only nod. "That being the case, knowing who you used to be, somehow you've gotten yourself involved in stopping them again. Which led you back here, because you may not remember, but somehow you know I'll help you, no matter what. That about cover it?" he finished.

"Yes and no."

"Oh?"

"To be honest, I don't know if I believe any of this. I was shocked spitless when I saw that you were here in San Francisco."

"Why do you not believe?"

"The sheer coincidence of it all! You just happen to be in the city! When I need to question you?"

"You don't believe there are forces that can arrange these things?"

"Okay. Fine. Why do you believe?"

"My grandmother, she was a powerful *bruja*. Could charm the warts right off your skin. When I told her the unit I had been chosen for she told me that you would be back. Santa Maria would not let you go until you succeeded."

"You believed her?"

"She'd never been wrong before."

"Well, there you go."

"*Sí.*"

After a moment, Sabine found her voice again.

"I am so lost." It was the only thing she could think of to say.

"You said that then too," Rodriguez said. "But you got us where we needed to go."

"Why me?"

"Why not you?"

Sabine made a helpless gesture.

"Well, how about this then. I asked my grandmother the same question. You know what she told me?"

Sabine shook her head.

"She told me, don't think you're special. You're not. But you are willing. Special called and you answered."

Sabine frowned hard in concentration.

"You mean—" she started.

"*Sí.* Anyone could have done what we did. What you are doing now. The world calls out for help. It's everyone's choice whether to answer that call or not."

"We answered."

"Si. And you're answering now."

"Do you know what's going on?"

"A little."

"Can you tell me?"

"I can tell you what you told me in 1944."

"What did I tell you?" Sabine shivered. Her own words? Out of time to herself?

"You told me it was simple. Newton and physics, except in men. For every man who creates, one to destroy. For every man who sought peace, one for war. And then the rest of us."

"The rest of us?"

"Si. The ones trying to keep it all from tearing the world apart," Rodriguez paused. "They want to remake the world, not so much destroy it. And they are so good at it now that no one opposes them."

"No."

Sabine felt it then. The Power on her skin, risen cat quiet with his words.

"I oppose it."

"And that is why you are here. Again. It is also why an old man finds his war is not over."

When the knock came at the door, Sabine felt no surprise to hear Edward's voice at the door when Rodriguez answered. She listened to his polite greeting and request for entry, all the while, cupping the white mug in her hand in Rodriguez' cozy yellow kitchen.

But then she'd taken great pains to leave the file with Rodriguez' information on her desk. Open. To the address.

She looked up at Edward with as bland an expression as she could manage. It was hard, because the Power on her skin surged towards him and she felt an answering surge from his own Power.

More going on, she thought. Not now. Too much to do.

"Get Rodriguez clearance and get him in, Edward. I need him."

"He's a very old man," Edward said.

Sabine took no time to note it for its interesting place as an opening statement.

"I know. And he's the only one who can help me."

For anyone else except Sabine, his pause would not have been noticeable.

"All right." He turned to Rodriguez who had come in to stand behind him. "Mr. Rodriguez, if you would be kind enough to come with us."

The old man smiled.

"I would be delighted."

ㄱ� Ⴅㄱㄱㄱ

Sabine left Edward and Rodriguez the minute they got back to IFHQ.

Stepping into her office, she glanced at the Tablet then glanced at her computer desk. The frame had indeed successfully translated the tablet. Sabine's skin tightened. She knew the hair all over her body had to be standing on end.

> *O Thou who know the Kingdom laid on the sacred Earth, know what price comes Sanctuary. Know that the Elder Ones only sleep and never die. Know that their Hatred grows even unto this day and*

know that their Servants ever strive to release them once more unto
the Kingdom.

She kept reading. It took a while. The tablet had been covered very closely in small symbol.

"Stupid, stupid, stupid," she bit out each word. "You stupid idiots."

A seeming outside and unstoppable force propelled her to her desk, but a corner of her mind observed with absolute certainty that what drove her was her own sense of urgency. The Power cackled on her skin like lightning, telling her in no words, time, every second, sped away from her, possibly too late to save them.

She wrote with none of her earlier intensity or frantic need for haste. She just put her thesis down, word by implacable word. Tried not to think of how the legacy and obsession of a dictator could still exist so long after the fact.

She wrote late into the night. Some of what she wrote permeated into other sections of her mind. Not the mind of the analyst that cracked the problem before her, but the mind of the human being.

All the pieces fell together. World War II. Hitler and his occult obsession.

The Holy Grail.

Her mind wanted to insist that it was myth. No such holy object could exist or its passage on the world would be noted everywhere. It could not pass silently.

But how was it not noted? she told herself. Legend abounded. Enough legend to terrify those who knew the truth and served in vigilance against the same legends.

No, they thought they'd really get the Grail, Sabine thought, her hand setting thin black lines of cursive script spooling over the pages. So much trouble from a story whose origins came from a history about a Roman senator's grandson become an Anglo war duke and his marrying of a Pictish queen.

She finished some time the next day. She didn't know the time. She didn't go to check. She finished typing the last of her notes into a cohesive report, the translation of the Monstrosity lying next to her, printed out and ready to go. It came out to about a hundred pages of text, once she had put in the appropriate footnotes, not counting the fifty pages of her own report. Of which half she had written in the last six hours. The other half already existed in various forms as she had struggled to crack the tablet.

In a perfect world, a team of analysts would be combing through her translation for years.

In her world, they probably had days to make heads or tails out of the parable. She put the period on the last sentence, sent the document to her printer and felt the crushing weight of exhaustion drop down on her. The combination of all-nighter and adrenalin that had fueled her final push drained out of her like water.

The printer finished and Sabine picked it up, heading out for the photocopier. She didn't notice the stares as she made her way to the photocopier. She had no idea that she looked like some haggard witch, clothes disheveled, hair disarrayed from the many times she had knotted a hand in it as she wrote.

She started up the machine and waited. Thought about getting a cup of coffee. The copier was warm from the high intensity light inside.

Her eyes slipped closed, the repetitive hum of the copier lulling her to rest, to just close the eyes for a minute of non-adrenaline non-movement.

She slept. Standing up. Her head resting on the hopper of an industrial Canon photocopier, as if it were the softest of pillows in the world.

She woke in Edward's office, on his couch.

She jerked straight up on the couch, tossing a white afghan off her legs in one violent motion. She would have propelled herself off the couch, except she saw what sat on the floor next to her.

All fifteen copies of her theorem.

Untouched. Beyond having been stacked neatly. But counting bright blue divider sheets told her that no one had taken a copy for themselves, unless they'd made a sixteenth copy after the fact.

She sat for a long moment, staring at it.

Eventually, she got up and went to look for Edward. She'd think later about the significance of Edward leaving her the opportunity to take the report into the Big Room herself.

It took far too little time to convene all the principles in the Big Room, in Sabine's mind. Edward had given the staff all of thirty minutes to scan Sabine's report. Time enough for her to get a digital projector and fake some slides of her more pertinent data. Even so, Sabine wasn't ready, not for a briefing on this scale or the thirty faces that looked back at her from around the conference table.

Tony and Andrew looked the most haggard, having come straight from San Francisco International Airport, but even they had the same expression as their colleagues, despite the fatigue. Each and every one, except for one, looked at her as if she were an oracle in truth.

Only Rodriguez, the oldest man in the room, looked at her normally, if the smile of complete confidence he gave her, could be called normal.

"We know what they want," she began.

"We do?" Edward asked dryly from the far end of the table.

"Yes. It's ridiculous." Sabine couldn't keep the fury from her voice.

"Do you mind sharing?" Edward's tone however was the epitome of mildness.

"They want to take over the world. Absolute rule all that crap. Well, no, let me amend that," she raised a finger to bring emphasis to her point. "They want the parts of the world with the most money. Majority of the third world need not apply except to supply sacrificial virgins."

"You're kidding, right?" Tony burst out. He and Andrew were struggling with the contents of her thesis, Andrew's head still buried somewhere in the middle of the thick report.

"I said it was ridiculous."

"Why is it ridiculous?" Edward wanted to know.

"Because their plan, if you can call this psychotic musing of a madman, a plan, is to unleash the equivalent of the elder gods at key points all over the world."

Tony's mouth hung open. Andrew looked ill. Marcus looked confused. The rest of the staff exhibited various shades of fear. Only Edward kept up a visage of mild curiosity. Rodriguez was her rock. He held a steady gaze at her and nodded for her to continue.

Sabine noted it only with her back brain and continued to rage.

"It's ridiculous! As if the Eldest will stop there! As if the Eldest won't eat them for lunch too! There's no rulership with these powers! There's only death and degradation!"

"I thought you didn't believe in god or, much less a plurality of gods." Edward again.

"Tablets don't crack in Enochian!"

Her breath left her, even as the rising tide of emotion that she had put off for the more than fifteen hours now claimed her. She struggled, found some emotional ground to stand on and shoved the adrenalin down. She let the data before her claim her and chose to be merely an analyst, not a feeling, thinking human, outraged at the pain only humans were capable of committing.

"You've all scanned the translation. With this information, they'll unleash the Eldest of the Elder Gods." Her hand fell uselessly to her side. "And that will be all she wrote."

"What do you mean?" Even soft, Edward's voice sounded too loud.

In less stressed conditions, Sabine probably would have noted with approval Edward's deft handling of her emotions. How he lead her out to the information still trapped in her head, no matter how much she'd put in written form.

"I said it. There is no sharing of rule." She struggled for the appropriate words, from her own education in comparative religions to the more recent crammed education she'd given herself on the Monstrosity and all things related to it.

"The Eldest gave way on the planet as we evolved as a species. We no longer required elemental, primeval force as deity. We grew more civilized, more sophisticated. Our masks for Universal Source grew in accordance."

She flipped open her own folder of notes.

"But old gods do not die. They merely sleep. Sadly, my old comparative religions professor would probably kill to see my report on this subject when I'm done, but the working theory I'm putting together is that the reason old gods never die, is a type of fail safe for the human race. If the human race were to devolve into some pre-civilized state, there would still be a working framework, a working mask for Universal Source to be known on the planet."

"We can't be up against gods!" Andrew blurted out.

"We aren't." Sabine replied, hard. "For the time being we are up against a bunch of deranged lunatics who have no clear idea of the kind of nuclear warhead they are messing with. If the translation of the Monstrosity is to be believed at all, they, this fucked up Lodge of the

Midnight Sun, are the followers that it speaks of who strive to return the planet to the Longest Night, whatever the fuck that means."

"Which lead me to another thread. I pulled some other data that I wasn't sure if you had checked or not. I wasn't kidding about the sacrificial virgins comment." A table of statistics appeared on the screen behind her, numbers in neat columns spread over a projection of the last five years.

"What's this?" Tony asked.

"Murder statistics of young adults between the ages of 14 and 21, correlated with reports of missing children of the same age, FBI and Interpol database figures, in areas near known Lodge activity, plus or minus three percent for outliers."

"Children," Edward sighed.

"Children," Sabine confirmed. "And I think I know why, but I have little proof to substantiate this theory. If they mean to unleash the Eldest, I think they're hedging their bets, by sacrificing young adults. They're stealing their places in the Summerlands, or whatever your working definition of heaven is, and sending the virgins to hell in their places. Never mind what the zombie hunters think will happen to these children. As you can see, just due to flat statistics, more girls than boys."

The silence grew too pointed. Sabine glanced up and saw shock painting faces white.

She continued her briefing, now well and truly in the grips of her data.

"The tablet in our possession speaks often of Sanctuary, though it is more concerned with the unleashing of the Eldest. The tablet is also self-referential as well as referring to two other tablets, confirming the intelligence we already had. One of the other tablets must detail this Sanctuary that it speaks of and I am guessing horribly that the second tablet must refer to the Chosen Ones who hold the keys to the Kingdom, who know the Chant of the World, whatever the hell that means."

"And you figured this all out," Philip spoke for the first time, unable to keep a tone of wonder from his voice.

"Mostly by inference and logic. Like all first theory, I'm sure I'm horribly wrong."

"So what are we realistically up against? Real world." Edward's voice now, direct and no longer mild.

He wanted a threat assessment, Sabine could hear that loud and clear. "Subtlety. The worst kind."

"What do you mean?" Andrew found his voice again.

Someone put a mug of coffee next to Sabine's elbow. She reflexively reached for it, but did not drink.

"From the standpoint of the so called real world, the rest of the world would go on just fine, once the Eldest are unleashed," Sabine paused, staring over the rim of her mug as she cradled it. "But for anyone who would be unfortunate enough to cross paths with them, the Eldest or their servants… They would wish that they'd been found by Jeffrey Dahmer. They'll spread. Their darkness, their hatred, their evil will spread. But probably all anyone will ever say is, oh, well, that neighborhood just isn't safe anymore and comment on the decay of society. It'll never be blatant. It'll only be blatant to the victims."

"Time frame." Edward's voice cut across the table again.

"Which one?" Sabine asked.

"What do you mean, which one?"

"The tablet isn't clear, there are several possibilities."

"Best guess then."

"Winter Solstice. December 22nd. The longest night of the world, at least for our hemisphere. Longest day, for the southern hemisphere."

"Not Halloween?" Edward asked.

"Trite," Sabine said with an edge.

"Sources…" Tony asked, his voice soft.

"Yes, I'm sorry. I had no time for a bibliography or a truly complete set of footnotes. But a great deal of this was, strangely or not strangely depending on how you look at it, discovered by Hitler and Himmler with his handpicked SS goons. They were the first ones to attempt to unleash the Eldest."

"Hitler believed all this shit?" Andrew asked.

"Don't laugh. So do you bozos."

"Okay, yeah, but the destroy and/or rule the world part?" He had a section of the translation open and pointed at one of her many footnotes.

"It is unclear. One translation says destruction, another says dominion. May mean both. May mean neither. It's language. Not math. It's not precise." Sabine's detachment cracked long enough to show irritation, though not at Andrew, but at the vagaries of human language. "I'm not an archeologist or a linguist. I'm a code breaker, for Crom's sake."

"Why Crom?" Edward's non-sequitur of a question nearly derailed her.

"Too many Conan books read at too impressionable an age."
From there on, there were no interruptions.

Sabine lectured and with as much thoroughness as she could
manage for the next three hours. She lectured on Himmler and his
obsession with the Teutonics and the Grail legend, on Arthur and the
Knights of the Round Table, on the believed divinity of the German
people and on Atlantis and fourth moons. Much of it just skimming. A
true decoction of her discoveries would have absorbed years of an
industrial think tank's resources. But she had no time.

Above all, she lectured on what the tablet said. She knew that her
ability to teach the information she had found would make or break
their ability to avert disaster.

Sabine finished.

For the first time in the time she'd been at IFHQ, everyone filed
out of the Big Room, leaving Sabine one of the last to leave. She
collected her notes, all her mad energy gone.

"No."

"No, what?"

"No. This time even you can't put yourself out in the cold, Sabine.
You stay in."

"Why?"

"They never would have cracked it," he stopped.

Her head came up from her papers, whip crack quick. He was pale.
Her eyes betrayed her and cracked her Game Face wide open. Fear? In
Edward?

"And the children would have kept dying." She felt her stomach go
cold and tight. Her own data got past her mind and into her body and
soul.

"Yes," she whispered.

"Then no. You go nowhere. We stop them. Even if it's the last
thing we do."

"It may very well be." From this fear, she spoke. "The Teutonics
failed to defeat the Slavs, y'know. They'll fail again."

"I don't want to believe any of this."

Shock silenced Sabine. Denial in Edward? A great deal of her own
certainty in dealing with the Monstrosity had come from her belief that
Edward at least believed in the myth and dark magick unfolding around
them.

"Want or don't believe?"

"Want."

"I…" Sabine cursed herself but found she had to tell the truth. "Our hind brain knows the truth, Edward. This shit is real. No matter how much we don't want it to be. No matter how much I don't want it to be. I cannot deny what I have seen."

"Nor can I."

"We do have luck and more on our side," she offered.

"How so?"

"The Lodge. They had all three tablets. And split them up. They didn't want them found together. That has to be a significant indicator in our favor."

"You're right," he said.

Sabine went back to her office and was ill-prepared for what hit her next. She no longer stood in the hallway of an intelligence think tank in San Francisco. She turned, shock and fear making her spin, taking in the rubble of the temple she'd seen in her Dreams. Dead soldiers all around her. Rubble everywhere.

Torch light, so much torch light glinted off of black helmets. Sabine blinked and saw the hall again. But she'd seen enough. She'd seen the British SAS soldiers filtering into the destroyed temple and knew what the vision meant to tell her.

The British fucking knew.

They knew all along. The vision faded and Sabine once more stood in the hall, the papers in her hand crumpled to destruction. She smoothed the paper, controlling herself with terror-fueled will power.

Dreaming. While wide awake.

Now what? How bad of a sign was it? If the feeling in her stomach were any indication, it was the worst sign in the world. Did she tell Edward or not?

She made herself sit down at her desk. She couldn't handle thinking on it. Put it all in a mental box and bent her mind to other concerns. Like how to stop the unleashing of the Elder Gods before she lost her sanity. Which she wasn't sure gave her much time.

Sabine stepped in her front door an hour later. No flash of iridescent blue wings greeted her. She hesitated in the door as a strange still feeling fell over her. It wasn't fear, but a foreboding of a kind that she could not identify.

She dropped her bag and it hit with a very real, very large, very loud thump that still failed to penetrate her surreal state.

She found the butterfly in her bedroom.

Dead.

It lay on her pillow, its wings stretched straight out, like a benediction.

CHAPTER XV – THE EQUATION OF MORALITY

Sabine hung the black frame on the wall behind her desk. Outside, the sky held a color of blue not unlike the blue of the butterfly's wings. It all framed the Bay Bridge in postcard perfection. She stepped down and contemplated the effect, brilliant blue winged creature now preserved between panes of glass, wings still outstretched in blessing. It seemed morbid, yet all too appropriate. When it had come time to deal with Zoë's gift, Sabine had been unable to even bury the insect in the safe house's yard.

Memory tickled. Zoë's voice in the great cavern.

"The ultimate power…" Sabine echoed.

What? she thought. *The ability to die quietly, alone, on a pillow in an empty house?* Her anger dissipated. Wouldn't it be a gift? A power after all?

Because there would be no quiet deaths for any of them if they failed.

The morning came and went. Sabine went to lunch. Found a place on the corner of Beale and Mission to smoke, undisturbed. Came back. The entire building seemed to hold its breath. At the same time, Sabine felt like she could hyper-ventilate with adrenalin.

"You need to get in on the brief with Tony and Andrew."

Sabine looked up from her desk. She hadn't been working on a damn thing.

"When?" she asked mildly.

"Now."

By the time she made her office door, Edward was gone.

She thought of stopping for a cup of coffee and a perusal of the vending machine in the break room, but decided against. Now usually meant yesterday, in Edward speak. Moreover, Sabine realized that she hadn't found out where Tony and Andrew had been.

She stepped over the threshold of the airlock into the Big Room, to find it empty. Not that Andrew and Tony did not count as occupants, but under normal circumstances at least half of the thirty person team who worked the room were in residence.

Not today.

"Have a nice trip, boys?" she tried to ask, but it sounded brittle in her ears.

"Hey Sabine," Tony said with a smile.

Andrew just waved.

"Where is everyone?"

"Not cleared yet."

"Oh?"

"We wanted to show you what we've got before we go to the main team. Especially after your rather spectacular crack of the stick of butter in your office and the equally huge brief you slammed us with."

Sabine grinned at Tony's description of the Monstrosity. It did have that buttery yellow color, she realized. Her smile faded though when she put together the relevant facts.

They'd gotten off a plane. Come to her briefing. Not slept. Insisted on having Edward grab her after she'd gotten sleep, but not gone to their own beds. Which could only mean one thing. They'd been up all night going over her material and correlating it with...

"Where have you been?" Her voice came out like ice.

"Germany," Tony answered and handed her a file. "Edward tells us that he told you that we found the Malice Twins. Well, that's not all we found."

"We found one of the key meeting places of the lodge," Andrew added, collapsing in one of the padded leather chairs. "It's a place called Wewelsberg Castle—"

"The German Camelot?!" Sabine burst out.

"Excuse me?"

"They've got Wewelsberg Castle as one of their meeting places? It's a museum. Associated with the Third Reich. Himmler and his cronies met there and did all sorts of stupid things. Supposedly there's a crypt in the basement that they called Valhalla. Are you telling me that you found them there?"

"Yes. But what's this about the Third Reich?"

"It showed up in my research when I was struggling with the code. It's in the briefing."

"I'm sure it is, but I'm afraid that my brain is certainly too fried to have much retention of anything," Tony cut in. "And yes, it is a museum, but that doesn't change that they own it through about a dozen fronts and are funding it through a series of Swiss accounts that we can't crack for the obvious reasons. They also have several of their members living there under the pretense of being museum staff. What you hold in your hand is the collection of surveillance photos we grabbed when we there."

Sabine flipped it open, leafing through the 8 x 10 glossies, with only a half a mind. The Malice Twins were recognizable straight off.

But so was the third man in the fourth photograph.

"Oh my god."

Sabine sat down hard, the picture in her hand, the rest of the folder falling from her nerveless hand to the floor. "I know this man."

"Who?" Tony and Andrew were immediately by her side.

"Him. The one in the really elegant coat. Corsico."

"Whoa!"

"What? You know him?" Both men rode over each other.

Andrew went for the phone.

"Edward. Big Room. Now."

"Where? Where did you meet him? When?" Tony demanded.

Sabine looked up at them, bewildered.

"I take it that this is enormously bad?"

Edward came in the door, not breathing hard, but clearly having run.

"She knows Corsico," Tony blurted out.

Edward pinned her with a hard glance.

Talk fucking fast, Sabine thought and braced for the interrogation.

"How?" The first mild word came.

"I met him in Milano."

"Where?"

"Behind the Duomo on the boulevard and later at the Sforza."

"What did he say to you?"

It went on. Edward asked. Sabine answered. She stopped him after ten minutes of questioning.

"Me knowing him is not the problem."

"Oh?"

"He's here. In San Francisco."

"When."

"Three, four weeks ago. Twice I've seen him and he's tried to talk to me. Corner of Market and Beale. My own questions are how and why," Sabine said.

"What do you mean?" Edward asked.

"Edward, Ari and I hadn't even run into you when I met Corsico. How could he have known, well, anything about me! And why? Why approach me?"

"I don't know."

"We have other problems," Tony interrupted.

"We do?" Sabine queried, more disturbed than she knew how to convey.

"The Preserver."

It was a name she had hoped never to hear outside of her terrible Dream. Yet, here Andy spoke it in broad day. But to show recognition was to admit to the Dream and Sabine was nowhere near ready to do that.

"Who…who is the Preserver?"

"We don't know. No one has ever seen him. But what's disturbing is that we had reports of him here in San Francisco, and yet, the day we went to the castle, less than a day after he'd been reported here, we heard that he was there at the castle. Which isn't possible. It takes at least fifteen hours to make that trip from here."

"How did he get there from here in less than a day? Does he have a double? A stand in?" she asked.

Edward kept his own silence, taking the photos from Sabine. He took a seat and stared at the photograph of Corsico and the Twins on the grass in front of the castle.

"Unknown, but we need to find out. If this man uses doubles, it will be tough to tune in on him, especially when no one's actually reliably eyeballed this guy. Put it on the list, Andrew."

"You got it."

"In the meantime, what are we going to do about the Twins?"

"Kill them," Sabine said.

Edward gave her a speaking look, roused from contemplating the photo in his hand, but Sabine wasn't up to reading the meaning. Tony and Andrew looked uncomfortable at her sudden venom.

"Did they spot you?" Sabine interjected before they could respond, not certain what prompted her to ask the question. Just a sudden feeling of dread gripped her and passed like a fleeting shadow so she went with her gut.

"Not as far as I know."

Tony's forehead crease at her question.

"But you're not certain."

"You can only be so certain in this work, y'know."

Sabine sighed.

"Yes. I know. But I have a feeling that we will be totally screwed if we're blown at this stage of the game."

"Why?"

"I don't know. Call it a frikkin' hunch."

"Works for me."

"This disturbs me far more than I can say," Sabine said.

"Why?" Edward asked.

"All of this, everything is happening at once. Again."

"That's usually how it works."

"Exactly. Right when someone has committed to a move."

"True."

"So what the hell have they decided to do?"

"That's what you, Tony, and Andrew have to find out."

"If they did spot us," Andy interjected. "I don't think they care."

"What makes you say that?"

"Everything that we've come across, including your own analysis, points to an extreme arrogance. They don't think anyone can stop them."

"That's brilliant of them," Sabine said, sour at the thought.

"Hey, I didn't say any of them had the sense any god gave to a gnat. Then there's this Preserver guy that the Malice Twins work for."

"What about him?"

"The little we know about him is that he's one of the true heavy hitters for the Lodge. In fact, the Twins may very well be his errand boys."

"Why is he called the Preserver?"

"We don't know. It may be a title or a calling, it's hard to say with these societies. Like High Priest of a coven, but weirder."

"How much time?"

"The usual. None."

"All right." She turned back to Tony and Andrew. "Show me everything."

Sabine didn't sit once more in her own office till the next morning. The day's previous events drained out of her when she did, leaving her empty and hollow.

No one ever talks about how the pawn really feels, she thought, her emotions gone for a moment. Sabine pulled the translation of the tablet out of its folder on her oak desk. Edward had offered to have the tablet moved to secure storage, with the translation complete, but she had refused.

"I like it here," she had told him.

So the Monstrosity remained, though now it was covered in the

occasional yellow sticky 3M note, marked with a hand written number
that corresponded to passage entries on her translation. At the moment,
she found herself drawn back to the middle of the tablet and Note 16.

Beware, Followers of the Black Sun. Come close to your moment and
One will be loosed to walk the World; One born to Unsing and Curse
your works and your provenance out of Time and the World.
Know that you will always face your Doom.

Sabine sighed.

"The Bible's clearer."

"Is it?" The intrusion of Edward's voice made Sabine jump out of
her chair to her feet. "I submit Revelations."

She cocked an eyebrow at him. "What can I do for you?"

"My daughter has lead me to understand that a cup of tea and
sympathy can be had in this room if it is asked for nicely enough."

It wasn't what Sabine had been expecting him to say. She opened
her mouth. Closed it.

"Yes. Tea can be found. Are...are you asking?" She hated herself
for stumbling over her last sentence.

"Yes."

"I'll get the pot."

In the end, he pulled up her rolling chair from the computer
station, she sat in her overstuffed chair and they sat the purple rose
teapot on the corner of the oak desk. The light coming in from the
window behind Sabine was fog light, diffuse at bare midday, but bright.

He always looks pale to me, Sabine thought, as she poured the tea.

Halfway through the first cup of tea and the silence that had fallen
between them as the ritual of tea and sugar bowl were observed, Sabine
felt and identified the sinking feeling. It wasn't a bad feeling, this one at
least.

She had missed him.

She watched as he drank his tea. She'd give him another fine trait,
much as she might not want to. He didn't babble.

"So. Tea. Where do I hand the sympathy?" Sabine found she could
not take the continued silence.

His lips crooked in a lop-sided smile. Had he always had dimples?
She wondered. Or did she only now allow herself to look at him and
love the face that she saw?

"Sympathy," he spoke the word as if he didn't know the meaning of the word. "Ah. Well. Here?" He waved his teacup at her.

"I don't think the tea needs sympathy."

He laughed, short and apparently surprised at finding humor. "No then. Just to me." He took a sip from the fine china cup. "I owe you an apology."

"An apology for what?" Sabine laughed.

"For not believing that you would crack the code."

"Really. I didn't think I'd changed that much."

"I don't understand."

"You gave me a code. An unusual, and at first glance, impossible code. How was I not going to keep at it until it cracked open or died trying?"

"For the same reason I supposed your true purpose in this building."

"And that would be?"

"I feared the worst."

The word fear was an interesting choice, Sabine thought. Here they were, both hostages to their own fears.

"You thought me a spy for the Opposition," she smirked.

"It had occurred to me."

"Ah, if only! No. No, Edward. I'd be way better off if that were the case. The gods hate me and have decided to use me as their personal bowling ball. At least, that's what Rodriguez tells me."

"I don't understand."

"That's okay. Neither do I. When I figure it out, I'll make sure that you're at least the second person I tell."

"The second?"

"If I don't tell Ari first, she'll kill me."

"You have a point."

Silence again. She spoke first again, but this time not from unwillingness to bear the quiet.

"Apology accepted."

"Truly?" he said it with little inflection, but she knew what it cost him to even ask.

"Yes. Truly." She looked over at the Monstrosity, unable to look at him in the gray fog light. "There's one thing we have in short supply, isn't there?"

"What would that be?"

"Trust. We have precious little trust."

Long after Edward left, teapot drained, Sabine sat and stared out her window. She thought about relationships she had held in the past. She picked up the phone.

"Hello?" Came the well-loved voice on the phone line.

"I need breakfast. At a pub. I'm fucking homesick for Europe."

"Don't you say hello anymore?"

"Why? No one I work with does."

The drive out to the Outer Sunset from downtown turned out to be more than pleasant. For one, no fog locked in the farther side of San Francisco, and the drive up Fell Street was roofed with blue sky and a warm sun. Traffic obliged and stayed clear too. She even found parking a half block away from the green awning of the Rain Tree, finding herself on the sidewalk outside its front door with time to spare. She lit up a quick cigarette on the sidewalk instead.

"How bad is it?"

Sabine turned to see her best friend dressed in jeans and a white sweatshirt, her curly hair swept up in a ponytail, little black purse hanging in her hand. Sabine grinned back and they hugged for a whole minute, Sabine careful to not burn her friend with her cigarette.

"Let me put it this way," Sabine said, when they pulled apart. "I'm running to the Ladies every fifteen minutes."

Ari sputtered with laughter. Sabine took one last drag and they went inside and found a table.

"Sweetie, try handing out more sympathy and less tea," Ari gasped.

"I will if they would stop asking for just a cup of tea and expecting me to drink with them," Sabine answered.

"Like Nancy Reagan said, just say no!"

That did it. They were unable to talk, much less order when the poor waitress came by their table.

"Tell me everything," Ari said, after they'd had time to drink half a cup each of their respective beverages.

"Oy, if I told you everything, we'd be here forever. I have a feeling they'd like to close eventually," Sabine replied.

"All right. Half of everything."

"I don't know where to start."

"Start in the middle."

"It's all going pancake shaped."

Ari stopped stirring her teacup. A brief look of sadness appeared on her face.

"Doesn't it always?" Ari asked.

"Yes. No. Yes. Oh, fuck it."

"Ah, in one of your decisive moods, I see!"

"Fuck you," Sabine said with a grin. "You know what I mean. Yes, it does seem to always go pancake shaped on us. No, because it's never gone pancake shaped on us like this before and yes! Because…well. Europe."

"Yes. Europe. Hence your craving for pub grub?"

"Call it a grounding exercise. Especially in relation to Europe."

"What about it?"

"Everything's going pancake shaped again."

"What about it?"

"I…Dream. But it makes no sense," Sabine started. "And now I'm freaking out, because I don't know what any of it means. I also don't know what the hell any of this has to do with me. Is it all Shakespearean sound and fury? Or is something… Gah! I don't know what I'm trying to say."

"Okay. Then don't start there. Tell me about Edward."

"Tell you what, oh spook like one?" Sabine asked with a lop-sided grin.

"Are things as tense between the two of you as they were? Does he still think you're one of the bad guys?"

"I don't know." She was slow to answer. "He apologized to me, y'know. For that very thing. But I don't know if he means it, or if his own institutional paranoia has him saying that to me, so if I were one of the Opposition, I'd be put off my guard. Which is all hysterical as hell, when I don't even know why I'm involved in the first place, except that I had a relevant talent for a relevant problem he had. I'd call it luck, bad or good, who cares, that bumped us into each other, but…"

She looked at her friend.

"What I remember of Europe tells me there's no such thing as luck anymore. An old man tells me the same thing. Says that things are moving that haven't moved in over fifty years and I'm a part of them. I fucking hate it."

"You Dreamt of Edward long before we went to Europe."

"Like I said. I don't believe in luck anymore."

"You just need a friend?"

"Yeah. I just need a friend."

"Well, okay, besides fate of the world kind of shit, how are things?" Ari tried.

"It's just weird. I spend time with Edward, but I don't know why. The work does not bring us into the same room that often."

She betrayed herself with something. Her face, Sabine thought later. She'd have to work on her tells, best friend or no. Ari could read Sabine no matter how hard she put her Game Face on, but that didn't mean she had to make it easy when so much was at stake.

"You're in love with him," Ari stated. "Aren't you?"

"Eh…" Sabine could only make the place holder sound; how did she explain? She couldn't find the words.

"He's married," she tried.

"Yeah."

"That's it."

"That's it." Ari waited. "He's married."

"Yeah."

"So?"

"So, that's the end of the conversation."

Ari sat back in her chair.

"Well, yeah. But…no. Because it doesn't have anything to do with whether or not you love him. And if that's the reason you've ditched me to go Inside."

"I have not ditched you."

"Have so," Ari said in her best five-year-old impersonation.

"Okay," she began when she managed to stop laughing. "Do I love him? Do I have to answer that one?"

"That is an answer."

"Yes, but I won't have said it."

"Why is that important?"

"Because. It is. And some things truly are better left off unsaid."

"Really."

"Really."

"I don't agree."

"No one's asking you."

"Okay, I can see that this is going to start a fight if I don't stop." Ari dropped her gaze.

"I'm sorry, Ari." Sabine slumped. "I don't mean to be so defensive. It's just not something I can think about. Ever."

"I know. It's not your fault." Ari's voice was soft. "I just can't stand to see you unhappy."

"I'm not unhappy." The absolute bitterness in Sabine's voice brought up Ari's head.

"Um. Excuse me?"

"I'm furious," Sabine said, recognition for the first time of what the thing that ate at her stomach was.

"Why?" Ari blurted.

"Because..." she trailed off and then the words when they came were acid. "I'm not real! I'm a freak!"

"What are you talking about?"

Sabine came apart at the seams, albeit in a very controlled and quiet manner.

"You get stabbed as a child by your mother and your teachers report you to social services. You just happen to be neglected and left on your own by two brilliant parents and they don't even see you. You're a shadow. So the shadows claim you. They live to find children like who I was. Intelligent. With no family center, desperate to belong," she paused for breath. "And oh, they give it to you. They give you family. The family of shadows. They give you belonging. You belong to them. But it's all lies. Maybe not all of it. Even they're human. Need tea. Need sympathy. But underneath it all, there is only one motivation. Make you loyal. Make you blind," she paused for another breath again, almost a pant, not a real breath.

"And use you till you die," she went on, stopped. Started again.

"But that's not the worst of it." Sabine shot up straight in her chair, pinning her friend with eyes that were too bright and blue. "The worst of it, oh gods, the worst of it is that, I got away, but I didn't, and haven't fit in the real world since. I've gone from one horrid relationship to another. Had no ambition. Hidden in my stories. But the shadows never let you go. They never let you leave. I was a fool, Ari. I didn't escape. They let me go. And they are going to use me. Till I die. And that's why it's the worst thing. Because I am happy, gods, happy! And furious! Because here, is the only place that I belong." Another breath. "Here... Here I am normal and real."

Silence like a stone. The two friends sat locked in their emotions and Ari was the first to find her voice. But it was voice that held its own anger and refusal.

"No," Ari said. "No, Sabine."

Silence tried to invade again, but Ari fought it off with another word.

"Never."

The moment passed, but only by force of will.

"Well, what about your dreams?"

Sabine blinked and shook her head. "Fuzzy reception day. Can't get a thing."

"So adjust your rabbit ears." The both dissolved into giggles, whipsawing on the emotions.

"Okay, okay. Breathe, stupid, breathe," Sabine wheezed. "Honestly, I'm just totally fuzzed out today. What do you get?"

Ari's took a deep breath.

Sabine rarely asked for this sort of guidance. She hadn't asked once during their time in Europe.

"They say... you're in trouble."

"Tell me something I don't know," Sabine commented.

"They say nothing will change until you find the hunger that is not a hunger. That you must face your heart's desire and steal its secrets from the heart of darkness." Ari's voice took on a dream like quality.

"Pardon?" Sabine queried.

Ari's voice returned to light normal. "Hell if I know what it means. That's just what they said."

"Great. Sometimes they're sooo helpful. Not."

"Yeah, I know what you mean," Ari sighed. "So, how is Edward?"

"Edward who? You're just not letting up on this one, are you?"

"That good, hmm? And no, I'm not letting up. Something has had to really go wrong to have you this upset."

"I don't want to talk about it."

"Okay."

The waitress came and cleared their empty plates.

"You are real, not because of what they made of you, Sabine," Ari said into this lull. "You're not a freak."

"Aren't I? Was what I did in Europe, normal?"

"I bet you some place, it is."

"Well, be that as it may, this is where I'm at. But enough about me. What's been going on with you? I see they didn't kidnap you back to the Holy Land after our little vacation."

"Ah." Ari looked distinctly uncomfortable.

"Ari?" Sabine lost her easy smile. "What's happened?"

"It's going pancake shaped all over."

"Ari, what has happened?"

"They're kicking me out."

"What?" For a moment, Sabine panicked.

"No. Richard and Amanda are kicking me out," Ari named her landlords.

"Why?"

"Because I won't, I can't buy the house! Besides, I don't know if I really want to live in Albany anyway. It's too far away from you and everyone," Ari sighed. "Boy, isn't this just pedestrian as hell?"

"Damn." Sabine shook herself. "So what? When?"

"All my stuff has to be out by the First."

"What?!"

"You keep saying that."

"Ari, that's less than thirty days' notice. And what about your lease agreement?"

"Broken."

"Wha—!" Sabine stopped herself. "No. I won't say it. I just can't believe that they're doing this to you. They promised you that you could live in that house for as long as you needed to."

"I know."

"When did you find out?"

"A week ago."

"Why didn't you call me and tell me?"

"Because, it's like you said, everything else is going pancake shaped. Losing a house and having to move just didn't seem as important as everything else."

"Does it have to be? Dear gods, Ari, this is awful. We just got home! You've only been in that house for not even six months."

"Believe me, I know."

"Are you going to sue them?"

"It's a waste of time."

"No, it's not! They screwed you over!"

"Why are you getting so lit up about this?" Ari asked.

"Because..." Sabine stopped. "Why are we arguing?"

"I don't know?"

Sabine sighed. "I don't get enough time with you to waste it in arguing."

"I didn't start it."

"Who cares? Ari!"

"I'm sorry. I'm sorry. *Beseder?*"

Sabine knew she had badly upset her friend. Ari didn't devolve into Hebrew for little things.

"It's okay. It's fine." Sabine took a deep breath and regrouped. "What's really bothering you?"

"You."

"Me?"

"Yeah."

"Why?"

"I don't know! I just know something is wigging me out. You go off about not being real and just in general, life sucks all around. I don't want anything bad to happen to you, Sabine."

"I don't want anything bad to happen to me either."

"Yeah, but you're no good at keeping yourself out of trouble."

"Neither are you."

They stuck their tongues out at each other.

"Still friends?" Sabine asked.

"Still friends."

"Crom, what are we going to do about your asshole landlords?"

"I don't know. But this is going to be damn bad karma for them."

"In spades."

Sabine finished her coffee and nodded a no thanks, when the waitress came to do another refill. "I just feel so lost, Ari. I don't know what to do about any of this."

"That's okay, sweetie. Nobody does."

"Ari?"

"Yes?"

"You won't leave me, will you?" The question was so unexpected, that Ari had to pin her friend with a long glance before answering.

"I've got your back. Forever."

Sabine nodded, once. "Okay. Then I'll figure it out." She met her friend's eyes. "For both of us."

Friday came too soon. Sabine had forgotten about the embassy party. She would have forgotten permanently if Edward had not stopped by her office at five in the afternoon and asked her if she didn't need to get home early to get ready.

The reminder sent her into a panic. She drove to the house like a madwoman and then stood in her postage stamp of a room, staring at her clothes. She didn't know what to wear.

In the end, she chose slacks. Black. An austere, tight fighting matching turtle neck sweater. She might have been wearing a lot of black lately, but it worked. She couldn't argue with that. No jewelry. Just black and her lengthening hair clipped up to the nape of her neck. She couldn't remember the last time she'd had a haircut. Her overall look was nothing fancy, but she'd be damned if she competed with Mrs. Quintaine on that woman's terms.

Her head hurt as she got dressed, a throbbing, percussive pain in her left temple. Which was a strange thing, since it coupled with a strange optimism that had stayed with her ever since she'd had lunch with Ari. She found painkillers in the bathroom and palmed four of them.

Edward's home stood lit up like Christmas, strings of white lights everywhere. A valet waited outside. She turned over her keys, even as she recognized that he was armed.

The front door stood open, more twinkle lights detailing the door. Inside, all was equally transformed. If the previous cocktail party had been elegant, someone had truly pulled out the stops for the embassy types. Floral arrangements covered every available surface and the scent of roses and heliotrope filled the air. Sabine breathed in deep, even as she knew that she was out of place, but felt still her happy optimism. Someone took her coat. A waiter handed her a glass of champagne.

Sabine hesitated. She didn't know whether she should step upstairs to her appointment with the children or if she should wait.

She decided to wait. The last thing she needed was to have a run in with Mrs. Quintaine. Sabine just knew that would be bad. She hovered near the wall just inside the front room and watched the dignitaries.

Or would have. If someone hadn't buttonholed her.

"Good evening."

The woman who spoke was a head shorter than Sabine, and since both wore high heels that made her tiny indeed. Her eyes dark enough to read as black and her dark brown hair lay piled on top of her head in a style that Sabine admired, but could never have achieved in a million years. Artless, yet immaculate. Diamond studs glittered in her ears and she wore an outfit that was so similar to Sabine's that Sabine regretted her choice. It was London and the Dorchester all over again. She might as well have worn a sign.

"Good evening." Sabine tried a polite smile.

"I am Irina Alexyana Romininov." The woman, Irina, held out her hand. She wore three gold rings on the last three fingers of her hand, Sabine noticed and without thinking, she took the handshake.

Lightning ran across her skin and she did everything in her power to keep her shock from appearing on her face.

"Sabine Parsons. You are from Moscow," Sabine said instead.

"You are familiar with Russia?"

"Once. Now I am afraid I am much out of the stream of current events.. The sleeping power, quiet since Europe, flared in this woman's presence, but not in warning.

Recognition.

"Among other places. I felt I had to come over and make myself known to you."

"That's very kind of you."

"And you? What is your specialty?"

Sabine felt her smile grow more fixed. "Ancient mythical languages," she settled on.

Irina lit up. The woman had a breathtaking smile.

"We are, um, counterparts, as I guessed." Her accent appeared even more pronounced for a moment.

"Oh?" Sabine cocked an eyebrow.

"I, my specialty. Mythical archeology."

"Really?" Sabine's eyebrow stayed up, as all her warning bells clanging away in her mental ears. "Should we be talking? Hell, should we even be seen talking?" Sabine figured she was blown.

"*Nyet*. But we should talk, you and I. Our associates would benefit."

"You know the Russian Caravan restaurant on Geary?" Sabine suggested. Her impulsiveness was sure to blow up in her face, she was sure.

"Know it? I love it."

"Great. You buy the vodka and I'll buy the blinis."

"Done."

"Three days."

They shook hands on the deal. Sabine hoped that Edward wouldn't skin her for making deals with what, at one time, had been the Opposition, even as she took the card that Irina pressed into her hand with the handshake.

She left her place by the wall and headed for the open doors of the balcony. The room felt too close and too warm. She needed a cigarette.

Edward found her there, staring out to the night dark ocean, smoking, a crumpled Silk Cut package perched on the railing. She rubbed her hands, over and over, pausing only to flick her ashes on top of the empty cigarette container.

"Weather's going to change. I can feel it…" Sabine didn't finish. She said it out loud, without thinking.

"You can, can you?" he asked, his voice neutral and calm.

"Um," Oh, what the hell, she thought and spoke the rest of her thought. "Yeah. In… in my bones. Literally. My hands to be exact. Could just be arthritis. My mother and grandmother got it young…" she trailed off because he had still not spoken. She turned, wondering why. He just looked back at her, his gaze steady and even.

"I just know."

"I believe you," he paused. "What does it mean? What does it tell you?"

"It tells me…" and here she took a deep breath. "Trouble is coming."

"Yes," he nodded. "I believe you."

He gestured for the door. "The children are expecting you. Eagerly, to be precise."

She smiled, stubbed at the cigarette, and preceded him into the house.

They got upstairs just in time to watch Phoebe Quintaine slap Jacob in the face.

Sabine stopped in her tracks. Edward stopped just in time behind her. Sabine could feel the awkwardness through his skin, but said nothing. Jacob's head dropped, hiding his face, but Sabine could see the red rushing to the stricken cheek.

"What seems to be the trouble?" Sabine heard herself say from far away. Behind Jacob, Sabine could see Michelle lighting up with joy, but damping it all as her mother turned to look at her daughter.

"Merely a disciplinary moment, Sabine. I'm sure you understand." Phoebe swept out, Edward trailing her. She left Sabine standing there. Who immediately dropped to her knees, her arms going wide as both children ran into them.

Jacob didn't cry. Neither did Michelle.

Sabine felt her face go still and sad. Her stomach knotted.

Did it never end?

No. Sabine shook her head. *No.* She held the children close to her. She vowed as she had at eighteen. She would never, never let anyone harm a child. Not anyone.

Even, if it meant her life for theirs.

"Come on." Her voice still sounded from far away. "Let's go watch some television. I'm sure there's a Discovery channel show on something interesting that we can find to watch."

"Sabine?" Michelle's voice cut through the distance. "Are you okay?"

"I'm fine, honey bunny," Sabine said, making her voice sound more real. "But if she ever hurts either one of you ever again, I'll kill her." The words were out of her mouth before she could stop them.

Jacob looked up at her with clear eyes.

"Promise?" was all he said.

Sabine returned to her house a little after two in the morning. The children had been put to bed hours before that, but Sabine had then been dragged into the embassy party proper by Tony and Andrew. She'd been introduced to Ms. Romininov again, and neither of them let on that they had already introduced themselves. By the time she'd been able to extricate herself from the party and all the political maneuvering, it has been 1:30 in the morning.

She briefly felt sorry for a number of the floral arrangements at the party. People had kept insisting on getting her glasses of champagne. She had dumped ninety percent of them in convenient containers.

She moved through the safe house leaving the lights off. Her head still ached though not with its earlier intensity. Only when she got into her room did she bother to turn on the light on her desk.

The light stopped her in her tracks, high heels held by the straps in one hand, her hand still on the desk lamp switch.

Cocoons everywhere.

Stuck to every surface of the butterfly plants and planters in her room. Stuck to the walls. Even the window over the bed. Hundreds of them.

Sabine thought of the butterfly now framed and on her wall in the office. Her heart felt squeezed in her chest.

Monday found her back at IFHQ, sitting upside down in her overstuffed chair, legs over the back, head lolling off the front edge of the seat. It was a habit she'd picked up as a child. The blood rush to her head seemed to help her think. It was either do that or obsess about lack of cigarettes. No one carried Silk Cut brand cigarettes. Apparently, they weren't imported. She wasn't desperate enough to smoke something else. Yet.

She stared at the Monstrosity while it gleamed in the light falling on it from her window. The weekend hadn't brought any new inspiration. She had an unsolvable problem in the form of being unable to know what the Lodge of the Midnight Sun had planned. Followed by the more immediate and mundane problem of what to do about Phoebe Quintaine. The suspicions that Sabine began to build about the woman did not make for easily slept nights.

If it hadn't been for the fact that she knew she wouldn't get any work done on Sunday, any more than she was getting done right that instant, she would have gone into her office. But instead, restless or not, she'd stayed home. Tried to read. Instead spent most of the day staring out her window at the far off ocean, through the cocoon bodies of her sleeping soon to be butterflies.

So when her eyes slipped closed the first time, she didn't mean to. She slept, upside down.

The Dream waited.

She opened dreaming eyes on the great hall. For once, she feared nothing, not discovery nor what might happen to her, nor around her this time. The Dream distanced her and kept her from questioning.

She stood many yards away from the altar of the Beloved. She started to cross the cold distance, for once looking around for more detail.

There was little to note. The great gray stone pillars. The black marble floor. The entrances that opened off the hall that Sabine knew numbered thirteen without having to count. She came to a halt before the Beloved, just as the coils parted and Zoë peered out at her.

"Hello, Zoë. It's been a while since you Dreamed me."

"You've done it." The hope on Zoë's eyeless face was horrible to behold.

Sabine took a step forward, arms wide, but Zoë and the Beloved withdrew at the same time, up and back.

"What's wrong?" Sabine dropped her arms.

"They would never have cracked the great tablet," Zoë whispered.

"You know, everyone keeps saying that." Sabine's voice edged towards irritation. "What's the big deal?"

"It's –" Zoë came at her in a rush; coils everywhere, hiding them from view. "No, no. I cannot say. Not for certain. But…"

"Zoë, what is it?" Sabine dropped her voice.

"If you find the Enchanter, this will all end. All of it."

"Yes," she said after a long minute. It would all end.

And with it, more than likely, Zoë's life.

Sabine opened her waking eyes, frowning. As if she needed more questions, she began to think, only to have a voice she knew very well break into her beginning process. But for once, Sabine felt no surprise.

"What did you Dream?"

Sabine knew she did not imagine the capital D in Edward's sentence. Nor did she imagine the hardness. For a brief mad instant, she thought of denying it all.

For her, there had to be one place where you told the truth.

She rolled her legs off the back of the chair and took her time sitting upright in her chair. Pushed her hair back, knowing it had to be a tangled mess.

"Zoë."

"The Oracle?!" Edward looked stunned, and went looking for a place to sit down.

It made two of them. Luckily Sabine already had a firm hold of her chair arms. What the hell? A shocked and outraged part of her brain gibbered.

Worse yet, before Sabine could frame a question, Rodriguez stood in her office door.

Edward used the old man's appearance as a chance to make his exit. More like his escape, Sabine considered, leaving her with the hot potato of a question. Edward didn't look good as he left either, but he also looked like someone with a mission. She hoped she'd have a chance to button hole him later.

How in hell did he know who Zoë was?

"Captain?"

"Yes, Sergeant." The words were out of Sabine's mouth with no conscious thought until the sound of her own voice jolted her to consciousness. "Oh, gods! Rodriguez!"

"Yes, sir?"

"Oh, please, I should be calling *you* sir! Please, please, call me Sabine."

"Old habits die hard."

"Now's as good a time as any. I'm sorry if it seemed as if I forgot you. I truly haven't," she said, gesturing him in.

"It is well. They had some questions for me," he said.

"I bet." Sabine couldn't keep the sarcasm from her tone.

"It is well. Truly."

"All right. Do you need me?"

He held out a small object. A small, leather bound journal, held together by a leather strap. Very old, the dark brown cover stained a darker brown and black in places.

"No. But you need this."

"What is this?" Sabine reached for the journal, her fingers closed on the spine...

The world tilted and fell beneath her feet.

She stood in front of a young Rodriguez. From the height difference, she knew that she once more looked out of Harrison's eyes. The journal in her, no, his hand stayed clasped in new leather.

"Write it down, Antonio. Write it all down."

"I did, sir."

Sabine snapped back to herself, frightened to death. "I—he—we spoke."

"It is well, Sabine." His first use of her actual name grounded her. "I have more experience in this, I think. But in answer to both of your questions, I kept my word, as you asked."

"You did. Gods, you did."

"*Sí*. Yes. You were right. They made us sign papers after the war, but they, Tony and Andrew, they say it is no matter. I would tell you anyway. You probably already know it."

Sabine found herself arrested in the motion of opening the journal and found herself caught up in Rodriguez gaze. His brown eyes were very clear and very understanding.

"Oh," Sabine breathed out. "I—I, no, he...Dreamed...too?"

Rodriguez tilted his head to the open door. Sabine knew from memory not her own that he meant her to know they had listeners. Again, memory not her own caused her to tuck her head down, chin to her chest in a swift, sharp movement. Only a tiny part of her froze in terror that she had body code of an OSS agent. Getting her go ahead response, he nodded.

"They said you wanted the Ahnenerbe records." The German word sounded strange in Rodriguez' mouth. "I remembered the book. I keep it with me always."

"Everything. The temple..."

"It was called the Temple of the Midnight Sun. You blew it up."

"And died."

"Si, yes, and died. But you succeeded."

"No, Rodriguez. No. Because here we are again."

"Exactly, Captain. Exactly." His words brought her up short.

"I have to read this right now. Do you mind?" She gestured at him with the book.

"That is the entire reason why I brought it to you."

"I'll meet you in the Big Room as soon as I'm done," she said, her head already down.

If Sabine had been able to slam the lock open into the Big Room, she would have. Only an hour had passed since Rodriguez had given her the journal. But it was long enough for her to get through the pertinent parts and to have some of her questions answered. Sadly, as usual, the journal had raised more questions than it answered, but she knew one thing.

She had to save Zoë.

"Edward, we need to send a wet team to Italy," she began without preamble.

Edward looked up at her from where he sat at the conference table. He wasn't reading anything, and for a moment, Sabine wondered what he was doing there, but realized that any order she had given Rodriguez probably went straight to Edward.

"Why?"

"You have to get the Oracle." If Sabine had wandered into the Big Room stark naked and announced that she was the Queen of Sheba, she couldn't have gotten a more immediate and sudden silence.

"It's out of the question."

"Why?"

"The mission would be too dangerous and for too little return."

"What? Is this some kind of fucked up survival math? One little girl sacrificed to the depraved pleasure of a madman isn't worth the risk of trying to save her? I know where she is!"

"What's the rest of the objective?"

"Does there have to be one?"

"Yes. For my people, yes."

"All right, asshole, since you can't seem to figure it out unless I feed it to you with a shovel! It's called the fucking end of the world as we know it. I don't mean the fucking Rapture. If anything, I mean the anti-Rapture."

"You can't know that."

"Yes! Yes, I can!" She flung the journal at him. "I was there!" A sane little distant part of her brain screamed, *what the hell are you doing?* If a part of Sabine's motivation existed from guilt from a life, long dead, well, she'd be damned if she admitted to it.

Edward leaned forward, his arms on the table, ignoring the journal. "You are talking about a fortified building with modern defenses. You are talking about waltzing into a stronghold of unknown resources. How can you justify the mission?"

"They're going to kill her."

"When?"

"Soon."

"When, Sabine?" His voice cracked with authority. The other people there might as well have been wallpaper for all the notice either of them paid.

"I can't be more specific than this!"

"It's not good enough."

"Look, I can tell you when or where, not both. Not in this sitting."

"Why not?"

"Look, just call it the Sabine Uncertainty Principle and leave it at that! My precog electrons don't have enough energy to go the distance. Chill and leave me alone. I'll tell you as soon as I know more."

"It's not enough, Sabine."

"We can't let her die, Edward."

"We can't afford to save her."

"With her soul, how many can they condemn? With her soul, how many bargain passes to Paradise can they steal?"

"But you said it can't work!" Tony blurted from the side, but Sabine didn't even turn her head to face him.

"Who cares what I fucking said!? It's what they fucking believe! We cannot, *cannot* leave her there. Not if any of you have any scrap of human decency." She swept the room with a glare.

Edward gained her line of sight and their eyes locked. The tension in the room had the quality of violence. The sane part of her brain noted out of the corner of her eyes, how everyone edged away.

She couldn't read him.

The moment stretched and broke. He picked up the journal. "I'll take it under advisement."

"Edward—"

"Time, Sabine. You have to give me time."

She shut her mouth. Even hard-edged and short, she knew a plea when she heard it. She closed her eyes and bowed her head in acknowledgement.

"Tony. Andrew. My office, now." They left and several other of the main team left as well. Sabine found herself staring at Rodriguez who just smiled at her.

"Did I do enough?" she asked the old man.

He nodded, knowing what her real question truly was.

"Everything and more, Captain. Be easy. God is with us."

Sabine let herself into her little house, drained and sick to her stomach with too much knowledge in her head and too much fear that had replaced her earlier well-being.

It was now her house, she realized, her key in the lock, not the safe house anymore. She'd been there too long for it to be otherwise. So with night coming on, the day ended, she stood in the open door and tried not to physically sag. She dropped her black bag and her leather coat on the floor.

No wings greeted her.

She was uneasy in spirit, so uneasy that her body felt ill and out of sorts. Her stomach kept cramping. She desperately wanted a cigarette. She paced the ten feet of one direction of the living room but found no solace. She made a cup of tea, but did not drink it. She looked in the refrigerator, but ate nothing. In the end, she found herself in the little bedroom. She took her mother's guitar from its hook on the wall.

Before she could lay fingers to strings…

…The guitar sang.

A clear, woodland sound filled the room. It went on and on, a tone only ancient resonating wood can make, until it faded away into a hum more felt in her hands than heard.

If tears fell across her cheek, she did not feel them. She played. For herself, for her mother, for everyone she'd ever known. She played the Ode to Joy and fragments of songs by the Eagles. Sometimes she just played random strings of scales and arpeggios in no order. And through it all, the guitar sang and healed her broken heart.

One lonely soul to another.

She rubbed her hands together. Playing had hurt, healing aside. She just couldn't seem to get her hands warm, no matter what she tried. She drank as much tea and coffee as she did as much for the warm cups as well as the jolt of stimulation that she needed so badly, now that she didn't have any more cigarettes. Made no sense really. Adrenaline made her heart race, but her hands stayed cold even while the rest of her sweated.

Oh well, she thought, and shrugged at no one. Just time to get another hot cup of something and tried to put her fear and heartache away from her.

The act of putting tea together and warming and filling the pot helped a little, but Sabine kept finding herself staring at nothing at all. Her mind wound up hard around the thought of what the Lodge had planned for Zoë, hell, for all of them. She knew their plans could not have changed much from the time when Arthur Harrison had lived and instructed his sergeant to keep meticulous notes.

She poured her tea and added sugar. Tears had helped, but she still hurt. She went back to her room, stepped in, preparing to put her guitar away and stopped.

In the space of time it had taken for her to make her tea, every cocoon had opened.

Every surface lay covered in new brilliant blue wings.

It was an impossibility. A living miracle. Sabine stood transfixed, tears running down her face, as the butterflies enveloped her, their wings brushing her like kisses of utter redemption and ultimate blessing. And ultimate salvation.

CHAPTER XVI – THE EQUATIONS OF SACRIFICE

The butterfly hanging on her wall now held even more wonder for Sabine. She had left an azure cloud bank of butterfly offspring at her house, flitting in the small rooms, with Sabine wondering if she had enough plants to feed them all. When she had gone to bed, they had settled everywhere, even hanging on the walls like a living wallpaper of blue wings.

The one on her wall in her office told her one thing with certainty. Transformation remained infinite, death merely one more step on the wheel. The sense of awe over this strange miracle did not leave her or abate in any way. It stayed and she wondered, her thoughts and feelings a turbulent mess.

The thought of turbulence sparked a thread of analysis.

She contemplated the tablet in her office.

Turbulence, she thought, *always precedes the breakdown of a fluid state.* It applied to Game Theory as well, which in the end, all analysis truly broke down into. She had told Edward that someone had decided to move. The turbulence in events proved that.

But it also meant a breakdown, somewhere, was also imminent.

Sabine lay down to sleep a few nights later in her meager bed, tucked in the corner of the postage size bedroom of the safe house, her sleepy mind fixated on one image which, for a change, wasn't the Monstrosity or some other oppressive thought. She fixed her thoughts on her first butterfly. Iridescent wings still spread in benediction, her mind ran in circles over its deeper meaning.

Sabine sat straight up in her bed the next morning with no memory of waking. Just one moment, asleep. The next, wide awake and her heart pounding as if it would leap out of her chest.

"Edward?" she whispered.

She didn't know what she dreaded, but she felt power on her skin. Her chest ached like it had in Europe. A glance at the clock: only an hour before her usual wakeup call of 6:30 AM. She scrambled out of bed an instant after that. Madly looked for clothes. She couldn't shake it.

Something was wrong.

Five minutes later, she stopped briefly, her hand on the door handle of her car, keys in the other.

This is crazy, she thought. *I'm rushing off to work over a feeling! Where's the rationale?*

The answer sprang up immediate, logical. Because lately her feelings were the only warming of impending trouble.

Breakdown, she thought and slammed the car door open.

She got to IFHQ in record time. Five minutes after that, stood in the doorway of Edward's office.

No Edward.

She stepped out into the hall. Looked both ways. There was no hall traffic. No one had really arrived for work that day. Night staff would be in the Big Room. No extraneous noises. Just the hum of the building's HVAC system, and the hum of the overhead fluorescents in the hall. Quiet enough, that she could have heard grass grow, if any were in the building.

She headed for the Big Room. "Where is he?"

Philip turned at the sound of Sabine's voice. He didn't wipe the look of concern from his face fast enough.

"What happened?" Her tone hard now.

"Nothing happened," Philip said, with an easy smile. "He's sick."

"Sick?" Sabine was brought up short. "With what?"

"Some bug or other. Nothing to worry about."

"Right," Sabine paused, her momentum draining away. "Anything else going on?"

"It's quiet."

"'Kay," she paused again. Turned around and went back out. The feeling didn't go away. Her heart while not feeling as squeezed as it had before, still hurt. She took a deep breath, trying to ease the constriction. Didn't work. She turned to go to her office, only to find Edward walking towards her and by default, on his way to his office.

"Edward!" Sabine didn't even bother trying to keep the relief out of her voice as she started towards him.

"Sabine."

Her concern rose another notch. He sounded exhausted. "You look like shit."

"Thank you for the compliment."

"You're welcome." She locked step with him. "What are you doing here?"

"Being sick."

"You came to work. To be sick." He nodded, lowering himself to his couch, the minute they got to his office.

"Why?"

"Couldn't rest at home." A thin layer of sweat lay on his forehead.

"You take any meds?"

He shook his head slowly in the negative, his eyes already closed. Without thinking, Sabine walked over and started to cover him with the white blanket. Its ever present attendance was becoming more and more clear.

The speed with which he grabbed her wrist when she drew near enough, entirely belied his illness.

"I didn't condone it," he said softly, though clearly he had been trying for more volume. His voice was the only thing that betrayed whatever illness plagued him.

"Condoned...?" Sabine frowned in confusion. "Condoned what, Edward? You're feverish."

"Phoebe. Hitting Jacob." If he had struck her, Sabine could not have been more shocked. She had forgotten the incident at the embassy party. Not for the reasons some others might have. She had forgotten and made herself forget, because to remember was to contemplate doing a violence to the woman Edward Quintaine called wife.

Her feelings must have been apparent on her face, because his grip tightened.

"I didn't condone it. I didn't know she had ever hit him." He took a deep breath, tiring. "It will never happen again."

Sabine felt the moment stretch, but she also could feel him through his skin with the sleeping power. He wasn't lying. He believed what he said. But Sabine knew something that Edward didn't, knew it the way only someone who had lived through it could know.

It wasn't the first time that Phoebe had hit Jacob and it wasn't going to be the last.

But he was sick. Then was not the time to lecture him or educate him on the nature of child abuse. She pulled free and tucked the white blanket around his body.

"I know it won't," she said instead.

He was ill enough to not understand the full implications of what she meant.

She made tea and carried it into his office. She also carried her log book and current notes. No one stopped her and no one asked. She sat with him. He slept. She worried. All in all, it should have stayed a quiet day.

But she fell asleep and the Dream had other plans for her.

Coils and coils of blackness, reflective as wet and warm as blood, from tendrils to limbs the thickness of tree trunks curled around her, but this time, not only did she know she Dreamed, she realized the continuing error she had been making.

She was not Seeing through Zoë's eyes.

Because chained to the great altar, lay Zoë. Sabine knew she once more saw the future, a future. A future where she would be chained to the Beloved. A future, a specific future that she feared above all others, though she could not name or explain why.

Zoë's death.

The thirteen hooded figures drew close. The coils drew her away, even as Sabine wished to close her eyes, but she could not. From the ceiling, she watched as they began.

The rape.

The vivisection.

Dismemberment. They took her apart at the joints, the bones and flesh then picked up by each person, still bleeding to make runes on the black basalt floor. All in silence except for Zoë's screams echoing and echoing in the great chamber, until her head rolled off the altar, decapitated from her tortured frame.

Sabine sat up, files spilling everywhere.

"Are you all right?"

Sabine blinked in the afternoon light coming through Edward's office window. Edward sat halfway up, propped on one elbow on the couch. He had been trying to get up.

"Sorry."

"Are you all right?"

Sabine sighed and started collecting the files. "I–" she shrugged. "The Dreams keep coming."

"Do you know what they mean?"

"Yes. No. Mostly no. Hell, I don't even know why I Dream, only that I do."

He lay back on the couch. "What did you Dream?"

Sabine finally looked him in the eye, her files collected. "What I always Dream," she replied after a time. "Death and dying."

He didn't answer, because the phone rang. Sabine answered it. "Quintaine's."

"Sabine, is he awake?" Phillip's voice was welcome in her ears.

"Yeah. Why?"

"Phoebe's left the children alone at the house. Can you get him back there?"

Sabine clenched her jaw, rather than burst out with a set of words she didn't want to explain to Edward. "I've got it covered." She hung up the phone and smiled at Edward. "You're going home."

"Why?" Edward asked, his forehead creasing in worry.

"Kids need you."

"Where's Phoebe?" His voice went hard in an instant.

Sabine clenched her jaw again. "Not at the house." She came over and helped him up, ignoring how it felt to touch him at all. "I'll take you back."

Sabine got Edward to her car with no fuss. They made the drive in total silence. She thought at first it would bother her, their total lack of conversation or lack of radio, but instead found it soothing after the shock of the latest Dream.

She parked in the drive of the Seacliff home and waited for Edward to lever himself out of the passenger side before breaking the silence. "Is there anything I can do?"

"I feel like I should be asking you that," he said, leaning on the roof of her car, gathering his strength. "As it is, I do have a favor to ask."

"Shoot."

"I'm in no shape to watch the kids. Can you stay?" An odd catch had crept into his voice, but Sabine was certain she imagined it.

She hesitated. "Sure. Sure, I can stay."

Jacob and Michelle were thrilled to see her. Edward took himself off to his room with little fanfare, leaving Sabine in the hall with the two children. Jacob stayed only a moment to smile at Sabine and then head off for his room. Michelle on the other hand, decided she wanted to take Sabine out to the garden, which she didn't even know existed. They headed to the back of the house, but rather than towards the double doors that lead to the terrace, Michelle lead Sabine by the hand down a long narrow hallway that ran beneath the stairs and next to the kitchen. They had gone a few steps, when an open door caught Sabine's attention. That and the several guitars that she spied on the inside.

"What's this?"

"Daddy's music room."

Sabine's eyebrows rose in curiosity.

Music room? she thought. "Can we peek?"

"Sure! Daddy doesn't mind. Not like Mommy." Michelle's brow clouded.

Sabine cursed Phoebe Quintaine for the hundredth time. "So, show me around already," Sabine said with a light voice and Michelle grinned up at her, her dark thoughts already forgotten.

"They're lovely," Sabine said, gently touching the neck of a very fine Stratocaster electric guitar.

"Daddy doesn't play like he used to," Michelle said.

Sabine cocked her head at the little girl. "I take it he played?"

"A lot, but that was when I was really little."

Sabine's lips quirked. To her, Michelle was still really little, but she remembered that at eight, she had thought she was terribly grown up as well.

"I wonder why he stopped," Sabine said.

Michelle frowned. "Mommy."

Sabine's eyebrow quirked at that one.

"Do you know how to play, Michelle?"

"No."

"Would you like to learn?"

Michelle's face lit up like a light bulb. "Could I?"

"Sure." Sabine searched for an acoustic and spotted an acoustic electric Ovation in the corner. She pulled it out and sat down on the room's overstuffed chair. As she suspected, it was already in perfect tune. Edward might not be playing where his children could hear him, but he had not abandoned this room. It was too clean and too lived in feeling. She put the guitar down.

"Come on, sit in my lap. I'll make the chords and you strum…"
Then Sabine's mind blanked, but after a moment's frantic searching, a
set of chords did appear in her memory.

"I'll be with you, darling, now…"

An hour flew by in the blink of an eye. Sabine had a transcendent
moment when after getting all the words down, it turned out that
Michelle had a perfect singing voice, clear as a crystal bell.

"Honey, that was beautiful!" Sabine exclaimed. In contrast with her
own more than serviceable and rather fuzzy contralto singing voice,
Michelle sounded like an angel.

"Mommy doesn't like music," she said.

"Your mother doesn't know everything." It was the only
diplomatic thing that Sabine could think to say.

"I'm hungry."

"I'll meet you in the kitchen. Let me put the guitar away."

"Okay. Hi, Daddy!" Michelle piped as she ran out.

Sabine followed through on putting away the Ovation, not yet
acknowledging Edward. She hoped he wasn't angry at her for taking
liberties with his music room. Finished, she turned to face him.

"'Sunshine of Your Love?'" Edward queried, his face an
expressionless and unreadable mask.

"I blanked. Only thing I knew chords for. Sue me," Sabine bristled.

Edward's lips twitched and smoothed. A smile? Did he just try not
to smile? Sabine wondered with a raised eyebrow.

"Oh no. I was just curious," Edward said and walked off down the
hall.

Sabine managed to not die of curiosity. Edward disappeared after
that. She spent time with Jacob and Michelle. Helped them build a very
advanced and rather silly, complicated log cabin out of Lincoln logs that
Jacob insisted on making toilet paper mummies to live in. The lack of
light and misty lamp light was the only indication that night had come
on and with it, an adrenalin spike for Sabine.

Tonight was the night.

The night she'd agreed to meet Irina.

She said good night to the children. Couldn't find Edward to say
that she was leaving, so she left her message with Jacob and Michelle.

"We'll tell him," Michelle said merrily. "But only if you come back?"

"Okay," Sabine agreed, managing not to laugh at her naïve blackmail.

Only when she let herself out, nodding to the man on station in the hall surveillance closet, did she feel a cold shiver that had little to do with fog and dusk.

Phoebe hadn't come home. Sabine had been some hours at the house. She shook the thought off. Personal shit had to wait. She had a game to go and play with an opponent she knew better than to underestimate. Cold war over or no, the Russians were still the Russians.

She found her car, turned on the engine and took a moment to orient. Gratifyingly, she realized that having taken Edward home, it meant that she was already out on the ocean side of San Francisco, already past whatever traffic could happen. From Seacliff, it was only a short and southward drive of fifteen or so blocks to Geary Boulevard, the Outer Richmond and the Russian Caravan restaurant.

Luck smiled even further. She found parking less than a block from the restaurant, which was a rare miracle in the city. Especially since she was already feeling a little twitchy and didn't really feel like walking, alone, two or three blocks for parking, which was the norm.

She was early. Sabine wrapped herself a little tighter in her black leather jacket and set off briskly for the restaurant. Got inside, to find it fairly empty. The old maitre d' seated her at one of the red leather circular booths towards the back and with a good view of the door, after she insisted. He asked her preference, and deciding not to wait, Sabine went ahead and ordered a bottle of pepper vodka and a plate of blinis and caviar. She hoped to stiff Irina with the bill.

Irina appeared five minutes later, dressed in cream turtle neck, long cream sweater and matching pants, brown spike heel boots clasped around perfect legs. Sabine had to smile. Irina was the picture book perfect model fashionable Russian woman and she knew that the cover must have been immaculate. Her very ostentation meant no one looked even twice at her past the moment of appreciation.

Irina smiled at seeing Sabine seated in the booth. Nodded her head in acknowledgement of Sabine's choice of the power position and quite willingly sat with her back to the door. Sabine quirked an eyebrow for half of a second. Unless the rules of the game had changed, Irina was putting her safety in Sabine's hands, an offering of peculiar trust.

The vodka and caviar came. Irina smiled again in appreciation of the selection. They'd yet to speak. They drank instead, both knocking back their shots almost in synch and Sabine managed to not gasp at the shock of ice vodka hitting her stomach like a Mac truck.

"I am thrilled that you chose to come," Irina said, another concession in the game, offering the first opening.

"I wasn't about to stand you up. Mythical archeology fascinates me."

"As do mythical languages for me." Irina refilled their glasses, wrapped up a blini and ate with relish.

"I make suggestion, yes?"

"By all means."

"Let us, as they would say, cut the crap and get to the point, yes?"

"Love to."

"Then, I shall start." Irina settled back further. "Did you ever ask why?"

"Pardon?"

"If they are so powerful, why mind control drugs?"

Sabine gaped like a fish on dry land. She hadn't even considered the question. Nor had she expected Irina to come out swinging with quite this particular take on cutting the crap and getting to the point. It also told her in one sentence that op sec was pretty much blown to hell and gone. Worse yet, consumed with the Monstrosity, Sabine hadn't thought of the cold cream jar from London in so long that the terror alone of remembering it was enough to make adrenalin and vodka mix in unpleasant ways.

Fuck, she thought. *Fuck. I've missed a fucking significant indicator. How screwed are we?* It didn't even occur to her to realize that she lumped herself in with Edward's group.

"Belief. Belief controls everything. Gods, magick, all of it. For their power, why haven't the Elders broken through by now? Science, pure and simple. Too few believe in them," Irina continued. Another depth charge of information. Sabine clung to her Game Face. Clearly, IFHQ was fucking late to the Game and everybody else already had their playbooks.

"Then why go after world leaders? Wouldn't you want to basically dump this in the water supply then?" Sabine questioned, deciding, fuck it. Op sec blown, let's blow it the rest of the way.

"People in places and positions and influence of power generate more energy, because of their collective power over others."

"Their belief or actions can generate more energy."

"*Da!* Yes! Now imagine that you control what they think, what they believe," Irina broke in.

"Yes, but that assumes that these pills work. Or that they even exist."

Irina looked somber. "Oh, they exist. They work. They have no antidote."

Sabine was arrested in mid-thought and beginning sentence. "None?"

"None."

"How is that possible?"

"They are not made through purely chemical process."

"How are they?"

"Alchemy."

"Great. Fucking lead into gold wasn't enough for them?"

"Isn't this just that? Worldly power, power over others?"

"Irina, why tell me this?"

"Someone had to get the back channels open, yes?"

"Yes," Sabine agreed and then awkwardness settled. "But it doesn't explain why you chose me as point of contact or, or anything."

"Don't you know who you really work for?" Irina's question was openly wondering.

"I thought I did, but something tells me that you are going to disabuse me of that notion."

"Supposedly, think tank for the US government on religious extremists and religious terrorist groups. In reality, we have known that Mr. Quintaine's group was the only sanctioned, if black, group meant to face this threat. But that was—"

Sabine cut her off. "Thirteen years ago."

"Yes. You know your history, but nothing happened in that time. They are losing their legitimacy, just as we are losing ours. We are just as mocked as your association, because we lacked results for all those years, but you and I, I think we know the truth, yes?"

"Which is?" Op sec blown or not, Sabine realized that her fear wouldn't let her play as fast and loose as she could or would.

"They are coming for us. *All* of us."

Sabine knocked back her shot. It burned on the way down and she gasped in reactive shock. It was also all she could think to do.

"It still doesn't answer, why me?"

"You are the one completely unknown and unpredictable variable.

The child prodigy, the prodigal daughter returned to the fold," Irina began, then suddenly leaned in. "And, I guess, but my gut says with certainty, that you have cracked the gold tablet code."

The vodka sat in Sabine's stomach like acid. "What tablet?" Her Game Face was full on and her tone was mildly pleasant. Her blood hammered in her ears.

"We know your people retrieved at least one of the tablets. We do not know from where. We know that the cracking of the tablet code had been a priority of the Lodge until two years ago, when suddenly, they stopped." Irina sat back and threw her hands up. "Why? Now you return, a tablet, or tablets, are recovered from where they are suppressed. You cracked it."

"And if I did?"

"You know how to stop them, yes?"

"I don't know anything," Sabine said evenly. "I don't know if I can trust you. I don't trust who you say you work for. I don't know you're motives and I suspect what I don't know."

"You know as well as I that a front assault is never intelligent against a heavily fortified position."

"What does that have to do with anything?"

"A wise man once said, if we do not hang together, we will most assuredly hang separately."

"Benjamin Franklin."

"Correct. If we do not help each other, we will all die. Or wish that we could."

Sabine said nothing. Her own analysis told her the truth of Irina's words.

"I can't just break op sec on your say so."

"No. You cannot. Discuss this with your not so dead Mr. Quintaine."

"What of him? None of this give me grounds to say or do anything Miss Romininov."

"My name is Irina," she smiled. "And you are right."

Irina threw a $100 bill on the table, severe overpayment for the vodka and the caviar that neither had truly enjoyed.

"Instead, I will give you proof of my good faith." She stood gracefully. "You have a mole among you. What I guess, the Opposition knows."

"Who?" Screw the Game, Sabine thought. If she's not bullshitting...

"Look to Mrs. Quintaine." Irina held out her hand.

Sabine answered the handshake.

"Allies are needed, Sabine. Allies and subversiveness. I know I will be hearing from you soon."

Out on the sidewalk, Sabine stood in the San Francisco fog, her head still spinning, her gut full of acid and leaden from vodka and fear. For once, she did not want a cigarette. Nicotine on top of vodka and adrenaline would have been too much. She had too much to take in and clearly had to make a command decision damn quick. She had to talk to Edward, but he was still down for the count. That left Phillip.

Boy, isn't he going to be thrilled, she thought, turning to go, only to immediately lock eyes with none other than Allejandro Corsico. Who she now knew to be associated with the Malice Twins.

Her Game Face came on in under a second.

"Mr. Corsico. What a lovely surprise."

"Miss Parsons! A good evening to you," he said with a small smile. Something was different. She could feel it.

"To you as well." Sabine started to pass him and would have been stopped if she hadn't dodged his restraining hand at the last minute.

"Must you go?"

"It's late, Mr. Corsico. I need to be getting home."

"Home? Or downtown perhaps?"

She should have kept walking. All her warning bells were going off. She hesitated.

"Downtown? You must think me pretty well off if you think I live downtown." She went for the prevarication with an easy laugh.

"Let us not play games anymore, Miss Parsons." Corsico's melodious voice took a firmer note than Sabine had ever heard in it before.

"Excuse me?"

"Was you dinner meeting successful?"

"Meeting? Oh! You mean Rina! Just getting together for drinks. She's an old friend from way back," Sabine said, her easy smile still in place though her heart wanted to pound out of her chest; she breathed in deep, pretending to enjoy the cold foggy air. "How about you? What brings you out tonight? The movies?" She nodded her head at the movie theater across the street, turning her body again, body language putting out the, oh gee, must be going now, message.

"You. I meant what I said, Miss Parsons. Or should I call you Oracle?"

Sabine gave herself credit. Her Game Face did not slip. She laughed.

"Oracle? You have an interesting sense of humor, Mr. Corsico. Good night." She was another three feet down the sidewalk when he spoke, his voice carrying clearly.

"Walk away from me, Miss Parsons, and all of your friends will be dead within the hour, starting with Edward Quintaine and Ari Doran."

Sabine stopped. She was made. She could feel it too. Which meant one thing. Time to play it for all it was worth. She stood a moment, her head down, before taking a deep breath, her head coming up and answering him that way.

"I know who you are."

"Do you?"

The Cast came upon them so suddenly that Sabine could neither counter Cast nor prepare. Just one moment, they stood on a street in San Francisco, fog bound and cold, the next minute, they stood in an opulent hall.

"You know nothing of me."

"Oh shit." Sabine didn't care that she spoke out loud. Corsico laughed.

"You *are* the Preserver."

"At your service." He bowed.

"All right. What the hell do you want?"

"You."

"Me."

"Yes. You."

"Okay. You've got me. Now what?" Sabine asked. A kaleidoscope of emotions swirled up and down out of her body. She'd felt the strength of his Cast. She knew she had little hope, but one thing she knew. She had to keep her mouth shut. In fact, she needed to die that way. So now, she just had to provoke him into killing her.

Where's a damn cyanide pill when you need one? she thought acidly and then even that emotion drained away.

She was going to die.

"Now? We talk." He turned away. Her emotions woke long enough to violently wish for a gun. It went away.

She Reached…

He gestured and Sabine gasped in pain, doubling over. Somehow, he cut her off from the Source. The severing was as painful as a jab in the side of her body, physical agony.

"Please. Join me for espresso." He never turned to face her. She straightened, forcing herself upright, forcing herself to breathe.

She followed him into an ornate sitting room, done up in what she was sure were real Louis XIV antiques. It was a large room, more study than sitting room. On every wall the head of a big game animal or endangered or extinct predator was mounted, all beautifully mounted and stuffed. They were all beautiful examples of the taxidermist's art. All done in the tastefulness of a Victorian gentleman's study. Horror tried to penetrate her detachment when she realized that some of the dates of the kills were after the time when these animals were protected. So he's a poacher, but of the kind that is beyond fear, Sabine thought, filing away the piece of datum for future analysis. As if she had a future for analysis.

He took a seat in front of the large marble fireplace and gestured her to the other, tapping the white linen covered table between the two chairs. A butler appeared with a silver tray and small white china cups. Sabine didn't have to look to know it would be espresso. The more accurate question was, was hers drugged?

"Talk about what?"

"What do you want, Sabine?"

"I want to go home, oh great and powerful Oz," Sabine replied. "What do you think?"

He laughed. "A wonderful sense of humor. Seriously, *columba mia*. What do you desire? We only wish to know which coin would tempt and induce you to join our organization."

Sabine's brain went into a hard disconnect. Incredulity flooded in, displacing her earlier calm.

"You're recruiting me?"

"But of course."

"Are you high?"

He didn't laugh this time. "It troubles me that you fail to take me seriously."

"I'd say I was troubled, but this just proves you don't know jack about me." She locked gazes with him and didn't like what she saw. Her mind ticked over, all new information with her trying to make the puzzle pieces fit. This entire turn of events was not something she had expected in her analysis. For one, she thought the Opposition knew nothing about her and in one night, she discovered they all knew too much.

"Why do they call you the Preserver?" she changed tacks.

"Shall I show you?" Out of the sitting room and through the hall he led her once more. Sabine followed, not knowing what else to do. She couldn't leave. He stopped in front of the doors at the very end of the long hall.

"I genuinely cannot tell you in words how much I have looked forward to this exact moment." He pushed open the doors and stood aside.

Sabine stepped in, past Corsico, brushing past him and his electric presence, only to lay eyes for the first time on the Preserver's Collection.

It was a museum, if you could use such a term for such a room. Done like a parlor, but it was much more like a whorehouse. Though to Sabine, a whorehouse would have had a cleanliness missing and devoid from this man or this room.

It was filled with naked women. Really, almost girls. All beautiful, but stuffed and mounted in the most obscene of positions and postures. On their hands and knees, with their legs spread wide, as if to accommodate any man's lust or abuse. But the one thing he could not seem to do, whoever the unknown taxidermist was and Sabine could guess who, even though he sculpted their faces into apparent expressions of lust and obscenity, he couldn't seem to remove the horror from their glass eyes. The horror of what had been done to them.

Worse yet, even at distance, Sabine could tell nothing was sewn up. They looked alive and frozen in positions that they could not escape, their bodies unprotected from any violation.

As if to prove her at that moment unproven assumption and horror, his art so cunning, Corsico laid a hand on one of the woman and began to stroke his fingers in and out of one of the bent over trophies' cunt as if somehow the poor thing could still feel it. He violated not just her, but Sabine as well, and Sabine couldn't keep herself from feeling his fingers even in her.

Fury and humiliation choked her, but she didn't lunge at him. She knew that was what he wanted. She clung to her rationality with all her will. Her analyst's mind told her to keep paying attention, so she did, even as she wanted to kill.

There were no signs of violence on the women. They either came to him willing and when the process was begun, it was too late or his skill could erase such trauma. And that was when her analyst and Dreaming eyes saw something far worse.

He somehow trapped their souls in the trophies.

Sabine saw the runes of power that entrapped the girls. The flare of the power through lines of sickening light as their souls beat against them, like the hearts of birds beating against iron cages.

Fury was replaced with complete horror. There was nothing she could do to stop him. She wanted to rip his heart out with her bare hands. She turned her back on him and the room, never caring if he attacked her at that moment. She could look no longer.

"They are preserved for all time, my pet," His voice was so melodious and beautiful that Sabine just could not rectify the statement with his voice. It was an obscenity, but then so was the room she stood in. In that moment, she saw the future and without benefit of mystical powers.

Corsico and all who were with him would do the same to the world. They would create a world that was a museum of frozen obscenity, terror and pain.

"And you... Your beauty, your power added to my Collection will go far to making it complete," his voice continued.

Sabine snapped. "You're insane on a number of levels. One, I am no one's idea of beautiful. Two, if you think I'll sit still for two seconds and allow you to do *that*," she gestured blindly and violently. "To *me*, you've got another thing coming."

He ignored her outburst. "I had to see you among them. A weakness, I admit, but I could wait no longer and we could not let the game continue. So it is all to my gain!"

"What gain? Do you mean to keep me?"

"I merely mean to give you knowledge."

Sabine seethed. She couldn't stop him. Corsico was too strong for her and too well trained in his Power. She only had instinct to guide her and from that, she knew she could not take him. He would foul her first Cast. Let alone the fact that she could only feel the Power, but could not Reach for it.

Which meant the women were doomed and that made her want to scream.

"You'll fail."

"Really? You're so sure?"

"History proves your failures."

"You judge history, little girl?"

"Damn straight, asshole."

His laughter was really starting to grate on her nerves.

"It also proves our successes." He ran his hand now down the flank of the supine girl.

Sabine shuddered. "It still guarantees nothing. You have no certainty of success, so I wouldn't be so sure or certain." Her bravado sounded so hollow in her ears.

"Why should I worry, Miss Parsons?"

"Hubris, you bastard. You should worry about hubris."

Again, the clear and bell like laugh.

"If I thought for a minute any of your pet incompetents had a hope in heaven of stopping us, I might worry…"

"That's the problem with hubris. It makes you blind."

"Ask Mr. Quintaine how well he did against us the first time."

The first time? Sabine felt frozen. Reality twisted around them, and Sabine found herself, alone with Corsico, on the sidewalk in front of IFHQ, the place where Corsico had seen her before. The fog lay even thicker here downtown. Sabine reeled at the displacement this time. His Casts came from nowhere. Unlike the Malice Twins, she didn't even feel a rising of the Power to his call.

"Fine. I'll ask him," she said, fighting for detachment, which was far easier now that her sight was no longer violated by the horror of his Collection. But she could not detach from the rage.

"Cliché and all, *columba mia*, but you are lovely when you are angry."

"I'm going to kill you." Her voice was iron, implacable.

"And I am going to possess you utterly," he said with great amusement. In a twist of warped and shredded reality, he vanished.

Sabine tried not to vomit all over the sidewalk.

She still stood there, swaying in the fog, when Mel, the reliable and staid security guard, found her and gently, unquestioningly, took her back inside the building and to the Big Room. It surprised her not at all to find the room full with a good chunk of what was the day staff in the middle of the night. Before Tony or Andrew, or even Phillip could say a word, she spoke.

"Someone needs to get my car. It's parked outside the Russian Caravan restaurant." Tony nodded to one of the junior analysts, who left.

Sabine stepped forward, adrenal exhaustion slowing her movements, and she sat down at the long conference table. "They fucking knew."

Silence. Long and awkward.

"They know what?" Tony tried when Sabine failed to elaborate.

"I need background checks run on everyone in this room and anyone associated with Edward Quintaine." She ignored the question and the fact that she had zero authority to order such a thing.

"Why? We ran them only a short time ago–" Andrew started and Sabine's control snapped.

"Do it again!" Sabine barked.

"What's going on?" Tony asked.

"I need a video debrief crew now."

"Sabine –"

"Now!" she yelled. Both men ran for the phones.

The video crew showed up. Sabine closed her eyes, fought for detachment, fought to recall the entire evening from the beginning. She began. She left nothing out. When she finished, an hour later, no sound came from anyone else in the room. Even breathing seemed muted.

"Oh my god," someone said.

Sabine focused on Amanda, the black haired magician on the team.

"Can you backtrack off of me to figure out where he took me?

"I can find it," The sorceress said with a grin. "Arrogant prick was a fool to take you to his stronghold." She exited the room.

"Why now?" Marcus sounded bewildered.

"The Jungians have a word for it. They call it synchronicity," Sabine replied.

"There is no reason for any of this," Raul Martin, the senior analyst in the room broke in.

"So? You were expecting reason? These people are out to gain control of the minds of every world leader they can get their hands on. Where in that equation do you find any concept of reason?"

"You have to be kidding. Wouldn't someone notice? Wouldn't someone else stop them?"

"Don't you mean, why won't someone else do this? Why would they? Magick isn't real, remember? Dark gods and darker demons are merely figments of certain deluded individuals' imaginations. Why in the name of anything would they choose to believe in something so patently insane?"

"You don't have to play the Devil's Advocate with me, young lady."

"And you don't have to condescend to me, you arrogant ass. If we are lucky and plan well enough, we may be able to spread the word, but the chances of it not being heard by the opposition are slim to none. You want to waste lives, you go right ahead, but I will have no part in it and I will certainly not allow it. There is too much at stake besides your piddly ass fears. So why don't you buck up and be a man."

"I won't be spoken to this way!"

"Fine. Get out."

"What?"

"Get out. There's no room in this for cowards."

Raul shut up and sat back in his chair. Sabine let her gaze slide right off of him and fixed the rest of the room with a cold look. No one spoke.

"I suggest we are adjourned," she said into the silence.

"Don't you think you were a little harsh?" Phillip asked, following her out into the hall.

"Define harsh."

"Never mind."

"That's more like it."

"We're fighting the forces of darkness!" Phillip looked pained and dropped his face into his right hand, as Sabine caught the tail end of a conversation going the other way down the hall.

"Did I fail to mention we have our share of idiots?" he choked out.

"What's his problem?" Sabine asked out of curiosity.

"Read too much Dion Fortune at an impressionable age."

Sabine tried not to choke on her laughter. Considering how many of the lady's books she had seen on the Research Library's shelves, she also knew sarcasm when she heard it. And laughed anyway till she finally did choke, coughing as well as laughing till her face hurt.

Humor was long forgotten when she headed back to the safe house. She had no idea how late it was and it surprised her not at all to see the sun rising in the East.

Tired as she was, her nerves were strung tight and taut as steel wire, tight enough that when the first feel of displaced wind and reality hit, she Reached and spun around, kicking the door open behind her, to leave an avenue of retreat.

The Malice Twins.

She felt herself go cold at the sight of them. Colder still at the cadre of men, though she struggled to call them that. Barbarians more accurately described them. Black leather and oily skin, like bikers gone medieval.

"Miss Parsons," the Twins spoke in cadence.

"Mr. Buonocore. Mr. Genge."

They moved. Sabine Cast before the two men could join hands. She felt their rising Power. There'd be no Wolflord and Pack to save her this time.

She Reached and screamed for a killing blow.

Genge fell and the horde ran for her. She ran inside the house, a step ahead of them, even as she felt a far weakened Buonocore throw something hot at her back.

She made it to her bedroom and yanked at the sash of her window, knowing that the drop out the back of the house was going to be steep and hard, but she could make it. She didn't have enough in her to Cast again, to stop the horde from grabbing her before she could make the drop, or they'd be out after her before she could make the back gate. Her legs weren't long enough to outrun them and she had nothing for another Cast.

In between her and her attackers, the butterflies swarmed, a diaphanous, fragile cloud of gossamer wings and frail bodies. They clouded in front of the horde just as the heat, which turned out to be fire, hit.

Her Chunnel Dream come to life.

Morning light filtered into the house, not sunset.

They burned and continued to fly, landing on the attackers, the attackers igniting as well from the thick oil covering their bodies. A wall of flame ignited in a heartbeat in the narrow corridor, five feet from her, flaming butterflies landing in hair and on clothes, burning where they landed and killing as they went.

"No!" Sabine screamed, above other screams, as each butterfly, every last butterfly burned, all to save her. All so she would have time to escape. Fragile bodies between her and death, for her life, for her chance to strike back at this evil.

She leaped out the window. She had to. They had sacrificed themselves so she could live. They had done it for her love, out of an impulse that humans knew by the same sacred name.

CHAPTER XVII – CONNECTIVITY

"Are you okay?"

Sabine turned away from watching the smoke plume rise off of a far off hill. The West Portal district of shops had yet to open, nor were there any commuters waiting to head into the tunnel that MUNI would take downtown. That left only her, Tony, Andrew, and a surprise: Rodriguez.

Tony and Andrew stood up in the same clothes she had last seen them in. If Rodriguez had been woken, she couldn't tell. He wore crisp khakis and a white shirt under an ancient leather jacket that she knew to be from World War II.

Which left her.

In the same clothes, smoke stained and sweat stained.

"I'm fine. Let's go."

Sabine resisted the urge to lay her head down on the cool surface of her desk when she reached it a few hours later. She knew if she did, she would fall asleep in under a second. Her brain felt packed in cotton wool. She clamped her jaw shut around another yawn.

Great. My life is either brutal adrenaline, or brutal exhaustion, she thought. "I need a vacation."

"Who doesn't?" Phillip asked from her office door. The bastard had the gall to not only look rested, but also immaculate in gray slacks, white shirt and matching gray tie.

"I also really need to start closing my office door."

"Why?"

"Because I'm tired of you guys sneaking up on me."

"Nah. We'd still be able to do it."

"Jerk," Sabine said. Phillip grinned.

She had a choice. Either appear cheery or start screaming. Or crying. She didn't know which was worse.

"Got a minute?"

"Whatcha need?" She pretended attentiveness.

"Yes, but really, why?"

"Why what?"

"Why take over the world through magick? Aren't there easier ways?"

Sabine opened and closed her mouth like a landed fish.

Of all the questions she had expected and dreaded, this not only wasn't the last one, it defied prediction. Yet because of its unexpected nature, not only did it sink in, but for whatever reason, sparked a new chain of logic.

"I was going to say, isn't it obvious," she began. "But I'm wondering if that isn't a fatal assumption."

"Me too," Phillip said.

"Shit. Why? Why do it this way? If they have a tenth of the power to raise the Elder Ones, hell, the abilities we've seen! Would they need to go about it this way?" Sabine talked to herself but Phillip answered her as if she had asked.

"We keep coming back to only one fact. Lack of data. And for that, there is only one remedy."

"Oh?"

"Get the answers. I'm backing your bid to take the Oracle." Sabine's eyebrows shot up. "Your Game Face is slipping."

"Fuck my Game Face. I don't understand."

"You're too close on this one to see the real benefits to rescuing the girl, Sabine. You only see what her fate might be—" She started to interrupt him, but he cut her off with a wave of his hand. "Might be. Which means you're missing key facts. Why rescue the Oracle?" he asked rhetorically. "Because who else has a damn good chance of knowing all their plans?"

Sabine sat and stared at him, getting a sudden feeling of elation and adrenalin as the ramifications of his words sank home. "I worship the ground you walk on."

"Don't thank me yet. Now, we have to convince Edward."

"Edward is flat on his back from backlash," the words left her mouth and the rest of her brain asked, how the hell do we know that?

"Well. Then now's our chance, isn't it?" he said with an impish grin.

"How long?"

"As soon as we have a fix on location and a complete brief for the wet team, they go. Considering we're looking at Italy, more than fifteen hours after we finish the brief," Phillip's smile softened. "Which means you need to get some sleep. I came in to give you a ride to my place."

"I'm sorry, Phillip, but, I don't think so."

"Hmm?" He frowned.

"No."

"Excuse me?"

"No. I'm going where someone can actually protect me, since this has demonstrated that you cannot," she said.

"I don't understand."

"If you need me, call Ari Doran's house."

"That's unacceptable."

"Everything I own is currently burning merrily to the ground, Phillip. I'll be at Ari's."

It was Phillip's turn to play the landed fish. The tension started to wind up, but unlike Edward, Phillip flashed his charming grin instead.

"Okay," he acquiesced. "But Edward's going to hit the roof."

"He can hit Ari's roof."

"In that case, get going. Your car is in the garage. You need sleep or you're no good to me. Are we clear?"

Sabine grinned at the Navy speak. "Yes, sir. We are clear."

"Dismissed then," he went on his way.

Sabine looked down. She didn't have her bag. She hadn't been blowing things out of proportion. Everything she owned was burning. Which meant she didn't have her damn car keys.

"Shit."

She went down to find someone who could hotwire her Acura.

"Sabine! Wait one!" Phillip called just as Sabine paused at the elevator, hoping the B&E team would be at her car, by the time she got down to the garage. Hell, she hoped her car wasn't still sitting in the Richmond.

"What's up?"

He handed her a clip on small-of-back holster, already fitted with a Colt Officers .45. She hesitated, but took it. He then pulled two extra magazines out of his pocket. She took them with the other hand and glanced at the loaded rounds. Silver cased and black slugs. Black Talon Glaser rounds.

"Wow. You don't fuck around."

"We may not protect you, but I'm counting on you to protect yourself. No matter how accomplished Ms. Doran may be." Phillip's somber expression froze her. "I'll let you go there, but this is my condition."

Weighted silence then between them. She nodded once. Pocketed the mags, pulled the pistol free of the holster, to check the weapon. Loaded. No surprise there. Slipped the pistol back, clipped the holster on to the back of her jeans, inside the waist band, and followed that with pulling out the mags in their clip holders, clipping them on as well. Pulled her shirt down over the whole assembly and tried not to squirm at the feel of the cold metal and resin grips pressing into the small of her back.

She couldn't remember the last time she'd carried a live firearm. Phillip nodded in satisfaction. Sabine hit the elevator call button. What else was there to say?

"Say hello to Ari for me," Phillip called as the elevator doors closed.

Driving across the bridge in a borrowed car, Sabine had enough time to feel the anger, the grief, and the elation all at once. Such a poison cocktail of emotions should have sent her driving off the Bay Bridge. It managed not to, but it did mean for the third or fourth time in her life, she cried as she drove.

In spite of the emotional storm, she managed to negotiate her way to Ari's without mishap. She parked in front of the small Craftsman home and sat. Looked at her watch. Not even eight in the morning.

Sabine sat. Took in the garden that Ari had so lovingly put in over the last year of renting from her so-called friends. Roses and lavender, all in their fall greenery, blooming just over. Even only green, the yard had a beautiful feel, and soothed some of the conflicting emotions in her chest.

She got out, went up the brick walk and knocked on the front door.

"Sabine?" Ari asked. She hadn't been up that long. She still wore green plaid pajamas, though she had managed to throw a white terry cloth robe over it all. She took one look at Sabine and held the door open.

"Everything?"

"Everything."

Ari sipped her tea, grief and disturbance clear on her face. Sabine poured herself another cup from the ivy patterned teapot between them. They sat in Ari's dining room at her grandmother's old mahogany dining table on matching harp-backed chairs. The room was dim and Sabine found she didn't mind. It meant that there were no direct line of sight windows, which unless they were being microwaved, made it more difficult for a whisker laser listening device.

"I am so sorry, Sabine," Ari said. "Are you okay?"

"I think so. But to be perfectly honest, I'm probably in shock," she replied.

"I'm sure. But all your stuff…"

"Probably the Universe's way of saying I had too much crap."

"Sabine…"

"I have to joke about it, Ari, or I'm going to start screaming. Or crying. Again. I'd rather not."

"So what are Edward and his boys going to be doing about it?"

"I don't know and I don't care. I have twenty-four hours and I have been commanded to sleep. Can I borrow your couch?"

"You're staying with me?" Ari brightened.

"You're stuck with me."

"Yay! I can do you one better! Why don't I tuck you up in my bed? I was just going to do some work in my office."

"That would be bliss. Whatcha working on?"

"Bills." Ari made a face. "Need to pay my bills."

"Ack!" Sabine pulled a face of her own. "I'll leave you to it."

"You want a nightgown?" Ari asked carefully.

Sabine looked down and took in her own appearance. The smoke. The clearly worn too long clothes.

"A shower might be in order too, I'm thinking," she sighed.

"Coming up."

Sabine woke hours later, with no recent memories in her head. Took in the early afternoon light coming in from the high narrow windows and the mess of a well lived in and loved room.

Ari's.

No rush of emotion greeted the realization. Numbness had set in. She wanted to be grateful, but found instead that she berated herself for yet another indication of how unnatural a person she had to be.

She thought a minute more about throwing herself into a really fine depression. Instead, she sat up and swung her legs out of the big four poster bed, the pink satin nightshirt that Ari had loaned her feeling comfortable, yet unnatural.

She wandered out of Ari's bedroom and through the small galley kitchen, but didn't find Ari. It took another moment of wandering into the dining room to find Ari at the front door, screw driver in hand, unscrewing something attached to the front door post. Sabine scanned the front room on her way to her friend and took in all the boxes and packing materials. She'd been so wrapped up in her own misery she hadn't noticed on the way in. She struggled mentally and realized that Ari only had another week before she had to move out.

"Have you found a new place yet?"

"Yeah. I found an apartment a little further into town."

"Nice place?"

"It's basically in the ghetto, but I'll live."

"Why such a bad neighborhood?"

"Only place I could find on such short notice."

"Assholes."

"Yeah."

Ari removed the small oblong box from the door post, pocketing the screws in her jeans.

"What are you doing?" Sabine asked.

"I'm taking my *mezuzah*."

"Okay. That assumes that I know what the hell a *mezuzah* is."

Ari cradled the oblong box in her hand reverently. "A *mezuzah* is a prayer box. It holds a passage from the Torah inside. It protects a house from harm and bars evil from entering."

"Hmm. Permanent ward."

"Yes."

The phone rang and Ari went to answer, leaving Sabine to contemplate the packing detritus. She didn't track her friend's conversation. In all truth, it was all she could do to stay vertical. Ari returned in less time than it really took to have any type of decent conversation.

"We need to get out of the house," Ari said bitterly. "They want us, me, out of the house so they can show it."

"Please let me hurt them."

Ari shook her head.

"All right. Give me a minute to get dressed. Have anything I can borrow?" Sabine asked.

"Raid the closet."

The ended up at Barney's, a small burger joint not five minutes from the house. Sabine didn't feel her brain come back to its usual speed till she pushed back from the table, food consumed, and cradled her coffee mug in one hand.

"It's been ages, it seems," Ari said.

"I know," Sabine answered.

"Sabine, what is going on? Be straight with me. Really going on. Corsico. The barbarians."

Sabine looked into her coffee cup. Nope. There was no answer there.

"It's all falling apart and into shit, Ari."

"Sabine…?"

"You remember that book. At Curios."

"Yeah. You had me drop you off at the idiot's headquarters right after. What about it?"

"It had a few answers, but made for a lot of questions too."

"Such as?"

"The kinds of questions that only the box that sits back in your homeland can answer."

If Sabine had slapped Ari, she couldn't have drained all the color out of her friend's face more effectively.

"No. Way."

"Way."

"That's…"

"Bad. I know. Very, very bad." Sabine sipped her coffee. "That's what's going on. That kind of shit. Not world politics, not the usual spy versus spy crap that we're so used to. End of the fucking world shit. That kind of stuff. And you and I, my friend, are stuck in the shit right up to our fucking necks."

"Why? What the hell does this have to do with us?"

"Okay, maybe not you, but definitely me."

"Why? Why even you?" Ari's outrage grew.

"That's the other problem. I don't know. And I know I'm running out of time to find out that answer."

"You want to tell me what you're doing at my place in the first place? For real."

"They can't protect me, Ari."

Ari's reaction was the last one Sabine could ever have predicted. She grinned like a fiend.

"You've come to your senses! You're going to make *Aliyah!*"

"No," She gasped out laughing. "But I trust you to keep me and yourself safe, more than I trust Edward."

"I'm still shocked that Edward let you come to my house."

"He didn't have any choice in the matter."

"Excuse me?"

"Backlash took him out. I don't know why. No one will tell me, but he's sick as shit and I told Phillip I was leaving. Where I was going too."

"And he let you? He was the gray guy in the gray suit, right?"

"That's him. He thought it was funny."

"You're kidding."

"Nope. My impression is that Phillip does occasionally only live for those moments when he can yank the shit out of Edward's chain."

"Well, he deserves it, that's for sure."

Sabine snorted her coffee. The acidness in Ari's voice had caught her off guard.

"Now, Ari. Be nice. Edward's had a hard time of it. We certainly haven't made his life any easier."

"I see no reason to change what I just said," Ari said. "But speaking of him, how are you getting on with the moppets?"

"Jacob and Michelle?"

"Does he have two other moppets I don't know about?"

"Not as far as I know," Sabine said. "We're fine."

"Wow. Yeah, I can tell." Ari was the Queen of Sarcasm, when she chose to be. "You're still stressing."

Sabine hesitated. She had not told Ari about Phoebe hitting Jacob, nor the conversation with Edward only a few days before. Ari's views on the treatment of children were no mystery to Sabine.

"Sabine...?"

"The kids have gotten really attached to me. They keep acting like there's something I can do to help them, when there's nothing. I have no home, Ari. I have a burned out house and a battle list of dead. That's not anyone's definition of home. I have two kids who look to me to save them from their childhoods and I can't save myself from my own. As an adult! I'm still dealing with it and I'm heading towards thirty! On top of which, my own childhood appears to be the spawning ground of all my current troubles. Yours too! I'm no use to myself. I can't be any use to them."

"You can be their friend," Ari said. "Just like you are my friend and that is a hell of a use, sweetie."

"It doesn't feel like much. Jesus and Astarte, I fucking hate the self-pity!"

"You're frustrated."

"Yeah… It seems so small and weird, Ari."

"What does?"

"I'm more worried about what all of this means for you and the kids than I am about what can happen to the world."

"That's not weird."

"It's not?"

"No. That's just personal."

"Yeah. It is personal."

Pulling into the driveway of Ari's soon to be ex-home, it took only a moment to see that something sat out of place. The front door stood wide open as did the side yard gate.

"Shit. They must still be here," Ari said, but then Sabine felt it. Something sick and twisted, the way that decay would feel; if a smell could ever translate to the sense of touch.

The .45 Phillip had insisted she take appeared in Sabine's hand a half second behind Ari's own Beretta. "Where the hell do you keep that?" Sabine asked in passing, not expecting an answer.

"I could ask you the same thing," Ari goggled at her friend.

"Controllers are silly ass ninnies," Sabine said.

"I've been saying that for years," Ari nodded. "I'll take the front. You take the back."

"Got it."

Sabine crept into the backyard. The wooden gate creaked alarmingly when she brushed past it into the darkening shadows of the side yard, but nothing moved. Nor did she hear anything other than wind and traffic off in the distance.

"Jesus Christ! Zombie hunters?" Sabine's voice was tight with disbelief and disdain. "Of all the stupid…"

Six people lay dead in the backyard on the grass, chests ripped open, ribcages open to the darkening day. Their hearts were all clearly missing, the blood turning the grass black. Sabine dropped her gun and her head briefly, keeping her lunch down by force of will. She was an analyst, damn it! Not operations!

She only recognized them because they had been in the reports that she had gone over. But recognition or not, it still left her with a hell of a mess in front of her. No sign of what took them out, except for the open back door.

But seeing them there, told her what to expect inside. Which made her realize that Ari was already in. She hadn't heard any shots yet though. If they were lucky, whatever had killed the zombie hunters' team was long gone.

She crept into the house, gun at the ready and was grateful that no reception committee awaited her. The walls of the house glowed, where not shadowed from the febrile kitchen light. A bare light bulb visible through the immediate left hand doorway from Ari's bedroom entry way, the shade for the lamp long gone, still swung on its cord from the swift passage of... something. Sabine noted the smears on the linoleum and berated herself for having agreed to go in alone.

"Ready or not, here I come," Sabine said to no one. She met back up with Ari in the dining room, having cleared Ari's bedroom and the bathroom, going through the connecting door into Ari's study and out. Ari had been there for a while.

Standing over the dead bodies of Richard and Amanda Pratt, her once landlords and friends. "Hah! See what happens when you kick someone out? You piss off the Shekinah and She removes her protection! Hah!"

Sabine dropped the gun to her side, but didn't put it away. "Ari, you are chastising two dead bodies."

"So?"

"And something was sent to kill you."

"Yeah, well I would have kicked its ass."

"Well, there is that."

Which was when the dead man shambled into the dining room.

Sabine didn't think. Two squeezes of the trigger sent two Glaser rounds into its head before Ari even had time to come up to bear.

Time slowed down. Dilated horribly. Sabine for the first time ever felt the sickening feeling of not being dispassionate in the place where she shot. Because the body dropped all right, dropped and ripping out of its head came a thing that she had only seen once before in her Dreams. Slaughtering a team of highly trained people sent to retrieve a large gold tablet that she knew all too well.

"Ari!!!" Sabine screamed.

She could see where the Glasers had flattened against the skull of the creature. It looked part snake and part like something that H.R. Geiger would have dreamed up, black scales and covered in clotting blood. The skull, shaped like an arrowhead, its body barbed like a spine, sharp and deadly black and wet looking, even though the blood, rising up out of the body, five feet of it. Black mirror eyes locked on Sabine and she wondered through the knots in her belly, so, this is what it's like to know you're going to die.

"יהוה סלי ומצדאתי ומפלמי-לי! אווי צורי אהכסה-

בו!"

It reared away from Ari and whatever she had screamed. Sabine had no idea where Ari had been hiding the flamethrower. She just followed the cry with torching it.

It made no sound. Just fell in flames, writhing like a slug that had salt poured on it. Sabine clambered over the dining table, and emptied the rest of her clip into it where it flopped on the oriental carpet that was never going to be the same, into the back of its neck. The Glasers finally penetrated and black matter sprayed the floor and embedded into the carpet.

It stopped moving.

She kicked it.

Then took a deep breath.

She'd been screaming the whole time.

The silence shook her more than the report of the rounds had or the flamethrower's dragon breath. She heard no sirens.

"Fuck," Ari said, her voice hoarse and raw.

"Oh man. It doesn't have a mouth," Sabine said.

"Yeah. So?"

"So what the hell did it do with the hearts?"

Ari looked green. "Let's let other people figure that out."

"Good plan." Sabine was certain she was just as green.

They both stumbled from the dining room and into the front room. It wasn't any better, Sabine discovering it was just as much of an abattoir as the dining room and backyard. The real estate agent that the Pratts had hired lay slumped over a card table set up with the flyers on the house and business cards. A couple lay on the floor. All had their chests cracked open.

Sabine went and sat on the brocade couch anyway, now covered in black goo, her .45 cradled in her left hand,. Utter misery and terror roiled through her gut. Numbness set in at the horrors in the house.

"I knew he lied, but I didn't think he'd move this fast. Try to kill you. Hell, try to kill me," Sabine said, closing her eyes.

"Hey. Hey! It's okay," Ari said down next to her. "I'm okay."

"Gods, Ari."

"I know. I know."

"I've got to call Phillip."

"Why?"

"This is going to blow shit for everyone, both us and your people. We've...we can't leave here like this."

"Right. You call. I'll get the plastic bags."

Sabine struggled up from the couch and found the phone. She heard Tony on the other end and didn't wait for him to get out more than the patter informing her that it wasn't a secure line.

"I need a containment and cleanup crew, pronto."

A half second of pause. "We're on our way," Tony said and she hung up.

Not even twenty-four hours and Sabine found herself in a in the back seat of a Lincoln Town car, going the opposite direction across the Bay Bridge, though this time Ari was with her and somebody else drove. They had left a full cleaning crew at Ari's place, who discovered that some of the reason why no alarm had been raised was due to the fact that the neighbors on both sides were dead. All killed by the creature that rode back in a different car in a body bag, to International Film for a full autopsy and analysis.

The cleaning crew was arranging to have all three houses go up in a freak fire.

Sometimes Sabine had enough sense to feel frightened at the resources of the people she now worked for. Ari sat with her arms crossed, staring out the window.

"What's wrong? Besides the obvious," Sabine asked, just as they drove through the tunnel on Treasure Island.

"I thought they were my friends. How could they have done this to me? And then to go and get eaten before I could get even!"

"Ari..." Sabine didn't know what to say.

"Even they didn't deserve this, Sabine." Ari turned and fixed her eyes on Sabine. "No one deserves this."

"No. No one deserves this."

They finished the ride in silence. Sabine felt the misery root deeper in her gut. Until surprise replaced it, when Andrew drove them right into the underground garage of IFHQ, Ari not dropped off somewhere.

"Um. Andrew?"

"Yeah?" he answered, parking the car with the rest of its identical brothers in one row of stalls.

"Ari's still in the car."

"Yeah."

"Weren't you going to take her to the Israeli Embassy?" Sabine asked.

Andrew caught her line of sight in the rear view mirror. "Oh no," he grinned. "Ari has won the booby prize. She comes in."

"Oh," Sabine said.

Edward Quintaine waited, Phillip right behind him when they came out of the elevator. "Ms. Doran," Edward said.

"Quintaine," Ari smiled.

Sabine felt her gut sink further. Ari being nice meant that she was out to sharpen her tongue on someone.

"We have a briefing room ready." He lead the way.

Debriefings. Nothing but debriefings, Sabine thought. *What the fuck was this going to do to figure out what the hell was going on?* She wondered. But then her analyst brain kicked in. It was the only way to figure it out.

The briefing room turned out to just be a small lead-lined conference room. The cameras were set to go the minute they walked in. Sabine headed for a chair, not waiting to see if anyone else followed. She wondered if she'd get in trouble for falling asleep. The adrenalin that her body had produced in the last forty-eight hours now left her feeling so exhausted that it might as well have been the same as if she hadn't slept.

"Those death snake thingies," Sabine started. "What are they?"

"They don't have a name," Edward answered. "In fact, we've never captured one before, alive or dead."

"Lucky me."

"Yes. Lucky you." And from the tone of his voice, Sabine knew that he meant a whole wealth of other meanings. "And how did you manage to kill it?"

"Ari yelled at it."

"Excuse me?"

"Ari yelled at it. I don't know what it was. Actually, what was it?" Sabine asked.

Ari had taken the seat next to her and stared at her interlaced fingers on the table top. "Hebrew," Ari answered.

"Okay. What was it?"

"*`The Lord is my Rock, and my fortress and my deliverer. The God who is my Rock, in Him I take refuge,*'" Ari quoted. "It's a... prayer. Song of David. I actually didn't expect it to work."

"Go David," Sabine said.

"But it did?" Edward leaned in.

"This isn't the first or even second time you guys have run into one of these damn things," Sabine said.

"No."

"Great."

"What made you think to try it?" Edward continued.

"A little voice told me to."

"Ah." Edward pushed back from the table, leaned back and Sabine knew enough spook body language to know he was doing everything he knew to appear unimpressed and unconcerned. "What else does the Mossad know about these things?"

"Plenty."

"Guys," Sabine cut in. "The Russians have already thrown their lot in with us. What's it going to take to get your fraternity in on this more than it already is, Ari?"

"James Bond over there not leaving us out here with our fannies hanging out."

"James Bond?" Edward almost smiled.

"Yeah, James Bond! What are you trying to do, get us killed? You knew that this thing was in this country."

"Quite the contrary. Though maybe we could change that for you," Edward said while Sabine stayed hung up on Ari's statement.

"Keep it up, laughing boy."

"Will you two cut it out?" Sabine asked. Ari looked contrite. Edward did not.

"Sorry," Ari muttered.

Edward didn't apologize.

"You know what that thing is?" Sabine turned on her friend.

"Probably no more than Quintaine does. It's somewhat demonic, so..."

"So, if you're devout, quoting appropriate scripture at it wigs it out?" Sabine found her mind clicking into overdrive.

"Apparently."

"What did you mean, he knew it was in this country?" Ari just looked at Edward.

Edward shook his head in the negative. "No, Ari. We did not know. Or I never would have let Sabine leave here, with or without me being conscious."

The words made Sabine feel a little better.

"What about Ari?" Sabine asked.

"It wasn't after Ari."

"You don't know that."

"Who else knows about these things?" Sabine asked two hours later, as the video crew wrapped up the equipment.

"The British for sure," Ari said, staring at her fingernails.

"As in MI5 or 6?"

"Probably only 6."

Edward again kept his own counsel, staring off at one wall.

"The data's good on this?" Sabine asked.

"Decent," Ari nodded. "Why?"

Andrew walked in, heading for Edward, but Sabine waved his attention her way. "Get me Nigel Lovejoy," Sabine said and swept out.

In the hall, Sabine found a person she realized she'd been hoping to spot. Phillip was just turning down the far end of the hall.

"Where are we in our time table?" Sabine asked.

"Ah!" he smiled. "A willing audience! Come into my office." He lead the way to the Big Room. "I watched most of the brief."

Sabine didn't need Phillip to elucidate that he meant on closed circuit television.

"Death snake thingies?"

"You have a better name for them?"

"Oh no. I actually thought it not only highly entertaining, but very descriptive. What do you think it would be in the Latin?" She punched him in the shoulder and he guffawed. "You're lucky," he said when they reached the Big Room, some of the humor leaving.

"What's that make the dead?" Sabine asked.

Phillip went to Andrew and Tony's stations, though neither man was in residence. He punched up a screen on one of the terminals and three of the wall screens lit up with various telemetry and live video. "We're in position in twelve hours."

"Son of a bitch, Phillip!" Sabine couldn't help it. When he had said he would move on her suggestion, she'd expected a month, at least weeks.

"What was it you said to me before you left? Ah yes. I don't fuck around." The man had to have the grin surgically attached. "We've had some assets in place for over a year now. This was just an optimal time to make use of them."

"Over a year?" Sabine's eyebrows climbed for her hairline again.

"You're surprised." Phillip sounded surprised.

"Yeah. Immensely. What the hell were you assholes waiting for if you could mobilize this quickly and with…" Sabine scanned the telemetry quickly. "Son of a bitch! Two special ops teams? With support?"

"You saw the after actions on the recovery of the Monstrosity."

"My informed assumption had been that had been an operation of some months in the planning."

"It was. But it executed in a small time frame. The Game has changed, Sabine. He or she who cannot step up at a moment's notice is stepped on," Phillip said, his own attention drawn back to the screens. Sabine scanned and realized that the whole room was plugged into this op on one level or another. Even Amanda sat in front of a set of screens, though in front of hers there was a white cloth, a candle stick with black candle and a large round orb of what looked to be either onyx or obsidian.

Phillip noticed her caught attention. "She's running the astral dark for us."

"She can do that?"

"Hell, she's the only reason we know where we're going. Well, you too."

"Me?"

"The place Corsico took you?"

"Yes?"

"When Ammie ran the geomancy on it, it popped up as the same place that we'd been getting hints of the Oracle's location."

"Where?"

"Sweetheart, he took you half way around the world. Milan."

"Milano?"

"Milan."

The Duomo. Suddenly all of her memories of Milan were in sudden force in the front of her mind. The Voice. Zoë. Everything.

She had to warn Zoë.

"Sabine? Are you all right?" She looked up at Phillip. She hadn't even seen him stand up and hadn't realized she was swaying again from the flood of adrenaline.

"I'm very tired," she lied.

"You need some place to lie down?" Phillip's concern was palpable and almost made what she was going to do unbearably hard. But op sec or not, Zoë had to know, she had to be ready.

"I'm just going to go to my office. Bring me an update later?"

"Sure. I'll wake you when it starts to get interesting."

"Thanks."

She ended up back in the hall. Scanning for Ari. She had no clue how to achieve her goal, but she had a theory and she needed her friend for it. Not spotting anyone she knew, except for Mel way down at his station, she headed for her office, hoping that Edward or someone would have thought to park Ari there.

Her luck was good.

"Where'd you go?" Ari asked.

"I need your help."

"Anything."

"Stars endure."

It was the first thing Sabine heard in the Dream. She pivoted, for a change tennis shoes on her feet, wearing the clothes she had gone seeking this Dream in. The black chamber stayed empty, the entrances dark and shadowed.

"Stars?"

"Stars endure," Zoë repeated. "In one way, one form or another, they go on. Don't forget."

"I won't." As with all of Zoë's foretellings, Sabine found it difficult to understand at first. Sabine walked in a small circle. She'd gone into the Dream for a reason...

"They are coming. I know," Zoë broke in.

"You already know."

"You had to come. I need you," Zoë said and Sabine's fears quieted some. Zoë's black eyes looked at Sabine, arresting her next question.

Into that dark chamber, the child oracle spoke softly in her so sweet, yet ancient voice, and said, "I give you my power."

The Gift streaked out of Zoë like a shooting star. It collided with Sabine like a meteor crash, square into the center of her chest. It raised her to her toes in a rigid jolt. Sabine screamed at the beauty of the energy, a scream of both violence and exultation.

She felt her mind split open and before her mind's eye, a million futures spooled into being. Staring straight into the center of the sun at noon couldn't have been more blinding. She felt her body shift, felt the cells of her physical form strain and reconfigure to something new. She screamed again. The coils of the Beloved caught her as she staggered.

"What's happening?" Sabine screamed. Her ears were deafened and sharpened simultaneously. She could hear voices and Voices and all screamed her name. Through this cacophony a child's voice cut, frail and frightened.

"Oracle, you must answer."

The Voice that Sabine had only ever heard come from and entwined with Zoë's voice now braided itself into Sabine's as her mouth moved instantly in answer.

"*Ask.*"

"What is to become of me?"

Surrounded by the black coils, the oil slick rainbows, the floor a distant shadow, Sabine's sight cleared long enough to see Zoë. Not the oracle, but the child.

The Voice twined through Sabine's own.

"*You are to finally become yourself. Have sight where none can see. Lead where none can follow. Sister and daughter, all that has been taken from you shall be repaid,*" Sabine said, the futures clear in her inner sight, yet no clearer could she speak. "*But you will have to face the darkness you fear most to reach Sanctuary. The Preserver will never rest as long as you live.*"

In the next heartbeat, the Oracular Source left.

Sabine mewled in pain as the futures spawned into infinity, stars spun above and below her. She fell from the coils of the Beloved through an endless void.

"You went very far out."

Sabine opened her eyes to find Edward behind her, cradling her head between his hands which rested on his knees.

She tried to speak and only managed to croak, "...stars."

"Give it a minute. You really did go far out. You're not all here yet," Edward said, brushing her hair off her forehead.

Sabine blinked, not comprehending why Edward sat as her Anchor and not Ari. She remembered going into the Dream with Ari as her touchstone. She didn't struggle to speak though, the after effects of the Dreamwalk keeping her temper from even thinking of activating. Instead, she watched Edward's face, whose eyes never left her own.

He looked haggard, an expression Sabine knew that in her living memory she had never seen before. Somewhere, deep inside her, something stirred.

"Did..." Sabine swallowed and tried again, even as Edward caressed her throat as he shook his head. "Did something go wrong?"

"Later," Edward said.

Again, Sabine was too relaxed to fight, but she spoke again. "Promise."

Edward went still. It didn't show, but in contact with his skin, Sabine could feel the stillness that went through him.

"Promise," Edward replied.

Sabine's eyes started to slip closed more and more, each time staying closed a little longer.

"Sleep, Sabine," Edward said and Sabine felt something reach up from under her and with a feather touch, pulled her into a warm blackness.

⚡ ε Z

"Is she okay?" Ari verbally jumped on Edward, the instant he walked in the door of the Big Room.

"Sleeping," he said and turned to Phillip. "Where are we?"

"Ten hours out. Teams are sleeping."

"Good. Keep me posted."

Ɓ7ᛞZ♭

Kevin Andridge led his six person team into a chamber Sabine could have described in forensic detail. The black basalt floor, the roughhewn gray granite columns that numbered the same as the entrances, thirteen of each and the long distance to the black altar. Described the darkness that concealed the ceiling even as unseen light sources illuminated the level they stood at, all in a gray light.

"Shit, and I thought fluorescents made my skin look bad," someone whispered from the back, probably Higuero.

"Cut the chatter," Kevin hissed.

Hand signals then, pairs of shooters crab walking from column to column towards the altar. Kevin had seen the complete mission profile and after action reports from the retrieval of the gold tablet. This place looked too much like that other temple and his heart raced up to the thought. But nothing could prepare him for the Beloved.

The coils of the Beloved floated down from the ceiling, defying gravity and description in its grace. From within its deepest coils came Zoë, cradled in it with infinite care and infinite love and yet a prisoner, her body invaded at every opening by her connection into the Beloved. The team drew back in horror.

But Kevin stood his ground, all fifteen years of him unable to comprehend what he saw before him, but he knew that Zoë saw him.

The Beloved gently set Zoë's feet on the ground before the altar. She had never walked in her entire life. The Beloved had carried her for all the years that she had been alive; cared for her in ways more infinitely patient and loving than any parent or adult lover could ever have. A being whose entire being was devotion and love had been hers, and with that same devotion, It gave her up.

Her legs shook even with the Beloved's support, but before she could even protest, the Beloved withdrew. It withdrew the life support tubes, the contacts, the invasive coils that had been as much her body as the Beloved, leaving bleeding marks and scars where they had been, but Zoë didn't notice. The Beloved rose to the ceiling and the shadows.

Zoë for the first time in her entire life stood alone.

Utter joy and sorrow and confusion and incomprehension sketched across her face. She stood for only an instant and fell. Kevin took a running start and caught her.

"Hello," she whispered, and her voice was human, frail, frail human, the power of the Oracle gone.

ℰ𝘓𝘕ℰ𝘓g𝘢𝟕𝙿

It was understandable in the end. Edward Quintaine had his mind on other things. But Phillip Dougherty was a man who planned for many contingencies. He had found a use for Antonio Rodriguez. As a babysitter to Jacob and Michelle Quintaine.

The house in Seacliff lay quiet. The normal surveillance team that lived in the front hall closet had been called back to IFHQ in preparation for the mission in Italy, though a low level security presence remained on the street. Inside, an old man sat on a couch with two young children, telling them stories he really shouldn't have.

"So Patton didn't rescue the 101st?" Jacob wanted to know.

"To this day, they will tell you that they did not need rescuing."

"Wow."

"I don't think I could ever be that brave." Michelle shook her head.

"Michelle," his faint accent stressed her name in ways that Michelle loved already. "I tell you something now. The truth is, none of those men, no one that I served with, ever felt brave."

"No?"

"No. We did what we had to do. It was important to protect our loved ones back home and to help the people there who had suffered so. Without us, they would have been under a great tyrant and many would have died. That is what kept us going, even as frightened as we all were."

"You were scared?"

"Oh, sometimes I think especially me. My Captain," his voice hesitated over that word, but he kept on. "Now he was a man that I often wondered if he ever felt fear. It was not till much later than I learned that of us all, he was the most frightened."

"How can that be?" Jacob asked.

"It was simple, *mijo*. He knew what was truly at stake.."

"How do you know?"

"Because he told me. If he had not, I would have thought as you, Michelle. I would have thought he felt no fear. But he knew a secret that I did not, though he did teach me. He knew that fear was never enough of a reason to stop when faced with a great evil."

Into this quiet, they heard the intruders before they saw them. Smelled them.

Rodriguez had both children on their feet, hustling them for the back door before either could wonder what the smell was. They made only ten feet.

"Magician..." A terrible voice, really many voices, hissed.

"Magician?" Michelle whispered.

Rodriguez turned to face the horror unseen in the shadows. "What do you want, Misborn?" Rodriguez said, his voice harder and from a younger man.

"Give us the children."

"No," he said and drew his weapon.

"Always you defy us." The Misborn came into view. Michelle gave a frightened squeak. They looked to be children no older than she, three in number. But children, living children, did not bleed from the eyes nor did they curdle the air around them.

"You should expect it now."

He waited no longer. Aimed and fired three rounds at the creatures, didn't wait to see what hit, grabbed Michelle with his free arm and ran. "Run, Jacob! Run!"

Jacob took off, leading the old man carrying his sister. Off the back balcony, a trail went between the houses and opened onto Baker Beach, all empty sand, sea grasses, the Golden Gate Bridge post card perfect behind it. Jacob didn't slow. He ran straight for Baker Battery, the World War II gun emplacement that sat hunkered down in overgrown ice plant and sand dune. He kept looking back. For an old man, Rodriguez kept up, setting down Michelle as soon as they hit the beach.

"Good boy! Into the bunker!" The ocean wind tried to rip Rodriguez' words away.

There was no sign of the Misborn.

ㄟ𝄢Ｖ乙𝈯7

Sabine stepped into what was becoming her favorite briefing room, briefing in progress, Rodriguez and both children in chairs before Edward. Phillip followed close behind and took up position by the door.

"Sabine," Edward said. There was no indication of his earlier exhaustion.

"Edward." she sat, smiled at Michelle, waggled her eyebrows at Jacob.

"Captain," Rodriguez said.

"Yo. So. Had fun without me, I see."

"We were getting bored."

"What happened?"

"A set of creatures that Rodriguez called the Misborn came to my house," Edward said.

Spook houses were sacrosanct. Someone had just broken the rules, big time. Especially with children involved. Terrorists did shit like that.

"The Misborn?" Something niggled at Sabine's memory and Memory.

"They knew him," Michelle spoke, her voice soft and frightened.

"You're okay, honey bunny. You're safe now," Sabine said.
"How?"

"World War II."

Memory unspooled in Sabine's head. Captain Harrison's Memory.

"Oh gods," she said, as it took her.

"You must radio out the second you hear the blast." She stood in Harrison's skin, in a cow bier of all places, in the German countryside. Rodriguez sat on a bale of hay, wounded.

"I'm coming with you." Rodriguez staggered up.

Sabine/Harrison pushed him back down. "You'll just slow me down. I need you here. That's an order."

"Sir."

"Antonio, I'm counting on you."

"I will not fail you, Captain."

"I know you won't. I know."

Memory shifted and became Waking Dream, the cow bier and later in the day. Sabine was herself. She knew only a mile away her previous Self crept into a cursed Temple, attempting to stop the evil she faced now.

Rodriguez was alone.

The children, two boys and a girl, stepped into the filtered light. Sabine felt her heart trip-hammer, even as she knew that this was long past, long since history. Rodriguez lived.

"Little boy…" the Voices hissed, but the mouths of the children did not move.

"What— Who are you?" Rodriguez asked, one arm still around his precious radio.

"We are Misborn." The hiss raised the hair all over her body.

It made Sabine's Remembering self, cringe. It sounded like someone trying to speak through a slit throat. Then they both saw the blood their eyes wept, the bloody footprints their steps left behind. Then the smell. Blood and flesh and shit. Fresh battle field or slaughterhouse.

"Sabine." Edward's voice. Hard, cutting through her Memory.

"Gods and little fishes," she whispered. "How did you fucking survive?"

Edward made a strangled noise.

"If not for the protection of my rosary, I would have died then." Only Rodriguez seemed unfazed.

"Faith again," Phillip commented.

"Yes," Rodriguez said.

"It doesn't tell us why they were after Jacob and Michelle," Edward said.

"They weren't after the kids," Sabine answered. "They were after Rodriguez."

"Why? They asked, demanded them."

"Only because they thought of them as important to Rodriguez. Like the radio." Sabine met Rodriguez' eyes with her own.

"Radio?" Phillip asked.

"Long story," Sabine sighed.

"This is not a wrinkle we need right now," Phillip added.

"You're only half right," Sabine said.

A waiting silence was the only response she received. "Don't tell me I'm the only one who sees it?"

"Sees what?" Phillip again. Even Rodriguez frowned.

"I'm not the only one who needs Rodriguez." Stone silence settled in the room, broken by a little girl.

"Not Mr. Rodriguez! No one gets to hurt him! Daddy! Do something!" Michelle erupted.

"Oy." Sabine came back to realizing that she was not in a room of adults. "I think we're done."

"Yes, we are!" Phillip said. "Michelle, you want to help me catch the bad guys?"

"Yeah!"

"Fine. You come with me. You too, Jacob." Phillip ushered the children out, Rodriguez following. Edward went to leave as well, but Sabine pinned him with her gaze before he could rise from his chair.

She waited for the door to close. "What happened?"

Edward did the one thing Sabine had never expected him to do. Ever.

He sighed. "Not to delay the grilling you clearly wish to give me, but to what particular what do you refer?"

"Ha." She took her own deep breath. "Your domicile is compromised. I got that part. I meant my…" *Oh, this is hard,* Sabine thought.

"Your Dreamwalk." It felt worse that Edward's tone was not in any manner accusatory.

"Yes. What happened to Ari?"

"She was losing you."

"Yeah. How did you get there?"

Oh ho, Sabine thought. Edward's face for half a second showed an emotion.

"I felt it." The words, so dry.

"Really."

"Yes."

"Well then. That's…very interesting."

"This isn't getting us anywhere," Edward said.

"You're right. Shall I tell you what else I know?"

"Why don't you tell me what happened on your Walk?"

Sabine smiled. Ah yes. A good defense was a good offense. But she knew how to play this game too.

"Zoë gave me her Power."

Edward's face this time did not shutter away his emotions, giving her only Game Face. He just stared.

"She what?" At least his voice showed no tells, Sabine decided.

"Zoë gave me her Power."

"What does this mean?"

"I don't know." It was again Sabine's turn to sigh. "I'm sure I'll get to find out in the worst manner possible."

The intensity of his gaze arrested any further thoughts in her head.

"I surely hope not."

"Edward," Sabine said. "We're not out of the game yet."

"No. We're not. But the Opposition keeps upping the ante."

"That's what they do. What they've always done."

"What will you do with this ability?"

"Use it," she said, an echo of the Oracular Source in her tone.

A couple of hours later, Sabine walked barefoot on the grass through a graveyard.

Thin autumn sunlight bathed everything in a gold glow through the overcast that had descended on the day. Sabine felt the cool damp of the grass under her toes, the soft grass and the deep stillness of the place resonate up through the soles of her feet.

In the time that she had been working for Edward, Winter had started to come again. It wasn't fully in, Sabine could feel that, but she could feel that September was already hinting at the coming cold, even in California. October would see Indian Summer come and give the lie to the longer dark, but for right then, Winter stretched fingers into Autumn.

Ari had tried to come with her. Sabine had to tell her friend in firm terms that not only did she have to stay at IFHQ, but she was counting on her to hold down the fort while she went to do what the Oracle inside her told her what to do.

Then Sabine had gotten in her car. Driven across the Bay Bridge, but this time heading for Piedmont and a necropolis of century and older graves where stone angels wept on monuments and others beseeched the sky.

So Sabine walked on the grass, barefoot as the inner promptings told her, among old marble and older headstones, feeling the promise of Winter in her bones. The prompting stopped. A wind came up instead, colder than Winter, but then the Dead always brought their own chill.

"Hello, Grandma."

"Hello, Sabine." She turned. A young, dark haired woman stood behind her, her hair styled in a perfect 1940s wave, a woman Sabine only recognized because she had seen the woman's face in old photographs.

"Grandma? What are you doing here?"

"You need my help."

"You're not buried here."

"No. But in the end, are not all graveyards one and the same?" Maria Elena, once Sabine's mother's mother, stopped by an ancient stone, the inscription long gone, wind and rain having done entropy's work. "This one will do for our purposes."

"You know why I'm here?" she asked, sounding doubtful

"How could I not?"

"Of course."

"You love them very much."

Sabine looked up and met her grandmother's translucent eyes. "I don't know what to do. I just knew to come."

"I know what to do."

"Show me."

"Your blood on the stone."

Sabine looked around, walked back to the road where she'd seen a broken beer bottle. A brown Budweiser bottle from the looks of it. Came back with a large piece.

"Tell me what you need," Maria Elena said.

The words came, Oracle speaking through Sabine's mouth, tearing, vibrating her throat. "By my life's blood," Sabine cut her palm in a quick stroke. "Protect the children, Jacob and Michelle. My strength is your strength—"

"—*Your strength is mine*—"

"My power yours to call—"

"—*Your power mine to call*—"

"Till Death unbinds us—"

"—*till Death unbinds us*—"

"Or Time makes us whole."

"—*Or Time makes us whole*," Maria Elena flared white and gold. "It is done." And she vanished from sight.

Sabine just stood there, watching her blood drip on to the headstone. "Goodbye, Grandma."

And as if from far off, she heard, "I love you, Sabine."

The thought occurred to her that she had been unsurprised to see her grandmother. What surprised her was the relief she felt that it had not been the shade of her mother who had come to her call for help. She didn't know how she would have handled that.

She turned back for the car. She needed to bind her hand and get back. Things were moving too fast now. Work to be done and she had done all she could to protect Jacob and Michelle from whatever waited for them all.

It'd probably kill her, Sabine thought, a sobering thought in its totality, but the next thought came clearer. *So. It killed her.* Hatred and grief welled up in her for a blind moment. Everybody died. Usually before you could do anything about it or you could make any amount of sense of what life meant in the first place.

Either way, she'd go down fighting.

Driving back ended up being trickier than driving to Piedmont. Traffic got sticky and ugly. Steering with one hand, while the other started to throb from pain, was a neat trick, Sabine discovered. She made it, a long hour later, but by the time she got back, Phillip waited.

"Yo, what? You bug the car?" Sabine asked.

"Why, yes! Funny you should mention it." Phillip grinned.

"I'm back. I'm back. Why the reception committee?"

"Did you get what you needed?"

"I think so," she said.

"What did you do?" Phillip asked.

"I asked my grandmother to protect Jacob and Michelle."

"Your grandmother is dead. Both of them are."

"I know."

To Phillip's credit, it only took him one half-second to put two and two together. "Are you sure?"

"Sure of what?" Sabine matched his tone.

"The backlash on that kind of spell can be major."

"Can it?"

"Yes."

"It's worth it."

"Just making sure you are aware of the consequences."

"I think I've been aware of that fact for some time."

"Fine."

"You need me?"

"We need to go out to Seacliff."

"What's happened?" Sabine focused in on him.

"What hasn't? You need to get changed. There are clothes in your office. Meet me down here in ten minutes."

Sabine managed to get back in seven, checking her watch. She'd thrown on the black suit she'd found waiting for her. She had no idea where they'd found it, since all she owned had burned.

"Get in." He pointed at another of the fleet cars when she stepped out of the elevator, a gray Oldsmobile.

"Is it bad?" She settled into the car's passenger seat.

"We can't get the team out of Milan just yet."

"Why?"

"We're going out to the house to find out."

"What's at the house?"

"We're meeting the Russians."

"We are?"

"We are."

"Wow."

"And you thought Edward wasn't listening."

"Oh, I know he listened. I didn't think he was going to act on it," Sabine said, staring out the window. Twilight came down on San Francisco, sodium lights coming on in the streets and painting the city in their orange glow against the deepening blue sky.

"Why the house?" she asked.

"They may be allies, but no need to let them inside the keep's walls."

"Op sec. Got it. They've already been to the house."

"Exactly. Oh, a friend of yours will be there."

"Ari?"

"No. Irina Romininov."

"Huh."

"Should be interesting."

"You have a warped sense of what is interesting."

Phillip turned onto California Avenue, heading west, a moment's lull in the conversation as he focused on the vagaries of San Francisco inner city traffic. "One other thing."

"Yes?"

"I listen. I re-ran those background checks. Myself."

Sabine took her eyes from the passing street view to give Phillip her full attention. "Don't tease me, Phillip."

"I did. I wouldn't tease about this." His seriousness backed up his claim.

"Who?"

"Phoebe."

"Phoebe? Mrs. Quintaine?"

"Mrs. Quintaine."

"Holy shit."

"That's not all."

"Isn't that fucking enough?" Sabine exclaimed.

Phillip reached into his jacket pocket and dropped the last thing Sabine ever expected to see again right into her lap, without taking his eyes off the road. A small cold cream jar.

Sabine didn't need to open it to know what would be inside.

"I found them in Phoebe's purse."

"Why tell me this?" were the only words she could find to say.

"Right now, you are my ally too, Sabine. I trust you." Sabine felt her heart go still. "There's no time to go into full details, but I'll get you a full brief. I am asking you to keep this between us for now."

He risked taking his eyes off the road long enough to pin emphasis of his statement with his stare. "She's been having affairs with a multiple of people who all have bad connections to our favorite brotherhood. At first, I thought her unwitting." He cruised up to the Seacliff house, parked, but neither of them moved to get out. "I have since changed my mind. She knows and is most witting. In fact, most willing. Those prove it."

His head jerked to the jar in her lap. "The only question that remains to be determined is who she was using them on."

"What are you going to do?" Sabine would not touch the jar.

"Well, I can't do what I would like to do," Phillip grinned.

"No, I guess you can't." Sabine stared out the windshield. "Edward would never let you kill her."

"I didn't say anything about killing."

"All right. Execution."

"Yes."

"I have no illusions, Phillip," Sabine said, taking the full weight of his stare.

"That's why I trust you."

"Oh shit. The children. Are they his?" Sabine asked. "It'll kill him…"

"There's no telling at this time. And it wouldn't matter. They're his as far as he's concerned."

"What about her?" Sabine surprised herself with her own cold tone. "Blood types and hair strands from all of them. DNA testing. Get on it," Sabine ordered.

"Later. For now, we need to get inside."

"Done deal." Sabine touched the jar. Picked it up and slipped it into the outside pocket of her suit jacket.

They made their way up to the house, shoulder to shoulder. Sabine felt a closeness to Phillip she'd not felt with anyone at IFHQ. Not even Rodriguez who her Past remembered and her Present cared for in some indefinable way. At that moment, Phillip was not only her friend, but her anchor. Who knew that a gift of trust would do that to her? she thought.

Inside, except for the security post, no one stood in the main house. Sabine glanced up the stairs, but saw no one. The children must have still been at IFHQ or somewhere else secure. Phillip went to confer with security and Sabine went deeper in. She spotted Edward out on the balcony, looking out, though little could be seen. Only the lights from the Golden Gate Bridge's traffic in the distance illuminated that bit of ocean.

He wore a gray tweed suit that was almost professorial in its look. A lavender rose with a sprig of baby's breath was tucked into the buttonhole of his lapel. He wore his glasses as well, which only heightened the look of academia, a look that Sabine was not familiar with on him.

Sabine found herself running. Stranger yet, she tried to hug him, but Edward kept his distance.

"Don't worry. I won't crush you," Sabine said, a frown crossing her forehead. It took her a half second to realize that there were possible layers of meaning to that statement.

"Your suit. I won't crush your suit."

He made some sound, but it didn't come out in words, but his expression was clear. He could care less if she crumpled him a little. His arm slid around her shoulders and he pulled her in close for an embrace. It wasn't tight, but it was firm and he did press her to the entire length of his body. There was nothing sexual about it. She lay her forehead against his shoulder for a moment, wondering why her eyes stung.

They stood there for a long moment. Sabine allowed herself to breathe him in. How she felt about him was becoming more complicated by the second. Sorrow, grief and a strange, twisted longing knotted under her breastbone. She pulled away enough to look up at him and was arrested by the look on his face.

His other hand came up to touch her face. "I just can't go on not knowing what it would be like to kiss you."

The world went still inside of her. Edward started to lean in.

Sabine felt awkward. He stopped, but saw something in her face and moved in again, this time, awkwardness even so, Sabine wanted this.

"Well, what have we here?" They snapped apart as if flung. Phoebe stood in the doorway.

"Hello, Phoebe," Sabine said.

Phoebe looked overdone, like some gaudy ornament from the court of the Sun King. The sequined gown she wore with her diamonds just was too much. Or maybe it had nothing to do with what she was wearing at all. Without meaning to, Sabine put a hand against her side, smoothing the black silk suit against her skin. It took all her willpower not to draw her gun.

CHAPTER XVIII - CATASTROPHIC FIELD COLLAPSE

Edward walked into the study on the first floor, a room that Sabine had never been in before. Done up in dark wood and pale cream walls, the only art in the room was a Magritte, specifically Son of Man. Sabine had been arrested by the placement of it as the only adornment when she'd been ushered in, having stood in the front room aimlessly until Phillip had collected her.

Irina Romininov waited in the study, sitting on a small tan leather couch in a pose both artless and graceful. Sabine grinned upon seeing her, wondering how many years Irina had studied ballet to have acquired such effortless body control. Martial arts did not give the same grace. Irina had grinned back, but her eyes were somber and dark, making the brown appear almost black in an already pale face. Today, Irina wore black leather pants and a sleeveless black turtle neck sweater, the pants tapering over stiletto boots.

Irina nodded at Edward the instant he came in and did not wait for him to sit. "We should not linger," she said.

"I thought we meant to meet and exchange information," Edward said.

"Which is why I come to the point immediately." She inclined her head to the left with a delicate frown. "The Lodge mobilizes even as we speak. They are not unaware of your operation in Milan, as you already know."

"What has happened?" Sabine interjected.

"Your team is trapped in the embassy by zombies," Irina supplied. Sabine shook her head. If she hadn't already had firsthand experience of the zombies in Ari's house, she wouldn't have believed Irina.

"Death snake thingies," she muttered.

"An accurate description of the nameless creatures. I am impressed." Irina gave a quicksilver flash of a smile. "But without support, they will have a difficult time of escape, nor can they draw that kind of attention to themselves. How had you planned to retrieve them?"

"We were going to mimic a terrorist attack. Car bomb the crowd," Phillip replied.

"Crowd?"

"To any onlookers, it currently looks like there is a demonstration outside the embassy. Only if you know what to look for can you tell that no one's alive," Phillip replied to Sabine's query.

"Holy shit, you can't do that," Sabine said. "It'd be on CNN in two shakes."

"There were reasons why we hadn't implemented that plan," Edward commented.

"You have no other plan?" Irina asked.

"None of our high powered are close enough. They'll have to sit tight. Unless you have an idea?"

"None of ours are close either." Irina got to her feet. "It changes nothing. Time is fleeting and we should not stay. The Lodge has mobilized something this way too. To this house."

"Do you know what?" Sabine asked, stepping in front of Irina.

"They look like children. We only have photos—"

"The Misborn. Again," Sabine hissed. "Fuck. We gotta go, Edward. Unless you've got a faith hidden in a jacket pocket, that's all that stops them. I thought you'd re-secured this place!"

"We did," Edward said, turning his attention to Irina. "Why should we worry? Our high powered are close here."

"Not high powered enough for them," Irina said, shaking her head in the negative. "We know next to nothing about them. Do you really wish a suburb of San Francisco to be the proving ground for what their true abilities are?"

Edward shot a wordless question to Sabine.

"I remember not even remotely enough," she answered the look.

"You must scatter, Mr. Quintaine. They mean to crush you. They know you've taken the Oracle, they know you have Miss Parsons. More importantly, they have deduced correctly your next move."

"They have?" Sabine wondered.

"They go to retrieve the other two tablets."

"What tablets?" All three of them said simultaneously.

"Please, do not all deny me at once," she sobered. "Believe me, my friends, we are all friends here. The threat is too real and too complete for me or my masters to care about international rivalries. We must hang together—"

"Or we will assuredly hang separately?" Sabine finished for her.

"Precisely."

"How do you know this?" Sabine asked.

"Our own network started turning up this information when you were spotted in Italy. We've tracked this far. Something has tipped them off. We do not know what indicator, but they have decided to move on your organization and one other."

"The zombie hunters." Sabine felt her brain light up. "Who the hell are the zombie hunters?" She worried that she had thrown a non-sequitur into the conversation, but Irina responded with a clear tell of her own. Surprise.

"How do you know of the Lesser Order?"

"Excuse me? The lesser order?" Sabine blinked.

"The Lesser Order of St. Dominis. They are pledged to destroy the undead and undying wherever they find them. They date to sometime after the destruction of the Templars, now operating as a sort of counter-terror group, but I have a feeling I can give you a history lesson another time. How do you know of them?"

"Let's just say I've run into some of them. Dead, but run into them. They had no sign of support though. I just found the bodies."

"They can teleport. That much their high powered can manage."

"Like the fucking Malice Twins," Sabine muttered.

"The——?" Irina shook her head. "No. We should continue on the road. I was not overstating when I said that we should not linger. I did not mean to keep you even this long. You must leave and soon."

"Where's Ari?" Sabine asked, her mind racing.

"Back at headquarters."

"Ari…" Sabine whispered.

"All right. We scatter. The usual, Phillip," Edward said, getting to his feet.

"Done. Ladies, with me, please."

"I need a fucking cigarette," Sabine muttered on the way out. She was utterly unsurprised when Edward pulled out a pack and handed her one and a lighter.

ꓶꓟwⳤꙄꓟ

Edward didn't go with Phillip and the two women. He went in search of his wife. He had a feeling that she hadn't left yet. He found her in the kitchen, even more out of place in her finery than she had been on the terrace.

"I need a favor, Phoebe." Phoebe put the water glass she'd been drinking from back on the counter next to the stainless steel sink. The kitchen was a study in modern efficiency. All steel countertops and steel facing on the cabinets. Minimalist and expensive.

"Well, out with it," she said, her tone pleasant enough.

"I need you to take the children to my mother's for a few days."

"I assume from your tone that you mean now." Her tone didn't change.

"Yes. Now."

"This is quite irresponsible of you, Edward. You know I have plans."

"Something has come up."

"Doesn't it always."

"Damn it, take them, Phoebe. For once in your god damn life, be their mother and protect them!" The verbal explosion set a silent shock on the room. Phoebe's eyes went wide in alarm. The sign of the outburst was gone as quick as it had appeared.

She nodded, if a little on the jerky side.

"Thank you. I'll call as soon as I know more. I would like you to stay there as well." He didn't wait for her answer.

ᒐ ᘓ ᔕ ᗷ ᑕ ᒪ

Sabine decided she was sick and tired of cars. Not cars generally. No. She hated being in them. It seemed that all she had done that day was drive or be driven from place to place and not once had she had a chance to just slow down. Have a cup of coffee. Scream at someone for the complete injustice of it all.

People who wanted to fuck up the world were now out to not just kill her but everyone she cared about, she realized. Well, she wasn't sure how she felt about Edward, she thought, as the buildings rolled by, street lights blinding her night vision. Her anger dulled.

This is worse than being out in the cold, she decided. When she had been outside, only having nightmares about Edward and his deadening eyes, it had been just that. Nightmares. You could get up in the morning, have a cup of coffee and wonder if eating chocolate ice cream before bed would ever again be a good idea. Nightmares weren't real. They weren't supposed to become flesh and blood and dress up in the clothes of three demonic children who left bloody footprints and violated the senses.

Phillip pulled into the garage of IFHQ. Sabine shook herself out of her reverie. She would have gotten out of the car without a word, but Phillip put a hand on her arm.

"It's not as bad as all that."

"What, I add mind reading to your abilities now?"

"No, just a familiarity with your psych profile. We always planned for this contingency."

"You did? Why?"

"It was only a matter of time, Sabine."

Sabine sighed. "Was it really?"

"Yes. It was. Really," Phillip yawned. "Use that analyst brain of yours. We oppose them. We have several things they now want. What else are the rules of the game?"

"Capture the flag," she said.

"Capture the flag," he agreed. "They have no choice. We've forced their hand. And that is fine. Only in a dynamic situation will we learn their full capabilities."

"And if it kills us?"

"Well, then the world's just fucked, isn't it?"

"I guess it is."

"Don't worry, Sabine." Phillip popped his door open. "It takes a lot to kill one of us."

"I sure hope you're right."

Irina leaned against her Beemer, when Sabine got out. "A lovely building you have. I am happy to get to see inside," Irina commented with a huge smile.

"Don't get too excited," Sabine said. "It's pretty dull."

Back upstairs, Sabine felt a little pain in her abdomen. She left the others when no one looked, Irina being introduced to the team, though outside of the confines of the Big Room. They'd moved to a conference room that was two doors down from Sabine's office.

She went back to her office, finding more casual clothes than the suit. Pulling on black jeans and black sweatshirt felt like pulling on comfortable skin. Afterwards, she made her way to the kitchen. Made a cup of peppermint tea and swallowed two little white pills from the kitchen pharmacy, peppermint tea chasing the pills.

Ari found Sabine in the kitchen, staring out the window at the San Francisco skyline. "I hear we're moving. Scattering to be exact."

Sabine took her attention from the view. "Our Russian friend informed us that the Misborn were sent out to the house again. She recommends we disperse as fast as possible. Apparently the Brotherhood finds us annoying enough now to exterminate."

"Good! I was feeling unloved." Ari pulled one of the uncomfortable green plastic chairs out from the single white circular table in the kitchen. "Did Edward say where we would be scattering to?"

"Your guess is as good as mine."

"Joy."

"You can say that again."

"What's eating you?" Ari asked.

Sabine started. Her gaze had gone back to staring out the window.

"I don't know," she answered.

"Any clues? A hint even?"

"No." Sabine shook her head. "Just a feeling."

"What kind of feeling?"

Sabine gave up staring. The sky was too dark to tell her anything anyway.

"The kind of feeling that says we're too late."

"Ah." Ari got up. "Phillip says we'll be ready to go in an hour, stupid tablet and all."

"They told you about the tablet?"

"Nope. I saw it in your office."

"Huge fucker, isn't it?"

"That's why you wanted the Enochian, isn't it?" Ari asked.

"Yeah. Freaky ass shit."

"No kidding. However, I didn't come to find you to discuss oogy tables. They've got dinner in the conference room."

"What time is it?" Sabine asked, realizing she had no recollection of where she'd abandoned her own watch.

"Close to ten o'clock."

Sabine nodded and followed Ari. Some intrepid soul had gone out and gotten pizza. Sabine picked at a piece, but found she had no real appetite for any of it. Meanwhile, everything and everyone around her seemed to be moving at an accelerated pace. As she sat with her sad piece of sausage and pepperoni pizza, several people wandered by carrying computers, and file boxes. She did nearly get up when she saw four large men moving the Monstrosity.

"Where are they taking it?" Sabine asked.

"To a safe place." Phillip came over and pushed her back down into one of the conference room chairs. "Aren't you going to eat more than that?"

"I'm just not hungry. I'll get something later." Sabine put the piece down; she'd had maybe three bites. "Phillip, I need my research."

"Don't worry, it goes with you. We need to keep that brain of yours cooking after all. Still have your weapon?"

Sabine leaned forward and lifted up her black sweatshirt.

"Hmm. How do you sit like that?"

"Like what?"

"I sit back with one of those holsters and I have holes dug in my back in no time."

"Dunno. Just fits." Sabine got to her feet. "I gotta go, Phillip."

"Where?" he asked.

"My office. Something doesn't fit."

"All right. Just be ready to go when I come to get you."

"I will be."

Back in her office, Sabine set quickly to work. A great deal of her files were gone, but the ones she had left on the oak desk were still there. She flipped through them randomly. She didn't know what she was looking for.

Her stomach continued to bother her, but Sabine ignored it, continuing to work. The discomfort had not even remotely prepared her for the first knifing pain that seemed to cut right under her rib cage.

It's probably nothing, Sabine thought. *It'll pass.*

Sabine doubled over onto her desk as knife after knife seemed to stab into her gut, teeth clenched against making any sound. Bent over, the pain wasn't quite as intense, but Sabine still couldn't make her eyes focus. She didn't know how long she stayed in the grips of her agony, but it faded a little, enough for her to unbend. Her now cold peppermint tea mug seemed to help. Sabine went in search of the vending machine for her floor. Maybe a little nibble will help, Sabine thought.

A package of Reese's peanut butter cups later, Sabine felt a little better. The candy had tasted like cardboard. She'd had trouble even wanting to look at them, but she attributed that to her reluctance to them being a little stale.

There is nothing wrong with me, she thought, because there couldn't be anything wrong with her.

Sabine made another cup of tea in the kitchen and went back to her office, dodging more people moving things now out of the Big Room. She was just glad she had been alone when it happened. The last thing she needed was someone thinking she was ill when she clearly was not.

⌐𝚺w𝔸ℰ𝚺

"We need to talk."

Edward looked up from his desk, pausing in packing his briefcase. "What is it?" Edward knew how rarely Phillip used those words.

"We have a mole."

"The Russians told us," Edward felt no need to invoke Irina Romininov's name.

"Phoebe."

If Phillip had shot him, Edward doubted the pain could have been more. "What?"

"Phoebe's the mole."

"You're sure," Edward said, but it wasn't a question.

"Sure and certain," Phillip said.

"Phillip, you have to find her. Now."

"Why?"

"She has the children."

He turned on his heel and went for the door, cell phone out, speed dialing, while he yelled, "Andrew!"

⅃ℰℱℬ�7

Two hours later, Phillip came to find Sabine.

She sat on the floor, under the window of her office, the computer and Monstrosity gone. In her lap, Sabine had the only report on Allejandro Corsico. She flipped through the scant collection of glossies in the file.

"We're ready."

"They're not here."

Phillip paused at the apparent non-sequitur. "Who's not here?"

Sabine looked up. "The Misborn. They're not in any of these pictures."

"I fail to see any connection."

"Irina said that they had pictures," she paused. "We don't have any, Phillip. None."

He frowned.

"The Misborn are not Corsico's," she said.

Phillip's face went blank.

"We're fucked. Someone else is in this game," she said.

"Time to go, Sabine," Phillip said and grabbed her arm to get her up off the floor.

The last of them, Sabine, Irina, Ari and Phillip came out of the building onto Mission Street, where Tony and Andrew had two cars parked illegally, hazards flashing on the mostly empty street. The rest of the floor had been empty on their way out. Stripped.

But the minute Sabine's foot hit the sidewalk, she felt it. Her skin tightened, went cold, then hot.

"Life has a value only when it has something valuable as its object." Corsico's voice echoed. Sabine stopped. The others went for the cars.

"Hegel," Sabine said, as Corsico came into the corner street light. He was alone. Sabine also knew that to be a lie. She felt others.

"Ah, you know your philosophers."

"I try. It's more that I collect quotations. That's one I've collected." A rising wind ran cold fingers through Sabine's hair.

Only Ari had ever seen Corsico before and only from a distance. Her hand reflexively reached for something, but Phillip had a hand on Ari's arm. Sabine was the only one on the sidewalk. No one was close enough to throw her out of harm's way this time.

Just her. And the Preserver.

"I see. And do you have something valuable as the object in your life, Miss Parsons?"

"What if I do?"

Ari's mouth started moving, but no sound came out. Sabine glanced at Ari and then away.

"What would you do to keep it safe?" Corsico asked, though he came no closer.

"I don't think I need to tell you that," Sabine replied.

"No? But what could you possibly have in your life that could be of any value, Sabine?"

"That's why you're the incompetent magician and we're leaving," she said and turned to go.

"We'll find out," he said.

"Oh good. Then I'll have a real reason to gut you all like pigs."

"You wouldn't dare."

Sabine spun and stalked towards Corsico. "Dare what? Dare putting you in your place? Dare to call your bluff? Please. You think your threats mean anything to me?"

"You've changed. Where does this fierceness come from, Miss Parsons? One wonders." Corsico remained unmoved.

"It's good to wonder. It keeps you up at night."

"What have you done, Sabine?"

"Whatever do you mean, Corsico?"

"What have you done that has wrought this change?"

"What does it matter?"

"Woman, you will answer my questions or your suffering will be used as a tale to frighten the Unbelievers for the next hundred years." The smile on his face belied the threat.

"I'd say that frightens me if I really believed you could do that, but, you know, I just don't. You people are pathetic. If you can even breach the Veil it'll be because the gods take pity on your incompetent asses."

"That is enough!"

"Not quite." Sabine stopped ten feet from Corsico and the .45 was suddenly in her hand. "You better run, motherfucker. Because the next time I see you, I'll kill you."

Phillip did not seem surprised. He shoved Ari into the back seat and Irina after her. Two sharp hand gestures had Tony and Andrew into the driver seats of the two Mercedes, leaving only him on the street, with what could have easily been a matching .45 in his own right hand.

"Time to go, Sabine," Phillip said.

"Run, motherfucker. Run," Sabine said and turned her back on the Preserver. Sabine didn't turn around when the twisting wind and jarring energy told her he was gone.

"I'm ready," she told Phillip and got in the last car's passenger seat. He just smiled at her and shut her door.

ℬ∞ⅬⰍ𝔍ℰ𝟟⋟

On Highway 1, heading south from San Francisco for the 280 Freeway, Phoebe Quintaine drove her red Infiniti, Jacob asleep in the front seat and Michelle asleep in the back. No other cars were on the road and she drove far too fast for that part of the road, which was at that point only two lanes and windy. Only the headlights illuminated the road and no moon shone to show the rest of the way.

Jacob woke a little. "Where are we?"

"Go back to sleep," His mother answered, the coldness in her voice something Jacob had long come to expect from her.

"This isn't the way to Grandma's."

"I said go back to sleep." The warning normally would have been enough, but his sleepy eyes widened into shock. His sister woke up in the back seat to see the same thing in the road that their mother had taken her eyes off of to scold him. Phoebe jerked her eyes back to the road with only enough time to see the impossible.

A man in a gray suit in her headlights.

The next instant they hit him, but the car buckled like tinfoil around him and his upraised left hand, in screaming metal, shattering glass and a flash of heat lightning inside the car.

� ᐱ759

At a Ramada next to the San Francisco International Airport, Sabine left her hotel room, shaking her head a little. The feeling of being out of sorts and dizzy hadn't left her since her interchange with Corsico. She rubbed her eyes and blinked blearily.

"I've just got to get some sleep," she murmured. She stepped into the hall and what felt like a sword slammed through her solar plexus like a runaway truck, sending her blind.

Not now! Sabine wanted to scream, but even as she tried to lock her jaw to keep from screaming, she vomited.

Bright crimson wetness hit the carpet between her braced hands. Too red, red so bright that Sabine had trouble making sense of it. She wanted to moan when her pain-numbed brain recognized it. She couldn't stop vomiting, but all she vomited was bright red blood spreading faster and faster on the beige industrial carpet.

She thought she heard screaming from faraway but the blackness hit with a roar like another truck.

ᛒᐇ763 ᐸᑕ 573

On a black highway in Pacifica, Jacob Quintaine struggled to get out of his seat away from the horror that remained of his mother. The steering wheel had impaled Phoebe Quintaine through the chest, but that was not what had him pulling futilely on the door release.

Darkness roiled out of their mother's crushed chest. Her head lolled over, eyes mad and wide as she reached out with a clawing hand. Michelle shoved herself into the corner of the backseat as far away from the blackness as she could, Jacob doing the same into the passenger side door when an actinic, translucent flash appeared between them and the darkness.

"They are not yours!" a woman's voice cried.

Michelle cracked open her eyes. Jacob stared at the apparition of the dark haired woman who stood between them and the dark. Between one heartbeat and the next, the dark roiled back into their mother with the speed of a whisper and a blink. Phoebe glared at the woman.

The woman was translucent and not, the form of her seeming to be solid, but when she moved, Jacob swore he saw starlight spill from the folds of her clothes in flashes so brief that he almost thought he imagined it. The starlight was in her eyes as well and she seemed to glow.

"Jacob, you need to take your sister and get out of the car." The woman turned to face him, all the while his mother glared impotent rage, gurgling horrible noises.

"Why should I trust you?"

"My name is Maria Elena. I have given you my true name. Sabine sent me to help you. She said to remember the fairy tale of the house of the godfather that she told you." At the mention of Sabine's name and the mention of the fairy tale, Jacob unfastened his seatbelt and managed to open the passenger door.

"I knew Sabine would help us," Michelle said.

Jacob gave her an encouraging smile. "Come on." He helped her crawl out of the back seat and out into the road. The woman stood outside already, between them and the open road. The cold night air had Michelle shivering in her thin dress, her pink sweater no warmth. Jacob tried to wrap his arms around her, but he was cold too. They shivered together like two small animals, stumbling for the side of the road.

"Come with me. I've got to get you off the road," Maria Elena said.

Headlights glared white hot and blinding from around the corner. Maria Elena threw her arms out wide, facing the lights. She flared like a flash of sheet lightning, a half dome of ethereal fragile light flaring into being between them and the car. Too fragile and egg shell thin, Jacob could not see how it was going to save them. They clung together as they stumbled to a frozen halt. Maria Elena kept them from falling yet never touched them and shoved them forward into moving again. The car swerved, the wind of its passing nearly toppled them to the ground, missing them by inches. They stumbled into the ditch at the side of the road.

"Just sit here and wait. The emergency people will be here soon," Maria Elena said.

"Are they really coming?" Michelle asked.

"Yes. They're coming. Try to stay warm."

Michelle curled into a hollow in the ditch. Jacob curled in next to her, the two children clinging to each other. The gravel in the ditch was even colder than the night air and uncomfortable to sit on. Jacob found that he was wobbly all of a sudden. Maria Elena stood over them, watching the road with a look that made starlight flash in her eyes like a lightning strike.

"Stay here. I'll be right back," she said and vanished.

"Are we going to be safe?"

"I won't let anyone hurt you. I promised Dad."

"Daddy's okay, isn't he?" Michelle shivered harder.

"Dad's fine. He wouldn't let anything happen. He'll find us. You'll see."

"I believe you. Who's that lady?"

"I don't know. But Sabine said something about true names once, didn't she?" he said.

Michelle nodded, her teeth chattering. "She said they had… power? That someone gives it to you, you have power?"

"Yeah. That lady, she said she gave us her true name and that Sabine sent her."

"She saved us from that car."

"Yeah, but we still gotta be careful."

"Yeah. Get closer. I'm cold."

"Me too. I hope they get here soon."

⚡ ⴹ ⴭ ⚡ ⴭ ⴤ ⴹ ⴔ ⚡

The oily, utterly black cloud that filled the car now made it impossible to discern Phoebe Quintaine's body in the interior. Maria Elena knocked lightly on the driver's side window.

"It won't work," she said.

Phoebe's face came swimming out of the darkness, pressing up against the glass, distorting the flesh of her face and making her look like a grotesque caricature of a woman.

"She has given us the children," the darkness hissed.

"They are not hers to give. She cannot bargain for her life this way."

Phoebe gurgled, the madness starting to give way to panic.

"You didn't honestly think that we would let you harm them, did you?" she said, shaking her head in disbelief.

"You cannot withstand us," it hissed again.

"I have other strength" Maria Elena replied.

The darkness attacked.

It geyser-ed out of the roof of the car. The dark arced to crash down on her. Maria Elena flared like a ghostly sun, wave after wave of sheet lightning thin as fog, stopping the wave like a brick wall. The darkness recoiled, stunned.

"How?!" It hissed in outrage.

"I said, I have other strength."

"It is not possible! You are shadow here!"

"Shadows cast their own light," Maria Elena answered and flared again, her hand flung up to the stars above. Starlight glimmered in the lightning. It rained down on the darkness and the ghost. The black hissed in rage, as the light shredded them apart, till all that was left was an empty night.

Ƀ�testꙄ

Help was not what came.

The air rippled and bent. The gray man stood before Jacob and Michele. Jacob thought about fighting or running until the tall thin man spoke.

"Move, and I kill your sister." His accent was thick.

Which is how, without a fight, Jacob and Michele vanished in twisted air with a man that Sabine knew as one of what had been the Malice Twins.

Maria Elena saw it all.

She also had no remaining power to stop him.

"Sabine. Oh, Sabine. I've failed you," she whispered.

7ɪwꙄɛɪ

"Edward, we've got other problems," Andrew said, as Edward would have gone with the paramedics who were taking Sabine to UCSF hospital.

"What?"

"We got the telemetry up on Phoebe's car. I mean, we tried to get the telemetry up."

"What?" Edward repeated. "What's happened?"

"It's gone. There's no tracking for the car. We lost it on Highway 1 in Pacifica." Andrew tried to motion back for the hotel room where they had set up their improvised command post.

Edward paused. Andrew took the decision out of his hands.

"I'll go. Find out what's happened. I'll take Tony."

Edward just squeezed his friend's shoulder and followed Andrew.

An hour later, at almost two in the morning, Edward rejoined Phillip, Ari, Irina, as well as Rodriguez, in the cramped, dark and horrid waiting room that the hospital staff of UCSF forced people to use when waiting for their ill and wounded to be treated. Ari was on her feet in a heartbeat.

"What's the sitch?"

"Tony and Andrew have gone to investigate. Find out what happened to Phoebe and the children. The rest are monitoring the post back at the hotel. How is she?" Edward asked, sitting down heavily in one of the molded seats bolted to the wall.

"Bleeding ulcer. They've got her in ICU. Say she's lucky she didn't kill herself." Ari sat down next to him. "But we know that's not what happened."

"We do?" Edward commented.

"Tell him, Phillip," Ari said.

"She put a protection spell on the children," Phillip said.

"What the hell inspired her to do something so foolish?"

"I'm thinking she was worried for their safety and apparently with clear reason," Irina joined the conversation. "Much as I wish to help you continue this conversation, I think I should be on my own way."

"Abandoning us already?"

"No. I must go for reinforcements. We're near enough the embassy that I should be able to rouse someone," she said, the only one not looking tired or otherwise worn out.

"I admit to being very surprised that you are so willing to help us," Ari said.

"Take care of your friend, Ari Doran. I think it's time you called your Bubbi, don't you?"

"Yeah," she said, though Irina was long gone. "I probably should."

"Can your grandparent help us?" Rodriguez wanted to know.

"It certainly can't hurt."

The doctor arrived, a young man in his late 20s who clearly had pulled the gravedigger shift for some insult to the governing resident.

"Are you here for Sabine Parsons? I'm Dr. Gens. She's resting well now, we've moved her out of ICU."

"When can we see her?"

"I wouldn't recommend that any time soon. She's very ill. In fact, if you'd like to go home, you can visit her tomorrow."

"I don't think so," Phillip said.

Phillip had stepped out of his corner and both he and Edward produced badges from inside their coats.

"This woman is under federal protective custody. We don't leave her and we see her now."

"All right. But this is a mistake," he said. "She's up on the fourth floor. Follow me."

Edward started to follow them, but paused.

"I'm going to get some air," he said.

"Are you sure?"

"No. But if I don't find someone to steal a cigarette from, I'm going to go insane," Edward said. "I'll meet you up there."

"Ah," Phillip responded with a grin. "Well, not to be mother, don't wander far."

"I won't."

Edward found a spot right outside of the ER doors to smoke the cigarette he'd bummed off one of the nurses. He had enough time to light it and take one drag when Otho Buonocore appeared in front of him. Enough time to register that he'd made a gross miscalculation, no time to draw or Cast, and time enough to get tangled in the Casting net the man threw on him.

"Quintus," Buonocore said softly. "Five times we call you."

The life left Edward's eyes.

⟁⟁⟁⟁⟁⟁⟁

Sabine fought for consciousness, fought through the pain in her gut and opened her eyes on a world that was too sharp and too tight around the edges.

She bled magick. Her spell on the children had spiraled out of control. But worse yet, she could feel Edward gone. She sat up, adrenalin making even the pain and drugs stand at bay. She pulled wires off and the IV out of her arm. She still bled. She knew she did not have much time. Someone would come running from hearing the monitors flat line.

She swayed on her feet, the hospital gown giving an unfortunate draft. She bled magick. So she knew what she had to do. She Reached through the pain, grabbed the wildness and shoved sideways in that place she created Castings. Her pain disappeared and so did the muzziness from the painkillers. For a brief time, (not enough), she would be okay. But it was not a true healing.

She grabbed, Reached again. It wasn't like she hadn't seen the Malice Twins do it enough times. But what she meant to do was far, far more dangerous.

She uttered her first and shortest prayer…

"Help me."

…and Twisted the Cast.

Sabine found herself standing somewhere she'd never been, in a condominium complex of all things. The darkness of the night didn't illuminate if the buildings were white or cream or some other indeterminate light shade. She hesitated, but her bleeding magick and the stirring Oracular Source pushed her forward.

She stepped up the three cement steps of the unit before her and knocked.

The door opened what seemed a long five minutes later, presenting a woman not much taller than Sabine. The woman had short, short blond hair and the most startling pair of blue eyes Sabine had ever seen. She wore a pair of white pajamas covered in cavorting white and pink sheep, and though Sabine was certain she'd woken the woman, there was no sign of sleep in her heart shaped face.

She took in Sabine swaying on her doorstep and sudden realization appeared on her face. "Ah. Is it that time again already?"

"Can—" Sabine realized she didn't know how to say this at all, but figured, with such an opening, she might as well press on. "Can you help me?"

"Yes. Come in." The woman stepped aside. "My name is Jain. J, A, I, N. Please don't misspell it. I've been expecting you."

"You have?" Sabine stepped in.

"Yes. Any idiot who can read the sky knows something was up," Jain said, mixing her tenses. "But first, I think, let's get you sitting."

Sabine stepped into a living space done in monochrome, nothing but white; except for the wall that faced the front door dominated by an enormous mural of a black dragon in flight that took up the entire twenty foot high wall to the sloping ceiling. Jain led her to a chenille L-shaped couch that divided the room from the smaller dining area.

"My name's Sabine. Do you always spell your name?" Sabine asked, the continuing wooziness making her slur her words.

"Beats having people misspell it."

"Oh."

Jain sat down on the white marble topped coffee table, facing Sabine, her knees spread, elbows resting on the knees as she cupped her chin in her hands. "Do you know why you're here? Actually, do you even know where you are?" she corrected herself.

"I—" Sabine took a steadying breath. "I asked for help. I don't know where I am."

"Sunnyvale. In California," Jain clarified when Sabine's eyebrows rose. "New to teleporting, are you?"

"Very new."

"How far did you Jump?" Sabine knew she didn't imagine the capital to the spoken word, Jump.

"A minute ago I was in San Francisco."

"Ambitious." Jain leaned even further forward. "Now you want to explain to me why you, a proto enchanter and Oracle are bleeding magick all over my living room?"

"Who are you?"

"*Cogito ergo draconis*," Jain said. "Suffice to say that this is no surprise to me." She got to her feet and went into the tiny kitchen that was accessed through the dining area. Jain put a silver kettle on to boil that had a dragon shaped whistle spout.

"There's only one form of help that I give," Jain said from the kitchen. "Swords."

"I'm sorry. I'm not following."

"That doesn't surprise me. You're just confused in general, aren't you? Must make you fun at parties," Jain said as she busied herself with a teapot.

"I guess I am. Confused that is. I don't know if I'm that much fun at parties. I don't know what I would need a sword for either."

"Oh, sure you are!" Jain returned with the tea tray. "The Source brought you here, yes?"

"Yes."

"Then a sword must be what you need."

"You're taking all of this amazingly well," Sabine said as Jain poured the tea while sitting cross legged on the coffee table, the tea tray next to her.

"After all I've seen, I'm surprised by little." Jain handed her a teacup. "Drink that."

"What is it?" Sabine might have been wounded, but not all sense had left her.

"Earl Grey, willow bark and dandelion root with honey."

"Oh. Thank you." Sabine sipped a little. Strong herbs cut under the traditional tea that she knew so well, but they didn't take away from the flavor. In fact, Sabine found knots in her shoulders letting go a little with nothing more mundane than a cup of tea in her hands.

"I feel I should warn you."

Sabine's hand hesitated on the way back down to the saucer with the cup. "Warn me?"

"I can help. But the price is high."

Woozy and all, on this Sabine didn't hesitate. "I'll pay it."

"You haven't even asked what the price will be."

"Whatever it is, I'll end up paying it anyway, won't I?" The words were bitter, but the tone was not.

"More than likely."

"Then I might as well make the best of it."

"I'll take that then." Jain held her hand out for the cup. "We'll just patch you up a little better, why don't we?"

"Can you?"

A tidal wave of a Casting answered her, grabbing Sabine in ice and fire as Jain's hair stood away from her head like a gold halo. Her back arched like a bow and her mouth tore open in a silent scream. Through the pain, she heard Jain speak.

"I said the price would be high."

Time had no meaning for however short or long Jain's Cast required. Days or seconds could have passed and Sabine would have been unable to tell. But she felt her gut knit. She felt her bleeding magick stop. She felt her connection to wherever she raised her own Casts back strong again underneath her skin.

Sabine slumped on the couch, panting, her skin doused in sweat, the hospital gown plastered to her sodden chest. As soon her eyes could focus, Jain slipped the cup of tea into Sabine's trembling hand.

"Drink."

Sabine did her best and managed to spill none of it. It was like drinking a warming fire.

"I'm afraid I have no facility for a gentle healing," Jain said. "I heal as I am, with Fire. It's not fun, but it gets the job done."

"I'd say thank you, but…" Sabine trailed off.

"It seems rather masochistic? Don't feel bad. Thanking me is not something you may feel like doing by the end of this all." Jain got to her feet. "Can you get up?"

Sabine finished her tea. She nodded when she discovered that the shakes, which were quickly fading, were all that remained of Jain's healing.

Jain lead the way up a short flight of stairs into the back of the condo. Opened a door onto a guest room done in russet tones and rummaged in a mahogany tall chest of drawers. Handed underwear, black jeans and a black sweatshirt to Sabine.

"We're much of a size, but I don't think I have any shoes that will fit."

Sabine looked down. Jain did indeed have the tiniest feet she'd ever seen on a woman. Jain smiled at her scrutiny and left, shutting the door on Sabine holding the clothes. She dressed, finding that even with sudden healing, her bones creaked. It took doing to get the simple clothes on. Jain had been right. They fit, and only just. She'd just have to make do without shoes.

She opened the door and Jain gestured for Sabine to follow further down the hall. "It's not the first time that you've come to me for a sword," Jain began as if no pause had been in their conversation. "And it won't be the last."

Jain threw open the doors at the end of the hall, revealing a display wall of red velvet, hidden halogen museum lights coming on. On individual velvet covered rods hung seven swords, though to call them swords was to do them great injustice. They were upon sight everything that a sword was meant to be. Beautiful in form and instantly understood as deadly. Sabine felt her heart beat harder in her chest for a moment. Whatever their outward appearance, they were also living myth, though she had no idea where she'd come by the knowledge.

The fabled Seven. Swords created for either the creation or destruction of the world.

And Jain meant to give one to Sabine.

Jain selected one from the far right end. Silver, light and smaller than the other seven, it shared more in common with a Roman gladius than with its later and more modern cousins on the wall. She turned and handed the blade to Sabine.

"Are we just doomed to repeat ourselves then?" Sabine asked. "Are we just idiots? Utter fools?"

"No. Is Winter evil for ending and giving way to the Spring?"

"Speak in modern English, please."

"It's all about choice. You can either choose to see it as doom or gift. Both carry weight. Both are a matter of perspective."

"A matter of perspective?"

"Well, consider. Angels, demons, is there a difference?" Jain asked.

"So far, in my admittedly limited experience, yes," Sabine insisted.

"A name you could give me would be Leviathan," Jain offered.

"The Bible says that makes you a devil, one of the Damned." Sabine didn't know what made her say it.

"Hey. Don't believe everything you read," Jain grinned. Sabine followed her back into the front room, the wonders behind her once more safely shielded behind their oak doors.

"What do you mean? You say I've done this before. Which means this isn't going to work."

"Depends on what you have planned, doesn't it?" Jain took a seat on the couch this time. Jain poured more tea. Not knowing what else to do with the sword, Sabine set it gently on the coffee table, all silver and sharp.

"How so?"

"That one," Jain indicated the blade on the table. "Is particularly good at unbindings. Of all shapes, sorts and kinds. It asked to go with you. I assume there's an unbinding ahead of you, but if you go after something else, it will not help you." Instantly, Sabine's memory supplied her with vivid images. Too vivid. Corsico's Collection.

"I see from your face that you know what unbinding you have in mind," Jain said.

"You said not to believe everything I read." Sabine changed subjects.

"Haven't you ever heard the cliché that history is written by the winners?"

"Yes."

"Same thing."

"The Bible isn't literal history as far as I know."

"Let's just say that it is…and it isn't."

"You speak in very irritating riddles."

"I must apologize," Jain breathed a slight laugh. "A peril of my genetics, you might say. Imagine if you will, not of history repeating, so much as spiraling. The same view, but from a different altitude. It's not that you or anyone is doomed to repeat anything. It's that in any given pass, any given life, you cannot achieve everything. Right every wrong. Know all of the truth of a situation. See things through another's eyes. You can only be yourself. You can only do the best with what you have."

"So what does this have to do with not believing?"

"What if this is all as it should be? What if everything is happening as it is meant to? What if everything you were told, in other words, read, wasn't the absolute truth, but…a truth."

"You're kidding."

"Life is its own perfection. Are predators evil?"

"No," Sabine said slowly. "But what of…" Suddenly, Sabine found she could not speak Corsico's name out loud.

"…someone I mean to…" she couldn't finish that sentence either.

"You mean it never occurred to you that this might all serve some purpose?" Jain seemed genuinely puzzled.

"You make it sound very Zen." Sabine gave up.

"It is. All manifests as it should. Even the one you seek to destroy is the perfect incarnation of whatever they need to be."

"What? Like some kind of Buddha of Destruction?" Sabine meant it flippantly.

"Why not? Jain asked. "All is one."

"You called me a proto enchanter." Sabine tried changing tacks again. Too much new information made her act petulant, she knew, but she didn't care. Anger bubbled under her skin too. While she minced words with this woman who she began to think was no woman at all, something terrible had happened to the children.

"Which you are."

"It means nothing to me," Sabine said.

"Really." Jain's eyes narrowed. "You know nothing of the Chant of the World?"

At that point, Sabine decided she just as well might chuck her

Game Face out the metaphorical window. "I only know of it. I don't know what it is." Sabine offered truth.

"Do you know where the word enchanter comes from?"

"I'm not big for the etymology of words."

"From the Latin, *incantere*. The words, enchant and chant derive from it, among numerous others." Jain didn't go on; a strange look passed on her face. "I have this feeling though."

"Feeling?"

"If you do indeed know so little of the Chant and Enchanters on top of only knowing yourself an Oracle, perhaps I've said enough." Jain contemplated her teacup.

Sabine found her hand on the sword before she knew it, her possession of it opposite her earlier reticence. "Even if that knowledge could help me?"

"There are more terrible and powerful things than little enchanters, Sabine," Jain said and for a brief moment, Sabine saw the Dragon. And remembered that there were indeed more ancient things than even the stones of the Earth.

"I'll remember that." She let go the sword.

"You do that," Jain said and smiled, once more, masquerading human.

Jain tipped the teapot, to find it empty. She tsked.

"Time for you to go, I think."

"You measure time in teapots?" The silliness of the scene made Sabine forget her previous madness as quickly as the vision of the Dragon had passed.

"Works as good as any. You came here under some duress and obviously with a need for speed. I've kept you long enough." Jain went and opened the front door. Sabine stepped out into the night and a rising wind. She looked up at the sky. Couldn't see the stars. She looked back at Jain framed in her doorway, suddenly looking small and very childlike.

"How do I find them?" Sabine asked, sudden panic dousing her in icy adrenalin, making new skin and new soul hurt, even as she realized that she'd told Jain none of her situation. Only come for help.

"The same way you got here," Jain replied.

"I don't know how I did." Sabine's hand tightened on the hilt of the sword till the knuckles went white. Jain said nothing. Just looked at her.

Sabine closed her eyes. Took a breath. Opened herself up to the night and the World.

And suddenly she stood in the waking Dream.

𝒳 𝒮 𝐋

Thirty odd miles north of Sunnyvale and back in San Francisco, Ari's first hint that everything had gone pancake-shaped, verily and how, were the first words out of her "brother's" mouth after she'd identified herself with her connected phone call.

"The box says don't lose her."

"What? Joseph?" All that answered was dial tone.

Ari felt the *chai* pendant around her neck heat.

"Oh. Beloved Shekinah."

She ran.

When she found her way to the fourth floor after haranguing one of the night nurses it was to find Phillip and Rodriguez trying to soothe a very irate doctor. Phillip managed to urge Dr. Gens to leave the hospital room with him, leaving Rodriguez to Ari.

"What happened?" Ari asked.

"Phillip said something moved. He has a rosary, did you know?"

"No, I did not know." Ari contained her impatience. "Then what?"

"He ran here. I followed. Then orderlies came, saying code blue. We came in. She was gone," Rodriguez answered.

Ari found that his succinct military reporting soothed her. It reminded her of her brothers, Israeli paratroopers all.

"Gone."

"Gone," he repeated.

Ari scanned the room. Took in the disconnected IV. The thrown off covers.

"She didn't take her clothes. She couldn't have gone far."

"If she walked," Rodriguez interjected.

"If—" Ari turned her attention back on the older man. His eyes were shut in concentration and not a little sorrow. His eyes opened when she did not continue her sentence.

"If she walked," he said again and Ari could tell he meant what he said.

"There's another way to leave this room," Ari stated it because she'd seen the other means of leaving. In Europe. But her Sabine could not do that.

"Mr. Rodriguez, how did she leave here? Do you know?"

"No, I do not know how she left here. But I know that she would have had to walk by the two of us in the hall and the orderlies and that I did not see her and I watched this door the entire time." He pointed at the room's one door.

No open windows, Ari noted. And they were on the fourth floor. Sabine had been in no shape to jump out or climb down. Even well, few people could manage such a thing unless truly desperate. Ari felt the *chai* pendant heat again around her neck. She knew the answer to this locked room mystery. She just didn't want to accept it.

"Even if she gets help, she will need more," Rodriguez said. "She will need your help."

"She will?" Ari queried.

"She will."

Phillip burst back into the room. "Did Edward come up here?"

Both froze. Rodriguez shook his head in a curt negative.

"Right." Phillip didn't pause. He went right back out the door.

"I do not know how to say this, let alone, ask. Is there a way you can follow her? I know you have a faith of your own. You said that prayer," Rodriguez said, his manner urgent.

Ari nodded. "It's lucky that I trust you, Mr. Rodriguez," she said. "Yes. There's a way I can find her."

"You know, they would not let us see the camps, Captain Harrison's team and the others," he said.

"Why?"

"Because after all we had seen… I don't think it matters, but I have always wanted to tell someone from your home, I know why Israel fights so hard. Why you are fighting so hard now. Why we fought so hard then."

"You do?"

"Yes. Because if we didn't, it will be all of us who go to the gas chamber next time. Save the Captain," he said and added, softer, "God bless you and protect you, Ari Doran."

Ari looked him in the eye and smiled as the pendant around her neck lit like a newborn star.

"She does," she said, and was gone.

ㄥ ૯ ℥ ℞ ⼑ ⼻

The Waking Dream left Sabine standing before Rodin's Gates of Hell in a great dark hall, not unlike the hall of the Beloved, her past Self, Captain Harrison, standing at her side.

"You'll need to do as I did. Get past the Guardians of the place and lay your charges," Harrison said.

Sabine didn't know how long they had been standing in the Dream. "I don't have any." She turned her head to look at Harrison.

"You'll do fine. We always do," Harrison said, his gaze fixed, but then he looked afraid. "Even if they keep coming back."

"You succeeded. They were stopped."

"But they are back."

"And we will stop them again," Sabine said, her fist clenching on the sword hilt in her hand. Harrison nodded and Sabine felt her split selves become one again.

She took one last look at the Gates, closed her eyes and spoke her need.

"Take me where I need to go."

ᙓ𝑳ᙈᙓ𝑳g𝒶𝟕𝐏

"Phillip, be easy."

"In all respect, Mr. Rodriguez, how am I to be easy about any of this?" Phillip had returned to Sabine's empty hospital room to find it missing yet another person. He'd gotten a less than satisfactory explanation already from Rodriguez, who continued with less than satisfactory comfort.

"Because there is nothing we can do for them now."

"That is not an option for me, sir. I have to find them." Phillip turned his back on the room, pulling his cell phone out, getting a pickup of his call off of one ring. "We have a situation. Quintus, Oracle and Sidecar are in check. Repeat. Quintus, Oracle and Sidecar are in check."

He hung up. "Why the fuck did they have to take her clothes off?"

"I do not understand," Rodriguez said.

Phillip turned to favor the older man with a wintry smile. "If she still had her clothes on, I could find her. She's wearing a GPS tag."

"You bugged her?"

"If I have learned one thing in this entire benighted situation, Mr. Rodriguez, it is that not knowing where Sabine Parsons is can be a monumental liability. Possibly a fatal one."

⚠⚠⚠⚠⚠⚠⚠

Warped space and reality deposited Sabine outside of a building she had only seen via satellite feed, though she had been inside once before. She had teleported half way around the world. She was in Milan…

…and in a flare of gold light, so was Ari Doran.

"Sabine!!"

"Ari?!"

"You tried to ditch me!"

"There's no time."

"I know."

"Where are we?"

"Corsico's."

"Why are we here?"

"He took the children."

"Oh, now he's going to die." They both contemplated the manse. Both noted the same thing at the same time.

"Where the fuck is everyone?" Ari asked.

"Good fucking question." Sabine's answer was just cold. Sabine didn't know what was worse. The fact that Corsico's home in darkness would be bad, but standing on the grass, with morning sun beating on her shoulders with not a soul about was far more chilling.

"What's the plan?" Ari asked.

"I'm going to go through the front door," Sabine stated.

"Ah. We don't have a plan."

"We have a plan! It's a really bad plan, but we have a plan." Sabine strode forward. "Let's put said plan into action."

"Joy," Ari muttered.

The minute Sabine put her hand on the doorknob of one of the double entry doors, she knew it was a mistake, but she couldn't pinpoint why. The Source was unclear. The same great hall opened in front of her that she remembered before. Ari whistled. Sabine looked at her friend.

"His cleaning bill must be a bitch."

They stepped inside.

"This is ridiculous. They should be climbing all over us by now," Ari said.

The manse felt… hollow.

Yet she knew that the Dream and the Source wouldn't have brought her here, Ari too, if Edward and the children were not somewhere to be found in the manse's confines.

"We'll need to split up," Sabine said.

"Bad idea, *sabra.*"

"Why?" Sabine hesitated.

"You know what happens whenever you split up a party! Hell, look what's happened to us!" Ari had a point. Sabine ground her teeth in frustration. She had to find them. She thought to open herself to the Oracular Source again, but just as she went to close her eyes, a flicker of heat haze appeared before them.

Sabine had the sword up and Ari had her gun out when the shade of Maria Elena appeared. "Grandmother!" Sabine gaped, horrified at the tattered soul that stood before them.

"I tried, Sabine. I failed. He took them."

"I know, Grandma, I know."

"I can lead you to them," Maria Elena said. "It's the only strength I have left."

"Grandma, what is this doing to you?"

"Shush, dear one." Maria Elena, once her living grandmother, made a soothing gesture with one transparent hand. "It doesn't matter. Help the children. I won't be made a liar by that horrible man." Maria Elena's shade floated more than walked to the grand staircase.

"Liar?" Ari asked.

"I told the children help was on its way and by God, help is on its way." Maria Elena's voice faded with each step she took.

"I see what side of the family you take after," Ari said.

Sabine paused at the foot of the stairs, her eyes drawn to the end of the hall that ran behind the staircase. Ari already ascended after Maria Elena, but Ari paused as well when she realized that Sabine wasn't keeping pace with her.

"Go on ahead," Sabine said, not taking her eyes off of the hall.

"*Sabra…*" Ari warned.

"I have to do this, Ari. And I don't want you seeing what's in that room."

"What room?"

"Go up and get the children."

"Sabine!"

"Do it, Ari. For me. Please."

Ari opened her mouth to protest. She nodded instead and went up after the ghost.

Sabine turned back to face the end of the hall. She quick walked, her bare feet silent on the marble parquet floor. Kicked open the door, the sting of the blow shuddering up her entire leg. She stepped inside the room that housed the Preserver's Collection.

Took in the contorted, frozen, naked bodies. Felt the bile rise in her throat in response to the eldritch creeping feel of the room. She raised the sword above her head and struck.

Again and again, the sword flashed out and down, now with a life of its own. The sword never hit resistance. Heads parted from shoulders as if bone did not even exist; torsos followed, severed in half. Sabine cut her way through the Collection, decapitating women, cutting through the sigils that held soul to undead frozen flesh.

She didn't know when she started weeping and shrieking. She only knew when she stopped. She stood in the middle of the destroyed collection and screamed one last time and heaved for air.

Blood. Everywhere and on her. She gave the sword a violent shake, blood spattering off in a sheet. She backed out of the room, closing the door. Ari stood with Jacob and Michelle. Before Ari could open her mouth to speak or Michelle or Jacob could move, Sabine was screaming again, but this time in warning.

"Get down!"

Otho Buonocore stood behind Ari, reality warping around him as he began to Cast.

Before Sabine could counter Cast, Ari Doran proved why she was one of Israeli's elite. In a move worn so smooth, the way only constant practice can make it, she drew. Her aim rock steady, she brought up a different weapon than her usual Beretta Jaguar. Sabine had enough time to register the Desert Eagle in Ari's right hand. So did Buonocore. His eyes went wide in terror and the Cast warped to different purpose.

The report of the Desert Eagle in the hall was like thunder.

The bullet never struck home. It hit Buonocore's shield and flattened against the invisible barrier. He stumbled and ran to a set of doors across the way. They ran after him, Ari towing the children, the Desert Eagle holstered. They burst into the next room, columns in golden marble against the walls, Ionic tops supporting the roof. No furniture graced this room. It housed only one thing.

Rodin's Gates of Hell.

Otho Buonocore was nowhere to be found. Michelle leaned into Ari, seeking comfort. Jacob stood on his own, his eyes never leaving Sabine as she walked to the pillar closest the Gates.

"I love you, Ari," Sabine said, panting as she leaned against a column, the smeared blood on her right cheek looking like an open wound, hair matted and wet from blood and other fluids. The sword in Sabine's hand seemed to eat the light and darkness in the room.

"Don't do this, Sabine, you don't have to do this," Ari whispered.

"I'll be okay, my dear one. Stay. Protect the children."

"With my life," Ari said with sudden ferocity.

Sabine grinned like a flash of lightning. She walked out into the hall to face what waited for her. The Gates opened, actinic white light blinding her and leeching all color out of the room, leaving only black shadows and everything else reflected white too painful to gaze at for long.

Sabine turned to look behind, the fire from the Gates blowing her hair in a black halo around her head. Her eyes blazed with unshed tears as she looked at the children.

"No!" Michelle screamed, tears streaming down her face.

"Sabine!" Jacob yelled.

Sabine's voice carried as if she were right next to them. The shadow of the Oracle echoed Sabine's voice.

"I have to go," she said, profound love in her voice.

Jacob broke down and tried to rush forward to stop her, but Ari held both children with a grip like iron, dropping to her knees, refusing to let go.

"I'll be back. Remember the story. Godfather Death will give me back what I want."

Jacob's mouth rounded into a silent "O" and he collapsed against Ari's arm.

"Yes," he heard whispered in his mind and spinning on her heel, Sabine turned and leapt into the maelstrom.

The Gates slammed shut behind her with a roar of wind.

In a gray place without borders, Sabine Parsons hung suspended, her thoughts gone. The light and noise of seconds before left only this grayness. A floor became solid under her, or always had been, it was hard to tell. At first, Sabine thought she stood again in the Waking

Dream, but then, her eyes adjusted and more became clear. She stood in an antechamber, Jain's sword throbbing in her grip.

A set of doors now visible before her, heavy and black, set in a gray stone portico. Sabine tugged with her free hand on the large iron ring set in the right hand door, but nothing moved.

"Fuck." She guessed where she had to be. There had been nothing of this when the team had been here. Sabine threw caution out the metaphorical window and flung open her mind to the Oracle.

"Show me what lies beyond." The heavy doors opened inwards to her, belying their heaviness or previous immobility. She went to step inside and a titanic force froze her to the spot. Sabine sucked in air, terrified.

Harrison's words came to her.

"You will have to get past the guardians of that place."

The Oracle had given her more than just the opening words to breach the ward on the doors. It told her also that a great work had been begun inside. Which meant the wards and guardians of the place were wide awake, which they hadn't been when Edward's people had been there.

Everything they had avoided, Sabine now by herself had to face.

"Bright Lady, you must leave your weapon here."

Sabine stepped back. Met no resistance and stared about. She laid eyes on a small stone gargoyle set inside the stone portico, just inside of the doors. Small and black, it looked like a small hairless man with no arms, only wings, carved out of black basalt.

"I am not the Lady. Why do you call me that?" Sabine asked.

"Are you not one of her priestesses?"

Sabine wanted to weep again. "I have forsaken Her."

"She has not forsaken you." The Voice was so gentle and in that moment, she saw the glow surrounding her own hand and the sword.

"Oh my," she breathed.

"You must leave your weapon here."

Without a word more, she did, laying the Dragon's Sword at the feet of the black statue. She walked unresisted into the great hall that she had only walked in Dreams. Thirteen doorways. She emerged from the farthest entry in the hall. The rough carved gray columns that vanished into a ceiling she could not see. The light that came from nowhere and everywhere, leeching all color from her skin.

Sabine looked down. Took in her clothing, shock making her shaky for a moment. Black sweatshirt and jeans, blood on her feet, on the back of her hands. Her bare feet on the stone.

Just like her Dream.

She ran for the altar. It took what seemed like forever to run the length of the hall. Edward Quintaine lay on the stone, hands clasped on his chest, eyes open and sightless.

"Edward?"

If it had not been for the wave of utter adoration that came with the caress, Sabine would have screamed. But instead, when the warm tendril touched her cheek, Sabine looked up and saw with her waking eyes for the first time the glory of the Beloved. The coils came down and tendrils stroked her face. Tears stung her eyes, feeling the grief and hope that now made up the Beloved. She walked behind the altar, trying to get closer. The coils plucked and stroked at her clothes, silent and entreating. Alive and yet not, love and devotion made animate in a machine that was less and more than any simple mechanical device.

"She is well. She's okay," Sabine choked out, stroking the Beloved. "But I still need your help."

A larger coil reached out and stroked Edward's face. No response.

"Is there nothing we can do?" Edward was just large enough that she knew she had no hope of carrying him out.

"There is nothing you can do."

Corsico.

Icy rage flooded Sabine. She detached herself from coils that now tried to hold her back, protect her. She walked out back in front of the altar, even as the Beloved, unable to pull her back made clear its own allegiance by obscuring the altar, and wrapping Sabine in Its embrace to the extent that she would allow it.

"We'll see about that," Sabine said, her grief gone. "I certainly did something about your little collection."

"What have you done?"

"You really shouldn't leave your little palace unprotected, you motherfucker. I'm afraid that I did some redecorating."

Corsico took a deep breath as if to retort and stopped. The next minute, a slow smile began to spread on his face.

"No matter, *columba mia.* What better way to start a new Collection than with you? Before I kill you and sacrifice Quintaine, I really must know. How did you get involved in all of this? I must know."

Sabine had no idea where or when he had entered, but so far, he was alone. "Where is everyone?" Sabine demanded.

"Gone."

"Gone?"

"My poor *columba*. If you expect me to divulge my evil plan, you are sadly mistaken. That is for second rate amateurs."

"Oh, that explains it then. You're third rate." Sabine poured all the acid in her tone that she could manage. "So why should I tell you anything?"

"Indulge me. You certainly will not get out of here alive."

Sabine began to open herself to the different source, not the Oracle. She needed to stall. Get time to raise power for a Cast. She would only get one...

"How did I get involved? All right, I'll bite. The weather. I kept seeing rainbows. Broken rainbows eaten by darkness."

"So you read the world, little girl. What of it? Such an interesting trait would not have been ignored for long."

"Probably true. But I think I am beginning to understand what it was trying to tell me."

"Do tell."

"It was just Someone's way of trying to get my attention."

"And did it?"

"I'd say so." Sabine cocked her head to one side. "So, how long have you had Edward under your control?" She was guessing, but she had to throw something out there.

Corsico threw his head back and laughed. Sabine flinched at the sound, the lovely caressing tone of it.

"Forgive me, *columba mia*. I remain unmoved. Too bad you won't survive to learn the answer to that question." Unfortunately, Sabine felt his rising Cast and knew that Corsico had felt her opening gambit all along. The hall exploded in fire and wind, stone chips exploding off of the columns. Desperate, she twisted her beginning Cast to shield not only herself, but the altar and the Beloved.

An invisible wave of force came hurtling at Sabine, taking the smoke, fire and dirt howling through the hall and turning it into a coherent wall screaming at her like a freight train. Her arms flew up to guard her face and eyes, and it hit her like a huge wave hits a rock, breaking apart into chaos, the smoke and fire spinning around her like a collapsing tornado. She rocked with the impact, but it did not fell her. The wave collapsed and dissipated.

Sabine dropped her arms slowly, small cuts on her face where some of the stone chips had gotten through.

"My turn," she said, one side of her mouth coming up in a chilling smile.

Something snapped inside of Sabine's chest. For the first time in her life, she threw her soul open all the way, Reaching for a Cast from as far as she could, her very bones straining at the power she hauled from the World.

Cast and counter Cast turned the hall into a circle of hell. Stone and flashes of lightning as each sought to weaken the other's grasp of their power. Sabine went off of pure instinct and rage, while Corsico stood as unmoving as possible, his cream suit now soot-stained and torn in places.

Sabine screamed, pulling a Cast from even deeper in her soul that drove Corsico to his knees. But she could not follow with a killing stroke. She fell to one knee. She could feel the Dragon's healing unraveling. Magick bled out of her skin.

"No," Sabine moaned. "Just let me kill him!" She dragged herself up, Reached again, Reached as deep as she could go. They staggered like prize-fighters in a ring of stone. Sabine braced her feet, going for the final Cast that would destroy Corsico.

"Oracle!" he screamed.

Sabine staggered. She staggered and fought the command.

"Oracle!" he screamed again.

Sabine lost the Casting.

"You must answer!"

"*Ask!*" Sabine screamed back, the howling energies stripping her voice thin, unraveling Cast and bleeding magick turning the hall into a gray tornado of eldritch forces.

"Are you my death?"

Sabine felt her mouth move and the Voice came.

"*You face your eternal doom,*" and her voice was the Voice of the Oracle.

And Something else.

He ran. He did not even make ten feet.

The Beloved attacked. It ripped itself out of the ceiling, out of the walls, stonework and basalt crashing down in noises more terrible than thunder. An explosion rocked the hall. Sabine felt herself lifted up by a coil to safety, even as the Beloved died. Who knew how many years of enslavement, of degradation, it had witnessed and suffered? Sabine felt the rage and sorrow as it lashed out. She screamed in grief, the Beloved's sacrifice washing over her in fire and pain.

The cacophony ended.

She struggled to sit up, surrounded in an oasis of safety behind the great altar, the smoke settling, the waves of explosions stopped. Her ears rang. Fine dust covered her and filled her eyes, her mouth and her nose. She swayed to her feet, spitting. The Beloved's bulk lay around her, shielding her in an egg shaped space, coils covering the altar, its final act before destruction.

Her throat broke with a sound she did not recognize as human.

Loss cracked the rest of the Dragon's healing. Sabine sobbed in pain and grief. Magick continued to bleed out of her. She threw herself on the lifeless coils. Tried to force the bleeding magick into the coils. Nothing. The black rainbows were gone from its flesh, dull and dark gray, no wet sleekness remained.

It was gone.

Corsico also.

Sabine screamed.

Time brought sense back to her. Bleeding magick and pain drove her to move. She shoved lifeless coils off the altar. Underneath, she found Edward. She put her right hand on her chest, looked down, fully expecting to see blood or something. Only the glow remained from her passing of the Guardian.

"Lady, help me," Sabine whispered, even as she saw water hit the back of her hand. She still wept. She put her hand on Edward's forehead and shoved her remaining magick into him.

"Edward, please wake up." The color came back to his eyes. Reason came back. Relief flooded Sabine's muscles. She swayed, weak as water.

"Sabine…" Edward's voice sounded dusty. He coughed, sat up.

"Are you okay?" she asked.

He nodded, face drawn and white. "Are you all right?" he asked.

"I am now," Sabine said, closed her eyes, and fell.

Darkness kept Sabine trapped.

She dreamt and Dreamt, trapped in the Dream, unable to swim her way free or break out of its tidal pull. She Dreamed and eventually gave in and gave up. But there was only one thing to see in the Dream. Lightning and a face. Rainbows devoured by darkness. And strangest of all, a double rainbow, a hope, but then darkness would take it, crushing the hope it brought.

Lightning always followed. But the lightning, if it could rightly be called such a thing, made itself out of a living darkness, blacker than night and no true light, and the face...

The face, a hideous, ancient woman with midnight black eyes. A woman, who unknown as she was to Sabine, struck such terror and horror in her, she would try to wake again. Only to fail. Be sucked back into the Dream.

Of broken rainbows...

Of dark lightning...

And a face of ancient evil.

EPILOGUE

UCSF Medical Center, San Francisco, California, The United States of America

Hospital rooms were not made for debriefing.

"Who is the Abbess?" Edward demanded.

It was the first thing that Sabine heard, swimming back up to consciousness. She had memory of other voices. The team. The dislocation of reality of someone Jumping space, teleporting a great distance. Shreds of conversation and Jacob and Michelle's voices shrilly speaking of a ghost and a darkness. She struggled to open her eyes.

"I don't know, Edward, and neither do my controllers. But we will find out." Ari's tone was tired but firm when she answered.

"I know who she is," Sabine said from her bed, opening her eyes. "I have Dreamed her."

Outside, lightning forked across a black sky.

www.ingramcontent.com/pod-product-compliance
Lightning Source LLC
Chambersburg PA
CBHW051443260626
47162CB00001B/229